PRAISE FOR *THE*

"The book's lyrical evocations of natural Florida, beautiful but perilous, ring true, as does its depiction of the entanglements of small-town life. Family dynamics are a strong point, and the author builds suspense skillfully as Loni unearths connections between past and present that could be lethal. This debut novel, set in rural Florida, deftly combines family drama and tense thriller."

—*Kirkus Reviews*

"With its atmospheric swampland setting, Hartman's debut brings to mind Delia Owens's blockbuster *Where the Crawdads Sing* (2018), while the mystery itself is on par with Stacy Willingham's *A Flicker in the Dark* (2022) . . . [T]he fast pace and short chapters keep the story moving for an enjoyable ride."

—*Booklist*

"Hartman debuts with a well-crafted and fast-paced family drama set in the Florida panhandle . . . [Her] depiction of the natural setting show her to be a talented writer, as do the well-executed takes on museum work, botany, and ornithology. Readers will hope to see Loni back for more."

—*Publishers Weekly*

"Hartman's first novel is interwoven with strong natural history themes, evoking the works of Barbara Kingsolver."

—*Library Journal*

"Steeped in the lush rhythms and murky shadows of the Florida wetlands, Virginia Hartman's *The Marsh Queen* is at once a gripping mystery, a devastating family drama, a romance, and a tribute to the natural world. Loni Murrow is a character who will stay with me for a long time. An astonishing debut."

—Lara Prescott, author of *The Secrets We Kept*

"Part romance, part mystery, *The Marsh Queen* unwinds its entangled story lines with measured grace. Virginia Hartman shares with her bird artist narrator a keen eye and a precise touch, as well as a wry understanding of the way the natural world comforts and sustains. This is a marvelous debut, witty and wise."

—Alice McDermott, National Book Award–winning author
of *The Ninth Hour*

"A unique blend of literature and mystery, with deft evocations of Florida's flora and sometimes malignant fauna, *The Marsh Queen* finds a compelling Southern-noir niche all its own and marks Virginia Hartman as a writer to watch."

—Louis Bayard, author of *Courting Mr. Lincoln,*
Lucky Strikes, and *The Pale Blue Eye*

"The setting is distinctive, Loni is like a girl detective grown up, and it crackles with trouble and action."

—Ellen Prentiss Campbell, author of *Frieda's Song*

"Subtle and complex, *The Marsh Queen* navigates the currents and backwaters of family relationships, the Florida swamplands, and a mysterious death that occurred twenty-five years before. Like Barbara Kingsolver, Hartman delves deep into the natural world to explore her characters, and in this case, the connections between one haunted woman and the waters that took her father's life. Fans of Delia Owens and Lauren Groff will find this a wonderful and absorbing read."

—Suzanne Feldman, author of *Sisters of the Great War*

"Loni Murrow, the protagonist in Virginia Hartman's harrowing urban-rural novel, knows that it's not that you can't go home again, but what wretched truths might await you there. In *The Marsh Queen* there are stories within stories, there are stunning family secrets, there's an almost gothic séance atmosphere—all of that is beautifully orchestrated. But at heart this novel is a kind of mythic journey; let's call it The Daughter's Search for Truth, Love and Redemption."

—Howard Norman, author of *Next Life Might Be Kinder*

"[A] deeply emotional debut . . . a strong, simmering story of family loyalty, strife, and secrets."

—*CrimeReads*

"The flora and fauna of panhandle Florida play a prominent role in the proceedings, especially in their interactions, willing or unwilling, with the humans around them. Virginia Hartman has an excellent eye for the natural world and the myriad roles people play in its display . . . *The Marsh Queen* is a love letter not only to the healing of family ties, but also to the natural beauty of the Sunshine State."

—*Criminal Element*

"Hartman convincingly portrays the beauty of the marshes, creating an atmosphere of serene beauty, but also one full of surprises and ultimately danger . . . [Her] love of this landscape, full of unexpected wonders, is inherent in her writing."

—*New York Journal of Books*

"[An] original and deftly crafted story of crime and family that is an inherently fascinating read—the kind of book that will linger in the mind and memory of the reader long after it is finished."

—*Midwest Book Review*

"The novel's framing details of Florida marshland, ornithology, museum work, and fine art are expertly and beautifully drawn. *The Marsh Queen* is unwavering in its lush, finely detailed, appreciative portrayal of a distinctive natural setting, and ends on a redemptive, even inspirational note."

—*Shelf Awareness*

The
MARSH
QUEEN

VIRGINIA HARTMAN

G

Gallery Books

NEW YORK   LONDON   TORONTO   SYDNEY   NEW DELHI

Gallery Books
An Imprint of Simon & Schuster, Inc.
1230 Avenue of the Americas
New York, NY 10020

First Gallery Books trade paperback edition April 2023

GALLERY BOOKS and colophon are registered trademarks of Simon & Schuster, Inc.

For information about special discounts for bulk purchases, please contact Simon & Schuster Special Sales at 1-866-506-1949 or business@simonandschuster.com.

The Simon & Schuster Speakers Bureau can bring authors to your live event. For more information or to book an event, contact the Simon & Schuster Speakers Bureau at 1-866-248-3049 or visit our website at www.simonspeakers.com.

Interior design by Jaime Putorti

Manufactured in the United States of America

10 9 8 7 6 5 4 3 2 1

Library of Congress Cataloging-in-Publication Data
Names: Hartman, Virginia, author.
Title: The marsh queen / by Virginia Hartman.
Description: New York : Gallery Books, [2022]
Identifiers: LCCN 2021048431 (print) | LCCN 2021048432 (ebook) |
   ISBN 9781982171605 (hardcover) | ISBN 9781982171629 (ebook)
Subjects: LCGFT: Thrillers (Fiction). | Novels.
Classification: LCC PS3608.A78748 M37 2022 (print) | LCC PS3608.A78748 (ebook) |
   DDC 813/.6—dc23/eng/20211022
LC record available at https://lccn.loc.gov/2021048431
LC ebook record available at https://lccn.loc.gov/2021048432

ISBN 978-1-9821-7160-5
ISBN 978-1-9821-7161-2 (pbk)
ISBN 978-1-9821-7162-9 (ebook)

for my children

and
in memory of
RJ and Alex

I was born upon thy bank, river,
My blood flows in thy stream,
And thou meanderest forever
At the bottom of my dream.

—Henry David Thoreau

There is a land of the living and a land of the dead
and the bridge is love, the only survival, the only meaning.

—Thornton Wilder

1

If I were a different person, I could move forward and never look back, never try to fathom the forces that shaped me for the worse. But there are times when a fog rolls in, slow as dusk, beginning with a nodule of regret. *I should have, why didn't I, if only.* I replay the day my father left us for good, the sun showing orange through the live oak, him pacing at the bottom of the porch steps, twelve-year-old me looking down with my baby brother, Philip, on one hip. I winced as I gently extracted a strand of my dark brown hair from his doughy little grasp.

Daddy bounced his feet on the bottom step and squinted up. "Look, darlin'. Miss Joleen next door can help your mama with the baby. So how's about it, Loni Mae? You comin' with me?"

My dad hadn't gone fishing in months. But he'd grown restless, knocking into furniture and slamming the screen door. There was a thrumming in the house like the wind before a storm.

That day, my mother said, "Boyd, go on! You're pacing the house like a caged animal."

I'd have given almost anything to be out fishing in the swamp with him, to draw every creature I saw, to watch and listen as before. But how could I? I had to stay. Now that Philip was here, I served a purpose in my house. I held him while my mother talked on the phone, while she rested or did housework. I knew how to make him laugh those hiccupy laughs. He was my after-school activity, my weekend amusement, my part-time job. My mother no longer shook her head at my hopelessness, nor raised her eyes to heaven.

Daddy turned, and his boots crunched gravel. He retrieved his fishing pole and tackle from the garage. I put the tip of my braid in my mouth and sucked it to a fine point as he walked out to the end of the dock, his khaki vest sagging with lead weights and lures, the tackle box a drag on his left arm. He turned and looked back for a minute, tilting his head so his face caught the light. I put my hand up to wave, but a shaft of sun was in his eyes, and he didn't see. He swiveled back toward the jon boat, stepped in, and he was gone.

He could have slept at the fishing camp, that faded two-room cabin that stuck out over a muddy bank, or he might have gone on patrol right after his swamp time. But on Monday morning, his Fish & Game uniform still hung in the closet at home, pressed and waiting.

Around three, my dad's boss stopped over. Captain Chappelle was tall and fit in his khaki uniform, his boots clunking up the porch steps. My mother was out the door before he'd reached the top stair.

"Hello, Ruth. Just came by to see if Boyd was sick or what."

My mother turned to me. "Go on, Loni. Get to your chores." Two vertical lines between her eyebrows told me not to argue.

I couldn't hear what they said, though from the kitchen I strained to make words from the low tones in the Florida room. I wiped the last dish and heard Captain Chappelle's truck kicking up gravel in the driveway.

The weather turned cool that night, sweatshirt weather, and still Daddy didn't return. Long after I'd gone to bed, I heard voices and went to the top of the stairs.

"I shoulda seen it, Ruth." It was a man's voice—Captain Chappelle. The Florida room's square panes of glass would be black now, the marsh invisible behind them. The darkened banister glowed with the light from downstairs, and Captain Chappelle's voice rippled with a watery sound. "Boyd hadn't been himself lately. I just never thought he'd go and—"

"No," my mother said.

"Had he been acting strangely around home? Depressed? Because these last few weeks—"

"No," she said louder.

Captain Chappelle's voice dropped to a murmur, but words floated up to me. *Drowned . . . intentional . . . weighted down . . .*

My mother kept repeating, "No."

"We'll fix it up, Ruth. Boating accidents happen every day."

"Not to my Boyd."

At the funeral home, I stepped away from the varnished wood box and listened.

Such a terrible accident.

> *What a shame.*

It could happen to anybody, out in a boat.

>> *You just never know when it's your time.*

So it was an accident. Those other words, floating up along the staircase, had just been a bad dream.

After the funeral, my mother and I took Philip home and we didn't talk about Daddy. If we didn't speak his name, maybe we could erase the knowledge that he'd never come back.

2

A body of approximately 150 pounds plunging into deep water from a height of approximately two feet above the surface, if weighted with an extra 15 to 20 pounds of, say, lead weights, will sink at the rate of approximately one foot per second. The person, regretting the lead weights, might thrash and struggle, or, not regretting, might succumb to the rate of sinkage until the dark and cold of the water takes over, until the moment when breath no longer holds, until the final, too-late regret, when the weight and the dark and the distance from the surface counterbalance any second thought, at which point the rate of sinkage becomes irrelevant, and the small fish approach and begin to nibble.

The glass tank before me contains a tiny diver figurine, air bubbling out of him, small fish hovering near, making me certain I will never again visit the National Aquarium, as close as it is to my work. My eyes move from the diver to someone behind me, a dark-haired young woman, hovering in the glass. I turn, but no one is there. I look back to see it's my own reflection, my adult self, for a second unrecognizable to the girl whose terrors have a habit of creeping into the grown-up I've forced myself to become.

Who would have thought that these seven or eight eye-level tanks recessed into the wall in a lobby of the Commerce Building could threaten everything that keeps me safe in Washington? Beg me as they will, the ichthyologists will have to find another artist. I'm sticking to drawing birds, from now until sweet goddamn eternity.

I take the two blocks back to Natural History at a clip, unfazed by a beefy guy in a dark suit who tries to stand in my way and breathes, "Hey, honey. What's your hurry?" At last, I enter my sanctuary, with its shining foyer. The public space of the museum is not my favorite, loud and full of tourists and school groups and hungry hordes. Their curiosity is endearing—they're acolytes for the natural world. And the marble gleams with architectural detail and precious objects all around. But on these, my gray days, entering the building carries the weight of death: all the specimens, thousands of carcasses of every species, stuffed or otherwise retrieved from oblivion so we can know them, yet all dead. The birds I draw and paint, all dead. On these days, my only defense is to imagine every pinned butterfly taking wing, every stuffed marsupial waking up, every preserved plant specimen blooming and carpeting the marble floor like a time-lapse forest, and every bird coming to life, flying up to the dome and away. On the days when the fog comes and hooks into my gut like a sharp-toothed parasite, these visions can save me.

The steadier, more consistent salvation, of course, is the work. I can lose myself for hours drawing, for instance, the common loon, with its inky head, white banding at the neck, and an intricacy of pin dots and fractured rectangles cascading across the wings. With the right precision, I can bring the deadness of a bird skin to a striking facsimile of life.

From the museum's foyer, I enter the drab back hallways and ascend to my studio, a well-lit office with an old metal desk pushed into a corner next to my drafting table. Vertical shelves hold drawing papers arranged by weight beside soft pencils organized by number and the pliability of their graphite. I've set the dark bottles of Rapid Draw next to an insanely large number of pen nibs and, next to them, my tubes of paint in rainbow order, ROYGBIV and all the gradations between.

I sit at my drafting table and look out over the Mall, the nation's vast green rectilinear lawn, punctuated with museums and monuments and a straight blond path. It took nine years to get an office with a window overlooking these American elms, soon to begin a fragile March budding, and toward the Smithsonian Castle. But it only took one day of work at Natural History to know I'd found my home. Yesterday was my thirty-sixth birthday, and my colleagues came in here singing, insisting I blow out candles on a little cake. They don't know the water is rising as I close in on thirty-seven, my father's magic number, his end point.

I reach for a paintbrush. On my slanted table today is a partially finished *Vanellus chilensis*, the southern lapwing, her slender black crest flying out behind her head. I refine the bronze sheen on the upper wings and fill in the gray, black, and white of the face. I need a size 0 brush for the beak, so I swivel away from the window to choose from among my clean, dry brushes, every bristle aligned and ready.

I'm at the tip of the beak when the phone rings. I set down the brush.

"Loni, it's Phil."

For a millisecond I think my brother has remembered my birthday. Then I come to my senses. "Phil, is something wrong?"

"Mom's had a fall. You gotta get here." He pauses. "And . . . you should plan for an extended stay." The fall broke her wrist, he tells me, but that's not the main problem. "She's been acting strangely, Loni. Her memory—"

"Come on, everybody that age forgets things," I say, cutting him off. I was home last year and I did notice her extra-short temper with me, but that's just an intensification of a lifelong habit.

"Tammy thinks it's the early-onset thing."

My mother is only sixty-two, and Phil's wife, Tammy, is no medical or psychiatric expert. I don't want my sister-in-law making any diagnoses. "All right. I'll see if I can get a few days off."

"No, listen, Loni. Take more time than that. This is major. And we need you here."

He so rarely asks. However, it's not the ideal time to miss work. The incoming administration has installed a cadre of nonscientists, mostly business majors hovering around the age of twenty-five, to examine the Smithsonian's efficiency quotient. I'd call them fresh young faces if they weren't so imperious and sour, masking their inexperience with the strict authority they've been given to boss our bosses. I might even have some patience with their youth if they weren't so determined to get rid of good people.

Ornithology's baby hatchet man is named Hugh Adamson. Last Monday, he gathered the staff together to spit out corporate-speak such as *downsize* and *consolidation*. "We'll be encouraging early retirement," he said. "We won't replace those who quit, and we'll enforce to the letter any and all violations of the leave policy."

Our office dress code is pretty relaxed, but Hugh wears a suit every day. The costume seems new to him, trousers straining against his thighs, perfectly starched shirt cutting into his neck. "Achieving downsizing via attrition," he said, putting a forefinger between collar and skin, "should not affect morale."

I snuck a glance at my boss, Theo, whose aging, mustachioed face was completely immobile. Federal employees are notably difficult to force out, but it seems these new bureaucrats will find a way. What Hugh and his fellows don't understand is that stern looks don't tend to motivate anyone in our line of work. The Institution encourages expansive thinking, and an ability to breathe in the atmosphere of your field is necessary for breakthrough science. People at the Smithsonian truly put their lives into what they do. But these young men—and they are all young, white men—are blind to everything but their own agenda. Which, at the moment, means conformity. Leaving for an extended stay in northern Florida will not fit their mold.

I head down the hall to consult the botany librarian, Delores Constantine, who has worked at the Smithsonian for the last forty years. She's the institutional memory of this place, and my role model for longevity in a job. She's also as prickly as a stalk of blessed thistle.

The hallway leading to Botany is lined with cabinets full of dried plants laid out on acid-free paper. Today, I imagine them as a vertical garden, orchids and epiphytes dripping from the sides, a phantom scent of humid forest.

I enter the library. "Delores?"

"Back here."

She stands on a rickety stool between stacked bookshelves. At eye level, the hem of her mauve skirt meets a pair of age-spotted shins. She lifts two large volumes above her head and hoists them onto a high shelf.

"Delores, can I help you there? I mean, is that safe?"

She glares down at me through cat-eye bifocals. "What is it you want, Loni?" She pushes the books into place and steps down from the stool.

I tell her about my brother's call, and what little I know about my mother's current condition.

She doesn't say, "Oh, kid, I'm sorry."

She leads me instead to her desk and moves a pile of books. Without sitting, she clicks the mouse, peering at the screen with her neck at what seems like a painful angle. "See this?" She points. "This is the FMLA form. Family leave." She gets up and whips a sheet off the printer, offering it to me with a blue-veined hand. "You fill this out, ask for eight weeks off, and go take care of your mom."

"Eight weeks? No possible way."

She puts a hand on a hip. "You don't have to use it all. Heck, the law gives you twelve if you need it. But with all the suits walking around this place, best keep it to eight."

"*Two* weeks in my hometown would be more than I can take," I say.

"Honor your mother, Loni." Delores has a daughter of her own, somewhere, but it's a pain point. They rarely talk. One of the few times it came up, she shrugged and said, "She doesn't like the way I give advice. But not everybody you love is gonna love you back." And then she went back to her work.

Delores puts a stack of books onto a cart. "You ask for eight, and if you use only two, come back and look incredibly dedicated to your work." She moves her lips into a canned smile, her eyes enlarged behind her specs. As a plant person, Delores may not seem like the most apt career counselor for a bird artist. In fact, she rarely thinks about birds. She's famous for tapping the side of her head and saying, "I only have so much space up here, kid. And it's botany, all day every day." But she knows more than anyone about how this place works.

"So go fill out that form and walk it down to HR," she says, giving me just the advice I need.

As I reach the doorway, she picks up another set of books and says, "Three things to remember: Number one, the Smithsonian will not pay you during your family leave."

"But—"

"Number two, check out the liaison program. I think Tallahassee has a museum that could use your help. They pay you directly, so you can preserve your leave status."

"Liaison program?"

Delores heads toward a bookshelf. "Look into it."

I nod, but then turn back. "What's number three?"

"Don't go a minute past the time you request. It's the French Revolution around here, and they're oiling the guillotine."

I go back to my desk, fill out the form Delores gave me, and search the Smithsonian website for "liaison program." Then I call Estelle, my truest Floridian friend, who always picks up when I call.

"Estelle," I say. "Is your museum part of the liaison program? With mine?"

"Hello, Loni. Yes, I'm fine, thanks, and you?"

When I'm moving slow, she's moving fast. And now, this once, when it counts, she wants to slow me down. I can visualize exactly where she is, at her curator's desk in the Tallahassee Science Museum, and I can even approximate what she's wearing—some stunning, jewel-toned suit, crisp-white-collared shirt, and complicated jewelry, her long red curls pushed back to accommodate the phone at her ear.

"Estelle," I say. "Please, just tell me."

"Yes, we are. Do you think I'd have my best friend working at the Smithsonian and not lobby hard for a connection? The Board approved it six months ago, and I believe I mentioned it to you."

"Right. I thought so!"

"There's a little excitement in your voice, Loni."

"Yep. So see if you might need anything from a wandering bird artist."

"You're coming home?"

"Just for a little while."

"Yay! And, as a matter of fact—"

"No need to commit right now," I say. "It's just good to know there's a possibility."

It takes me three days to get the forms stamped and approved and my own boss, Theo, mollified. He sits at his desk to sign the papers, then tosses the pen down and drags his hand from graying mustache to chin.

I try to reassure him. "Theo, I plan to come back quickly. Two weeks, max."

"Uh-huh," he says.

"I'll be back for the forest fragmentation project." It's a program that's been years in the making, requiring careful documentation of bird populations and countless illustrations. "I promise."

I pack my art kit, a tiny tackle box into which I place my favorite pencils, a quill pen and a few nibs, a matte knife, my Arkansas stone, and more crinkly tubes of paint than I'll ever use. I stuff my sketchbook and a few other small items into my large cloth bag, and then I turn out the office light.

My fellow illustrator Ginger comes running toward me from Botany, her long body waving side to side and her wild hair moving like a feathery bunch of fennel in the breeze. "Loni, with you gone, who'll defend me against the Bug People?"

As departments, we aren't very respectful of one another. The geologists are the Rock People and Delores and Ginger are the Plant People. Here in Ornithology, we're the Bird People, the ichthyologists are the Fish People, the entomologists are the Bug People, those in Paleo are the Bone People, and Anthro is just Anthro, because otherwise we'd have to call them the People People. Ginger is a botanical artist, but she spends a lot of time hanging out by my office door procrastinating. She is usually either comforting me about my latest dating failure, telling me I'm beautiful and wasting my time on jerks, envying my long straight hair that doesn't frizz like hers in D.C. humidity, or moaning about the Bug People, who continually ask her for illustrative favors.

"Eight whole weeks!" she says.

"I'm not staying that long." I hold up my art kit. "And I'm working while I'm there." After Estelle and I talked, she called me back to say she'd finagled some funding for a few key drawings of Florida birds.

Theo steps out of his office at the end of the hall. The skylight amplifies his padded frame, and he smooths his salt-and-pepper mustache. Theo has been a mentor since my first Smithsonian expedition, when our team of scientists walked into a muddy Peruvian cloud forest looking for the *gallito de las rocas* (*Rupicola peruvianus*), the bright orange bird with a tall bouffant. I trudged behind him for miles, my energy nearly spent and two sips of water left, nothing to focus on but his waistline bulging over fatigue-green khakis, wondering how a pudgy guy twenty years my senior could have so much more stamina. Then he pulled up short and raised his right index finger, pointing toward the tangerine-colored bird we'd come to see. Without Theo, I'd have walked right past it.

He tries to sound hard-nosed. "You filed those FMLA forms?"

"Yes, boss."

"And you got the official notice from HR?"

I nod.

"Any last words?" he says.

"Don't let them eliminate my job."

"Just get back on time, Loni. That's all I have to say."

"I got that message." I give him a pat on the arm, the limit of physical affection allowed by federal employee guidelines, and push through the door to the next hallway.

Who is there to greet me but our man Hugh Adamson. He wears a bright red tie that buckles where it meets a gold bar. "Ms. Murrow, a word?"

I've never been expert at concealing my feelings, and I'm afraid that in Hugh's meetings I haven't been as stoic as Theo. Either because I've asked an irritating question or two or because my face has betrayed me, Hugh regards me with particular disdain.

He looks down at a clipboard. "Ms. Murrow, I see you've requested eight weeks off under the Family Medical Leave Act. As today is March 15, that will make your return date May 10. Please know that May 10 means May 10, and if you report to work on May 11, rather than the previous day—May 10—you will be, regrettably, terminated."

I give him a fake smile, closing my eyes and keeping my lips together lest I say something unfortunate about the number of times he has said "May 10," or about treating his elders like fucking idiots.

Perhaps he intuits what is on my mind, because he lowers his otherwise prepubescent voice and says, "Do you think I won't do it?"

"I beg your pardon?"

"I see how you look at me during meetings, like I'm a little shit who doesn't know what he's doing."

"Hugh, I don't think I've—"

"Well, you just better come back on May 10, Loni, because on May 11 your ass will be in a sling and we'll be waving you good-bye."

I nod and proceed past our young despot. I've never really understood that expression, *ass in a sling*. In this case, it could be one of those giant slingshots drunk college boys use to hurl water balloons at unsuspecting passersby. Perhaps Hugh was his fraternity's Slingshot Chairman. Maybe he'd like to pull back and fling every scientist in his small realm of power from a turret of the Smithsonian Castle.

To regain my equilibrium, I head for the corridor of bird skins. These are not taxidermied birds, not cute in any way. Still, it comforts me to open the wide, flat drawers and see them there, even if they are tied at the feet and devoid of the life conveyed in the average field guide. Ornithologists, it turns out, are both preservationists and murderers, learning how to scoop out a bird's innards and keep the feathers on. But a bird skin, if properly prepared, can serve as a reference into the next century and beyond. Like this drawer full of cardinals: juveniles, males, females, specimens with winter plumage, summer plumage, and every variety within the varieties.

I close the drawer and continue wandering the corridors, soaking in the fluorescent dimness and the preservative smell that could be slowly pickling our brains, lulling us all into unpaid overtime and an odd reluctance to leave. The noisy museumgoers never see this labyrinth behind the gleaming cases and stage-lit dioramas—never need to know about Botany's desiccated stalks or Anthro's disassembled people filed away in labeled bins: "Skulls," "Femurs," "Tibiae," and "Fibulae." In Orn we have dead birds ceiling to floor, but at least we don't separate them into their various bits.

I'm almost to Rocks when I push on a pebbled-glass door leading to the main rotunda, its taxidermied elephant frozen midcharge. I turn a circle, tilt my gaze up past the balcony toward the dome, and whisper a prayer to the natural world to bring me back healthy and whole, and well before May 10.

3

Revelers in green stumbled from pub to pub as I drove away yesterday from springtime in Washington, a collage of the organic and the man-made—redbud and sidewalk, dogwood and car. Small trees in the easement showed feathery pink blossoms.

I've left the delicacy of spring for a hot, sodden green, the cruise control carrying me south through Virginia and the Carolinas, Georgia, and farther on toward the place where Florida's panhandle curves in and resort beaches fade into a coastline of dense mangrove and fingerling waterways. Slightly inland from the Gulf sits my hometown of Tenetkee, where the water transitions slowly to land.

I pull into town and a droplet of the old familiar wish to be anywhere else diffuses through my rib cage. I roll down the windows. The air is heavy with moisture, the wind redolent with rain. I stop for one of only six traffic lights in Tenetkee and rummage in the cupholder for a covered rubber band to pull my hair off my sticky neck. At the third stoplight, I pull into the parking lot of St. Agnes Home, or, as we kids used to call it, the Geezer Palace. I wish it really were a palace, for my mother's sake. The building has a Victorian façade, gingerbread cheerful, with a concrete ramp leading to sliding glass doors.

I sit in the parking lot and watch the automatic doors open as someone approaches, then close after the visitor passes through. I check myself in the rearview, combing out my hair and dabbing some makeup over my freckles. I rarely wear foundation, but I'd like to avoid advice from my mother about "fixing myself up." Little good it does—the makeup just forms beige-colored beads of sweat that I wipe away with a tissue. At least my eyes look okay—the whites clearly defined against the green irises. I thought they'd be bloodshot, given all the hours I've been driving.

I sit for a few more minutes staring at the outside of the building. Because Mom broke her wrist, she went into St. Agnes for physical and occupational therapy. Phil hinted on the phone at the possibility of a permanent move. I was skeptical, but he reported a level of chaos in the house I could hardly believe of my fastidious mother: open food containers in the linen closet and soiled clothes stuffed into bureau drawers, burners left on, midnight rambles through neighbors' yards, and an insistence on driving after several costly collisions. Last year when I was here for a few days, none of this was evident. But I suppose while Mom's wrist heals and she recovers in the Geezer Palace, Phil and I can figure it all out.

When I arrive at her room, she's sitting in a vinyl chair, her arm in a cast and a sling.

She starts in right away, the aging debutante with a voice full of mint juleps and brass nails. "Awright now, Loni, take me home."

No *Hello, darlin', it's been a long time, how good to see you.* No kisses or tears.

"Hi, Mom! Long time no see!"

"Don't switch the dern subject, you're here to take me home, now let's go."

Phil's wife, Tammy, who's a beautician, has styled my mom's hair into two stiffly sprayed, soup can–sized curls ascending an inch above her center part, the gray tips curving down and touching her temples. Without any intention, my sister-in-law has given my mother the look of the boreal owl, *Aegolius funereus.* If, as Tammy claims, she tailors each of her hairstyles to the personality of the client, what might this one indicate? Wisdom? Insomnia? The hunter's instinct?

My mother stands. "I've got my purse, now let's go."

I search the room for a distraction. "Hey, look! Tammy hung up your wedding picture."

"Yes," my mother says, "and when I tell Daddy how you have incarcerated me here, he's gonna whup your hide."

It takes my breath for a second, Dad spoken of, and in the present tense. She's not only mixed up the years, she's trampled the unwritten family rule: nobody talks about Daddy. And *whup your hide*? That would be his phrase, not hers.

She opens the bathroom door with her good arm. "I'm fixing my hair, and then we're going." She shuts the door harder than necessary.

Her open suitcase on the bed looks like it's been stirred with a wooden spoon. She's been packing to go home, but I reverse the process, hanging a blouse in the spartan closet, then folding and arranging the other items back into dresser drawers. I'm about to close the empty suitcase and put it under the bed when I see a piece of pink paper in the elastic side pocket and pull it out.

Dear Ruth,
   There are some things I have to tell you about Boyd's death.

Boyd, our father, who aren't in heaven. My eye darts to the signature. *Henrietta.* I reread the first line, then scan the flowery penmanship.

   Rumors flew around . . . I couldn't tell you then . . .

My mother opens the bathroom door, and I slip the letter into the back pocket of my jeans, nudging her suitcase under the bed with my foot.

"Not a Q-tip in this whole establishment!" she says.

"Hey, I can go get you some." I'm out the door before she can fuss anymore about going home. The Tenetkee Pharmacy is only three blocks from the Geezer Palace by sidewalk—a block and a half if I cut through the park—and I can read the letter on the way. The glass doors slide open and I step into the heat, almost colliding with a tall, fit older man.

"Well, hello, Loni Mae."

I see the chest of a Fish & Game uniform and my heart bing-bangs before I lift my eyes to the face. He's a year or two older than my mom, but his hair is still dark, and he seems young for his age. He beams a broad, gleaming smile.

"Captain Chappelle!" I reach up and give him a hug. "Wow. Sorry. You caught me by surprise. No one's called me 'Loni Mae' since . . . you know, my dad . . ."

"Oh, so well I do." He pauses. "Boyd's passing will never leave me, no matter how many years go by."

Hearing Dad's name in public is like a blaring car horn. In my short trips to Tenetkee, I rarely run into my father's old friends.

"Where you headed?" he says. "I mean to stop in and see your mama, but I'll walk with you a ways." Chappelle descends the concrete ramp with me. "I heard you were livin' up north."

I recite the basic details about Washington and the Smithsonian, looking up at my father's former boss, still straight-spined and robust. I once overheard Daddy say, "I'd trust that man with my life."

"Have any chirren?" he says.

The sun is behind him, and I squint. "I beg your pardon?"

"You know, sons and daughters?"

"Oh, no, sir."

"Married?"

"No, sir. Not yet."

"And you like that Washington, huh?"

"Yes, sir." *Yes, sir. No, sir.* I'm speaking like a child, a slight Florida twang creeping in with my Southern manners.

"It's a shame about your mama," he says. "Me, I've just decided my age won't get me."

"Looks like it hasn't."

"I'm in that gym every day, fightin' it off!" He flashes that charismatic smile.

There's a lull before my mother's training kicks in. *Ask him something about himself.* "Um . . . how are your kids?"

"Oh." He looks down. "You know, I don't hear too much from Shari. She's up in Alabama. And Stevie, well . . ." He swallows. "Stevie was killed, you know . . . car accident . . . back in January. . . ." He stops and presses his lips together.

Shit, of course I heard about this—a head-on collision, Stevie just out of rehab, his car on the wrong side of the highway. "Oh, no. Oh, I'm so sorry."

Chappelle takes a breath and tries to recover, his voice husky. "So I'm alone, now, at the house. After work, I go lift all the weights this body can stand, then do yard work till nightfall." His face brightens a bit. "Hey, why don't you come see my garden? Your mama always liked the plants, didn't she? And you remember where I live."

"Yes, sir, I do." There I go again. Loni the child, talking to a grown-up. This is what I'm reduced to in Florida.

"Well, you stop by then, hear? Mondays are good. I take Monday off now—flextime, you know." He points a finger at me. "So when you comin'?"

"Um . . . Monday?"

"Good girl."

We reach the drugstore, and he looks at his watch. "I'll leave you here and go visit with your mama. If I'm gone when you get back, I'll see you Monday, right?" He walks away, a boat leaving me in its wake.

I pull open the glass door of the Tenetkee Pharmacy with its faded decal—a penguin surrounded by icicles. "It's COOL in here," it says, a remnant of a time when air-conditioning was the rare miracle. I get my mother's Q-tips, pay, and leave. I stand again in the unremitting sunlight, clutching the Q-tips so hard the plastic buckles. I hate coming home. No matter how short the visit, the place always confronts me with my father.

Main Street is empty because it's too damn hot to be out. I walk past Elbert Perkins Real Estate with its closed vertical blinds. Then Velma's Dress Shop, crackly yellow cellophane lining the plate glass and turning the strapless black-and-white prom dress on the mannequin to sepia, like an old newspaper.

I shoulda seen it, Ruth, the young Captain Chappelle told my mother on that rare cool night when I was twelve. *Had Boyd been acting strangely? Depressed? 'Cause there were lead weights in every pocket* . . .

I turn away from Velma's.

Across Main, the faux-Georgian columns of mighty Town Hall bespeak a grandeur that never came to pass for little Tenetkee. And catty-corner, defying any attempt at architectural unity, sits my brother's accounting firm, the façade gleaming with smoked glass and metal trim, the affluence borrowed, I suspect, from the lawyers who share the building. I proceed toward it. Phil's early success is surely due to the confidence of the unquestionably loved child. He's only twenty-four, and he's already joined Kiwanis, made himself known to the town fathers, and taken up golf, all things necessary to gain the maximum number of accounting clients in this town and beyond. Phil has what other people call charm. It's not fake, exactly, but I know him better than some. I feel like pulling on the shiny square door handle of his fancy building and shouting inside, "Do this your goddamn self! I left this town for a reason!" But then Phil's partners and the lawyers across the hall would all look up and mutter, *Oddball sister. Nouveau-Yankee. Thinks she's a big shot.* So I cross the street instead.

A fug of frying onions envelops me as I pass the F&P Diner, whose initials have inspired sophomoric jokes for generations. As the sniggering boy behind me in tenth-grade English finally explained, "F & P, don't you get it? It stands for what their beans and biscuits make your arsehole do."

"Gross!" I said, turning back to my studies just in time to get "the look" from Mrs. Abbott. She was new to town and wore a girdle that made her double-knit dress into a three-tiered cake. We were reading *The Winter of Our Discontent.* Steinbeck sent Mrs. Abbott into raptures. She asked us about the book's ending, and I raised my hand. "I don't understand," I said. "What was he doing in that place—was it connected to a dock? And why does he bring razor blades?"

Already annoyed that I'd been talking in class, Mrs. Abbott shook her cheek fat at me. "He's going to commit suicide."

"But he doesn't!" I flipped the pages. "It's right here! He says . . . page 298 . . . 'I had to get back.'" I looked up at Mrs. Abbott, my face hot. "So you're *wrong.* He goes home to his children."

"Young lady, get up out of your chair." Mrs. Abbott's eyes narrowed. "You will not speak to me in that tone of voice. Please leave the room." That meant *Go down to the dean's office and await your sorry fate.* At the doorway I turned and gave a last look to Estelle, who scrunched her mouth around her braces in sympathy. Mrs. Abbott prodded me like a prize calf, and with her trailing, I proceeded across the dull black-and-white tiles toward what we called "The Room of Doom."

I sat in the hall, my heart pounding, while Mrs. Abbott conferred with the dean. When she came back out into the hallway, I expected a lecture from the dean, detention, and then another lecture from Mrs. Abbott. Instead, she gave me an awkward squeeze on both my arms with her pudgy little hands. "I'm sorry, Loni. I'm so sorry."

It dawned on me that day as I walked down the hallway and slammed my locker, as I ate my inedible lunch, that other people knew something I didn't. Until then, I'd made myself forget the words that had floated up to the top of the stairs the afternoon my dad didn't come home. *Intentional . . . weighted down . . . depressed . . .* Afterwards, everyone talked about "the accident," which meant that Captain Chappelle's words hadn't meant what I thought. He must have said *un*intentional. But there in sophomore year, four years after the fact, I saw it all clearly. No one else in town had played that mind game. Mrs. Abbott's stupid squeeze told me that she, the dean, and every greasy-haired, half-grown kid hurtling past me in the hallway thought of my dad like the Steinbeck guy with the razor blades. Except the Steinbeck guy came back.

Our church taught that if you committed suicide you went to hell, did not pass Go, did not collect $200 of insurance. We got the insurance money. So what about heaven? Did Saint Peter see the form marked "Accidental Death"?

I reach the Geezer Palace and hold out the Q-tips to my mother.

"Loni, I'm glad to see you. Listen, I'm congested." She exaggerates a breath. Not a glance at the Q-tips. "Hear that? Phlegm. Next time you and Daddy go to the swamp, tell him to bring me some bayberry leaves. I don't want a whole tree, just a handful. Got to inhale the vapors."

What does she have, ESP? I'm thinking about him, so she has to think about him? For her, he's just out doing his swamp time. Which would make me, what, ten or eleven?

I yank us both back to reality. "Mom, I got your Q-tips." *And what about our rule? Don't mention Daddy.* She should follow the rules.

My mother says, "Nothing like that bayberry when you're congested."

The folksy Wise Woman thing isn't exactly an act—she learned about herbal cures from Dad's mom, Grammie Mae. But it wasn't inborn. At sixteen, my mother made her debut in Tallahassee with the white gloves, the big dress, and a daddy dance at the Cotillion. Both her parents were professors at FSU—her dad in zoology and her mom in classics—and they were preparing for Ruth to be a concert pianist. All that ended when she married my father.

Grandmother Lorna would finish teaching a class called Philosophical Approaches in Ancient Greece and drive the hour down to our place in Tenetkee to say things like, "Ruth, just because you married Boyd doesn't mean you have to turn into him."

But my mom adapted to her rural surroundings, picking up more from her mother-in-law about herbs and country gardening than she ever learned from her own mother about the cultivation of roses.

In her tiny room at St. A's now, she says, "So tell your daddy about the bayberry, won't you?" She sinks into the vinyl chair. "He never comes to see me anymore."

Yeah, well, he never comes to see me anymore either, and good riddance. But I take the thought back, quick. It wasn't good riddance, it was stupid, unnecessary riddance that took the ground from beneath our feet.

"Mom, I have to go. I'll be back tomorrow." I kiss her cheek, soft and cool. She's definitely not feeling well, or she wouldn't allow it.

Panic blooms on her face. "You mean I'm supposed to sleep here?"

Part of me wants to whisk her out of this room the size of a galley kitchen and back to the house on the marsh with the sleeping porch, the Florida room, and the unattached garage smelling of mulch and clay pots.

"Yeah," I say. "You sleep here. Just until your wrist heals." A possible lie. I turn to go.

She says, "What's that sticking out of your pocket?"

I put my hand to the back of my jeans. The letter. I forgot to read it. "Oh, yeah . . . my uh . . . shopping list." Lie number two. "See you tomorrow!"

This time, as the sliding doors shut behind me, I reach back and unfold the pink paper.

Dear Ruth,
    There are some things I have to tell you about Boyd's death. Rumors flew around, and I suspect they hurt you. I couldn't tell you then, but now it's time. If you don't mind, I'll stop over in a day or two so we can talk.
    Yours,
    Henrietta

Henrietta. I try to put a face to that name, but I can't.

I refold the note, and step down the ramp and into the parking lot. A man with wispy white hair and uneven gray stubble approaches me, moving faster than his age would suggest. Shouldn't he be inside? He calls out my last name. "Hey! Murrow!" He's suddenly up in my face. "You better look out, or you'll be floatin' facedown in the swamp like your daddy."

I inhale.

The man snarls like an animal. "Get outta town, girl."

A young guy in purple scrubs comes around the corner of the building, flicking a cigarette butt. "Hey, Nelson!" he barks. "You are not allowed on the premises! How many times do we have to tell you? Move along!"

The old man jumps back and away from me. He heads across the parking lot and toward the street, but then the wispy head turns, and his rheumy eyes catch mine.

Do I know him?

He climbs into a battered blue pickup, peels out, and he's gone.

4

I pull onto the gravel driveway in front of the familiar white two-storey and carry my small suitcase up to my old bedroom. At the top of the stairs, I step over a spilled pencil holder, an old leather box, and a Weeki Wachee snow globe, then weave my way between full and half-full cardboard boxes. Phil and Tammy have already started packing up my mother's house. Who told them to do that? Mom's room is in a similar disarray. I smooth the wrinkles from the creamy chenille bedspread that's been here since before my father died.

My blouse sticks to my back like wet plastic. There's no breeze coming in the windows, only hard sunlight making the walls and floor look flat and unfinished, though every surface is painted, papered, varnished, and area-rugged.

Tammy has book boxes marked "GIVEAWAY" stacked in front of the window AC unit. The books are among the few things in this house I'm attached to. Whatever she and Phil are planning, I won't let them give away the books.

I hoist one of her heavy "GIVEAWAY" boxes to get to the air-conditioner, but then I get an idea. I take the box down the stairs, out the screen door, and down the porch steps until I reach the trunk of my car. I have no plan besides preservation. I go eight times up and down the stairs in my rescue mission. The ninth box has no lid. It's filled with paperback mysteries and true crime. I set it down on the back of my car. Am I being unreasonable? Almost every one of these is book-marked with a slip of paper. My mother used to say to my father, *"Why don't you read something good?"* and he'd give her a blank look, then go back to his mystery. I'm surprised she saved these.

On the top, though, is a bird book, rubber-stamped *Professor Thaddeus (Tad) Hodgkins, Department of Zoology, Florida State University.* I pull it out. Next to the illustrations, in Grampa Tad's fluid script, are dates and locations of sightings, weather conditions, and notes on the bird's behavior. Priceless marginalia.

Grampa Tad wasn't the one who taught me about birds—that was my father. Still, I like to imagine the first conversation between the balding, tweedy professor and the country boy who'd come to court his daughter, the two of them stiff and formal at first, Grampa Tad asking questions like, "What time will you have her home?" and, "You're not a fast driver, I hope?" until, somehow, they hit on the subject of birds. Then, the older man's face changes. He cocks his head back to listen, saying, "I know, I know, and the pileated woodpecker . . ." and they're off, the speech of the younger man still a bit more country than the professor would like for his daughter, but "The boy knows his birds!" Grampa Tad says, looking to his wife, who gives him a frown, the two men's faces rippling into smiles, my Grandmother Lorna disgusted with the both of them.

I go back upstairs and bring down the heaviest carton yet. As I shift the load to open the screen door, the box slips and spills its contents. I stoop down and put them back in one by one. A small spiral-bound book lies open, exposing a handwritten page, and I look closer. The wind picks up, and I put my hand on the page to hold it down. I'm half in the door and half out, and as I read I kneel on both knees, then sit, then lift the book and lean my back against the doorjamb.

Trouble sleeping again. Mind racing with what if and what if again, driving me to distraction.

And Boyd's snake of a father turned up today to ask for a loan but in the end spewed poison, only thing he ever does, his rare appearances. Want to stop thinking about him and the effect he has on Boyd.

Doc says sleeplessness an effect of pregnancy, best to lie on left side, one pillow under belly, another pillow between knees. Still listing toward the front. Impossible to rest body or mind. Want to tiptoe downstairs to play a nocturne, but Boyd might wake. Or sit among my herbs, bergamot and lavender, but the screen door will squeak. With my hands in the soil I could—

Wheels on gravel make me look up. Phil and Tammy. I toss the notebook into the box, get to my feet and lift, letting the screen door slap. Phil cuts the engine just as I close the lid of my trunk. *Act friendly.* I throw my hand up in a wave.

Phil unfolds his long self from the driver's seat—a khaki flamingo. How can he be the same fireplug-shaped little kid who used to play in this yard, dragging around his favorite toy, a wooden abacus? Tammy climbs out of the passenger side, eyeing me the way a sharp-shinned hawk eyes her prey. I walk toward them.

"Hey!" I call, a greeting I never use in Washington.

"Hey," Tammy says, not taking her eyes off me. In her spandex dress, she's all angles, except for a tiny potbelly and her streaky blond bangs curving stiffly toward her eyebrows.

Phil seems taller and lankier every time I see him. He inherited my father's light brown hair, but his sideburns are cut short and sharp, his hair layered on top, a modern man-cut clearly maintained by Tammy. He leans down to give me a pro forma kiss on the cheek.

I flick my eyes toward the house. "You started to pack up, huh?"

"Yeah," Tammy answers from behind us.

"You're already moving her out?" I ask my brother.

There's a silence, broken by my sister-in-law. "Tell her, Phil."

"I found some renters."

"Whoa!" I say. To hell with acting friendly. "Did we talk about this?"

Tammy says, "Now, Phil wrote up an inventory . . ."

"An inventory?" I look at my brother.

Tammy goes on. ". . . so we can sit down like civilized human beings and decide who gets what."

I wheel toward her. "You are unbelievable!"

Her eyes go big and she looks to Phil. He raises his palms toward her, and she spins and click-clicks toward the house, her spiky heels struggling for purchase on the gravel driveway.

Phil half-sits against the hood of his car. He's always acted overly sure of himself. His squarish chin and deep-set eyes made him "a catch" for the likes of Tammy. But to me, he's just a pale, skinny kid jingling the change in his pocket. I know every nervous tic he's got, the leg shaking under the table, the finger tapping, the extra energy that leaks out at the edges. Mom used to call him "the percussionist." And even though I'm twelve years older, he seems to have appointed himself the decision maker.

"You rented out the house? Without consulting me?"

"Loni, you weren't here." Jingle, jingle.

"I came as soon as I could! You told me to take more time than I usually do, which I organized, with some trouble! But meanwhile, you just made a bunch of decisions without me."

He pushes up from the hood of the car. "Look, Elbert Perkins approached me with an attractive offer for the house. These people actually wanted to buy, not rent. I got them down to a short-term lease. I mean, why let an asset sit idle?"

"An asset? Phil, this is our family home. Our mother's home."

"Loni, she can't live alone anymore."

I let this sink in.

"And you know what the fees are at St. Agnes?" he says.

Our family's little accountant. I've always been too easy on him, because being left fatherless as a baby is something you never recover from. But I won't go soft this time. Even when he gives me that charming grin and hooks an arm over my shoulder.

"Come on, sis, it'll all work out."

Where does he get his infuriating optimism? The pink letter in my pocket burns hot, and half of me wants to share it with him. But we have that rule. *Don't talk about Daddy.* My brother steers me toward the house and its uncontainable chaos.

5

Thank God, they finally left. As dusk falls over the marsh, I walk outside. The gap-toothed dock has lost a few more boards and several new houses encroach on our clear vista of sawgrass and stream. My mother's herb garden retains its pleasing angles. The winters are mild enough here that the garden thrives year-round. Her basil is like a shrub, and the rosemary would be a tree if she didn't constantly cut it back. She seems to have kept the garden in trim even while the interior of the house turned toward ruin.

I tilt my head back to look up at the juncture in the live oak tree where two thick branches meet at the trunk. That used to be my thinking place. My mother worried I'd fall, but Daddy said, "Ruth, let her be. That's Loni Mae's own nest."

Up there I honed my sense of hearing, as my mother and our neighbor Joleen Rabideaux sat on our back porch drinking tea and sneaking cigarettes. Joleen was shaped like a potato on two toothpicks, and she'd rehash every sensational crime from Pensacola to Port St. Lucie. Her husband was the Fish & Game dispatcher, so maybe that's where she got her news.

I once heard her say, "You think Boyd goes away to his fishing camp too much? Well, my Marvin talks all day on that two-way for work, and when he comes home what does he do but get on that ham radio? And when he's not doin' that he's tinkerin'. He said to me yesterday, 'Joleen! I found a new frequency!' I went into our spare bedroom and he had a so'd'rin' iron in one hand and radio parts scattered all around. Boyd may drive his boat around on his days off, but Marvin ain't with me when he's with me!"

Another day she said, "Not everyone in the department is on the straight and narra, mark my words." I imagined words on a paper marked with red pencil, like in school. *Mark my words.* "Marvin's on that radio, and he knows."

Once when I was about seven, my mom rushed out of the house and told me Mrs. Rabideaux would be right over. I'd never been in the house alone. I waited and waited. I checked the pantry for daytime ghosts among the flour, oats, and dry beans. I went into the Florida room and felt the terrazzo floor cool on my feet, and upstairs to the sleeping porch, where the house seemed to breathe, sucking the screens in and out. Then I ran outside to the live oak and climbed up to where I knew I was safe.

After a while, a voice below crowed, "Hey there!"

Mrs. Rabideaux had opened the screen door and was calling inside. She wore a sleeveless red calico dress that looked like an onion sack. I came down from the tree and stood behind her until she turned and jumped.

"Well, ding-dangity!" she said. "Like to give me heart failure."

She and I played nine games of Parcheesi. Toward the end, every time it wasn't her turn she leaned back in her chair and rolled her eyes to one side. Finally, we heard my dad's Fish & Game truck in the driveway and turned to see my mom driving. Daddy was in the passenger seat with gauze wrapped around his arm and shoulder.

He told Miss Joleen, "I caught old Garf Cousins dumping trash into a sinkhole and gave him a fifty-dollar ticket. Don't you know, Garf pulled a knife on me? Musta been drunk."

Joleen said, "Well, you're in the right." Without thinking, she slapped him on the shoulder, and he winced.

He saw my reaction and made his face recover, though his voice took longer. "Don't worry, Loni Mae. It's just a flesh wound." He tried to smile. "It'll go a lot worse for Mr. Cousins. He's likely to go to Raiford."

Garf Cousins did go to the state penitentiary, and he hated our family for years. He sent Daddy a death threat from prison, which only made him stay longer. But whatever became of Joleen? I bet she'd have known this letter writer, this Henrietta. As I recall, Joleen and Marvin moved away not long after my dad died. One day they were home, and the next day gone, the house emptied out and the door ajar. Their place still sits derelict right down the road.

In my childhood bedroom, I climb into my old single bed with the gingham cover and turn on the reading light. Where some people read to fall asleep, I doodle. In my sketchbook, I draw the back porch as it looked from the live oak, Joleen with her round face and thin hair pulled back in a ponytail. My mother sits across the wicker table, a secret cigarette in the ashtray before her. I try to draw my mom's face, but I can't get it. I rub at the features with my eraser and try again. Then again.

In Florida, pictures tend to arrive in my sketchbook unbidden. The ones that disturb me get crumpled. Already in the trash are three studies of the strange man who accosted me in the Geezer Palace parking lot. Plus a sketch of our dangerous dock. Rip. Crumple. Toss. To the troublesome drawing of my mother, I say, *Look up at me!* But I can't get the *gizz* of her.

The word "gizz" would shock the Tallahassee Ladies Guild, but despite its homonym, it's a common usage among bird artists. Like "gist," but with more substance—a life force, the spirit that reaches beyond the brushstroke to the vitality of the bird. You can't actually draw it, but if it's not in your picture, you've failed. I've always been better with creatures than humans, but you'd think I could capture the *gizz* of my own mother.

People tell me I look like her. So I try again, focusing on the features we share: the straight-line lips, the point of the chin, the dark-chocolate hair. Of course, mine hangs straight to the sides of my face, so in the drawing I give hers a different style and the gray creeping in at her temples. Still, all I get is a modified self-portrait. Me, at her age.

I flip the page and try a different scene—my young mother at the piano, her long hair down, dented from the pins that held it close all day. She wears a white cotton dressing gown, more glamorous than the ironed shirtwaists she wore during the day. If she's playing a nocturne, then outside the picture my father must be at his fishing camp deep in the swamp. The notes she's playing don't make it into the drawing, but if they could, they'd convey her longing.

In my drawing, I turn her around on the piano bench. But still she resists. "Come on, Mother!" I say aloud, but the face turns out annoyed. It's late, so I throw down the sketchbook and turn out the light. The patter of the rain on the roof becomes a hard thudding. Nature is pouring out her pitcher. I imagine piano music downstairs—my mother's fingers dancing on the keys. Did she play a nocturne on that last night, assuming my father was warm and safe and dry at the camp? When really he was none of those things. Merely gone.

6

MARCH 18

In the morning, I step out to water my mother's herbs. How could she keep these so perfect while everything else fell away? I pull out the long hose, twist the spigot, and spray first in one direction, then another. Fragrances rise up—the thyme's spicy astringency and the fuzzy menthol of the sage, the chamomile's daisy-petal smell and the piney cool rosemary. The lavender, not yet in flower, is surprisingly mute. I direct the mist toward the basil, and the aroma jumps up like a lemon tree eating a pizza.

I go back inside. In the dining room are the items Tammy has removed from the sideboard: lace-edged linen napkins and a matching tablecloth that were once Grandmother Lorna's, gold-rimmed Limoges china that never left the cabinet, a set of teak bowls, and all the other lovely things my mother owned but scorned, because of the acrimony between her and her own mother. A piece of scotch tape holds a multi-page spreadsheet to the wall, titled "*INVENTORY*." I lift a page, skim, and let it drop, turning back toward the room and scanning for something pink—an envelope, I hope. The one that held that letter, ink bright and paper fresh. All I need is a return address.

An explosion of noise at the door gives way to running feet and small voices calling, "Aunt Loni!" as the two brightest lights in town barrel toward me. My nephew, Bobby, is skinny and quick at age five. "What did you bring?" He knows I visit Natural History's museum shop before any trip to Florida. His sister, Heather, more sophisticated at six, brings up the rear, swinging a patent-leather purse. Her brunette pageboy ruffles when I squeeze them both tight, and they follow me to my bag. I wrinkle my forehead. "Um . . . did you think I had something for you?"

"Yes, you do!" Bobby declares. His crew cut is soft to the touch.

"Yes, I do," I admit, pulling out a shark hat with white felt teeth pointing downward. He puts it on and looks in the mirror above the sideboard to see a plush shark eating his head. He runs in circles screaming, "Aaaah!"

For Heather, I've brought a smooth agate geode that glows in the palm of her hand. "Sort of matches your eyes," I say. It's shot through with brown, gold, and a speck of greenish-blue.

Those agate eyes look up at me. "Way cool." She gazes down again into the geode as if to divine a great secret.

Tammy strolls in, letting the screen door smack. Without preamble, she says, "Do you know somebody named Henrietta?"

I give her my full attention. "Why?"

"This lady came over here while we were packing boxes, said she needed to talk to Ruth, it was important, blah, blah, blah."

"Did she say her last name?"

Tammy puts a hand on her hip. "Hm. I don't think so. Anyway, I told her Ruth would be very happy for a visitor at St. Agnes." She looks at herself in the mirror above the sideboard and pushes her hair up on both sides.

"What was she like?" I say.

"Who?"

"Henrietta!"

"You don't have to get so excited, Loni. I don't know. She was old."

"Well, that narrows it down," I say.

"She drove a nice car, Coupe de Ville, pearl pink. Suh-weet." She turns away from her reflection. "Hey, there's another thing you should know."

"Yes?"

"We're telling your mom there's an electrical problem with the house."

"What?"

"Well, all she ever says is, 'When can I go home? Take me home, take me home!' And what do you say to that?"

I open my mouth to answer, but she keeps going. "My friend Deedee, she works with these people, and she says you tell a person a story—like the roof is damaged, or the wiring is being fixed, and that's why she had to move out for a while. And then, because of her *condition*, she'll forget where she used to live and be fine in the new place."

I actually laugh in her face. "Really? Sorry, Tammy, but I'm not making up a cheesy story. Whatever we tell her, it should be true."

"Okay, you try that. But remember, some people *without* master's degrees are smarter than those with."

I'm on simmer, and before I reach boil, I break Tammy's gaze and call to the kids in the next room, "Hey, you all! You ready for ice cream?"

"Yogurt. Get them low-fat frozen yogurt only, Loni."

I turn from Tammy and take two damp little hands in mine.

The fancy Lodge at Wakulla Springs has an old-fashioned dining room where they've never heard of frozen yogurt, so alas, we have to order good old ice cream sundaes with whipped cream and maraschino cherries, served in chilled metal goblets on paper doilies. I'm all for healthy living, but how often do I see these guys? Between cold spoonfuls, Heather tells me about the antics of some of the boys in her first-grade classroom, how her teacher should probably try the stoplight system they had in kindergarten to make students behave better, and who her best friend is. Bobby gives all his attention to his ice cream.

I look around the dining room. The older woman at the table by the window could be Henrietta, and I'd never know it. My niece brings me back. "Who's your best friend, Aunt Loni?"

"As a matter of fact, Heather, my best friend is named Estelle, and you know when we met?"

A shake of the head.

"When we were just your age. And we're still friends. In fact, I'm going over to see her tonight."

A man approaches our table. It's Elbert Perkins, the real estate guy. He's big and ruddy faced, with a barbecue belly. He wears boots with dress pants, the way a Texas rancher might. "Hello, Loni," he says. He must be seventy, but his voice is resonant and deep. He fingers a crisp straw cowboy hat.

"Oh, hello, Mr. Perkins."

He gives a condescending wave to the kids and then says, "How's the house coming?"

"You mean my mother's house?"

He nods once.

"Great, thanks."

"If you want me to get my reclamation crew in there, they can clear it out for you, save you the trouble, for a small fee. Have it done before the end of the month, no muss, no fuss."

I look at his third shirt button, which is mightily strained. "No, I think we've got it all under control, thanks."

"You sure now?"

I nod my head, hoping he will leave. The children study him as if he is an alien being. He finally says, "You just let me know," and ambles over to his own table.

The kids and I finish and walk out into the warm air with the cold still sticking to our smiles. I drop them at their music lesson as instructed, then park on Main. Calmer now than the last time I walked past Phil's building, I pull on the square metal handle, walk into the air-conditioned deep freeze, and approach the receptionist, who sits at a rounded chrome desk. I look down. "Hi, Rosalea."

She smiles blandly. Rosalea Newburn was a year behind me at Wakulla High. "May I help you?" she says.

She knows exactly who I am, she just holds a grudge because of an ancient dispute over a boy in school. Plus, she's Tammy's friend. God knows what's been said about me. Her jagged eighties hairstyle with plenty of mousse tells me she's a regular at Tammy's salon.

"Rosalea, could you please tell my brother I'm here?"

"Do you have an appointment? Because he's with someone."

"I'll wait." I sit on the leather couch and flip through the magazines. *Florida Today. Boar Hunter. Southern Living.* Rosalea gives me the fisheye. Can she really still hate me because of Brandon Davis? I didn't even really like him, just went to prom with him because he asked me. How could I know Rosalea had a famous crush on him, had memorized his schedule, and stalked him on the stairwell every day? He was my lab partner in biology and we sang silly songs to dispel the grossness of dissecting a fetal shark—"Mack the Knife," and the *Jaws* theme, and "I Believe in Spiracles." At first when he brought up the prom, I put him off, telling him I had to check with my mom. But when Rosalea and her posse heard he'd asked me, they started calling me "giraffe" for my long legs and thin body, and otherwise orchestrating a flurry of angry notes and gossip about me, at which point I found Brandon in the hallway and said, "YES! I'll go." I made a long green slip dress on Estelle's mother's sewing machine, and Brandon picked me up in his father's car. When he arrived, he'd already downed half a bottle of Southern Comfort, so I pushed him over and took the wheel. Later that evening, at the end of a sloppy drunk dance, he leaned in for a kiss and threw up on my new green dress.

The following Monday, Brandon switched lab partners and joined Rosalea in tormenting me. They stuck with the giraffe theme, sprinkling hay on my seat in homeroom, putting kibble through the slots of my locker, and posting a picture of a giraffe next to my campaign poster for student council president. They were so pissed when I adopted the giraffe as my campaign logo—*Vote Loni: A Head Above the Crowd*—and won.

I look up from *Boar Hunter*. The woman is still glaring at me from behind the round chrome desk.

Estelle keeps me up on all the hometown gossip, including Rosalea and Brandon, who married after high school. Sounds like Brandon doesn't do much these days but sit and eat junk food and watch TV. He works a few hours a week at the feed store, but Rosalea mostly supports them on her receptionist's salary.

The office door opens and out prances Tammy, Phil's important client. She walks past me with a, "Hm, Loni." Not *thank you for entertaining the children*, not even *hello*, but not exactly *kiss my ass* either, so I'll count it as progress.

"You left them with the piano teacher?" she says.

I nod. "Yes, ma'am."

Phil comes out of his office. "Loni, come on in."

Tammy leaves to get the kids, and Phil closes the door behind me. I plop into the chair opposite his desk. Here is the inner sanctum, the place where Phil gets to pour himself into the numbers he so adores.

"Ready for the financials?" he says.

I put my elbows on the desk and straighten my spine. "First I want to know every decision you've made without me."

"I'm sorry. Things happened pretty fast." He sets his pen down on the blotter. "I promise I'll keep you in the loop from now on."

"*Before* you decide stuff," I say.

"Yes."

He moves the pen and spreads out several sheets of paper. "So look these over and see what you think." The documents indicate the establishment of a trust. Into it will go payments from an annuity established long ago with my dad's life insurance money, Social Security benefits, the rent from the house, and the dregs of a small inheritance from Grandmother Lorna. My mom has a widow's pension from the state and a slim retirement benefit from the public school system where she taught music after Phil started kindergarten, setting her face like stone before every cacophonous band rehearsal. I expect these funds to add up to more than they do. Phil and I agree to make monthly contributions to augment the total, but considering how long she's likely to need care, the whole enterprise will be quite expensive.

"You're absolutely sure she can't live on her own?" I ask.

"Not without twenty-four-hour help," he says, "and that's even pricier than St. A's. I've been managing her bills, but she's a sucker for every charity that calls."

I read through the documents. What would my dad have thought? I can't ask that of Phil. He hardly even knew Daddy. At least I got twelve years with my father. To Phil, Boyd Murrow is an abstraction, a picture in a photo album, someone who tickled his son's chubby little chin and then turned and fell off the earth.

"Are you renting the house furnished?" I say.

"Mostly. Some pieces we'll, um, store." He taps his foot under the desk.

Store in his new townhome, he means. But my mom can't use the furniture, I can't transport it, and maybe Phil and Tammy need it. They've been married six and a half years, since right after their high school graduation. Until recently they lived in a furnished rental apartment, so in a material way they've struggled. And why wouldn't they, starting a family before they even knew what life was? Phil has no idea I helped my mother pay his in-state college tuition.

"You guys take the furniture," I say, blessing a done deal. "If we can't keep the renters from descending, I just want to save the books and anything that's sentimental for Mom. It's still her stuff, after all."

He rolls his pen between his fingers. "*All* the books?"

I shrug. "We'll see."

"So." He picks up one of the sheets of paper. "You remember Bart Lefton, right? His law firm shares our office suite here, and he helped me with the trust document."

A body passes by the smoked-glass wall of Phil's office. "Hey, Bart!" Phil gets up and opens the door. "Bart, Loni's here. Have a second?"

Bart Lefton enters and shakes my hand. He has the broad face and sandy-haired complacency of a Florida boy gone to seed. He and Phil hung around together as teenagers, though Bart was a few years older and never one of my favorites. I'm surprised he made it all the way through law school.

"Good to see you, Loni. Can't stop, though. Got a big case comin' up. Phil, you goin' over those . . . right. You're in good hands, Loni." He winks at me and leaves, closing the door behind him.

"So." Phil starts over. He picks up the document again and reads it silently, then aloud, as I imagine he does with his other clients to prove he understands the gobbledygook. "'. . . Successor trustees'—that's us—'shall have discretionary powers to administer funds for the benefit of the grantor, spouse being deceased.' Wait a minute," he says. "Rosalea misspelled 'deceased.'"

"As in 'spouse being deceased,'" I say.

"Mm-hm." He makes a note.

"That would be Dad," I say.

He looks up. I'm breaking the family rule.

I worry a rough cuticle on my right thumb. "Mom's been talking about him like he's still around."

Phil nods.

I say, "Do you remember anything of him?"

He lowers his chin. "Well . . . I think I remember him holding me above his head and making me laugh."

Phil got that memory from a photograph, and I know which one.

"Other than that, nothing," he says.

I have a flash of my father in the hallway of our house, holding Phil as a minutes-old newborn, the baby still covered with whitish crud, me frozen in place with the towel Daddy sent me to fetch.

I clear my head of the picture. My memories are complicated, but at least I had moments with my father, even if they seem now like a series of cascading smiles and frowns hurtling toward a terrible end. Phil has no real recollections. But he's also been spared the most dreadful knowledge. His is a clean, easy story—a father who went out into the swamp, fell out of his boat, and drowned.

Mine is a father who left us on purpose, who broke faith. But I don't need to share.

"What do *you* remember about him?" Phil says, my boomerang of a question hurtling back at me. Of course he would ask. No one has ever opened this door for him. The family rule has deprived him of even a shadow-box cutout. He wants to know something, anything.

"He was an excellent fisherman," I say. "He knew the swamp really well."

"Hm," Phil says.

Is he waiting for me to say more? It's deep, this hesitancy. For me, talking about my dad is like touching an abscess. Fresh pain, long after the wound should have scabbed and mended.

"So I guess you need me to sign these," I say, looking down and scanning the pages.

"Yeah." He picks up the phone. "Rosalea, can you come witness a signature?"

Rosalea comes in, jutting out her hip as she watches me scratch the pen at the bottom of three pages, then signs where she has to.

"Okay, then," Phil says.

Rosalea leaves, and my brother walks me to the door. "Hey, you know Saturday after next, when everything has to be out of the house?"

Sweat pricks at my armpits.

"That Sunday, when we're all done, want to cookout at my house?"

My heart lifts at the invitation. I'd planned to leave that Saturday night, get back to D.C. on Sunday, and be fresh for work the following day. "Wow, that's a nice . . ." I trail off. It would mean two entire days with my sister-in-law.

"Tammy has some hen party that Sunday," he says, "so it'll just be me and the kids. And you, if you come. Burgers, you know, simple stuff."

"I'd like that," I say.

"Around four?"

"Okay." I turn to leave, contemplating where I might sleep that Saturday night, once the house is taken out from under me. Maybe Estelle's.

As I open his office door, I turn back to my brother with a sudden idea. "Hey. Were you at Mom's when that lady Henrietta came around?"

"The one with the pink car?"

"Right. Did you catch her last name?"

A blank stare.

I don't tell him how urgent it is I speak with her, or how her letter sparked the most dangerous of emotions—hope. "Well, if you happen to think of it, tell me, okay?"

A scant nod from my oblivious, happy brother.

7

Next stop, the Geezer Palace, with a few more toiletries. Five minutes of putting them where they belong, and thirty-five additional minutes filled with my mother's pointy complaints. "Gosh, Mom," I say, finally, "I hate to go, but I'm running late for Estelle, and you know the traffic on the way to Tallahassee."

I love the road leading out of Tenetkee. First, because it leads out of Tenetkee. Second, because it runs right through an oasis of unspoiled Florida landscape—the Apalachicola National Forest. It has two narrow lanes with slash pines on either side growing straight and skinny, with branches that start about seventeen feet up. My windows are open and the sun flash-flashes between the trees.

Back when I left home for college, this road represented the wider world. At Florida State, I discovered who I could be when my mother wasn't around to click her tongue. Back then, I was running away. Today I'm running toward.

My windscreen is spotted with the conjoined pairs of lovebugs (*Plecia nearctica*) that hover thick over the road, mating as they fly, oblivious to the two-ton machines that hurtle toward them and spoil their bliss. I squirt the windshield cleaner, but my wipers only smear them into a sticky rainbow shape.

I pass the tower of the state capitol and pull up to an apartment building on Monroe Street that's beige and modern, with good landscaping and a shiny entrance. No need for the *Saved by the Bell* sleeping bag I used to bring to our youthful slumber parties. Estelle now has a guest bedroom.

I grab the box of Coconut Treats I've brought and slip them into my cloth bag. Just as I get out to reach for my overnight case, someone runs toward me in heels.

"Wahoo!" Estelle tackles me with a skinny stuffed-animal hug. She's all high fashion, as usual, a brown pencil skirt and sleeveless top with a flounce at the waistline. That long red hair holds a curl even at the end of a humid Florida workday.

I sling my bag over my shoulder, and Estelle walks backwards, talking rapid fire. "I want to hear more about the ride down, and how your mom is doing. Are Phil and Tammy behaving?"

I texted her yesterday, but she wants the news up to the minute. While I talk, she keeps sticking her head sideways in front of me and saying, "You're here!" and giving me a goofy smile.

We reach her apartment. Estelle's decorating scheme is warm—polished wood floors and thick woolen rugs, cream-colored sofas and pillows in hues of tree bark and clay.

"I'll put your bag in Roger's off . . . I mean, the guest room," she says.

"Where's Roger again?"

"Work travel. Houston." Her boyfriend is a journalist. He's nice enough, but I'm relieved I can just deal with Estelle on her own. Her voice echoes as she walks into her bedroom. "I'm gonna change. Make yourself some tea, or whatever you want."

I fill the teakettle. Estelle is very welcoming, partly because we're friends and partly because of her years-long quest to get me back to Florida. When I first moved away, she would call once a month to do interpretive readings of the Help Wanted ads in the *Tallahassee Democrat*, enhancing the job description with the promise of abundant straight, cute, single men who were awaiting my return. She still calls once a month, and the frequency of contact keeps our friendship fresh in spite of our differences. She's into fashion, me not so much. Her parents moved to Florida from Baltimore, my family's been here for generations. She's in my field, but she also went for an MBA. If she hadn't been in that seat in front of me in the first grade, a lifeline in the dangerous world outside my yard, we might never have been friends at all.

She emerges from her bedroom in paisley Pashtun pants and a lime-green shirt with tiny mirrors. Estelle's after-work thrift ensembles are as carefully chosen as her expensive work clothes. I open the Coconut Treats.

"Oh no. Already? Is it a guy?"

Estelle knows my romantic history, which is mostly catch-and-release.

"No, not a guy," I say.

Throughout our friendship, chocolate has had pharmacological applications, and Coconut Treats equal intensive care. They're only available at Stuckey's, a store by the highway on-ramp that stocks hostile tourist trash like real baby alligator-head paperweights and amputated-claw back scratchers. I wouldn't go in there if it weren't an absolute necessity.

"Then what?" She sits down on the couch.

"This place!" I say.

"My place?"

"No, home. Tenetkee. And of course, *The* Home. I ran into my dad's old boss as I was coming out of the Geezer Palace yesterday. I hate being confronted with . . . you know . . . all of it." Estelle is the only person I ever talked to about my dad's death. I peel the cellophane from the box of chocolates. "Hey, in school did any of our friends have a mother named Henrietta?"

She wrinkles her mouth. "Not that I can think of. But I can ask my mom. Why?"

I pull the pink letter out of my pocket. "Look at this."

Estelle skims it, subvocalizing, "*Boyd's death, rumors, hurt you.*"

She looks up. "Well, this is good news."

"Estelle, how could anything that has the word *death* in it and the word *Boyd* in it be good news?"

"This letter says, *now it's time*. So this lady must have some information you didn't have before. Like . . . what rumors does she want to dispel?"

"Yeah, that's the little flutter I got when I read it. But I've worked really hard against self-delusion, as you know."

She hands me back the pink paper.

"And by the way," I say. "I got your list." I put away Henrietta's letter and take from my front jeans pocket the sheet I folded sixteen times, as if making it physically smaller would reduce its burden.

"Yay!"

"Estelle. You're kidding me, right? There's no way I can draw eighteen birds for you."

"I pay by the bird." She smiles.

"I can draw one bird, maybe two. But I plan to be here only two weeks, and most of that will be spent clearing out my mother's house."

Estelle leans back into her couch pillows. "The only way you'll clean out that house in two weeks is if you pull up a dumpster and throw everything in."

I picture that kind of havoc and feel a little sick.

"You need to break up the task with something you're passionate about." She pulls at a red curl, knowing-it-all. "Such as drawing birds."

I roll my eyes but hold out the Coconut Treats, then take one myself. We chew our chocolate and let the sugar-cocoa-tryptophan-endorphins seep into our brains. She leans back again and gets a far-away look. "Do you remember our plans when we were in grade school?"

"Of owning a store full of beaded bracelets we made ourselves and having girl-children who were best friends?"

Estelle brightens. "Exactly! So this can be a version of that!"

"What can?"

"You and I working together."

I take another bite. Chew. Swallow. "Here's why not, Estelle: A) No girl-children."

"Not yet."

"B) I don't live here."

"Not yet."

"C) You want eighteen birds in two weeks."

Estelle sips her tea. "Hey. I'm just trying to give you what you like. But if you want to spend the whole time agonizing over Ruth's Lladró figurines . . ."

"Shut the hell up!"

She stops mid-chew. "Touchy, are we?"

Estelle knows about my short fuse, but I need to watch it. "Look, I'm a little raw. So please, no jokes about my mother or her belongings."

"Jeez. Got it."

"And I'm not saying no to *all* the drawings. The list is just too long, and the longer the list, the more likely we are to fight."

I have a tendency to clash with curators. When I get comments like, *The head is too compact and the tail should be longer*, I have to decide which part is worth contesting. But I also wake in the night with corrections they didn't even see, like the goshawk's wing that needed to be a millimeter higher to give the bird the truest sense of flight. Curators are vexing, but my own sense of perfection is what makes me hard to work with. Even if no one else notices, I want to step back and be satisfied.

"You? Fight with me? I can't envision it," Estelle says, pulling at one eye. "Let me see if I can cut down on the number. But please don't say it won't work, because nobody can conjure birds the way you can."

"Empty flattery."

"Yeah," she says. "Really, you suck. That's why I wanted you for this."

"You're aware I procrastinate and I'm grouchy around deadlines."

"Tell me something new, honey." She checks her fingernails. Then she looks up, that light of genius in her eyes. "I've got it. We make a pact. We can fight at work—constructive creative disagreements. But outside the museum, peace shall reign. The personal and the professional shall not overlap."

"What about our popcorn nights?"

"All shop talk is banned during *that* sacred ritual."

"Is that really possible?" I say.

"Well, if you're such a royal bitch at work, we have to do something to preserve our friendship."

"You're so demure."

"I know, Loni. Just a little old Southern belle, like you."

8

A week later, after sweating gallons of salt water while sorting and packing in my mother's house with Tammy, and many hours at the Geezer Palace listening to my mother complain, I go over to Estelle's Tallahassee Science Museum. She sets me up in a studio vacated by Bridget, her artist out on maternity leave. I know it is part of Estelle's plot to make me her minion, but there's no denying the relief I find in a cool, darkish place where I can shine a single lamp over a drafting table and just draw.

The museum is out on the edge of Tallahassee, surrounded by a nature trail and far enough from downtown to feel like the indoors and outdoors might have something to do with each other. A small residential area on the other side of the woods is hidden from view, so the museum retains the appearance of being the only man-made structure around. The exhibit space has displays on the original inhabitants of Florida, both people and creatures, and an entire room devoted to birds.

Before I start to draw, I carry in the ten boxes of my mother's books and stack them against a small couch. My car has served as their safe haven, but I've used up a lot of fossil fuel carting them around, and I'm glad to find an air-conditioned spot where they won't be in danger from Tammy. A window with a Roman shade reveals palmetto and cabbage palm and offers some good natural light. Now to Estelle's list. I tack two sheets of drawing paper to my table, one for the main drawing, and one for other ideas. An art professor at Florida State first suggested this method, and sometimes the random thoughts and pictures that spill onto the second sheet are even more useful than the subject at hand.

My model is a bird skin of the mangrove cuckoo, borrowed from the FSU Orn department. The cuckoo is number 2 on Estelle's list, and I'm starting there because FSU's specimen for her bird number 1—the purple gallinule—was ill-used, with matted feathers and a dullness that didn't do the living bird justice. The mangrove cuckoo skin is in better shape. With a light touch and my #6B extra soft pencil, I outline the teardrops of white at the cuckoo's tail. I work fast, going for something more than simple accuracy. Next, I mix colors. The white breast graduates downward from light cream to darker buff.

When I look at the clock, three hours have passed. I get up and stretch, then cross the studio to look over my mother's books. I notice the little notebook that opened itself for me in the wind, and pull it out. Across the front in large, handwritten letters is the word "GARDEN." I open to a random page.

Need more color. Try sunflowers, flax. If the blue does not clash with the purple, pink, white of my periwinkles. Mae gave me these first cuttings. How I miss her. Once weeding together among them she said, Bet you're glad for periwinkles, and I said, They do grow well. She said, Boyd's never told you? and I said, Told me? She stood up to straighten her knees. Mae, in that blue calico house- dress and white ankle socks. She said, Periwinkles got a love charm. Eat 'em with your truelove, and your future's set. I laughed, but she said, You don't believe it's real? Your Boyd had the lovesickness, bad. Didn't sleep, didn't eat, was sure you wouldn't come with him. Asked me for a cure but he had to do it. You probably never saw the white petals he mixed in that egg salad.

Mae was a true believer in such things. Well, love charm or not, I would have followed Boyd anywhere. Even now sometimes, when he's acting like a damn fool, I come out here and crush periwinkles under my nose, and the smell takes me straight to that picnic, the tang of Boyd's egg salad, and the taste of his kiss.

Whoa. I get up, find a door to the outside, and take a sweaty turn on the nature trail. The "GARDEN" on that little book is misleading, and probably meant to throw off busybodies like me.

Am I surprised she kept a journal? She was always proud of the column she wrote for the *Flambeau* during her days at FSU. And she was forever correcting my grammar—though never my father's. But regardless of her abilities as a writer, her journal is not mine to read.

I come back inside, stuff the notebook deep into the box where I found it, and start on the next bird. Wigeon. Round head, short neck, black spot on the bill. I saw this bird more than once with my dad. I do hate thinking about him, but my mother's journal has of course brought him to mind.

Once, in a patch of open water away from the trees, he sat in the stern of the canoe baiting his hook with a live worm, spearing it in two places. The wind stuttered across the surface, lifting ripples. The marsh grass made a *shh-shh* and the breeze gently turned our canoe.

"Now look what I'm showin' you, Loni Mae. This is how you pierce the worm without killing it." His thumbs were broad, with nick marks on the pads.

I looked away, feeling bad for the worm. "Daddy, who taught you to fish? Was it your daddy?"

He pulled the tip of the rod back behind him, cast forward, and let the reel spin. A small *plash*. "Well, Loni Mae, I guess I about taught myself."

"What was Grampa Newt like when you were little?" I wondered if he was better back then, less scary.

Daddy looked out over the flat water. "Loni Mae."

"Yes, sir?"

"You know the best thing about the swamp?"

I shook my head.

"It's so *quiet*," he whispered, bringing his thumb and forefinger together in front of his lips.

He meant me. *Hush*. The wind blew the marsh grass, and a frog called like a bell. Over Daddy's shoulder, three brown birds, one with a shiny green eye-stripe, took a few running steps on the water, flapping their wings and catching air. They called, *Whoee-whoe-whoe?*

"Loni Mae." Daddy's voice was one of the sounds of the swamp. The birds gained height, and he looked where I was looking. "Wigeons," he said.

I take the drawing off my table. Marsh grass waving, webbed feet taking off from water, a pair of thumbs with nick marks. Rip, crumple, toss.

Estelle appears at the studio door, wrapping the end of a red curl around her finger. "How are you coming on the purple gallinule?"

"Blechh," I say. "You should see the bird skin they tried to give me."

"Loni, you're in Florida. Purple gallinules live here. Go find one. I need that drawing by Monday."

I glare at Estelle. "You mean a field trip? Because, as a matter of fact—"

She talks over me. "It would keep you from losing touch."

I bristle. "What's that supposed to mean?"

"It means I'm your friend, and I know what's good for you."

"It means you're a naggy curator."

She sticks out her tongue. "Wanna get lunch?"

"Can't. I have plans."

*   *   *

My lunch plans involve a squashed peanut butter sandwich from the bottom of my bag. I eat it as I drive toward the canoe place recommended by the FSU Orn guy. I asked him when he lent me the bird skins. So it wasn't Estelle's idea. I thought of it first.

On the way, I stop in at Nelson's Sporting Goods for a binocular strap. This place has been here since my dad's time. The decor is all dark wood, taxidermied deer heads, hunting rifles, and male mannequins dressed in camo. A fish in its fighting posture hovers over a wall of lures. My dad would bring me with him sometimes while he hung around with the shop owner, Mr. Barber, and the clerk, Mr. Phelps. Who shot what size deer, and did somebody say it was a doe, at this time of year? Who had a nice meal of that fish he should have released? But it wasn't all so he could hear about people doing wrong. They talked about what lure was working for bass lately and under what conditions, what phase of the moon affected the fish, what color the water was, what reel, what cloud pattern. Mr. Phelps swore he got more bites when he wore a special hat.

I find the binoc strap, then wander the store aisles the way I used to when my father and the other men were talking. The place smells of pipe tobacco. The man behind the counter is withered and squints a little, but I don't think he's Mr. Barber. He's talking to a customer, but as I pass, he looks up and gives me an almost imperceptible nod.

When I was eleven or so, I could disappear among the dark greens and browns of the store, knowing better than to touch the perilous hooks or the massive, multi-tiered tackle boxes. I could hear the men talking, this time about weather patterns, another time about low-flying planes dropping bales in the swamp. I wondered who needed hay way out there.

"I tell you one thing," Daddy said. "If I find those guys, I'm hauling 'em in."

I was near the end of an aisle. I looked up and said, "Wouldn't it get all wet? The hay?"

The three men's faces turned toward me, and they all stopped talking.

"Hey, Loni Mae," my father said. "Hey . . . why don't you come show Mr. Phelps and Mr. Barber what you drew today?" He turned to them. "We saw a fish eagle, and don't you know this girl drew a pretty good likeness."

I went red. I had to obey, but my sneakers weighed a hundred pounds each. And then my knapsack zipper stuck. I got it open and pulled out my sketchbook.

Mr. Phelps raised an eyebrow.

Mr. Barber opened his hand. "May I?" He took the sketch pad from me and laid it before him on the counter, looking it over with a wrinkled forehead. Then he switched his eyes to me. "You drew this?" he said.

I nodded.

"You didn't copy it out of a book."

I shook my head.

"I'd like to purchase this, young lady. How much will you charge me?"

My scalp tingled. "You want to—?"

"What's a fair price?" he said, never smiling, just negotiating a business deal like I was a fishhook salesman. I looked at Daddy. His face had a faint smile and a question mark.

I didn't want to sell it. "Ten dollars," I blurted. He'd never pay that much.

"Sold," he said, and ripped the fish eagle from the pad. He opened the register, took out a ten-dollar bill, and put it in my hand.

Daddy put his arm around me and said, "I never knew you were such a tough businesslady." He looked at Mr. Barber, grinning.

It was my first sale. When we went in the store again it was framed and hanging on the wall.

I look for it now, the osprey my father called a fish eagle, drawn with a child's hand. But it must be long gone, along with Mr. Barber.

I'm in front of an array of squishy rubber lures: Twin Tail, Curly Grub, Mister Twister, Honking Pono, Ole Spot, Super Salt, and one hot pink Hi-Floating Bubble Gum Worm. Daddy would have known the exact use of each. I just like the names and colors. Despite his efforts, I never learned to fish.

Beyond the rack of lures, the guy behind the counter pats a full paper bag and tells his customer about fire ants. "You got to spread this stuff around the nest just before dark," he says. "Otherwise, the workers come home, see a bunch of dead bodies lyin' around, and go build a home somewhere else."

The customer buys the poison and leaves. The shopkeeper eyes me like I might steal something, so I grab the Hi-Floating Bubble Gum Worm and take it over to him. Between my thumb and forefinger, it has the consistency of an earlobe. I lay the lure on the counter with the binocular strap and meet the man's squinty eye.

"Still seeing any stripers or sunshines?" I say.

He's surprised at the question. "None nearby, worth bragging about. And, I hate to tell you, honey, but this won't snag you a striped bass."

I take my change, grab the binoc strap, and stuff the squishy pink lure into the pocket of my jeans. "Oh, I know. This is for something else. I wouldn't use anything but a topwater plug for catchin' stripers." I'm not even sure how I know this.

There's a change in the shopkeeper's face. R-E-S-P-E-C-T. Worth the $2.75 I've just spent on this silly lure.

The canoe place is another half hour on, at least ten minutes of it down a bumpy shellrock road. The bearded guy behind the splintered counter looks up without smiling. When I tell him I want to rent a canoe, he sits down and grabs a little form and a stubby pencil. "So how many of y'all are there?"

"One," I say.

"Just you?" He lifts his eyes without tilting up his head.

"Yeah, just me." I pick up some bug repellant from the shelf.

"Have you ever canoed before?" His pencil hovers.

"Yes," I say.

"By yourself?"

I turn to him. "Yes. I have."

"Well, I'll need your signature and a credit card."

"How are the mosquitoes?" I dig out my Mastercard.

"Alive and well." Still he does not smile.

I sign his waiver, hand over my credit card, and fill in his form with Estelle's address. If I write down my own address, this guy'll think I'm a tourist, and to native Floridians, there's nothing more ridiculous. I like to think I've lost my Florida accent, but in these parts, Standard American English is treated with suspicion. The guy runs my credit card on an old manual device that needs a carbon paper form. I didn't know anyone still used those. He lifts the card up, and I reach for it, but he cups his hand around it.

"If you don't mind, I'll hang on to this till you come back. This or your license."

Handing over my D.C. license will put me in the Yankee category, but I don't like the idea of leaving my credit card. "So what's to keep you from shopping online with it the whole time I'm gone?"

He straightens up. "It's called integrity."

"Wow. Okay." His eyes are clear and gray, a hint of gold near the pupils. I don't know why I should trust him, but I do.

He hands me a poorly xeroxed map of the complicated, meandering waterways. I follow him through the building and toward the dock. He's about my age, pretty fit, and not bad looking except for the Grizzly Adams beard. His faded blue work shirt is worn thin and looks as soft as an old sheet, tapering into his jeans in a not-unpleasant way, the rolled cuffs revealing tendons taut from lifting canoes. He reminds me of all the hometown boys I could have made mistakes with, if I'd wanted to stay a hometown girl.

At the dock he turns and hands me a paddle. "Now, this is how you get into a canoe," he explains, like I'm a beginner. "You stay low. If the canoe overturns—"

"Look, I'm not gonna tip your nice aluminum boat."

"Okay, then you know never to stand up in a canoe."

"Yes, I know that." I roll my eyes, which actually seems to reassure him.

"Have a good time," he says, smiling suddenly, showing me a row of perfect teeth behind the beard. He stands and watches me get in.

I put my paddle in the water, and despite my bravado, my hands tremble. For a minute I forget to twist the shaft of the paddle at the end of each stroke, and the bow points slightly right, then slightly left, the way it did when my dad first taught me to canoe. I don't look back at the bearded guy, because I'm confirming everything he thinks. But it doesn't take me long to smooth out my stroke. "The water teaches you," my dad used to say. The open lake is flat, and soon the paddle slips cleanly through.

The guy calls out behind me, "Don't get lost!"

I look back, then forward again. I steer the canoe parallel to the mangrove trees that hang low to the water in thick clumps. A dragonfly does a halting dance at the bow of the canoe, and the cicadas sing out a metallic whine—rising, falling, and rising again. I dip the paddle in, and let the canoe glide into a narrow waterway. Jesus bugs move on the skin of the water, leaving tiny wakes. The scene has its charms, but I haven't forgotten the dangers of what's below—crabs and cottonmouths, gators and gars. This is the brown water that swallowed up my father.

Back when I convinced myself of the "accident" story, I still couldn't square it with my dad's own boatmanship. So I cycled through different scenarios. He hooked a fish, got tangled in his line, and lost his balance. He fell from the canoe and hit his head on a cypress knee. Or, he had to get out and search for a catfish trap that got loose from a float, forgetting to take off his heavy vest. In another of my theories, he waded in to pick a swamp iris for my mother and got sucked into one of those bottomless mudholes. His body was found a few yards from the upturned canoe. For a while I combined the catfish trap story with the bottomless mudholes, and settled there. I just had to stop wondering. I had to help my mother with the baby.

I round a bend and catch a sudden pocket of cool air, a welcome pleasure in the still heat. As quickly as it comes, it's gone. I reach the paddle to gather new water, and hear my dad's instructions: "That's it, Loni Mae. Stretch forward and draw the water to ya. Push down your top hand and make your lower hand the pivot point. Now glide."

Slipping past a patch of reeds, I slow to look for the purple galli-nule, *Porphyrula martinica*. My father called it a pond chicken. No dead bird skin can capture the way this creature walks weightlessly over lily pads and floating reeds. That's why I've come out today, after all—to get the *gizz* of one purple pond chicken. I skim close to every clump of bulrush, wild rice, and pickerelweed. For a moment, the only sound is my paddle and the water. Then here come the moorhens, cousins to the gallinule, swimming around me. Their beaks are white, and their feathers are black, where the gallinule's are blue, violet, and rainbow-shine green. They start up with their high, collective cackle. "Listen to 'em laughing at us," my dad would say.

"Get out there," Estelle said, "before you lose touch." What exactly was that supposed to mean?

I spy a limpkin among the reeds, poking its tweezer-like beak in the mud for apple snails. Crying birds, they call them, because of the baleful sound they make trying to get a mate into their nest. It almost sounds like a baby's wail. I do a quick sketch of the limpkin's long legs and slender, curving bill, the variegation of its brown and white feath-ers. Then I paddle on.

I come around another curve and see a fishing camp that resembles my dad's—an old white wood building on stilts. This one can't be his, though. Ours would have rotted and fallen into the water long ago. Still, I beach the canoe.

No one's around. The angle to the swamp water is different from our old place, but I try the door, and it opens easily, without a squeak. There's a shiny coat of paint on the floor of the screen porch.

I move into the front room, but I hear something behind me, a low voice, and I turn to see, through the screen, someone bending over my canoe. Shit, I'm in his house, and if he's got a weapon he's got a legal right to shoot me dead. As quietly as I can, I slip back to see if there's a kitchen door where ours would have been. I step on a floorboard that creaks, and the man darts up, looking my way. His white hair flies up. It's that same old guy from the parking lot. I stumble backward, find the kitchen door, and descend the three steps to the damp sand. I peer around the corner of the house. He's gone back to inspecting my canoe, and I don't want to startle him. I get some distance from the side of the house, and then, to show I mean no harm, I say, "Howdy!"

The man stands upright, quick, and his eyes wander all over my face and beyond. Though he's old and maybe lost, he's still bigger than me.

I want to say, *I am Loni, the small and meek.*

He nods, like he heard my thought. When his face relaxes, I get the same sensation as before, in the Geezer Palace parking lot, like he's someone I should know. He looks back toward my canoe. "Where'd you get this piece a crap?"

I smile. "I know, not the lightest boat on the water. It's a rental."

He turns his eyes sideways toward me. "That sonofabitch Adlai Brinkert rent you this monster?"

"Is that his name?" I study the old man's face.

"You heard what I told you before, didn't you?"

I take a minute. *Your daddy . . . floating . . .*

He snarls, "You don't know who I am."

"No, sir."

"Come here," he says, walking toward the building I just snuck out of.

I hang back.

He holds the screen door open. "Come on, child!"

I gesture toward the canoe. "I've got to . . ."

"Nobody's gonna steal that thing. Come on!"

I step, like a sheep, up the stairs.

He leads me into a back room with cots just like the ones in our old fishing camp. He points to the wall. "Reco'nize that?"

There's a frame, and inside it a pencil drawing of an osprey.

"I kept keepin' it, waitin' for you to get famous, but you hadn't, had you?"

I turn to look him in the eyes. At St. A's, the guy in purple scrubs shouted at him, 'Nelson! . . . Move along!' Nelson. Nelson's Sporting Goods. "Mr. Barber?"

He smiles big. He's missing a tooth just behind his right canine. "But don't tell a soul you saw me. Not a soul, hear?" He grabs my arm and squeezes, hard. His face returns to the wild trouble I saw in the parking lot.

"No, of course." I eye the door. "But why not?"

"Because they want me dead, that's why! I know too much."

"About . . ."

"You just study good, little girl, and get on outta town before they come after you, too. It's impossible to fight them! They get their hands on you, they start by pullin' out all your teeth." He points to the hole in his mouth where a tooth used to be. "That's their torture chamber. It's too easy to end up like my friend George Washington—full set o' dentures. Did you know they can put tracking devices in your fillings?"

"No, I didn't know that. But Mr. Barber, remember the other day in the parking lot, you said something about my dad," I gulp air and swallow, "um, floating . . ."

"Facedown, that's right and you better watch your back because . . ."

"But people who drown . . . don't they sink?" I close my eyes, but still I feel it—brown water everywhere, a weight on my chest.

"Yeah, yeah, I heard the rumors. Let me tell you, Boyd didn't off himself any more than I would. And I wouldn't! Because then they could say I was crazy! No, they got to him." His grip on my arm tightens again, and his pupils narrow. "How'd you find me, anyways?"

He is squeezing my arm so tightly my hand starts to tingle. "Actually, I'm a little lost." I try for a smile. "I could use your advice about how to get out of this swamp."

"Oh. Well, you just need to get back to that rascal Brinkert, right?" His hand relaxes and lets go.

"Yeah. He gave me a little map, but . . ." I move toward the door, trying to act casual.

He follows me out and over to my canoe. "Oh, that's deliberately meant to confuse you. You listen to me, I'm the one who knows." He points. "You take this branch for about a hundred yards and then there's a wee narrow passage that looks like it goes nowhere. You go through there and then you're out in a big ol' lake. Cross that, go to about three o'clock, and you'll see a cut in the bank. Paddle through, and before you know it, you'll see Adlai Brinkert's little operation up ahead." He smiles again, showing that dark hole between his side teeth. Then the smile is gone. "But don't ever come back here. And don't tell anybody about your daddy."

"What . . . what shouldn't I tell?"

"You know." His eyes burn into me. "Now get on out of here."

I nod my head and start pushing the canoe toward the water.

Mr. Barber follows. "Until they stole my shop from me, I was everybody's friend. Everybody."

The canoe is mostly in the water now, and I step in and sit. "Trust no one," he says. "That's my motto." Something smolders in his unfocused stare. He gives the bow a hard shove, and I paddle slowly backwards, but I want to hear more. With deeper water between us, I call, "Mr. Barber, please tell me what you know about my dad!"

"I said git!" He walks to the side of the house and picks up a shotgun. He doesn't aim it at me, exactly, but he cradles it, and I pull water in the direction he told me. I move toward the almost-hidden passage. When I turn, he still stands stooped and wary, holding his gun, watching me as I go in through the trees and away.

I come out into an open lake, just as he said. A few hooded mergansers swim by the canoe at a safe distance, ignoring me. This is one of the birds on Estelle's list, and I'm glad for the distraction. I set my paddle in by the gunnel and take out my sketchbook, careful not to lose sight of the cut in the bank at just about three o'clock. I'm far enough from Barber that the adrenaline has abated, but can anything he said be right? I draw the merganser's dark rounded crest, the beak like a needle-nose pliers, and a bright yellow eye. My dad called this bird "the one with the mohawk hairdo."

The birds paddle at their ease as I draw, and the canoe turns, drifting toward the gently soughing marsh grass.

A large splash not twenty feet away sends the birds flying. A heron calls the alarm, her squawks like bursts of static as she rises. An alligator has tried for a meal and missed. Death or its potential is always lurking in the swamp.

I take up the paddle and navigate toward that cut in the bank. The map from the canoe shop is like a diagram of the capillaries of the brain, and I don't think this lake is even on it. I fold it up and follow the directions given to me by the man who is good friends with George Washington.

"Don't get lost!" the canoe guy shouted.

"Don't lose touch!" said Estelle.

"Don't tell anybody," Mr. Barber warned.

"Tell your daddy to come visit!" said my mother.

Mr. Barber is not the most confused person in Florida.

I follow his directions as the sun scallops gold edges on some thin, lacy clouds just above the highest trees. It takes a while, but I finally pull into the wide waterway with the canoe shop in sight. The fringe of clouds has dispersed into a line of blue-gray fuzz like lint from the dryer, and the sun has dipped below the trees. Grizzly Adlai Brinkert stands at the end of the dock waiting, the tapered shape of him a silhouette against the pink layers of sky. I'm surely keeping him from his supper.

It's been my strangest day yet in Florida, but I did not find the purple gallinule, so I'll have to come back. I coast in toward the dock with an old familiar fatigue in my back and arms. Adlai reaches out a rough, strong hand, and I take it.

9

MARCH 31

Almost the end of my second week here. Tomorrow the tenants move into my mother's house. All day in the stifling rooms, Phil and Tammy and I have packed stuff up, breathed dust, and wiped grime from odd corners. I've cleaned the floor, vacuumed lint from the baseboards, and swept away cobwebs from every window casing. There's still so much left to do that we actually called Elbert Perkins, the real estate guy, to see if he could ask the tenants to push back their move-in date. They said no.

I'm on a stool, a rag in my rubber-gloved hand, wiping inside the kitchen cabinets. "You're telling me she was putting dirty dishes in the cupboards and nobody noticed? Yechhh." I get down from the stool to rinse out the cloth.

Tammy is behind me. "Look, Loni, we cleaned a lot for your mother, but we couldn't keep up with all her weird little habits."

I throw the rag in the sink and pull off the gloves. "Really, Tammy? And she speaks so highly of *your* weird little habits."

Phil tilts his head at me.

"I need a break," I say.

He nods his head up and down. "Yes, you do."

Outside, the sun strikes the marsh in shafts of yellow, like stage lighting. I reach into my car to grab a sketchbook and pencil, then walk over to my live oak tree, touch the bark, and look up. It's not a decision, really, I just stick the sketchbook in the waistband of my jeans, clamp the pencil between my teeth, and climb.

Though I'm bigger now, the flat place where the thickest branch meets the trunk is still the right size for sitting.

Leaves shake-shake around me as fine lines gather on the page: marsh grass bending in the wind. The far-off whine of a motor sounds like my dad's old five-horsepower. Before he let me come along, I'd wait for him up here, tuning my ear for the buzz of his little jon boat, at first no louder than a mosquito.

He'd come into sight and disappear again behind the long grass, following the waterway's snaky approach, surprising a white heron. When he was almost to the dock, I scrambled down and ran to the end. He caught me up by the middle and swung me on his hip sideways like a feed sack. Through my swaying hair, I could see green lawn. He pretended to stagger, even though I wasn't heavy. At the house, he set me on my feet. "All right, Miss Skinny Bones."

My mother stepped down from the back porch. "Scruff," she said, putting her hand to his jaw to feel the stubble.

My father put his face close and rubbed her cheek with his. "Tell me you don't like it."

"Go shave, you," she said, trying not to smile.

On one side of my sketchbook, I've got marsh grass, a white heron, the boat gently bumping the dock. On the other side, porch steps and a woman's hand on a stippled cheek. I stick the sketchbook back into my waistband and shimmy down. After I pull out the hose and water my mother's herbs, I feel ready to go back inside, and I ascend the stairs to my mother's room. I sigh at all there is still to pack. Phil stands by the window looking out over the marsh, and I join him. "I hate this," I say.

"I know." He hangs his wrist over my shoulder.

I say, "Like, what will happen to Arnold?"

He smiles. "The armadillo?"

"He was so happy under the porch."

"Loni, Arnold decamped to the woods about twenty years ago."

"He and the litter of babies he gave birth to," I say. "Remember the space heater you lugged down there to keep Arnold warm?"

"Mom was none too pleased about that."

I say in my mother's voice, *"You'd burn down the house for that ugly old creature?"*

We both smile, and then we're quiet.

Phil says, "The people moving in seem like they'll take good care of the place." For the first time, I sense some regret in him as well. But it's short-lived. He unhooks his arm from my shoulder and turns, and we resume our practical chores.

Earlier in the day, I insisted on packing boxes by category and using proper packing materials, but by six o'clock I'm assembling cardboard and dumping things in without any sense of order, the curios wrapped in dishcloths, doilies, and pillowcases. I thought, since I've spent the last two weeks denuding the house, that we'd have only a few small things left to pack, but the number of items seems to grow as our energy wanes.

We finally seal the last box, and Phil says, "Has anybody checked the attic?"

All three of us slump over.

We carry down nine more crumbly cartons. By the time the U-Haul truck plus our two cars are packed full, it's 9:45 and dark. At 10:00, we pull up at a mini-storage place, supposedly owned by a guy Phil knows. The security lights buzz with insects and illuminate rolltop garage doors on the other side of a sturdy chain-link fence. No one's here, and the gates are locked tight.

"So why is it called 24-Hour Storage?" I say.

"Well, they *keep* stuff around the clock," Phil offers. "I thought it also meant the gates would be open around the clock."

"Crap!" I shout, striking the fence so hard it vibrates. A train passes, drowning my futile curse.

A shiny black four-by-four rolls slowly past us, a tough-looking guy with tattoos staring in our direction.

"Who the hell is that?" I say.

"I don't know," Phil says. "Either a criminal or the neighborhood watch."

"And in Florida," I say, "one's as bad as the other."

Tammy glares at me.

The vehicle stops a few hundred feet down the road, and its reverse lights go on. We each scramble to a separate driver's seat and take off.

In my rearview, a heavily tattooed arm comes out of the four-by-four's window with something long and black. I pray it's not a rifle, and I step on the gas.

10

April Fool's Day, and the foolish pair of pink fluffy slippers I found in Estelle's guest room make a *scuff-scuff* noise on her kitchen floor. She took me in last night at eleven, and I slept a whopping four hours, waking at 3:00 a.m. with a double helix of thought spirals. One practical: what to do with my mother's cargo, how to phrase a call to Theo begging for more than the two weeks I promised, and how to draw all of Estelle's birds before I go back. On the other strand of worry: the reverse lights on the four-by-four, the pink paper with the flowery script—*some things I have to tell you*—and the unfathomable Nelson Barber saying, *Boyd didn't off himself. . . . They got to him.*

At 4:00 a.m. I come out into the living room to puzzle over several remote controls until I find the very-low-volume button and a *Beverly Hillbillies* marathon on the Nostalgia Channel.

At six, I boil water for tea, and when I come back to the living room Estelle's boyfriend, Roger, is standing by the apartment door with a black gym bag observing Miss Jane Hathaway in her khaki bird-scout uniform setting out to find the wild kookaburra. Roger has dark curly hair and far more teeth than could possibly be necessary. He blogs for several Gannett newspapers, including the *Tallahassee Democrat*, and his writing has a notably ironic tone.

"*The Beverly Hillbillies?*" Roger says.

"Yeah," I say. "Call it therapy for the sleep-deprived."

"Really?" He shakes his head. "A bunch of hicks jumping around acting stupid?"

I stiffen. My acquired Yankee accent may sound like his, but I don't appreciate it when people from up north move south for the warm weather and then disrespect southerners. I recite the thesis from my freshman television studies paper. "Listen, Roger, *The Beverly Hillbillies* is based on a classic archetype: the stranger in a strange land."

"Oh yeah?" he says.

I lean against the kitchen doorway and hook one pink slipper over the other. "You see, the viewer identifies with the residents of Beverly Hills, who live by the rules of the 'regular' world. But Jed and Granny and Elly May reverse our expectations. We end up empathizing with *them* because our own cultural norms prove cold-hearted and illogical."

"This is so interesting," he says, checking his watch.

"Yes, it is, Roger, because we come to understand that the naïve but kind 'hicks' are wiser than those who consider themselves sophisticated and smart."

His jaw is slack and his eyes fixed. "That's a lot of bullshit for this hour of the morning."

He's totally missed my rebuke, poor stupid smart-man. "Also," I say, "I like it when Granny runs after Jethro with the frying pan."

He half-laughs, thinking I'm the stupid one. Estelle appears at their bedroom door, eyes unfocused.

Roger says, "I'm off to the gym. Hey, uh, Loni, how long you staying?"

I glance at Estelle. "Um, not . . . very long."

"Because," he says, "I have a friend in the rental office, and he can probably help you get a place." He looks back at Estelle. "As short-term as you want."

"A place. Um, thanks," I say.

He leaves, and I hang around in the pink slippers for a couple more hours. Estelle goes back to bed. When she finally gets up she says, "Sleep okay?"

"Fantastic," I lie.

"I'll be out in a sec," she says, then takes another half hour.

She emerges in a hand-painted silk kimono with her hair still damp. She starts cracking eggs into a bowl. "So, where do we stand?"

"I think Roger's afraid I'm moving in."

"Are you staying awhile?"

"I was planning to go back to D.C. as soon as the renters moved in. But there is still so much stuff. And I can't just take it all to Goodwill. It needs sorting."

Estelle whisks the eggs. "Uh-huh."

"And remember I told you about that old guy who accosted me in the Geezer Palace parking lot? I found out who he is. He's Nelson Barber! He even kept a drawing I made as a child, which would be kind of endearing if he weren't so scary. And he said to me, flat out, 'I don't think your daddy offed himself.' Of course, his scenario involved a conspiracy and somehow . . . George Washington's teeth."

Estelle slides a shimmering omelet onto a plate. "What?"

"He kind of rambles."

She puts out two place mats and indicates I should sit. "Hey, speaking of rambling, I asked my mom if she recalled a Henrietta."

"And?"

She shakes her head. "She gave me a long story about several other mothers of our friends, but couldn't think of a Henrietta."

"Yeah, well, if Tammy didn't recognize the lady, she must live out of town. Because every woman in Tenetkee comes to Tammy's salon. But if Henrietta knows something new about my father, I think I have to find her."

The door to the apartment opens and Roger dumps his gym bag in the foyer. "Ready?" he says.

I look at Estelle, then back to him. I've just taken my first bite of Estelle's exquisite fontina cheese and chive omelet, and it's tucked into my left cheek. "Who, me?"

"Yeah. Charlie's in right now, but he leaves at noon."

Estelle says, "Roger, she's eating."

He says, "You can microwave it when we get back."

I swallow the fluffy bit of egg that will never be as tender as it is right now. "Wait. Who's Charlie?"

Charlie turns out to be Roger's friend in the rental office, who shows me a clean one-bedroom, partially furnished, in a building two blocks away. He says I can rent it for two weeks minimum. The price is cheaper than one week in a hotel, so I say yes and write him a check. I know I'm rushing in, but it'll save me from being an unwelcome camper in Roger's home office or, worse, a "guest" at Tammy and Phil's. Having a room or two where I can park the remaining boxes of my mother's stuff will also save me from standing under a bare bulb in a scary, isolated mini-storage cage with a "Keep," a "Toss," and a "Give-away" bin.

Yesterday I said to Tammy, "We should hang on to the things Mom might consider important."

She just stared at me.

I trudge back to Estelle's to get my overnight bag, and from there I call Theo on his cell. Children laugh and call in the background. I'm interrupting his Sunday with the grandkids.

"Theo," I say, acting casual, "I'm glad I caught you. Listen, I know I said I would limit this family leave thing to two weeks . . ."

There's silence at the other end.

"But I've run into some hiccups, and I need to, um . . ."

"How many more days?"

"I was thinking seven. If I work steadily, I can be . . ."

"Seven more days," he says.

"How's the forest fragmentation project?"

"Proceeding without you," he says.

"Oh."

There's a silence.

Then I say, "And how is, you know, Hugh?"

"Proceeding with . . . consolidation."

I want to know more, and at the same time, I don't.

A small voice in the background says, "Grandpa, come on!"

"Well, it sounds like you have to go, Theo. Expect me on April 9, a week from tomorrow. Okay, bye!" I glance up at Roger, who hovers as I dial my brother.

In an hour, Phil and Tammy arrive down the street with the U-Haul and the other jam-packed car, and we unload everything from my car and their two vehicles into the "furnished" apartment, meaning it contains a bare bed, a paisley love seat, and a rickety kitchen table. After we set down each box, Phil pulls a Sharpie from his back pocket and numbers it, calling out in order as he writes. As the count goes up, so does my stress level. When we get to thirty-one, even though Tammy has all the items she wanted from her precious inventory, she pokes around making sure there isn't something good that she's missed. As she heads out, she says, "Have fun with the junk!"

She leaves, and Phil goes downstairs for the last box. I sit on the paisley love seat wondering which box might contain some sheets to put on the mattress. Hanging on the kitchen wall is a yellow rotary phone with a wire leading to an old-style answering machine. I get up and lift the handset and hear a dial tone. I'll have to make sure I'm not charged for this line.

Phil comes in with the last box. "Okay!" He takes out his Sharpie and announces, "Thirty-two!" with a smile. He probably doesn't realize the number is actually forty-two, since I've got ten boxes of books sequestered at the Tallahassee Science Museum. His accountant's brain would hate the imprecision. He wipes the side of his face on his sleeve. "See you at four, right?"

"Four? Oh . . . oh right." The barbecue. "I'll be there," I promise. I go to the window to watch him take his loping steps down the walkway to the street. The dork just left me with thirty-two boxes of junk to sort through, and still I can't wait to go to his cookout.

11

On my way down to Phil's, I stop at the Geezer Palace. We were all so occupied with the house yesterday that no one came to see Mom, and somebody should come every day. She still hasn't adjusted to being here, and why would she? I found a book about herbs among the boxes and I've brought it to her, because it has a few catchy rhymes she might remember.

"Mom," I say. "Look what I found!"

She stares at the book. It might as well be the Hammurabi Code.

I push on. "It has those little poems in it—about the plants and their special qualities."

Her face is devoid of curiosity. The hairstyle Tammy so carefully teased into shape is flat on one side.

I open the book. "Remember this one? It's by that famous female author, Anonymous."

No reaction.

I read aloud.

"Lemon balm soothe
all troublesome care
reviveth the heart
and ward off despair."

She actually mouths the last line with me, nodding. I breathe. These rhymes have stuck with her when maybe other memories haven't. I leaf through and find another. "Here's sage. And I know you have a giant patch of sage in your garden. I orate.

"Sage groweth best for she is wise
Who keep a happy home.
The man who sees his garden thrive
Will never die alone."

She sours. "Well, you and I both know that's not true." She's looking directly at me, and she's all there.

My enthusiasm for this book drains away. "Well, Mom, I gotta go." It's not a lie. I've got to get to Phil's.

"Well, that was a quick visit," she says, frowning.

On the way to Phil's development in Spring Creek, I pass a pearl-pink Coupe de Ville going in the opposite direction. Henrietta! At the next cutover I make a U-turn and try to catch up. Finally, the car stops at a dusty gas station, and I pull in on the other side of the pump. A long-haired teenage girl gets out—maybe a granddaughter?

I say casually, "Is that Henrietta's car?"

The girl looks at me like I'm a weirdo. "Who's Henrietta?"

"I don't know, maybe your gramma, your auntie?"

"My auntie?" She gives a little snort. "Lady, you must be from around here, right?"

I resent the *Lady.* "Yes I am, and you?"

"I just drove here from New Jersey. Maybe you could help me with directions? I'm trying to get to Fernandina Beach, and my GPS is saying 'no signal.'"

I take out my Florida map from the glove compartment.

The young woman laughs. "That's funny," she says.

"What?"

"I didn't know anyone still used those."

And who's the one who's lost? While I give the poor child the path to her swinging spring break, I steal glances at the car, even walk around back to glimpse the license plate, once she seems confident enough to get on her way. Yup, New Jersey.

My not-so-high-speed car chase and friendly traveler advice has made me late for the barbecue. As I near Phil's place, I pass a large cleared acreage of white and gray sand, every tree piled in a smoldering mound. It's the Florida commonplace of "slash and burn," which to me sounds a lot like "rape and pillage." Four feet of green sod borders the lot by the road, with baby palm trees at regular intervals. "Coming Soon!" the sign reads . . . Harmony Villas, Belcrest Estates . . . whatever it's called, it means lost habitat and more ugly plasterboard houses in this state's Monopoly-game future. I speed up and swerve to avoid a dead possum on the road, its red entrails exposed and gleaming. Manatee Lagoon is on my left.

I pull up to the guard gate. "Murrow," I say to the rent-a-cop in his Smokey Bear hat, and he lifts the black-and-white barricade. All the townhomes look alike, but Tammy has distinguished their door with a needlepoint pocket holding a squat pencil and pad of paper. Above it is a cheery rhyme lettered in yarn: "If we're not here, we're out in the boat, so be real nice and leave a note!" Four tiny people wave from a small yarny motorboat.

I knock, and when Phil opens the door the cool from the AC rushes out. He has on a red cook's apron and holds a plate of raw hamburgers the same color and pong of the possum on the road.

"Come on in, Loni."

I hesitate. *What's wrong with me?* My good-looking, clean-cut brother is inviting me in. I should be glad.

"I was just about to throw these on the grill," he says.

We walk through the living room past the coffee table with magazines in a fan shape, and move toward a shining rectangle of green just beyond the sliding glass door, which Phil opens with the sound of an air lock, and we're out again in the bright light.

Phil's friend Bart Lefton, the lawyer, sits at the plastic table holding a beer bottle. Bart smiles his broad, phony-looking grin. I suppose Phil needed a buffer—couldn't just have me over and no one else.

An arc of water rises behind them. Bobby and Heather, in their swimsuits, are throwing themselves at a blue plastic Slip 'n' Slide. "Hi, Aunt Loni!" Bobby waves while Heather slides. He's pink-cheeked and soaking. I'd love to join him and his sister, jumping in the water that sprays up in diamond droplets and falls on the wet grass.

Heather reaches the far end of the plastic, stands up, and calls to me, a dark tendril of hair curving toward her mouth. Six and a half years ago, when Phil and Tammy were seniors in high school and Tammy got pregnant, I figured, there goes my brother's future. From D.C., all I could do was fume. After Heather was born, I came down to tell them both exactly what I thought. But then that baby wrapped her fingers around my pinky, and my anger evaporated into mist.

Bobby surface-dives on the long sheet of blue, trusting every time that the ground will be there to meet him. Phil starts the meat to spatter and smoke.

"Where's Tammy again?" I say.

"At a scrapbooking thing," Phil says. He turns. "What do they call it, Bart, a crapping party?"

"Yeah." They laugh like sixth-graders.

Phil catches me picturing it. "Actually, it's 'cropping.' They cut up photos and put them into special books. Bart's girlfriend Georgia does it too."

"Yeah, it kind of consumes all their free time," Bart says.

Phil half-turns from the grill. "Tammy's fixing up some of Mom's old photo albums."

"Tammy has the photo albums?"

Phil jiggles the spatula. "Now, don't get mad. We made copies for you." He flips a burger, and a flame from the grill rises high. "Yesterday she came across some newspaper clippings I'd never seen. They were in a folder in the back of an album. Wanna see?" He hands me the spatula. "Watch the burgers a minute. And we also have to talk money. New development." He hands me the spatula and disappears behind the sliding glass, leaving me outside with Bart. I push a corner of the spatula into the meat.

Bart says, "Loni, you don't have a beer!"

"That's okay, Bart."

"It is not!" He goes inside.

The kids run and slide and laugh. Bart comes out with three fresh beers, and Phil follows with a couple of manila folders, taking the spatula back from me and tossing the papers onto the table.

Bart holds one of the beers to his forehead, then to his temple, closing his eyes at the cool.

I sit and reach for the file on top. The clippings are old and jumbled and clearly not what Tammy wants for her scrapbooks. The first caption says: "Wildlife Officer Boyd Murrow rescues an injured bird." In the picture, my father stands at the base of a tupelo tree. It's hard to tell, but it's probably a white ibis he's helped in some way. He's small in the picture, but smiling. I hear Nelson Barber's words as if he's looking over my shoulder. *See there? Boyd wouldn't off himself.*

I move to the next clipping. "Local student wins full scholarship." God, what a picture. I'm a senior in high school and look like I have no poise at all. My long hair hangs like two barely open curtains on each side of my face, and I have the slump of a tall girl trying to attract a short boy. My mother, about the same height, stands straighter. She has her arm around my shoulder, but I sulk, leaning my rib cage as far from her as possible so there's air between us.

The next one says: "Stork Undeterred by Storm" and, in smaller letters, "Local Couple Has a Tornado Baby." My father holds Philip, healthy and bigger than a newborn, but still swaddled, in front of a downed loblolly pine in our yard. My brother was born without benefit of a doctor or even a midwife. I didn't know till later that the low-pressure system of a tornado can bring on early labor. I was terrified by the sound of the wind, my mother's screams, and the slimy, howling thing that had come out of her. But I did what I was told, fetching towels and fishing line for tying off the cord. Once the wind died down, I tromped through the flooded garden for the comfrey my mother instructed me to get, and I mixed the crushed leaves with Crisco as she directed, watching her rub it on the tiny body before she swaddled him in a large flannel. Then we picked our way over downed branches to the truck. My father held the baby and supported my mother. I had never seen her so weak. I got in the cab, and my father handed the baby to me, putting the little head carefully in the crook of my arm. All the bumpy and blockaded way to the hospital, I looked down at that creature who'd come too early and I prayed he'd live.

Phil says, "How do you like it cooked, Loni?"

I come back to the overbright barbecue. Phil is waiting for an answer, oblivious to everything that's led to this excruciatingly regular day.

"Um. Well done," I say.

The clippings are all out of order. "Officer of the Year Boyd Murrow." My father, in a freshly pressed uniform, stands in front of a flag of the State of Florida shaking hands with a young and handsome Frank Chappelle. In the background stands another officer, a thin, scowling guy with protruding ears. "Lieutenant Daniel Watson, outgoing Officer of the Year."

The last clipping is the oldest: "Engaged: Ruth Hodgkins–Boyd Murrow." My mother's long hair curls at the ends. She has a spray of freckles across her nose and a smile like a teenager, though she'd soon graduate from college. My father seems barely able to contain a wild happiness banging at him from the inside. They're so young, life all in front of them. Ready to build their nest.

"Look at the second folder," Phil says, frowning.

Bart wanders over to the fence bordering the canal.

The file contains yet another exciting spreadsheet. Phil narrates: "All Mom's income, including our contributions, versus the monthly rate at St. Agnes."

"Right. You showed me at your office."

My brother wants me to love numbers the way he does, but I can't. I keep my own budget, but there's no joy in the counting. I skim the details he's broken out. The only difference is at the bottom.

I glance up. "This added up before. Why doesn't it equal her St. A's fees now?"

"Because before," he says, "it had her annuity."

"So where is it?"

"Makes me sick to think about," he says.

"What happened?"

"Somebody scammed her. Must have been right before she fell. She cashed in the annuity to cover some bogus outstanding charges they made her believe she owed."

"Wait, the whole annuity? Who? How?"

"Yes, the whole annuity. Seems it was an overseas group. Fairly low-tech, but they hit the jackpot with Mom. Now they're long gone, leaving us to pay taxes and penalties on cash that somebody else is enjoying."

"Well, we have to report it! We have to catch those people!"

Bart has ambled back to the table, and I look to him, then to Phil. Their calm tells me they've already reported it, and we're unlikely to catch the thieves.

I slump back against the plastic chair. Dementia sucks. I imagine my mother on the phone with the scammers, bullied and confused.

"However," says Phil, "Bart and I have a plan."

I look at Bart's broad face. He may be a lawyer, but this is truly none of his business. He rolls his beer bottle between his hands and smiles with self-satisfaction. "While your smart brother Phil was researching retirement benefits for state employees, he came across a remarkable fact."

My brother opens a package of buns. "Kids! Come get dried off now!" They run up and Phil ruffles Bobby's wet hair with a towel, then wiggles the cloth between Heather's toes to make her laugh. There's a tenderness to his fatherhood he's been able to cultivate without a role model. "Now, go get dry clothes on," he says. "And don't leave those wet bathing suits on the carpet!"

The kids scamper inside. He turns to me, smiling.

I don't smile back. "You were detailing our financial ruin."

"Well, this is what I'm trying to tell you. I did some research on state benefits, and there's a tidy sum the State of Florida still owes us."

"Oh yeah?"

"See, being law enforcement, Dad was in a high-risk category. In addition to the percentage of his pay Mom got from Workman's Comp, Fish & Game was supposed to give her another twenty-five percent, since the accident happened on duty. Plus, there's a $300,000 lump sum payment for officers killed in action. And we never got that."

"Whoa, whoa, whoa, Phil, that's . . . no. That's not . . . a good direction." I see my father on the dock that day, the weighted fishing vest, the heavy tackle box.

"Why not?"

I could tell him. Get him alone, tell him the truth.

Bart Lefton's voice scratches on my eardrum. "We just make a petition through the courts . . ."

"Bart, could you excuse us?" I say. I do not move.

"Oh, sure!" He looks to me, then Phil. "I just . . . I need to uh . . ." He slides open the glass door, then shuts it behind him.

"Phil. . . . Dad wasn't on duty the day he died."

"Oh yeah, he was." He taps the table. "I saw the paperwork. It says: 'On Duty.'"

"What paperwork?"

"The incident report."

"What is an incident report?" I keep my voice even.

"Loni, don't get all sensitive, now."

"I am not getting sensitive." Even though the sun is about to go down, the humidity has risen, and the trees have begun to buzz with cicadas. "I just want to see this 'paperwork' you're talking about. I never saw any 'paperwork.'"

"Because you never looked into it, and we have." Phil shakes his head almost imperceptibly.

"So why don't you show it to me?" My voice is not louder than it was before.

He stares me down and enunciates like I am in kindergarten. "Because I do not have it. It is at my office."

"Well, I want to see it," I say. "Everybody knows he wasn't on duty! He was out doing his swamp time." I control the waver that threatens my voice.

"Swamp time? What the hell is that? And how is that different from 'On Duty'? He patrolled the swamp. And why are you getting so mad? You're all pink."

"It was *his* time. I mean, R & R."

A high-pitched, "Yoo-hoo!" comes from the house. Tammy, back early. I'm boiling from the inside out. I've got to cool off before I deal with her. Phil said she wouldn't be here, and that was a lie. And then he has to go talking bullshit. The sprinkler cascading over the grass patters on the long blue sheet of plastic. I get up and run, hitting the Slip 'n Slide otter-style, and skid to a stop, my face and clothes wet, like the eye-level grass.

12

It seems Tammy never intended to miss dinner, only the cooking part. She and her girlfriend Georgia emerge through the sliding glass. If Georgia were a bird, she'd be Gambel's quail—a little unsure of what to do, yet determined to follow. Her rounded hairstyle echoes her overall shape, following Tammy's rule that each hairdo should fit the client.

"Is supper ready?" Tammy asks, and she and Georgia titter as if it's an absurd question to ask of men.

I get up from the Slip 'n Slide and come toward them.

Georgia looks me over with a question but just pats her sphere of caramel-colored hair. "Hi, Loni."

I grab a towel, and after some more chitchat Bart and Georgia say an elaborate good-bye, protesting that they never intended to stay for dinner. "Just beer," Bart says, laughing.

When I'm passably dry, Phil and I set the table inside to escape the mosquitoes. Heather sits across from me, bearing a decided resemblance to that picture of my mom in the clipping. The slightly upturned nose, the spray of freckles. This child called my cell this morning and left a voice mail, hesitant but clear: "*Um, Aunt Loni, this is Heather. Um, can you bring your bird books with you?*"

From across the table, she stage-whispers, "Did you bring them?"

"Not now, young lady," Tammy says, and bows her head to say grace.

I wink, then bow my head low. While we eat, Tammy corrects the children's manners. "Heather, no elbows." To Bobby's wiggling, she says, "Mister, will you sit still? You look like you're preparing for takeoff."

I laugh.

She looks at me, her eyebrows in a V.

I turn to my brother. "Phil, you still running?"

"Sure. You?"

"Yeah." I don't tell him it's all gone to hell during my time in Florida.

He says, "We should run together sometime." It's a platitude. He'll never follow through.

Tammy looks from one to the other of us, waiting to be included.

I say, "Want to join us, Tammy?"

"Oh, no. You will not see me exercising outside in this heat." Glad to be asked and glad to refuse.

After dinner, Phil goes upstairs to give Heather and Bobby their baths, and I help Tammy clear the table. I promised the kids I'd read to them, so I'm eager to finish quickly. I set the last plate and glass on the counter, but Tammy blocks my way out. She points to a dry-erase board on the wall. "Now, Loni, I want to show you my chart. Since you'll be staying for a while . . ."

"I'm not—"

". . . I'll go on Mondays and Wednesdays, you can go on Tuesdays, Thursdays, and Saturdays, and Phil will go on Fridays and Sundays."

I check the clock above the door. "And we're going . . . ?"

"To the Home, dear."

I brush past her into the dining room.

"Don't walk away from me."

"I'm helping you clear the table!" I can hear the kids thumping around upstairs. I pick up the salad dressing and grab my cloth bag with the bird books, slinging it over my shoulder. If I don't go up soon, I'll miss my chance to read to them. I put the Thousand Island bottle in the fridge.

"The chart, Loni."

I close the refrigerator and turn around. "Well, Tammy, I really won't be here for very long. So why don't I just go every day?" *I want out of this kitchen.*

Tammy puts her knuckles on her hip. "Oh, so this is one of your in-and-out trips again?"

"I beg your pardon?"

"I thought you were here to help. But I guess it'll be like normal. You swoop in, grab your mother's good graces, then run and leave us to wipe her butt."

"My mother's good graces? Tammy, you can't be talking about *my* family."

"Oh, it's *your* family. The one you usually ignore?"

I blink. *Do not ignite.* "So, don't the people at St. Agnes wipe . . . if she needs it . . ."

"And how would you know? You breeze in, complain about all the new 'cardboard' houses in town—meaning ours—and then breeze out, lettin' your mother think you're such a success you can't possibly spend another minute in Podunk."

I let out a bitter laugh. "Oh, Tammy, you're a little out of touch. My mother has never considered me a success."

"Out of touch? I think that would be you, Miss Smithsonian Institution. I'm the one who noticed your mother was losing her mind!"

Dinner has congealed into a hard, flammable greaseball in my stomach. "Here's what I think of your chart, Tammy. It's so plain. How about some graffiti?" I pick up the dry-erase marker and write in big letters: *Tammy is a fu*—. My bag falls from my shoulder to the elbow of my writing arm, making my hand drop. If I finish my thought, I'll go out into the hot night, banging the door behind me. Bedtime will pass with no bird books, no reading, no auntie.

I put the strap of the bag on my shoulder and continue to write. To the *fu*— I add *rious tornado!* and I draw a whirling storm behind the exclamation point, raindrops coming off it in every direction, dousing my fire. I cap the pen and turn to my sister-in-law. "Now, if you'll excuse me, I have an engagement with some natural history enthusiasts."

I go up the stairs, still shaky. Heather and Bobby jump up and down in their pj's and chant my name. "Aunt Lo-*ni*, Aunt Lo-*ni*!"

Phil, unaware of my fight with Tammy, passes me in the hall, touches my arm, and says in a low voice, "Start with Bobby."

Despite the jumping, Bobby must be worn out from the Slip 'n Slide, because the Very Hungry Caterpillar hasn't even eaten the plums when I look to see my young listener breathing shallow breaths, eyelids closed.

When I go into Heather's room, she's sitting up in bed. "Did you bring them?"

"Hmmm, I must have forgotten," I say.

"You did not."

"Oh, here they are!" I pull a few of the books from my bag.

She chooses one of Grampa Tad's field guides, and asks me about the picture of the black skimmer, a shorebird with red feet and a severe underbite. "They scoop up fish with the bottom part of their bill," I tell her.

She turns the page, and I read, "'The Cuban bee hummingbird is the smallest bird in the world.'"

"Way cool." She turns another page. She is wide awake.

"Heather, I'm supposed to be putting you to sleep."

"All right," she says, and lies down, her great-grandfather's book open at her side showing the weaverbird and its burlap bag of a nest. "Can you sing to me?" she says. She's stalling, but heck, I hardly ever get to do this.

"Rock-a-bye, Heather, on the treetop . . . ," I sing, and she laughs, too old for this one. But I soften my voice and slow down the tune until her face stills. "When the wind blows, the cradle will rock . . ." I scan the book next to her, the intricate weave of the nest hanging tenuously from a branch. "If the bough breaks, the cradle will fall . . ." As I form the words, I understand this song as I didn't before—a bird's nest, falling. "And down will come birdie, cradle and all."

Her eyes are closed, but she says in a soft voice, "Not birdie. Heather."

"Yes, Heather." I kiss her forehead, gather the books, and tiptoe out. "Sleep well."

Phil sees me to the front door, Tammy coming up behind him, quick. "What did you mean by 'furious tornado'?" she says. "And do we have a deal? Are you going on your assigned days?"

Phil gently prevaricates. "Loni tells me she's written it down, and she's all set with the schedule." He's asking me to be a pacifist in this house. "And, Loni, I'll keep you posted on the filing." He cocks his head.

He's talking about the thing with the state, the misguided . . . "Phil, no."

"Good night, Loni." And my stupid little brother closes the door.

13

I mope around the bare apartment all morning being unproductive. Finally, I call Delores Constantine in the Botany Library. I miss the Smithsonian.

"Hyello," she says, likely doing two things at once.

"Delores, it's Loni."

"Well, land o' Goshen. How you doing, kid?"

"I'm fine. Still in Florida."

"Yup."

"How are things there? Any drama?"

"Oh, I stay out of the drama, you know that. But we had a shipment of samples come in, and I'm helping catalogue them, as usual." I know even as she talks, she is looking through the bottom of her glasses at something botanical.

"Shouldn't the interns be doing that, Delores?"

"Yeah, but if I leave them alone, they just mess up my system. So it's good to be looking over their shoulders. What's up?"

No such thing with Delores as calling just to talk. "Not much."

"How's your mom?"

"Not great." *Honor your mother, Loni.* "Did I ever tell you she had an herb garden?"

"I don't think you did."

"It's still thriving." I see again that light in my mother's eyes when I read her that first herbal poem. "Say, Delores, you know that section with the old herbals on the bottom shelf nearest your desk? None of those are available online, are they?"

"Afraid not. Why?"

"Oh, I just thought I might find something in there I could bring to my mom."

"Like a nosegay?"

"Sort of. My dad's mother had all this herbal knowledge and I know my mother absorbed some of it. If I could find a few gems and share them with her, maybe—"

Delores continues my thought, "—you could connect."

"Yeah, that's . . . yeah."

"I'll see what I can find. You're near Florida State University, right? We could do interlibrary loan. Listen, I gotta go."

"Okay, Delores. Great to hear your voice."

14

In the lobby of St. Agnes, the TV is on and tuned to *The Florida Report*. I tend to get drawn in by television, since while I was growing up my mother was anti-TV. I've carried in a box of her things, and I set it on the counter to watch the animation of a reel-to-reel tape and audio from a 911 call—a woman shrieking to the operator, "The bedroom floor just collapsed, and my brother-in-law is in there! He's under the house!" The picture cuts to a small concrete home surrounded by police tape. A yellow-haired reporter with dimply knees walks toward the camera, intoning, "A man is asleep in his bed, and suddenly, a giant sinkhole swallows him, without a trace. His brother calls his name, but he is gone." They show the brother, his face distorted by grief, saying, "My voice just echoed down into that hole."

My TV trance is broken by a touch on my shoulder. It's Mariama, one of the several West African women employed by St. A's. She's about ten years older than me and a few inches taller. She smiles gently with her lips together. "How are you?" she asks. Mariama is the hall manager for the dementia care unit, and I met her yesterday, when my mom was moved from the rehab wing to this one. Today, she's wearing practical maroon scrubs and sneakers, and her hair is pulled back to accentuate a high forehead. Her Sierra Leonean accent is full of rounded vowels and soft R's.

"Oh, I'm okay, I guess. How's it going here?"

She begins to walk in the direction of my mother's room, and I pick up my box and follow. Mariama says, "Your mother does not want to participate in activities. That is okay. It is all new."

"She's confused," I say. "She still doesn't understand why she's here."

"I know, and she is younger than most. I would be confused too." Mariama smiles. "When she gets the look that says, 'I don't know where the 'eck I am,' we will distract her. But we need to know what kinds of things she likes."

"Well, she plays the piano, or used to. Can't do that until her wrist is healed, I suppose. But she likes classical music." *What else does my mother like?* "She can do a crossword puzzle in pen," I say. "She likes books. I can bring more of her books."

"Good," Mariama says. "This is good. You are giving us an arsenal of distractions." She says "ah-senal."

"Oh, and gardening," I say. "She knows about herbs."

"Does she? That is useful to know." Tiny half-moons of gold glint against Mariama's earlobes.

A woman with a walker bleats, "Marian! Marian!"

I shoot Mariama a look, but figure I'd better stay out of it.

She raises an eyebrow. "That's our Eunice." She takes a sharp left to attend to the woman.

When I get to Mom's room, she dispenses with any niceties. "This room is all wrong. And I can't find any of my things."

I put the box on the floor and take out a cream-colored bundle. "Right, so I brought some of them. Here's your bedspread." I turn down the polyester brown-and-gold cover from her single bed and unfold the chenille, draping it over the sheets. I glance up to see her staring at me with that *You-are-hopeless* look.

"Well, it is a little big," I say, "but it's so soft and nubby."

She crosses her arms. "It'll drag on the floor and be filthy in a day. It doesn't belong here and you know it."

I stop, then fold it back up. "I'm sure what you meant to say, Mom, was, 'Thank you, Loni, for doing me that kindness, but I'm not quite sure it will work.'"

"No, it won't."

Friction strikes a match. "All right then, keep the ugly one." I ball up the chenille, grab my bag, and walk out the door, sweeping through the lobby past Mariama.

"Halloo?" Mariama says, but if I open my mouth I may breathe fire.

I throw the bedspread in my hot car. There's nothing to keep me from driving off. Except that I left that box in the middle of the floor and Mom's likely to trip over it. I stand for a minute inhaling the heat, and then I go back.

On the screen in the lobby, the same yellow-haired reporter sits chatting with the anchorman. They can't still be talking about the sink-hole, can they? Big story in a small town.

Mariama is in the hallway, a pile of clean laundry in her hands. "Hi!" I say. "I'm sorry I ignored you."

She sets down the towels. "Oh, you were in a hurry. I understand. But I forgot to ask you if you have a fiblet?"

"I beg your pardon?"

She enunciates each syllable. "A ter-a-peutic fib-let."

Maybe it's her accent, but I have no idea what words she is saying to me.

"Let me explain," she says. "Some families tell their loved one something that isn't exactly true, but helps the resident ease in. Not all families do it, but if they have one, we like to jump in on the same chapter."

"Oh, like a fib?"

"Yes, but a little one. A fiblet."

I look away, then lower my voice. "My sister-in-law wants me to tell my mother the electrical system in her house is broken . . ."

Mariama's face relaxes. "Yes, the electrical story. That's a good one."

Don't tell me Tammy was right.

"It feels too weird," I say, "lying to my mother."

Mariama begins to walk, and we pass a vase of zinnias. "I know," she says. "Ruth is the one who taught you never to lie."

I nod.

"But your job now is to make her life easy. And so, the fiblet helps."

A man in a doorway strains to stand up from his wheelchair.

"Oh no, Myron!" Mariama lifts her eyes and hands, and I detect an edge of annoyance. But she scuttles to his side and gets him to sit back down. "You mustn't fall," she says.

When I get back to my mother's room, she says, "What's in there?" She points at the box on the floor. She's forgotten the bedspread, forgotten my pique.

"A few of your favorite things. Just like the song."

She pushes air between her lips. "Pff."

"And a few that are probably extra. So let's make some decisions." I take out a hot-water bottle, a loofah, and about eight hairbrushes. "Which of these do you want to keep?" I say.

"Well," she says, "all of them!"

I drag the box over by the vinyl chair where she sits, and I try for logic. "No, I mean, you can't use more than one hairbrush at a time, so which is your favorite?"

"They're all my favorites."

A bottle of aspirin at the bottom is two years expired. I chuck it in the trash.

"Don't throw that away!" she says. "I can still use those."

I tighten my lips, lifting out the tissue paper separating toiletries from clothes. I hold up a dress I've seen her wear on many occasions.

"That's not even mine!" she crows. When I hang my head, she says, "Your part's crooked." Faultfinding is so familiar to her, it doesn't even require working memory.

Her attention drifts to the window, and I put the dress and some other clothes on hangers. At the bottom of the box is another item I didn't notice, because it was buried by the clothes. I unwrap the tissue paper to see it's leather—a holster? The snap is rusted and the leather warped, like it's spent a long time in water. My father's. Oh God. Was it with him, on him, that day? My mother turns and looks at it, then at me. I wrap it quickly and put it back in the box.

15

I go again in search of the purple gallinule. The bearded canoe-shop proprietor is out in the parking lot when I drive in, pulling paddles from the bed of a truck. "You from D.C.?" he says as I get out.

"No. Why?"

He looks at my D.C. license plate. It shouts: *Tourist! City slicker! Greenhorn!*

"It's a loaner," I lie. "My car's in the shop." Why do I care what this guy thinks?

He follows me in, takes my credit card, and sets me up with a canoe. But he keeps an eye on me.

Early-morning steam rises from the water. I paddle to a different part of the swamp today, where the cypress trees grow, as my dad used to say, "keepin' their feet in the water." The canopy is high, like a cathedral, and I glide through a landscape of light and shadow. Ferns cascade from the trunks amid pink lichens the size of measle spots, and the cypress knees stick up from beneath the surface like the hats of submerged gnomes. I spot a delicate "Florida butterfly" orchid, with a heart-shaped blotch at its center, clinging to a trunk.

I spend three hours searching unsuccessfully for the gallinule before I give up and glide back in to the dock. The canoe man doesn't meet me. Inside, he's talking to a fellow with mutton-chop whiskers, a frayed denim vest, and scary sleeve tattoos of serpents and knives. I glance out the door to see a black four-by-four parked diagonally in two spaces. The mutton-chop guy looks at me, starting with my face, scanning down to my feet, then up again. He turns to Adlai. "So, I'll do like I told you," he says, slips out, and climbs into the black truck. I watch him after he goes, to see if the truck rumbles like the one that scared Phil and Tammy and me.

Adlai comes from behind the counter. "See anything good out there?"

I turn toward him. "You mean in the swamp? Sure. Always. But I'm trying to find one bird in particular."

He stares out the window.

I realize I'm still holding my paddle. "I'll just go hang this up."

"Unh-uh. Don't do my job." He takes it and brushes past me. "I'm underemployed as it is."

What's bugging him? He hangs the paddle outside, then comes back in, banging the door. I wait for my credit card.

I'm supposed to meet with Estelle, my taskmaster, in Tallahassee. But when I get to the science museum, she's not in her office. Her assistant tells me she's over at University Press.

"*'But don't let her leave'* were her exact words!" Estelle's assistant is young and enthusiastic, and right at this moment I can't remember her name.

"Okay," I say. "I'll be in Bridget's studio."

"Oh, I'm sorry," she says. "Estelle told me specifically, *'Don't let her start any projects!'*" Still with the smile.

"So here I wait." I seat myself across from her in a deep, boxy chair. It is very much like the chairs in the FSU library we used to call the "Circle of Snooze." How many times did I dream, openmouthed, in those chairs? I drum my fingers on the upholstered arm. The smiley girl keeps smiling. If I had a smartphone, I'd check my email, but my phone is deliberately dumb, so I search in my bag to find something, anything, to read. My hand touches a small notebook—my mother's *GARDEN* book. I intended to give it to her today, but in the midst of her contentiousness, I forgot. I open it, if only to avoid the sparkly smile of Estelle's assistant.

Rosemary— funeral flower
Lemon balm—consolation
Self-heal— soothes wounds

Parson's Nursery had no self-heal. Rosemary, then, for remembrance. Not likely to wilt like those forget-me-nots. Boyd said, Why're you so upset, Ruthie? They're just plants! How can he not understand? He was there, he held her. Forget. Me. Not. Now he palms my belly and says, Think it's a boy or a girl? and When should we tell Loni Mae? Oh, I know it has been a year. I know this is a new chance. But terrible things can happen still. So I come out to the garden and sweat. Ruthie, he said yesterday, do you think you should be diggin' so much out here? I heard of this thing, toxo-somethin'—but I interrupted him and told him, Boyd, the word is toxoplasmosis, and I'm fine as long as I wear gloves. Then I watched his face close down. I should know better than to correct him. But he will not keep me from the garden.

"Hi," Estelle says. Her scarf floats behind her as she sails past. I close the notebook, lift myself out of the deep chair, and follow her into her office. "Glad you brought a book," she says. "Sorry about that, but I was meeting with the head of University Press." She sings out, "It's so exciting!" She reaches her desk and sits. "Where do you want to eat? Great Earth or French's?" Estelle is in fast-forward. She moves a paper to the side and looks up. "Hey, why are you all blotchy?"

"I'm not blotchy." I put my hand to my face. "And . . . Great Earth is fine."

"So," she says, "we got the book project!"

Her brain is at gig speed and mine's still on dial-up. "Which one is that?"

"First let's see your drawings," she says.

I set them on the desk, and she handles them with just her fingertips, spreading them out and lingering on the mangrove cuckoo, then the wigeons. At the limpkin, she nods slowly. She does not say, *And where the hell is the purple gallinule?* Only, "These are good." She looks up and smiles. "But what's wrong with you?"

"Nothing's wrong with me."

"Quit lying."

"Estelle, weren't you telling me about . . . a project?"

"Okay, but let's go, because I have to be back here for a one-thirty meeting." She grabs the cute purse that matches her rose-colored pumps, and I shuffle after her in my canoeing clothes.

At Great Earth, we scoot into a high-backed booth in the corner. Estelle is saying something, but I'm still hearing the voices of my young parents from the journal, and contemplating my mother's need for self-heal and forget-me-nots.

"Why do I feel you're not listening?" Estelle says.

"No, I am. Tell me more about this exciting project." I want her to talk so I don't have to.

She draws a deep breath. "We've been commissioned by the legislature to come up with a textbook for fifth-graders on the natural history of Florida. It's a prototype for all the primary schools in the state." Estelle can say "prototype" and mean it.

"Uh-huh."

"Loni, this is what I've been pushing for! We're going beyond museum catalogues into real publishing. Books that reach people." She narrows her eyes and leans forward. "You know why we need to do this book, Loni?"

The "we" gives me a sharp pain in my right temple.

"Because a thousand people a day move to Florida, and they're flushing their shit, and filling in swamps, and building ugly townhomes, and using too many highway on-ramps, and their closest encounter with wildlife is roadkill."

"Now you sound like me," I say.

"But they're also creating a new generation of Floridians. And those kids can either grow up to throw their Big Mac wrappers at the manatees they run over with their ski boats, or" —she slows her voice— "they can open their eyes to your luminous birds, know the feral wetness of the swamp, embrace this amazing, wild ecosystem that's all around us, and save it before it's gone."

"I just tuned in to your station, Estelle."

She smiles. "We need to convert the great unwashed!"

"You mean the great, fifth-grade unwashed?"

"You *were* listening. Now, I don't want to pressure you," she says as a prelude to pressure, "but there would be a lot of work for you in this. A lot of bird drawings . . ." Her face is open, expectant.

"Well, what a shame I won't be here for it." I put both palms down on the table.

She glances at her menu. "I just want to plant the seed. No need to tell me right away."

"I'll tell you right away. Can't do it."

"Never say never, Loni."

"Estelle, quit trying to make me a permanent Florida resident."

Our waiter comes up behind me. His voice is sandpaper. "Hey, ladies. Decided yet?" I'm eye level with his arms, which are decorated with blue snakes and knives. I look up at his unsmiling face. He's the guy who was conferring with Adlai in the canoe shop. Drives a black four-by-four. I quickly order a bowl of pumpkin soup and hand him the menu.

He looks at me steadily. "I'm Garf. If you need anything." Then he turns and shambles toward the kitchen.

I turn my head slowly toward Estelle. "Oh my God. His name is Garf. He must be Junior. The son."

"What?" she says.

"Garf! As in Garf Cousins Jr.!"

"Our waiter? I don't think he's your type, Loni."

I roll my eyes. "No, I mean, who else would be called Garf?"

Estelle sits back. "Want me to ask him?"

"No! His family hates my family. His dad threatened to kill my father!" I glance back toward the kitchen. "Let's talk about something else. Just act like we're having a nice, relaxed lunch."

"Is that not what we're doing?" she says. "How are Phil and Tammy?"

I breathe in. "I'm trying not to let Tammy rile me. And Phil has this weird idea about getting more money from the state." I lower my voice. "But I don't like it. It could blow everything up and give my brother a lot more information than he actually wants to know. Not to mention, empty our coffers rather than fill them. I tried to discourage him, but Phil, as you know, doesn't take my advice."

Blue snakes and knives appear again as Garf sets down our food. Has he been listening? He hangs next to the table a minute too long.

"Thank you," I say.

"You're welcome, Miss Murrow." He gives extra emphasis to my last name and smiles, showing nicotine-stained teeth.

As he retreats, Estelle resumes talking in full voice. "And would it be such a bad thing to find out what really happened? You've got two people saying maybe it wasn't what you thought."

"Shh. What two people?"

"That pink-stationery lady and the wacky swamp dude."

I put my napkin on my lap. "Two very reliable sources. And what if 'what I thought' is confirmed in black and white for my formerly happy brother Phil?"

"Loni . . ."

"I mean, look at me. What I know about it has already made me bonkers, looney tunes, warped . . ."

Estelle bites into her sandwich.

"Stop me anytime."

She finishes chewing.

"Don't you think Phil will find out at some point? And then he might resent you for keeping it from him."

"Maybe." I taste a spoonful of the golden soup. Mace and tarragon, a hint of cayenne. *And the lemon balm, to console me.*

We finish eating, pool our money, and leave it on top of the check. Garf Cousins Jr. leans against a doorjamb, eyeing us as we leave.

16

I take a different route toward Tenetkee this time, and I pass Concrete World, with its troops of plaster deer lined up next to a battalion of birdbaths. I'm dying to tell someone my one original joke, which goes like this: I plan to open a liquor store next to Concrete World. (pause) I'll call it Spirit World.

The car radio is tuned to an AM station. The over-the-top DJ announces *Another rockin' set on The Mighty 1290!* They play a lot of news and jingles, but also the songs I once turned up loud as I drove this road through a carpet of spiky palmettos with my high school friends. I'm headed toward Frank Chappelle's house, because he did ask me to visit, and because he might be the only person who can sway Phil from his fool's errand. Phil said the incident report said "On Duty," and logic tells me Chappelle would have been the one to fill in that box—a gentle perjury to get us a few benefits we might otherwise have been denied.

I don't have his phone number, but it used to be okay in my small town to drop in on people unannounced.

Captain Chappelle's house is constructed of large, storybook stones with a chimney, out of place on this street of frame two-storeys. Tall Australian pines line the easement. These trees are common in Florida, but invasive, brought in long ago to dry up the spongy land. Their feathery tops sway in the breeze, saying, *Shhhhh.* In the driveway, next to a Fish & Game Suburban, sits a silver Cadillac, not this year's model, but not bad. A green-and-white-striped canopy shades the porch, with an overhanging vine of sweet honeysuckle.

The doorbell gives a curt buzz. At Fish & Game family barbecues, Shari Chappelle used to answer this door. She was a slender high schooler with long auburn hair and perfect hostess manners.

I hear someone moving inside, and then the door swings open. A tall man stands behind the screen, staring down severely.

"Hi, Captain Chappelle."

His face changes to a smile. "Why, hello! Come on in, Loni Mae."

I wish he wouldn't call me that. It was my dad's nickname for me. But I'm the one imposing here, dropping in without calling.

It's dim inside, and Captain Chappelle turns on a floor lamp. This house was luxurious in its time, but the damask curtains hang limply now, and dust motes shine in the light from the window. "What a welcome surprise on my day off," he says. "I expected you before, but no matter. Would you like something to drink? I have cranberry juice." He walks toward the kitchen, turning sideways.

"Sure."

He brings back two filled glasses, sets them down on coasters, and motions for me to sit. "I can taste the cranberry," he says, as he takes the seat opposite. "Not much of anything else, these days."

"No?"

He doesn't elaborate. "It's good to have company. The house is awful quiet. Stevie and I . . . were housemates the last few years, you know." His face clouds.

I hesitate, then say, "It must be hard without him."

Chappelle looks beyond me. "You have no idea."

"I'm so sorry."

"Well, enough of that. The last time we spoke I invited you to see my garden." He puts his palms to his knees and stands.

"Yes, I'd like to."

We proceed out the back door and down a set of wooden steps. His pace is quick and his back broad, without a hint of the extra weight most men his age take on. Close to the house, the yard is dotted with crabgrass and dry patches.

"Don't look at this part. Here's where it starts gettin' good." He points to the hydrangeas growing in profusion, tall puffballs the size of cabbages, green and purple and pink. "You know, you can grow different colors on the same plant," he tells me. "Depends on how acid you make the soil."

Orange and red camellias line the garden's perimeter. They have no scent, as if to balance the heavy sweetness over the front porch. "I drove past your mother's house the other day. You all renting it out?"

I nod.

"So where you staying?" he says.

"Oh . . . up in Tallahassee."

He turns his head at an angle. "Tally? Where? And *why?*"

"Where? Well, right there on Calhoun Street . . . the building's called 'Capitol Park' for some reason. Sounds like it should be either a big green meadow or a seven-storey garage." I laugh.

"And why Tallahassee?"

"Oh, I'm doing some work up there. Hey, is that rhubarb?" I point toward the once-neat lines of dark green leaves and red stems.

"You like rhubarb? I'll cut you some." He takes a folding knife from his pocket and flicks it open.

I protest, but he's already on one knee, shooing and cursing the horseflies as he slices the stems. The stalks bleed red juice onto his hands.

"My wife used to make the best rhubarb pie," he says, and looks off ahead of him, his wrist resting on a knee.

His divorce was a subject of gossip when it happened. One day while he was at work, his wife, Rita, packed up the kids and took off. There was something about money—I never understood it all, but I know the effect it had on my father. One night he said to my mother,

"How could she break a fella like Frank Chappelle? And take his *children* away?"

Stalks of rhubarb succumb to his knife.

"My father thought the world of you, Captain Chappelle."

He glances up. "Well, that was his folly," he says. "I'm not that good a man."

I don't know what to say to this, so I plunge on.

"Captain Chappelle, when my father died—"

He interrupts me without looking up. "It was real sad, when your daddy passed."

"Mm-hm. You were so good to us, afterwards, arranging for all those benefits, and making sure we were provided for."

He looks at me from where he kneels. His eyes are still a sharp blue, and his gaze is steady.

I swallow. "I just want to tell you, I know what really happened." I blink.

He stands and looks down. He's got to be six-three, a good eight inches taller than me. His face is in shadow as he holds the pocketknife in one hand and the dripping stalks of rhubarb in the other.

"Loni Mae," he says, "you can't believe everything you hear."

"No, I suppose not," I say. The sun is blinding, and I try not to look up. "Um, could we go inside?"

He walks to the back steps and almost lets the screen door slap before I catch it and slip through. He takes a seat, still holding the stalks of rhubarb. I sit again in the rattan chair.

"Captain Chappelle, here it is. My brother Phil doesn't know the . . . specifics of my father's death, and, if possible, I'd just as soon leave that as it is."

He says nothing.

"But he has this idea that since Dad died 'on duty'"—I make air quotes with my fingers—"my mom's entitled to some other benefit from the state she never got. He wants to file . . . I don't know, paperwork or something to try and get it. I tried to tell him that Dad wasn't really on duty when he, you know . . . died, so it might not be a good thing to pursue. Phil wouldn't listen to me, but if it came from you—like, if you told him what you'd done . . ."

He shifts in his chair, looks away.

". . . with the paperwork, the incident report, back then . . ."

He stares out the window.

I babble on. "I don't want to put you in a difficult position. It would be totally off the record. And since Phil was so little when it all happened, all you need to discuss with him is the on-duty/off-duty thing. The rest . . ." I shake my head, "I should be the one to, you know, tell him . . . if . . . when it's time."

His strong jaw relaxes, and he smiles. "Sure, Loni." His tone is comforting. "I'll talk to him. If you're certain it's unofficial."

I nod and pull a scrap of paper from my bag. "Here. Here are his numbers. Work and cell." I set the paper on the coffee table between us.

He gestures with the rhubarb. "Now, you know how to cook these, don't you? You have to boil 'em till they're soft, with plenty of sugar, or they'll taste bitter." He gets up and moves toward the kitchen.

"Um, Captain Chappelle?" I say to his back. My tongue feels like a dry biscuit in my mouth, but it's now or never. He's the one person who might have some insight about the *why* of my father's death.

"I wonder if I could ask you . . ."

He's already in the kitchen, pulling out a sheet of white freezer paper to wrap the rhubarb.

"Um . . . you know the night you came over to tell my mother . . . what happened . . ." I'm behind him now, at his kitchen counter. "Could I ask . . . I mean, before that, at work, how . . . how did my father seem?"

He turns his head, still wrapping the stalks. "I don't know if you knew your granddad Newt much, your father's father?"

"Only a little."

"Old Newt was a rambler and a gambler, and . . . how does that old tune go?" He smiles, but it's not a song I recognize. "Anyway, no offense to your family, but Boyd did not get along with his daddy. Newt was a scamp who took off early and only came back when he was low on liquor and the funds to buy it. Well, after I saw you at St. Agnes, I got to thinking about that awful day when I lost my best friend and you lost your daddy. Something occurred to me that I never connected, but don't you know that old Newt had been hangin' around town just before . . . the accident. I wonder if he upset your daddy some kinda way, made him reckless enough to, uh, have that mishap. 'Cause you know how good Boyd was on the water."

The brown water that entered his lungs. I close my eyes, open them.

Captain Chappelle is studying me. "He was a good man, Loni Mae."

He puts the wrapped rhubarb in my hand. "I'll be expecting a pie the next time you come." He walks toward the front door, and I follow. "How's your mother?"

"Oh, she's okay, I guess."

"Don't get old." He opens the screen door. "That's my motto."

I'm already on the porch, spit out of his house into that sweet honeysuckle air. "Well, I'll drop in again," I say. As I get to my car, I wave my white package. "Thanks for the rhubarb. And . . . don't forget to call Phil!"

He watches me get in. I back out of his driveway, using all the manners my mother taught me. "Bye now," I wave, all rhubarb pie and sugar. I'm leaving with one package I didn't want and one answer I did. So why do I feel like I just stood up in a canoe?

17

Though I'm barely awake in this strange, bare apartment, I'm aware how rapidly the extra week I begged from Theo is slipping away. I have to focus on the main task: distilling the contents of these many cardboard boxes. I sit on the paisley love seat and inhale their scent, like cedar shavings from a hamster cage. I slice open a carton labeled "CLOTHES" and pull out a few more dresses to hang in my mother's narrow closet. Below the dresses are pants and tops, some in better shape than others. At the bottom is her white, gauzy dressing gown. Would she use this now? Or do I relegate it to the land of secondhand goods?

My first decision of the day, and I'm stymied. I go outside for some fresh air, but it's a sauna, and I don't walk far. In the lobby, the metal mailbox for my unit 2C is already marked with a sticker reading: "L. Murrow," as if I'm in for life.

Back in the apartment, I lie down, hanging my feet over one armrest of the love seat. Instead of making a decision about the dressing gown, I close my eyes and drift, letting my mental film projector run.

I'm nine, maybe ten. A stuttering light frames my old bedroom window. I should be asleep, but for a split second the room is bright as day, then dark, then light, then dark. Out the window, someone's flipping a switch on the whole sky, on and off, on-on and off in uneven rhythms. A drizzle begins with a low rumble, but no crack to the lightning. There are clothes on the line, tiny doll clothes whipping in the wind. The screen door bangs and my mother rushes out in the dark-light-dark. Her gauzy white dressing gown flares out behind her.

My father stands at the door. "Ruth," he says. "Ruth, leave them."

She reaches up to retrieve a small shirt. Another slow roll shakes the house and then large, pelting raindrops begin to fall. My mother drops her arms to her sides. The light still flashes, and the storm sounds like cannonballs against the roof, but my mother doesn't move. She just stands under the clothesline getting drenched. Her hair, the dressing gown, the laundry, droop with the weight of the rain.

My father comes slowly down the steps into the downpour. He takes her in his arms and holds her for the longest time.

I reach for my sketchbook and draw a thin streak—the clothesline from above. A few more strokes from my pencil reveal arms reaching up, then long hair cascading over a gauzy, floor-length robe.

The drawing takes me where it wants until I reach my mother's face, obscured by a tiny shirt. It's a problem of perspective. I rip the sheet off my sketchbook, crumple, and toss.

I sit for a minute, tapping my pencil. Then I get up to retrieve the balled-up paper, smooth it out, and start over, using the crinkly sheet for reference. This is a problem I can solve. I draw the scene again. My father coming down the steps into the rain. The sag of the clothesline, the hem of the dressing gown, muddied and sopping. I draw my mother's arms, the stoop of her shoulders. But her face resists me.

I look up at the cardboard boxes. I'm getting sidetracked. *Remember the main task.* I set down the sketchbook, get some shopping bags, and stuff them with things for Goodwill. When I get to the dressing gown, I hold it up, give it a last look, then pack it in the box to take to her.

At St. A's, I unpack the dresses and the robe. As I hang them in her closet, my mother says to my back, "Thank you, dear."

I turn around. "I beg your pardon?"

"I said thank you, Loni."

I go over and feel her forehead. "Are you okay, Mom? You're not running a fever."

"Well, of course not."

"It's just, you never um . . . never mind." I pick up a hanger.

"I never say thank you?"

I shrug my shoulders.

"I haven't always treated you right, have I?"

I'm not ready for this. People do this on their deathbed.

"You are like your father. He always took care of me."

I get a flash of him embracing her in the rain. And then another flash, only ever seen in my mind's eye: my father standing up in his canoe, his fishing vest full of weights.

"He took care of you," I say, careful to keep the question out of the statement. *Except when he didn't.*

I sweep my hand under the tissue at the bottom of the box I just unpacked to make sure I haven't missed anything. If only I could find something to tell me my father was good, that he actually did take care of us, that he didn't find us too much to bear. I fold up the tissue, fold up the box, and gather my things. My mother follows me out of the room and into the common area. The TV is on, as always. It's the movie *Notorious*. She sits and I linger, because it's my favorite scene, when Cary Grant finally comes to take Ingrid Bergman away from Claude Rains, who's been feeding her poison, and in her weakened state she says to Cary, "You *do* love me, you *do* love me," and Cary says, "Long ago. All the time, since the beginning." It gives me chills every time I see it.

In the parking lot, I look in vain for my car. Where the hell is it? Then I remember—I parked on the street by the park. I pass the F&P Diner, rummaging for my keys, and I reel back . . . *uggh!* . . . to keep from stumbling over a pile of, what are they? I look more closely. They're doves—six or seven of them—all dead, clumped together on the sidewalk next to my front left tire, and mutilated, necks hanging at funny angles, feet cut off.

"My God!" I say aloud.

I stoop down and see they're strung together with a length of thin cotton. Hanging from one that still has a foot, there's a card like an old-fashioned price tag. I turn it over. Written in cursive are the words, *Fly Away, L.M.*

L.M.? Those are my initials. A young guy, maybe in his thirties, is hurtling himself toward me with a rapid, speed-walking gait. He's skinny, with a ginger mustache and short, curly hair. "What are you doing?" he shouts at me. "What have you done?" He gets pinker as he gets closer and lets out a scream. "My babies!" He points at me. "Murderer!"

I stand up. As I turn, a diamond-shaped divot in the diner's Venetian blinds snaps shut.

The ginger man is crying, keening and squatting down to touch the birds. Then he whips out his cell phone and punches in three numbers. Without taking his eyes from mine, he says into the phone, "I want to report a killing! And I have caught the murderer!" There's a pause. "I'm on Water Street right next to the park." Another pause. "Good. We'll be here." He stands up slowly and says, "Now, don't you try to escape. I've got the law coming."

"Sir, I didn't kill these birds."

"You did."

"No, they were lying here. I love birds. I wouldn't . . ."

"You came to my loft, yonder"—he points—"while I was at work, and you stole my birds! Why did you do it? Why did you *tie* them? Oh, poor things. You're a monster! I trained them since they were squeakers! They always came home. Every one of 'em."

There's the blip of a siren, and a squad car screeches to a halt next to my car. Town Hall is close enough that the cop could just as well have walked.

A burly black policeman emerges from the patrol car.

"Lance?" I run and give him a hug. His uniform is polyester, scratchy and hard.

"Loni? I didn't know you were in town. Phil tells me nothing. What are you doing here?"

The face of the red-haired guy scrunches. "I tell you what she's doing! Acts of murder!"

"Right," I say. "Something creepy's going on."

Ginger-man says, "She killed my birds!"

Lance turns to him, looks down at the birds, then again toward me.

I shake my head. "No. I didn't. But look at the tag."

Lance crouches down and turns over the little card. He's built a bit like my boss, Theo, only younger and more solid. He reads out loud, "'Fly Away, L.M.' Who's L.M.?" He looks up at me. "Is that you?"

I lift my shoulders. "I can't imagine why . . ."

Lance looks down again at the tag. "It could also be someone's signature." He squints up at me and the ginger guy. "Alfie, you got anybody mad at you?"

"No. Except for this crazy bitch, nobody would do that to my birds."

Lance stands up to his full, football-playing height and rests his hands on the gun belt around his waist. "Alfie, I'll thank you to keep a civil tongue. You don't want to get hauled in yourself, do you?"

Alfie shuts up, but a voice in my head says, in the cadence of Mr. Barber, *Get outta town, little girl.*

18

I wake in the wee hours with the image of those contorted doves, their broken necks and chopped feet. I deal with dead birds all the time, but in an orderly way. When I try to go back to sleep, the day's events start to swirl.

After Alfie's profanity-laced statement at the police station, Lance scanned some databases and the tiny Tenetkee phone directory—which is still in print—to see if anyone besides me might be implicated by the initials "L.M." He got no usable results, but he said he'd keep investigating.

"Hey, can I see that phone book?" I said. I ran my finger down the pages looking for Henriettas, but there wasn't a one.

At my request, then, Lance got out his phone and showed me the latest pictures of his twin girls. As I say, my trips here are short, so I don't often see Phil's school friends. But Lance and Phil have always been close, and now they even live in the same townhome complex. Our paths have crossed here and there through the years. Lance knows I wouldn't kill Alfie's birds.

As I left the police station, an overweight blond guy passed me on the street and said a lilting, "Hey, Loni."

I didn't register at first who he was. One front tooth was whiter than the rest.

He said, "Rosalea told me you were in town."

"Hey, uh . . . Brandon." Brandon Davis, now married to Phil's scratchy receptionist Rosalea Newburn, had put on considerable girth since the last time I saw him.

"Whatcha been doin'?" Brandon said.

"Oh, you know, just here visiting my mom . . ."

"Been to the police?"

"What?"

He lifted his chin toward the door of the station.

"Yeah . . . nothing, really."

Now Brandon would tell Rosalea, who would tell her girlfriends, and by the time the story got around town, it'd be me in leg irons and an orange jumpsuit, clearing weeds out on the highway.

Brandon smiled a little too gleefully. "Bird trouble?" He must have just talked to Alfie. He put his fist to his mouth to suppress a smile. "Okay then, good seein' ya!"

It would be nice if I could quit replaying the day's strangeness and just get back to sleep. I look again at the clock. Four a.m. In my bare bedroom, I turn on the light, get my sketchbook, and draw the dove massacre in gruesome detail. I know these birds. They mate for life, they can average 90 miles per hour on a 400-mile flight, and they come home no matter how far or unfamiliar the release location. But someone reduced them to inert and broken body parts, oozing and foul, just to make some twisted statement, with my initials on it.

I get up and look at my creased face in the bathroom mirror. My hair is a rat's nest. I pull at it with a brush, even though no one will see me. It's still the middle of the night, but I'm wide awake, so I might as well do something that will make me tired. Yesterday I brought all the book boxes over here from the museum.

I open a carton. *Journeys Through Bookland*: "KEEP." These stories and their two-color illustrations held me in thrall throughout my childhood. *The Arabian Nights*, Lewis Carroll, "The Pied Piper," "Lochinvar," all condensed just enough to make a child curious. And a few of Andrew Lang's fairy stories. There was one my dad told me, setting down the book, since he knew the story by heart, about a fairy queen who lived in the center of the marsh. She was both beautiful and terrible, angry at times and kind at others, and rarely seen by mortals. Mostly she took the form of a great blue heron, surveying her kingdom and all the creatures in it. She disdained most humans, except those she helped make the passage into the next world. But if a living person had a sincere wish and she deemed it noble, she would rise up out of the swamp in her true form, with her Spanish-moss hair and her eyes like the sharpest sunbeams, and she would ask the human to perform a nearly impossible task. If they did, she would grant the wish.

Out the window, the sky has begun to turn pink. I can already tell my "KEEP" pile is going to be too large. I need to be more cold-blooded, so I can get home to where I belong, my cozy apartment in Logan Circle, D.C., with a mohair Irish blanket thrown across the couch and the scarlet ibis painting by my friend Clive Byers on the wall. I miss the driver of the 54 bus who says, "Good morning!" every day when I get on at 14th Street and, "Have a nice day!" when I get off at Constitution, and I miss my Smithsonian colleagues and their deep investment in the natural world. After work, I also have the occasional date, even if the fish in that sea generally get thrown back. But here in Florida I'm a solitary sorter, a duty-bound daughter, a contrary sister. The faster I can do this task, the quicker I can get back to my own self.

I open a small bound reprint of Gerard's *Herbal* to a page marked with a snapshot—me, age eight or nine, with a galvanized watering can and a big smile. Behind me is the old hand-pump in our yard that reached down to a spring. On a good hot day, my mother would let me open my mouth in the gushing water and take a sip.

As I put the photo back, another falls out. Me again, maybe a year later, after a growth spurt. I'm only about ten, but I look like a malnourished fourteen-year-old with milk teeth. Not quite as carefree. I stick it back with the other one and read the page it marked:

> Calendula (marigold). A cure for childish ailments.

Calendula. Didn't I see that in my mother's *GARDEN* journal? I'm trying not to trespass, but what if I could make a connection between this copy of Gerard's *Herbal* she consulted and her own handwritten notes? It might help me get at the essence of her. After all, the marginalia in Grandpa Tad's bird books show me his interactions with his environment. Maybe in a similar way, I could consider Ruth's little book a natural history artifact. I dig the journal out.

> *Marigold (Calendula) — Herb of the Sun.*
> *Not a perennial. Apricot color like cosmos, but cosmos = rangy and tall, a weed. Calendula = composed. Loni's flower—Boyd brought them in a pretty pot to my hospital room after her birth. I save the seeds each year and replant, though she takes no heed. Gerard's Herbal says the petals are edible. So maybe a marigold cake for a sunnier attitude toward her mother? I do not think I deserve her pouts. I will admit I was angry. That doctor and his infuriating calm, the church woman who shoved her live baby at me, and Father Madden with his worthless bromides. One more little angel in heaven, he said, and then he patted my hand and said, You'll have another. I wanted to scream at that priest, You understand NOTHING! I ONLY WANT THIS ONE! ONLY HER! And all the while that I simmered, Loni played, oblivious and untroubled. That was worst of all.*

I shut the book. A familiar compression tightens right around my breastbone. I look again at those two photos of me. Number one: the helper in the garden. Number two: the clueless pest. From a certain point, no matter what I did, I could not please her. Did anyone even bother to tell me she'd lost a baby? And there I was, a galling annoyance, awkward and gap-toothed, while she grieved a perfect, lost girl-child.

Books are spread across the floor of the apartment, and I haven't accomplished a thing. I lift a volume of John Baldessari prints that used to sit on Grandmother Lorna's coffee table, and I page through, stopping at a black-and-white photo I used to stare at a lot. A young guy stands in front of a palm tree in a suburban neighborhood. Under the photo in block letters is the word WRONG. Now I see it's a visual joke—a parody of those old Kodak tips for good snapshots. The tree appears to be growing out of his head. Baldessari's label goes deeper, though. That must be why this picture fascinated me. I knew what this guy knew. He wasn't doing anything, and yet he was WRONG. Thanks for that, Mom. You helped me appreciate art.

I get up from the floor, change out of my pajamas, and pull on some clothes. Somewhere, people are doing meaningful things. It's way too early, but I need that little studio in the back of the Tallahassee Science Museum. Estelle was right. It's good to have someplace to go.

I park by the edge of Sullivan Road. Even at this hour of the morning, it's muggy and ripe, but I'm not the only one out. A woman far ahead of me in a polka-dot dress and sneakers bobs along with purpose. She's short but stubby, a potato on two toothpicks, just like Joleen Rabideaux. I look again. Could it *be* Joleen Rabideaux? I run to catch up. Judging by her gait and the blue-veined calves, she's about the right age. There's only the slightest chance, but if it were Joleen, I could ask her to fill me in on Henrietta, and help me decipher that letter. I could also find out why the Rabideauxs moved away in the middle of the night. I gain on her, and she looks back, but I'm still too far away to tell for sure. She ducks into a shellrock path between some trees. I reach the place where she turned off, but there's no sign of her. She has completely disappeared.

*   *   *

The AC inside the science museum gives me goose bumps. I set up the skin of Estelle's bird number 5, the marbled godwit—a migratory visitor to Florida, like me. I draw the beak twice as long as the head, tapering down to the width of a knitting needle, then fill in the back and wings with terrazzo mottling, brown and black and white. It has long legs and an exquisite neck. I hope this bird gets a prominent place in the exhibit.

On my second sheet, a young woman kneels on black soil, her back to the viewer, dark hair in a chignon. She pulls at the weeds that crowd her precious bee balm, betony, dock, and rue. She wipes her cheek with the back of her wrist, avoiding the dirt on her glove.

I should go see my mother today, but to be honest, I don't feel like it. Yes, she's an oldish person, displaced from her home, who might count on someone to come and break her solitude. But that journal entry . . . *I simmered while Loni played* . . . gives new color to my lifelong wariness.

Godwit. I draw the bird flying blessedly north, displaying her gorgeous cinnamon wings.

If I do go to St. A's, I'm taking my sketchbook. I'll try to get the *gizz* of my complicated mother. If she's right in front of me, how can I help but capture her? And as long as I'm drawing, how can she hurt me?

19

At St. A.'s, I do try for the calm life sketch, but my mother keeps saying, "Why have you brought me here? It is like a prison! Did I do something wrong?"

I attempt a few distractions—a crossword puzzle, books—but nothing soothes her. Finally, Mariama pokes her head in. "There you ah! Ruth, lunch is ready, and it's very yommy today." She cajoles my mother into going with her.

Can it be only lunchtime? Because I woke so early, I feel like already today I've lived a thousand lives. I take to the road with the slash pines and nearly fall asleep at the wheel.

Adlai gets out a boat for me, the tendons in his forearms spindling as he grips the gunnel. When I lean down to help him push the canoe toward the water, he turns with a frown, as if he doesn't want my help. But once I'm settled in the canoe he says, "Hope you find it this time," and gives a little sideways nod. Did I tell him about the gallinule?

When I'm deep in the swamp, I wonder if I'm approaching Mr. Barber's place. Why didn't I ask *him* about Henrietta?

I emerge from a narrow passage of trees into open water and pull hard against the wind. A man fishing from a little jon boat lifts two fingers in a wave, the boatman's minimal acknowledgment. He has on long sleeves, a hat, and shades, but mutton-chop whiskers like the waiter from the Great Earth. Could it be Garf Cousins?

I paddle quickly toward a side passage and reach a stand of bulrushes. But I slow the canoe, because at last, I see the bird that's been eluding me. Like a stilt walker, the purple gallinule clutches one vertical bulrush with each of her bright yellow feet. She doesn't notice me, because she's lasered in on the snail she plans to eat.

With my paddle across my knees, I let the canoe coast in as close as I dare, and reach in slo-mo for my sketchbook. The gallinule's candy-corn bill—yellow at the tip, orange toward the eye—points at the waterline, and the blue and green of the feathers glint in the sunlight. I sketch the light blue cap and the oval body, hinting at its iridescence. The bird pokes her head sharply into the water, swallows, and begins to meander. She walks across floating lilies, pad to pad, and then into the reeds until I can't see her anymore, no matter how I steer the canoe. When she's gone, I look at my drawing. "Hee-hee!" I say aloud, sketching a few more quick studies to indicate her motion and the intensity of her stare, with notes on the deep iris blue of the head and breast, the aqua of the back and wings graduating to olive at the tips, and underneath an inky black.

I wish I had someone to share this moment with. In grad school a group of us sometimes went on expeditions, and we all looked like Miss Jane Hathaway in *The Beverly Hillbillies*, only with ripstop REI gear instead of her khaki bird-scout uniform. We had a lot of "hee-hee!" moments.

I push away from the reeds and paddle on, knowing I could easily lose my way in spite of this cerebrum-shaped diagram. "LOST IN THE SWAMP!" shouted a recent headline in the *Tallahassee Democrat*—a little girl wandered off with her dog at her side. The German shepherd lay on top of her all night to keep her dry and warm. More often, though, the people "lost" in the swamp are there on purpose. Like Nelson Barber. What is he up to? And what is he running from? This vast tangle of muck has always made a good hiding place for ne'er-do-wells, like those guys my dad and his friends talked about, dropping bundles from airplanes. And the scoundrels who were there to retrieve them.

Once my dad and I were motoring in his little jon boat toward the fishing camp, where he kept his canoe. The motorboat was for getting there, the canoe was for fishing. "Can't sneak up on the fish with a putt-putt," my dad liked to say. We weren't far from the camp when we passed two men in a shiny new Boston Whaler. Usually, my dad would have smiled and said, "Y'all doin' any good?" partly to get the fishing report and partly just to affirm the brotherhood of fishermen everywhere. But this time he didn't smile, only gave a short little nod. He looked back at them after we passed, and they were watching us, too. He dropped me at the camp, locked the door, and said, "Loni, now you stay here. I'll be back shortly." Then he sped off.

I walked to the front of the little house, where it stuck out on stilts over the water. Then back toward the part anchored in the sand, live oak branches huddling around the windows. Then again to the front. Water lapped the pilings below me. I did this several times. A fish plopped, a tree limb creaked. Underneath I could hear frogs and crickets and wind and water. When my dad was with me, these sounds felt like a soft blanket to rest my thoughts on. But that day they told me how far I was from home. I touched the screens and the weathered walls, and knew—I couldn't get myself out of that swamp if my life depended on it.

After a long time I heard shouts, but out there, sounds seemed close when they were far away, and far away when they were close. I heard my father's voice. "Hands up in the air!"

Then I heard another boat, and more shouting. Finally, after what seemed like a long silence, Daddy's little five-horsepower buzzed around the bend, and I ran to the door. He unlocked it, drenched with sweat and grinning.

"Well, you finally ready to fish?" he said, as if I'd been the one making him wait.

"What happened?" I said.

"Oh, just some fellas that got tired of jail and thought they'd take a vacation. I got Captain Chappelle to come help me take 'em back where they belong."

"Those guys we passed?"

He nodded.

"How'd you know?"

"Just a hunch."

"What hunch?"

"Did you notice the tattoo? Big ol' Jesus on his arm?"

I hadn't.

"They always get Jesus in prison." He didn't explain, just shook his head, smiling. "Time's a wasting, girl, let's fish!"

The next day it was in the paper how Daddy had spotted the escapees from Raiford in a stolen boat and gone for backup. He and Captain Chappelle made the arrest. My dad used to say his job wasn't always exciting, but there was ever the possibility.

The sun is low in the sky now, and as far as I can tell, I'm nearly back to the canoe shop. I pass through a dark tunnel of mangroves and glide under a particularly low-hanging branch. Damn if it doesn't fall into the canoe, but there are no leaves on this branch, and it's moving!

I need, right *now*, to get this brown, shining danger back into the water. It's either a large, harmless water snake, or it's a cottonmouth, and the only way to know is . . . *shit!* The big white mouth comes at me for a strike. I bat at the head with my paddle and deflect it, and maybe I've stunned it too, but no time to think—I use the paddle's blade like a spatula and scoop that critter's body right out of the boat as fast as I can. His head comes back toward me as I do it, with amazing muscle control, and I flinch, leaning left while he thrusts right, just as the rest of his body slides backwards into the brown water and his head is pulled back and away. And then I paddle like hell.

I'm at the dock without realizing what choices I've made to get here. Adlai smiles as I approach the desk.

"How was it out there?" he says.

"Oh, my God," I say. "You won't believe what just happened."

He glances beyond me to see if I've wrecked his canoe. I start to tell him about the snake, and I'm short of breath, words spilling out and the adrenaline prickling my skin as I describe it.

A smile creeps onto his closed lips.

"You think that's funny?" I say.

"No, I just like your way of telling it. It's, uh . . . animated." He stifles a smile.

"Hey," I say, "this is no time to make fun!"

He blinks. "I'm not, uh, I just, uh . . ." He turns his attention to the stubby pencil in his hand. "I should write up your ticket."

The last few minutes bounce around behind my eyes.

"So that'll be eight dollars," he says, finally. He looks up from the receipt.

"You can just put it on the card," I say. "Wait. What time is it?" I check my watch. "I kept it out all afternoon. Isn't the half-day rate eighteen?" I set down my sketchbook on the counter.

"That's all right, ma'am."

Ma'am? "Well, *sir*, I'll pay for the time I was out."

He twists his mouth like he's eaten a bad walnut. "Please don't call me sir."

"So . . ."

"Call me Adlai," he says.

"As long as you don't call me ma'am."

He waits.

"Loni." I extend my hand.

"I know." He gives me the same firm grip he offered when he helped me onto the dock.

"Charmed," I say. "Now, what's with the eight dollars? Am I the hundredth customer or something?"

"Funny," he says, with no trace of a smile. "You been here several times in a row, on weekdays, which is my slow time. So, call it a bulk discount. For you and your passenger there." He nods at my sketchbook lying on the counter. "Anyhow, today you deserve a reward for your bravery and quick thinking!" He raises his eyebrows.

His amusement is annoying, but his smile gives me something I must have been waiting for—a glimpse of what's behind all that fur. He's younger than the beard makes him look.

20

APRIL 5

Today I've been sorting for hours, and I need a break. I lie down on the chenille bedspread. My mother's journal is in my bag. It won't be good for me, and I shouldn't look. But curiosity wins out. I reach for it and read.

Marjoram – contentment for a departed soul
Lavender – protector of children
Lamb's ears/betony – 'Sell your coat and buy betony.'

Lavender at the center with low-growing marjoram to circle around. Culpeper says to plant marjoram on a grave, though I have no grave. Soft lamb's ears for the outermost edge.

Pulling up lavender to transplant to my circle, I have come across a baby bird, just fallen, its breath recent. The limbs are splayed, face extending forward, beak a hard yellow smile that is too big for the head. The tiny body is all soft potential. But the life has left it. Boyd would say, Bury it, Ruth, before the ants come. But I need a minute more. Just as with her. To hold her and not say good-bye.

The chick's eyes—closed and big, head soft, skin transparent, like wet tissue paper. Dark spots below—heart, organs. Her skin was like that too. Dark streams visible, blood recently in motion. Little bird, I will put you to rest beneath my new circle, with marjoram planted above. One grave in place of another.

I lay my cheek against the chenille bedcover, mine now since my mother rejected it. In this bare-bones apartment, it's a refuge of familiarity. When I squint, the cream-colored bumps resemble a scale-model cotton field. I reach for my sketchbook to draw this miniature crop, but my drawing hand yields something else instead: a baby bird, just fallen.

In the journal, my mother is coping with sorrow. She is breaking the physical down into its component parts, trying to make sense of the ineffable. Though I'd never say we think alike, I recognize the process. It's what I do at my drafting table every day.

Might she have written this way after my dad's death, too? In the small pockets of time when I wasn't at school or helping with baby Philip, she and I went to opposite ends of the house. I hoarded my grief. What did she do with hers?

I skip to the end of the journal, but the final entry is dated before Philip was born. And Dad left us six months after that. Could there be other journals? I go into the main room and search through all the book boxes, without any luck.

I do find something, though. Between the pages of a true-crime paperback, I notice a makeshift bookmark with some handwritten notes. It's a windowed envelope with a Florida Power & Light return address. On it, in my father's handwriting, it says: *Marvin > extra 2-ways.* And the letters *FGC LED*, and below that a series of scribbles I stare at for a minute before realizing they are driving directions: *Rte. 319 to 263, R at Commonwealth.* I have so few artifacts of my dad that this scrap of paper feels like something precious I should save. I can see him cramping his left hand around his pencil and overslanting every letter.

My phone buzzes. It's Phil.

"Hey, wanna take a run?" he says.

So it wasn't a platitude. He actually meant it when he said we should run together. "Well . . . yeah," I say. "Right now?"

"No, like five thirty? Start from my house?"

"Okay."

We hang up. Phil, inviting me, is still so unfamiliar.

I look at the envelope, then at my watch. Before I meet him, I might just have time to see where these directions lead.

21

Where the hell are my running clothes? In D.C.—at least before Hugh Adamson came along—I ran three times a week on my lunch hour. The last time I ventured out, our young efficiency expert was waiting at the door of my office when I returned, telling me I was to take a one-hour lunch, which I had just exceeded by ten minutes.

But those runs in D.C. keep me sane. They also keep me in shape for our inter-Smithsonian softball games, and I'm the Natural History team's chief female slugger. And being able to hit means nothing if you can't also run. Hence my Monday, Wednesday, and Friday jogs. Usually, I start by crossing the National Mall to the Smithsonian Castle. I run past the Air and Space Museum, then up and around the Capitol building. I do my kick at the end past the East Wing of the National Gallery, and then cool down through the sculpture garden. In the summer I'll sit and watch the arcs of water rising from the fountain there. It's a circular pool as big around as the whale tank at SeaWorld, with eight arcs of water growing steadily from the circumference until they come together in the middle, as high as the surrounding linden trees. After the arcs reach their peak, they gradually diminish till they're hardly a spurt. I watch them rise and fall till it's time to go back in.

Now in Florida, I wouldn't even think of running at lunchtime. Any outdoor sport has to be strategically timed to avoid heatstroke.

At the bottom of my suitcase, my shorts and running shirt finally reveal themselves. I put them on, grab my shoes, and leave early for Phil's.

On the passenger seat I have that Florida Power & Light envelope. If my dad took Route 319 to 263, he was coming toward Tallahassee. But he hated Tallahassee with a passion. I head toward Capital Circle, where Route 263 swings by the airport. It's not a part of town I frequent, and I wonder what brought him out here. It's removed from the university and looks industrial in that wide-open, pine-dotted way of the outskirts of our little state capital. I turn right at Commonwealth, as my father's written directions instruct, but there's no street number, and I'm hard-pressed to see where he was going. The Coca-Cola bottling plant? Boys Town North Florida? There are a few things that certainly were not here in my dad's day—a software company and a biotech facility with a large footprint. I drive for a bit and then turn around. On the way back, I see the smallest of signs, Florida Fish and Wildlife Conservation Commission, and the Fish & Game insignia. I pull in and drive down a very long service road and through a parking lot in front of a low building I didn't even notice before.

I pick up the envelope. *FGC LED*. I squint to see what's printed on the glass door. "Fish & Game Commission, Law Enforcement Division." Was he up here for a training? I look at my watch. It's already five. I get out and try the door, but it's locked. I go back and sit on the hood of my car with my sketchbook.

The building is inanimate, which is not my strength. I draw the rectangle of the door, and copy the letters painted on the glass. The five o'clock sun reflects off the façade, and small trees dot the parking lot. This drawing is making me late for my run, but I want to understand. An officer comes out the door jangling a large set of keys as she turns the lock. She's about my age, and in a rush. I hop off my car and approach her.

"Excuse me, Officer . . ."

She turns.

"I wonder if I could ask you, what, um, is this office responsible for? I mean, the Law Enforcement Division."

She looks out toward the parking lot, then at her watch.

"Sorry to bother you, just . . ."

She recites what must surely be a script. "We do trainings, record keeping, whistle-blower reports, enforcement data, inspector general audits, a weekly newsletter, things like that. If you come back during regular hours . . ."

"Sure, right."

She hurries off, maybe late, like me, to meet someone.

The Manatee Lagoon complex adjoins a municipal park. As soon as I knock, Phil answers. We walk down the path toward the park, and he stoops to tighten his laces. Lance Ashford comes out of his door in uniform.

"Hey, Phil. Hey, Loni," he says.

"Hi, Lance."

He gives me a pointed look. "I hope you're staying out of trouble."

I haven't mentioned the weird dove incident to Phil. Lance shakes my brother's hand and hits him on his shoulder. To me, he says, "You keeping this guy in line, Loni? You always were so *strict*." He gets into his patrol car and I step to the driver's side window. In a low voice I say, "Any developments on the, um, homing pigeons?"

He shakes his head. "We found some long white hairs caught up in the string, but they could have already been on the sidewalk, or some shaggy dog could have come by and sniffed the birds before you found them."

The only shaggy white-haired dog I can think of isn't a dog at all.

"So, not much, sorry." Something in front of his car catches his eye and he smiles. Lance looks through his windshield and waggles the fingers of his right hand. I follow his gaze and see his two little girls on the other side of his picture window making faces and giggling.

I walk to the park with Phil. He tightens his laces yet again. Maybe running helps keep him sane, too. I mean, he's an accountant. That work would drive me out of my bird.

"Ready?" he says, looking up with the same smile he's had since kindergarten. I'll never forget the day I left for college, six-year-old Philip looking up at me saying, "I don't want you to go." I should have stooped down next to him, told him I'd come home often, and that he'd never ever lose me. Instead, I turned around and got on the bus, running from a crucial moment that's colored our relationship ever since.

But exercise can form a bond, or at least that's what I'm hoping. Phil's longer-legged than me, twelve years younger, and works out all the time, so he has an advantage. I haven't jogged for almost three weeks, and I have to push to keep up. We go a short distance, curving around a small lake.

"This a good pace for you?" he says.

I gulp enough breath to say, "Yeah, this is fine!"

He points to his phone.

"See, it lets me track the length and duration of each run, plus energy burned, based on my BMI." The guy loves to measure.

"Um, could we slow down just a little?"

He does, thank God. Then he says, "Well, Bart filed the action today. He says he doesn't think it will take all that long."

"Bart . . . did what?"

Phil's not even breathing hard. "You know, the thing with the state. He said it's better to do it through the courts, kind of a mini-lawsuit, so Mom can get her money quicker. Once we establish that Dad was on duty . . ."

I stop on the path. "Phil, I told you not to do that! Didn't Captain Chappelle call you?"

"Captain . . . ?" Phil keeps going, turning and jogging backwards until I start running again.

"Frank Chappelle," I say, catching up. "Daddy's old boss."

"Why would he call me?" He turns forward again.

"Phil, you get Bart to unfile that action, or—whatever he has to do to stop it."

"Why? What's the matter?"

"Fraud is the matter, brother. If we get money based on Dad being on duty, we're falsifying . . . stuff." I'm trying to sound like I know legal jargon, but I'm just sputtering. In all likelihood, the fraud committed twenty-five years ago will be exposed by this stupid "mini-lawsuit," with an emotional ripple effect I can't possibly articulate.

Phil keeps his steady pace. "Loni, like I told you before, it says right on the form: 'On Duty.'"

"And is it signed by Frank Chappelle?"

He shrugs his shoulders.

"So, you're telling me you don't care if it's based on fraud."

A high call rings out from above. *Teakettle, teakettle, tea!* A Carolina wren.

"Loni, if we don't do this, how'll we pay for Mom's upkeep?"

"Upkeep?" I breathe out. "That's cold."

Phil pounds along: footfall-breathe, footfall-breathe, the percussionist's rhythm. "You know what I mean. Are you planning to take it all on?"

"Let's sprint," I say. I go to my top speed, but Phil moves past me like he's just stepped on a skateboard. These are the things families fight about, in the end. Money, truth, and loyalty. But mostly money. If he keeps pursuing this, the cash from those death benefits could evaporate, and Phil might learn some truths he isn't prepared for. Oh, why the hell didn't Chappelle call my brother?

22

I take a shower, then get Chappelle's number from Information. I call, but there's no answer, no answer, continually no answer. All he had to do was tell my brother he wrote "On Duty" to get us some benefits. Was that so much to ask?

I call every hour. I call into the night. I call like a spurned lover, hanging up and then dialing again. It gets ridiculous, and I finally go to bed. I get up first thing in the morning and call again.

That's when I figure it out. He was trying to tell me, when I was there, but I was too polite to ask what he meant. When he offered me cranberry juice, he said he couldn't taste anything else. Doesn't that happen to people when they're sick, or even dying? He seemed so vigorous. But what if he's fainted? If he were to fall over, who would help him? He could lie there for days and no one would know.

I drive to his house. The sky is overcast, and the hanging vines shadow the porch like a scene from a noir movie. I buzz the doorbell, wait, then knock. I wait some more, knock harder. If the man is dead, he won't answer no matter what I do. I open the screen door and try the knob. I still can't believe people in Tenetkee do not lock their doors. I enter on tiptoe.

"Captain Chappelle?"

What if he's alive and I surprise him getting dressed? That would be awful. I call out louder. "Captain Chappelle?" And then I see him, fully clothed, but on the ground. Legs in the hallway, the rest of him stretched out on the kitchen floor. *Shit.* I lean down and put my head to his chest. His heart is beating, but his face is bloody.

"Captain Chappelle," I say in a loud voice. His lip is swollen and there is blood on the counter above him. He has a large welt on the side of his head that matches the shape of the doorjamb. I get the phone and call 911, because even little Tenetkee knows what an emergency is.

When the ambulance comes, I ride with him to the hospital. His eyes flutter open on the way. "Loni Mae!" he says. He seems unsure of what's happening. It's not the time to say, *Please do not call me that.* "I must have passed out," he says. And then he passes out again. We get to the hospital and they take him out of my reach. I sit and fret like a caring loved one, even though we're not even related.

After a long time, a doctor comes out to the waiting room. "We've treated Mr. Chappelle and he's stabilized." He scans my face. "Were you there when . . . he was injured?"

"No, I found him," I say. "I called his house, and when he didn't pick up I went over, and he was lying there . . ."

The doctor eyes me. I suppose they have to check for elder abuse. I start to feel guilty, even though I had nothing to do with his injuries.

The doctor looks briefly to his notes, then back at me. "It's possible he could have sustained these injuries in a fall, but I have to report when we suspect . . . something else. You say there was blood on the kitchen counter?"

"Yeah, I thought he must have, I don't know, fainted. Hit the door-jamb, then the edge of the counter, then . . ." I wouldn't even believe me if I were the doctor. "Can I speak to him?"

"He'll be asleep for a while. Why don't you go home and come back later? We'll take good care of your . . ." He pauses, waiting for me to define the relationship. His face asks: *Father? Uncle? Sugar daddy?*

"I'm a . . . family friend."

"All right. Well, no need to hang around too long, but before you go I'd like you to talk with Yolanda." A young woman in scrubs steps up from behind him. "She'll take down your contact information."

Yolanda takes me into a little room and not only writes down every bit of my information, she also asks questions like, "How long have you known the patient?" and "Are you the patient's primary caregiver?" and "Does Mr. Chappelle depend on you for shelter or financial support?"

When she asks if I have access to his bank accounts, I say, "Look, our families were friends. I don't even live in this town. I'm the Good Samaritan here, for God's sake. I'm not . . . whatever you're implying."

"Okay, Ms. Murrow. Not to be upset. We just have procedures we have to follow."

Geez. I grab my bag and leave.

23

They call it a drip, fluids, hydration. The morning sun strikes the bag of clear liquid hanging next to Captain Chappelle's bed, connected through the plastic tube to the needle in his hand. Apparently he was severely dehydrated, which could have made him black out. But I can still feel the young doctor's suspicious glance. It kept me from returning yesterday, but I'm here this morning in spite of my own resistance.

Frank's eyes are closed, and one is swollen purple where his brow hit either the doorjamb or the counter as he fell. The butterfly bandage on his lip makes him look like a pugilist who lost a fight. Beeping monitors measure his vital signs.

And what is my place here? Until recently I was a busy natural history artist with an enviable job in a fast-paced city. These days I'm in a sleepy town visiting frail older people, one in assisted living, and now one in the hospital.

The nurse said I've been his only guest. He has no one even to pick him up off the floor of his house. I'm not at all comfortable in this role, and I hate seeing Captain Chappelle tethered to all these tubes and wires. But I'm glad the monitors show signs of life.

Finally, he opens his eyes. He looks frightened at first to see me. Then his confusion clears. He rasps out, "Loni Mae."

"Captain Chappelle."

He reaches up a hand, and I clasp it. His grip is strong. "Well, girl," he says, and pauses for a breath. "I don't know what would have happened . . . if you hadn't come by."

"Actually, I came to your house to ask you—"

"You're like my guardian angel," he croaks out.

I sigh. "Well, after my father passed, you were *our* guardian angel."

There's a long silence. "What happened to your daddy, Loni, I'm sorry."

"It wasn't your fault."

"Yes," he says. "Yes, it was. I saw him, how he was, there . . ." He closes his eyes and seems to sink into a state deeper than sleep.

"Captain Chappelle," I say. Then louder. "Captain Chappelle!" I touch his shoulder. "Frank?" I want him to complete that thought.

The monitors beep a rhythm. I say his name again, but he is dead asleep. Not dead, though. So I may have another chance to ask him what he was about to say. I sit with him until visiting hours end and a nurse shoos me out.

I head back over to the little studio in the Tallahassee Science Museum. It's quiet on the weekend, and the after-hours security guard already knows me. He gives me a salute.

I raise the Roman shade. At the drafting table, I do not immediately draw. Chappelle's words swim by me. *I saw him, how he was, . . .* Why couldn't he have finished that sentence? Once and for all he might have given me an answer for why my kind, funny father left us to fend for ourselves.

Concentrate. Bird. I set up my tiny dead model of the savannah sparrow and consult my grandfather's field guide. "Savannah sparrow. Able runner. When surprised will drop into the grass and dart away." In the margin, Grandpa Tad has written in his neat penmanship: *10/2/72 half mile due north Wakulla Springs.*

Estelle's list focuses on the more distinctive Florida birds, but this one is as common as they come. Still, I try to honor its small dignity with precision, its yellow eye shadow and the brown streaks in the white breast. I draw a blade of cordgrass for the sparrow's perch, trying for a sense of motion as the breeze makes the long stalk bend and bow. The sound of the wind fills the drawing, and with it comes my father's voice.

"Look at that, Loni Mae."

I looked away from the little bird swaying on a reed, and toward the dripping fish at the end of Daddy's line, struggling and curling its tail up toward its hooked mouth, first one side, then the other.

Daddy grinned. "Gotta be a two-pounder."

The fish's spotted body moved silver-blue-green and gold in the sunlight. Daddy removed the hook from the fish's mouth and held its tail, ready to bash its head on the side of the boat.

"No!" I said, and the fish jumped out of his hand and into the well of the canoe, flopping and flailing.

My dad baited another hook and watched me watching the fish. Its gills went in and out, in and out, and after a few minutes, it moved with less energy. The colors faded, it struggled less, and finally, its eye glazed over.

My father said, "The other way's better for the fish."

Later, at the fishing camp, Daddy lifted a fillet, dredged it in flour, and put it in the sizzling pan. Before I started coming with him, I'd never seen him cook, never wondered what he ate out at this damp wooden building where mosquitoes bit us in spite of the screens, and frogs sang close and far, close and far all night.

I ate a bite of the fish he'd cooked, swallowed it, and said, "Wish we could live out here all the time."

Daddy reached for the ketchup. "I don't think your mama'd do very well without her garden."

I let my fork hover. "Mama could stay back. With her garden."

Daddy turned his head my way. He chewed and angled his head to one side.

When I got in my cot, Daddy said, "You know, Loni Mae, sometimes a person can be impatient with you, but that does not mean she don't care for you." He tucked the covers around me. His flannel shirt smelled like dinner and fresh air and old leaves. "Good night, darlin'." He kissed me on the forehead.

Footsteps above me. Museum visitors, perhaps. Next to my marsh sparrow, my second sheet of paper contains the crosshatching of a screen, my father framed by weathered white beams, and a patch of blue ceiling above. This is where I knew him best. For once, I don't rip my second sheet, don't crumple or toss it. Instead, I pack up and turn out the light.

24

In the morning, I sit at the wobbly kitchen table in this apartment that will never feel like mine. I told Phil I wanted to see the form, the incident report, the basis for his "mini-lawsuit." But now that I'm holding the number 10 envelope that contains the form, I don't know. I retrieved it on my way in yesterday from the mailbox in the foyer that says: "L. Murrow 2C," and it has been here on the kitchen table ever since, unopened. What am I afraid of? I slit the envelope and grab the trifold sheet, two papers stapled together. It doesn't sear my fingertips. It won't scorch my retinas. Unfolded, it's just a bad photocopy of a state form. A lot of little boxes. My eyes travel to the phrase in all caps: "DEATH BY ACCIDENTAL DROWNING." Yes, it says "On Duty," and yes, it is signed *Capt. Frank P. Chappelle.* I flip to page 2.

"ADDENDUM TO FORM 537b." Just another standard-issue document. About halfway down, under "Comments," there's a hand-written note: *Wallet of deceased found on land, approx. one hundred feet from site of body. Contents: Fla. Driver's License, Fla. Fishing License, Fish & Game Law Enforcement Badge/ID, 2 photos. No cash found in wallet.* This addendum is signed by a Lt. Daniel J. Watson.

I stare at a chip of paint on the windowsill. What does that mean, *wallet found on land*? Did it wash up on the bank? Did Daddy throw his wallet in some last renunciation of the things of this world? I don't want to picture it.

To change the image in my head, I get out my list of birds. Next to work on: the belted kingfisher. I'll need to buy some chromium-oxide green for that shaggy crest, or maybe Hooker's green mixed with cobalt blue, a touch of ivory black. Hell, I don't know.

I get up, go to the apartment window, and stare down at the patchy grass. Grackles dart about, pecking at the ground for bugs, chirruping over the hum of the air conditioner.

No cash found in wallet. What was this guy Watson suggesting? My dad wouldn't need money out in the swamp. I pick up the form. Watson dated his signature a full two months after my dad's death. I flip back to the first page. The date after Chappelle's name is a few days after the "accident." My brother never even mentioned this second page. And who is Lt. Daniel J. Watson?

For a minute, I stare straight ahead. Then I scrabble among the papers on the floor until I find the folder of old clippings. I turn over a few before coming to the grainy shot of my dad and Chappelle shaking hands. *That's* where I saw that name. The caption says: "Lieutenant Daniel Watson, outgoing Officer of the Year." He stands in the background, unsmiling.

Estelle answers my knock. "Can I use Roger's computer?" I say. Fortunately, Roger isn't home. I sit down at his deluxe two-screen computer and type into the search box: *Dan Watson, Tenetkee Florida.*

Estelle loiters in the doorway of the guest room. "So, what's happening?"

I shove the accident report at her. "Look at the second page. Now why would the wallet be found on land if he himself were . . ."

She completes my thought. ". . . in the water. Are they saying he was robbed?"

I swivel toward her on Roger's ergonomic desk chair. "The swamp is not generally a place where you get asked for your wallet. Though who's to stop someone if they did? My dad and I did come across those escaped prisoners once."

"Oh yeah." She nods, having heard that story soon after it happened. She looks over the accident report again, and sets it down beside me. "I'll be in my room if you need me."

I turn back to the screen. My search for *Dan Watson, Tenetkee, Florida* turned up no worthwhile results, so I key in *Dan Watson*, with no location, and I get a thousand different Dan Watsons, smiling profiles and news articles and sundry other mentions. I try *Lieutenant Daniel J. Watson*, and I get a site called Officer Down Memorial Page. It's a listing of law enforcement officers killed in the line of duty. So it looks like Lieutenant Watson will not be enlightening me about my father's death.

The site gives Watson's age at the time of death (*32—even younger than my dad*), the cause (*gunfire*), the incident date, and status of the perpetrator (*Not Available*). Next to this index is a thumbnail description of the incident: *Lt. Watson was shot in the face while attempting to arrest a person illegally hunting at night. Lt. Watson was taken to FSU Medical Center, where he succumbed to his wounds. The suspect is still at large. Lt. Watson is survived by his wife.*

I shouldn't do it, but I can't help myself. I put my dad's name into the site's search box. The index says: *Officer Boyd Murrow. Age: 37. Cause: Drowning.* Thumbnail description of the incident: *Officer Murrow drowned while on boat patrol.*

That is all.

I get up, pace the room, sit back down, and hit the X at the top right of the screen.

At the bottom right is today's date, April 8. That seems impossible. I told Theo I'd be back without fail on April 9.

I call him on his cell.

"Loni, if you're about to say you're not coming in tomorrow . . ."

I swivel away from Roger's fancy computer screen. "Yes, I am about to say that, Theo, and I know that is not convenient for you, but—"

"So maybe I should just trust the paperwork you filed, and not trust you. The paperwork says eight weeks, which is hard enough to—"

"You can trust me, Theo! It's just that I have a delicate situation down here and—"

"Look, I'm not allowed to give people on family leave a hard time. But Loni, I got a big project going on here. And I suppose you know that if you go one day past your requested date, Hugh Adamson will be doing the Snoopy dance as he fires you. I would very much like for that not to happen."

He cares. He's pissed, but he still cares.

"Me neither, Theo. Me neither. But don't worry, I'll be back *way* before May 10."

"Way before," he says, disbelieving.

"Before. I promise." Should I tell him he's my favorite boss ever? Should I tell him that his respect and his concern are qualities I value more than almost anything? "Theo," I say.

But he has hung up.

Estelle appears in the doorway. "How can I help?"

"Distract me. Cheer me up. Make my life simple."

She thinks for a minute, then says, "Come on."

I follow her into the living room, where she lies down on her soft, cream-colored carpet.

"Come," she says, and she scoots over so there's room enough for both of us to stare up at the ceiling. Then she modulates her voice so it sounds like a yoga instructor's. "Now close your eyes."

"Estelle—"

"Don't talk. Just do."

I comply.

"Now, picture a time when you were completely carefree."

"Estelle—"

"I know what I'm doing. Oh, but I forgot the first thing." Her voice goes slow again. "Take a deep breath."

I breathe in, then out.

"Now another."

I do.

"Let the floor support you. You don't need any of your muscles. Let the floor do all the work to hold you up."

I inhale deeply.

"Now, let the picture develop, blurry at first, your carefree moment. Where are you? Who else is there? Don't answer. Just let the picture develop around you. Absorb this image of contentment."

I breathe into a fuzzy picture. My own smallish hands, holding a very fine needle. I pick up tiny glass beads with the tip of the needle and let them fall one by one onto a clear thread. A young Estelle sits across from me. She has a slender needle too, and dips into the tray of tiny glass beads, sparkling like grains of sand.

When I open my eyes, Estelle is gone. Slowly, I sit up.

She comes out of her room. "Refreshed?"

"Yeah, that was good. How long was I out?"

"About twenty minutes."

I get up from the floor. "Thanks, friend." I pick up my bag. "Hey, wanna hear something my mother wrote?" I pull out the *GARDEN* book and open it to a page I marked with a sticky note. Estelle plops on the couch to listen.

I read:

Loni's little friend Estelle is over, and the girls are galloping around the yard, gnawing on stalks of sugarcane Boyd brought home from his trip. They are laughing at the top of their lungs.

Estelle smiles and nods. "That was us."

I keep going:

It is good to see Loni enjoy herself, instead of her usual mope. Watching her gives me a sense of who she is in the world. Compared to little Estelle, she is tentative, but funny—trying to match her friend in games and wits. She has a freshness to her, an openness she rarely shows me. Yet one night last week when I came in to say good night, she asked me to read to her, something we haven't done for a long while. I picked up a book of fairy tales, sat next to her with my stocking feet on the bed, and we let our imaginations roam around the same territory. After I'd read a few pages, Loni leaned up and kissed my arm, just like that, and then looked up, her face like a frightened rabbit's. I went back to reading, not really seeing the words. Is she so afraid of me? Have I closed myself off to that sweetness? I came to the end of the section and said, Shall we stop there? We could not have finished the book in one sitting. But when I suggested reading again, she said, Oh, that's okay.

In her present mood, laughing with her friend, she seems young and silly but also self-possessed, a mystery-child, growing in a way that might have nothing to do with me. I will insist on the reading. We will do that again.

Estelle frowns. "So did she?"

"Did she what?"

"Read to you again."

I get up to avoid Estelle's hard gaze, and put the book back in my bag. "I don't know. I don't think so. My dad read to me, sometimes. I mean, I could read myself, so . . . that's not really the point."

"Yes it is—"

"I just thought you'd like it because it shows you and me together at that age." I come back to the couch and grab one of the pillows.

Estelle's socks are decorated with pictures of fried eggs. "What grade were we in then, third? Fourth?"

"Something like that. No, she was pregnant with Phil, so we were about eleven."

"Hm. Even then, your mom was a little . . . I don't know . . . edgy?"

"Yeah, but maybe she was . . . trying not to be." I play with the trim at the border of the pillow. "Anyway, I shouldn't be reading her journal."

"However, if it gives you insight into your relationship—"

"Estelle, you're getting that 'I am your shrink' tone."

"Well, you should listen to me, because I'm wise."

"Hey," I say, "I just thought you'd like a picture of yourself as a child."

"And that's the only part of that I'm allowed to comment on?"

I stare at her.

She twirls her hair. "Okay, then. Weren't we cute. Gallop gallop, gnaw gnaw. Hilarity ensued."

"That's better."

25

I'm in Nelson's Sporting Goods comparing two sets of fingerless paddling gloves when I get a rank whiff of body odor, and before I know it, the man who used to own the store is right next to me.

"You had to go and fuck it all up, didn't you? You couldn't just let lyin' dogs lie, or shittin' dogs shit."

The last word lands a spray of spittle on the side of my neck. I turn to see white wispy hair and a scratchy, unshaven face. From the shelf to my left, Mr. Barber has picked up a hunting knife with a sharp, serrated edge. He turns it, watching it shine in a shaft of sunlight.

I take the half-second when his eyes are elsewhere to dart toward the counter, where the squinty salesclerk can see what's happening. Nelson Barber moves to follow.

The skinny clerk begins to talk past me in a high twang. "Now, you put that down, Mr. Barber. 'Cause I sure as hell know you don't have money to pay for it."

Nelson calls out to him in a deeper, scratchier voice, "And why is that, huh? I tell you what I do have money for. A box of shotgun shells, and you best sell 'em to me."

The salesman sings out, "Barber, you been told more than once not to set foot on this property. And the last thing I'm gonna sell you are shotgun shells."

Barber says, "I have a right to defend myself against attackers, not to mention turkey vultures like you people! Takin' a man's livelihood out from under him! Fuckin' vultures!"

Another man comes from the back room, and he and the salesclerk hustle Nelson out of the store. The larger man wrests the knife away from him as Barber looks back at me. "I told you who not to trust! But here you are!"

The bigger man gives him a mighty shove, and the white head whiplashes.

The store clerk shouts, "Get outta here, you old lunatic!"

My pulse throbs in my temple. I'm glad the knife is out of his hands, and glad for the distance from him. I clutch the gloves and watch until he's gone.

I thought today I might try to paddle toward Barber's place, to ask him about Henrietta. But knowing that he came to find me, I decide against paddling at all, and instead retreat to the apartment to sort. Death by a thousand decisions is better than death by hunting knife any day.

26

I've lined up the books along the baseboards, spines up. I'm possessive about books the way my mother is about her stupid hairbrushes—I want to keep them all. But here's why: A personal library is like a fingerprint. When I dip into these volumes, I travel through the lives of my mother, my father, my grandparents.

I pace the apartment's perimeter reading the spines. I categorize and rearrange them. But unless I buy a country estate with a paneled library and a rolling ladder, I must make some painful decisions.

Among my dad's paperback mysteries, we've got *Born in a Swamp*, and the Mangrove Mysteries series. I suppose I should donate these. Someone might enjoy them. I read the back cover of *Born in a Swamp*. It does sound like the pulp my mother always rolled her eyes at. I'm usually more respectful of books, but I toss this one to the corner and it splays open. When I stoop to set it right, I notice a small piece of paper that's fallen out. Another bookmark, a faded receipt from Parson's Nursery and Garden Shop. On the reverse, though, in my dad's handwriting, it says:

Frank > Elbert > Dan
Walkie-talkies
who else?

There's a loud ringing, and at first I can't figure out where it's coming from. With the slip of paper still in my hand, I walk toward the wall phone in the kitchen. "Hello?"

"Ready for another run?"

It's Phil. I forgot I gave him this number. I've used up all my free cell minutes, and the rental office never disconnected this old landline. The phone number's printed right on the handset, so why not use it?

"Sure, Phil. I'd like that." We agree to meet tomorrow morning. I hang up and carry the little Parson's receipt to the table and set it on a blank page of my open sketchbook. Then I go and get the newspaper clipping of my dad receiving his award, with Dan Watson looking on. I sit at the wobbly kitchen table and begin to draw—Frank and my father shaking hands, Dan, in the background, scowling. I need to understand more about their faces than the flat, grainy image gives me. My sketch adds definition to Frank Chappelle's angular smile, to the upward cant of Daddy's chin, to the strength of their handshake.

I put the drawing on the fridge under a small apple magnet left by the prior tenant. Under a similar plastic pear, I display the receipt with my father's handwriting.

On the way to the Geezer Palace, I notice a roadside flower stand, and I slow the car, then stop.

In her room, my mother sits watching *The Price Is Right*. I wasn't in favor of bringing in the small television set, but Tammy overruled me. When the show finishes, I turn the TV off, and my mother frowns.

"Hi, Mom! I brought you some tulips."

"I hope they're not from up north." Vinegar in her mouth.

"I don't know," I say. "I bought them on the highway."

"You know full well yellow is not my favorite."

I press my lips together. *Do not react.* In the bathroom, I run water into a vase and then put my wrists under the cool stream. I count to thirty, arrange the flowers, and come back out, setting them beside her.

She says, "Those are nice. Where did they come from?"

Note to self: always wait her out. "Look, I also brought you some books."

"Oh, Loni, I don't have the patience to read anymore. My eyes get so tired."

So what the hell will she do all day? Watch game shows? "All right then, I'll read to you." I open one of her poetry books and read a favorite passage. "The work of the world is common as mud—"

She interrupts me. "That's um . . . that's um . . . Marge Piercy." And then she goes on to recite the next three, transcendent lines.

I nod. "You got it, Mom." So she's not completely gone. I just have to stay calm when she's cranky, and read to her. Maybe my dad was right, all those years ago, when he encouraged me to see an invisible reservoir of good in my mother. It's like waiting for those cool pockets of air in the steaming swamp—they're unpredictable, but ever welcome.

27

As we start our run this morning, Phil presses the button on his watch. I actually keep up with him for a change. Again, we circle the small lake in the park near his house.

"You know," he says, "it's only a 3K path. We should try to go around twice."

"Or," I say, "we could take a detour into the neighborhood, go up and down a bunch of streets, lose complete track of how far we've gone, and then come back to the path."

He swallows. "If you want to do that . . ."

I laugh. "No, Phil, I'm just messin' with you. Twice around is fine."

He seems to relax a little, as if running two perfect circles will keep his life in order.

He asks about the drawings for Estelle—how many I've finished. For him, it's all about the count.

"Well, I've turned in three, but I just finished three more."

"So, six," he says, as if I don't know arithmetic. "How many left to go?"

I'm conscious of my breathing now, trying to catch the rhythm of his stride. "Well, with much persuading, she cut the list to fourteen. She started with eighteen, which was just—"

"So you're almost halfway done."

I tick my head to the side. "Yeah. Thanks, Phil. I like the way you put that."

We run for a while in silence. Then he says, "Am I allowed to talk about the lawsuit?"

"Allowed?" I say. I try to match his steps.

"Well, I know you're all mad about it, but I don't see why."

"Phil, I'm always mad."

He glances at me, unsure whether I'm joking.

"Bart says it's looking easy. The paperwork's in order, and our odds of winning are very high."

"Phil, I told you it wasn't a good—"

"It's just that . . . well, Loni, I don't know how to say this, but . . . I'm not sure Dad's death was an accident."

Oh shit. My foot catches on an uneven spot in the pavement. *This is it.*

"Did you see page 2 of that form?" he says.

I nod.

He takes in air. "The wallet, on land, a ways from the body . . . weird, huh? Bart thinks, maybe . . . foul play."

I say nothing, only pump my arms harder.

"And then the guy who wrote that addendum was killed. Never been solved."

Our feet thud against the blacktop, and that "Officer Down" page hovers before me like a hologram.

Phil keeps talking. "So, I'm just an accountant, what do I know? But I diddled around on the computer at work, and damn if this guy's name doesn't come up."

"What guy?"

"Lieutenant Dan Watson, who found Dad's wallet. Seems our firm used to do his taxes. Still does the widow's. Wasn't she your math teacher or something?"

"Watson? I don't . . . think so." A blue heron lifts off from the lake, wings large and slow, lofting upward.

"So I go to the year he died, which wasn't easy—all those old returns are on fiche. But listen," he exhales. "The husband has died, so the widow files a Form 706."

Tales of accounting.

"She doesn't have to pay tax on community property, you know, from her husband, but funny thing is, she also files a 709."

He's all bright eyes, like when he was little. I can't decode accountant speak even when I'm standing still.

"Loni, Form 709 is for gift tax. She got a very big gift that year and it wasn't from her dead husband."

"I'm gonna slow down," I say. "You keep going. I'll meet you at the end."

He shortens his stride and stays with me. "Loni, somebody gave Watson's widow a house the year her husband died."

"Who?"

"Well, not so clear. Usually, the donor pays the gift tax. But in rare cases, the donee is allowed to pay it."

I wish I knew what he was talking about.

Phil jogs on his toes. "And while I was looking through those tax records, Bart got ahold of Dad's inquest report."

A drip of sweat stings my eye. "His what?"

"You know, autopsy, investigation notes. . ." He says "autopsy" like any other word. Ice cream, running shoes. "And here's the strange thing, Loni. There was no investigation. Just that report that declared it accidental, and the weird note Dan Watson added two months later."

We're nearing the end of our second circuit. I want him to shut up and let me think. Accident report. No inquest. Mrs. Watson's house. What does it all mean? *There are some things I have to tell you about Boyd's death.* The elusive Henrietta, wherever she is, could help me out here.

"Time for our kick," he says.

"Wait," I say and I chase him, not because I want to run fast, but so I can understand what he's just told me.

He finishes his sprint and walks in circles.

I catch up and hope to breathe again soon.

"So, here's what I think we do," he says. "First, talk to Mrs. Watson."

I nod, still slightly oxygen-deprived.

"Okay then?" He raises his eyebrows.

I gasp out, "What do you mean, okay?"

"You'll go and talk to her?"

"Oh, no, I didn't say that."

Phil says, "Well my firm does her taxes, so I can't talk to her. You can be casual. She was your teacher."

"No, I don't think—"

"You're the prodigal daughter returned. Of course you'd have questions."

"Prodigal?" I say. "Look, Phil, even if she was my teacher, I wouldn't have a clue what to ask." I'm still catching my breath.

"Leave that to me." He puts his hand on my sweaty back. "Thanks, Loni."

I pant a little more slowly and study my brother's slender face. What in the hell have I agreed to?

28

"Mrs. Watson?"

The house is modest, stucco over concrete, and slightly bigger than the neighbors'. Two pink metal chairs sit beside the front door. A voice from an oval shape behind the screen door says, "Yes?"

"Hi, Mrs. Watson, I'm Loni Murrow. Boyd Murrow's daughter."

She straightens her neck. "That's a name I haven't heard in a long time."

I feel like I'm selling World's Finest Chocolate for the band trip to Palatka. "Mrs. Watson, I'm real sorry to bother you. Do you have a few minutes?"

"A few." She does not invite me in.

"It's nice out here on the porch," I say.

"Mm-hm." She stays put. Her gray hair has a big barrette on top, the hair behind it teased into a little mound. My sister-in-law's handiwork, no doubt. This lady was definitely not my math teacher. That was Ms. Watkins, not Watson. I have no excuse for being here.

"Ma'am, believe me, I do not want to bother you." I'd turn around except for the list of questions in my pocket, handwritten by Phil. If she has new information, I do want it. And if it's awful, I can choose how much or how little to share.

"Mrs. Watson, I know people around here hate to talk about the past. And I'm the same. I usually say, 'Look ahead, not back!'"

Blank silence.

"But of course, my father, you know, he passed away . . . in the swamp."

"Mm-hm." She looks beyond me.

"It was a long time ago, but I'm, I'm trying to find out about one little detail," I peer through the dark screen, "and I wonder if your husband ever—"

"My husband is gone, dear. He died some years back."

"Yes, I'm so sorry about that. I was just wondering if he ever mentioned—"

"Young lady, I think it's time you left me alone."

"Well, there's just one thing, Mrs. Watson . . ." I open my number 10 envelope and take out the xeroxed paper with her husband's signature. But she has already shut the wooden door inside the screen. I wave the paper at the place where she stood.

"Mrs. Watson. Mrs. Watson!"

Well. That was a waste of time.

I suppose if I were a good daughter, I'd use this moment in town to go see my mother. But in my bag is a photo Tammy took of her whiteboard, and it says today is not my day. So I might as well do what I want.

29

Adlai lifts down a fiberglass canoe. "No more aluminum for you!" he says. "Company policy—any customer who rents for three and a half weeks running gets an upgrade."

He reaches for an ash paddle.

"God, that's way too long," I mumble.

He turns. "I beg your pardon?"

"Oh. I mean, 'Lucky me!'" I change the subject. "Hey, are you named after Adlai Stevenson?"

One raised eyebrow tells me way too many people ask him that. "It was my granddad's name."

"It's nice," I say, to make amends.

He nods and walks outside. We guide the boat till it bumps alongside the dock, and he steadies it. Just as I'm about to step into the canoe, an egret flies low over the glassy water. The bird is white all over with delicate wisps at the head and tail. We both stop to look. The egret tucks her long neck close to her body, and her wings nearly touch the shining surface. It's a mirror—egret above, egret below. She's followed by a series of dark circles, the air from each wingbeat lifting the water.

"What's that one called?" Adlai asks, though he surely must know.

"Snowy," I say. "Snowy egret."

"And you could draw that?"

"Maybe."

His gaze follows the loft of her wings as she rises toward the trees. "That's about my favorite sight," he says. When the bird is gone, he turns to me, extends his palm toward the canoe, and says, "Your chariot awaits."

I get in, and he pushes me off. I look back toward him. "Thanks."

He taps a finger to his forehead in a little salute, then puts both hands in his back pockets and watches as I turn forward to paddle.

Resist, Loni. Resist.

Some of what I pass is familiar now. Or again. I keep thinking I might round a bend and come upon a spot where my father and I fished. But these waterways may not even intersect with the ones he and I canoed. Of course, all the water is connected somehow, even if only underground. And today, thanks to my boss back in D.C., I'm here to investigate those watery underground connections.

When I called Theo this past Sunday to say still three weeks were not enough, I stupidly said, "You know, if you need me to draw anything, I can always work from here."

He sighed. "Oh, I've got plenty of work. But I don't think I can assign it to you. Human Resources has its rules about family leave." I could hear him shuffling papers, and then he seemed to perk up. "Now if you wanted to *volunteer* for something . . . strictly pro bono . . . Bob Gustafson in Geology asked me for a favor."

I thought, *Rocks? When was the last time I drew something for Rocks? And for free?* And also, *Who's drawing the birds while I'm gone?*

"Gustafson needs a sketch of a sinkhole and a few submerged Florida caves. And since you're already down there—"

"Theo, I don't think—"

"Hey, you wanted something to do. Just don't mention it to Human Resources. Or to our friend Hugh."

"Right. Since Hugh and I have daily chitchats."

I agreed to do it in the end, but really, it made no sense. When I hung up, the churning in my stomach was a subtle reminder of my job's virtues and compromises.

The water Gustafson wants is not the surface water I'm paddling over, it's water that flows through the swiss cheese of limestone below the Florida soil. The underground rivers that feed the swamp are a part of the peninsula's Precambrian past, but putting them on paper does not sound like fun. Still, I agreed to it, so once I'm more or less lost in the twisting waterways, I take out my sketchbook. I'll start with swamp water, because it's what I know best.

It's not my favorite, my mother taught me to say when I detested something on my plate and a grown-up asked how I liked it. *It's not my favorite* kept me truthful and polite. I was never allowed to say *I hate it*. So may I say, drawing this water *is not my favorite*. I don't even do my own backgrounds, if I can help it. I draw the bird, and someone else draws the parching desert, or the coniferous forest, or the majestic snowcaps where the bird thrives.

But I sit in the canoe and try to depict the swamp water, seeing if I can inhabit my subject. Shape? Nonexistent. I know what's on it and what's in it, but the water itself I can only suggest. Tint? It's a tea-colored mess full of catfish, crawdads, bottom-feeders all. Not to mention the gators and snakes. In fact, let's not be polite. Not only is it *not my favorite*, there's a lot I *hate* about this water. I hate the mud and the way it stinks when the water's down. I hate the way it grabs at your boots, slurping and smacking when you pull them out. I hate the way the ground quivers at every step, the way it's not exactly earth and not exactly water.

But I draw it as well as I can, along with the bow of a canoe and some reeds beyond. I draw the canoe's insides, the ribs and front thwart, the handle of a paddle leaning against the gunnel. A boot, a pair of boots, and then a pair of khaki work pants grow up from them, a flannel shirt with unevenly rolled cuffs, reddish hair on the forearms, the scruffy weekend stubble. The ears, the eyes . . . my father.

My canoe goes *thunk*. I've drifted into the bank.

So many good reasons to hate this water. The canoe in this picture is not the one I'm in now. It's the one he and I spent so many hours in, the one he was in just before he met his Maker. It's the canoe I killed.

After the funeral, Captain Chappelle offered to sell the canoe at auction, and my mother agreed without argument, and without asking me. I never told her I went to that auction. It was two towns over. I took all my money, which added up to one hundred and thirteen dollars and fifty-seven cents, and I went on my Schwinn Varsity. It was a long way. I sat in the auction yard until the canoe came up. It was the last thing to be auctioned, and I bid on it. I ignored the people who stared and snickered at me with my braids, my high voice inching up the bid every time the big fat man on the other side inched it up some more, my face hotter with every bid.

Finally, the round-bellied man sighed and said, "One hundred dollars."

And I said, "One hundred and thirteen dollars and fifty-seven cents!" And everyone laughed a big one then. My face burned and my heart pounded, not because of the laughter, but because I had won. No one could bid more than that.

There was a pause, and then the man said, "One hundred and twenty dollars."

I looked at the auctioneer, and I said, "No!"

I think the auction guy was probably a dad who could see no one was there to help me, no grown-up, but he couldn't say anything because that was it, I'd lost it. Since it was the last item, everybody got up to go home. They'd had their fun. But I stood by the canoe that by all rights was mine, and when the fat man came over, I sat in it.

The auctioneer said, "Come on, little lady, let the man have his boat."

But I stayed.

I said, "I'll pay you the one thirteen and I'll trade you my bike," which was almost brand-new, I'd gotten it for Christmas.

The man looked over the bike. I wanted to say, *You're too fat for the canoe anyway*, but I didn't think it would help my sales pitch. He must have had a kid, because he was eyeing the shiny paint and squinting at the spokes, and then he held it by the saddle and twirled a pedal. I'd have thrown something else in, but I didn't have anything else.

He finally turned back to me. "You got the money in cash?"

I nodded.

"Kid, you really want that canoe, don't you?"

I said yeah, and he said, "Well, you got it." And he chuckled all the way to his car, pushing my Schwinn by the seat, *tick-tick-tick*.

Then the auctioneer put on his hat and frowned. "How you gonna get it home?"

And I said, "I'm not," because I hadn't thought that far ahead. He just shook his head and walked off.

I sat in that canoe until the sun started to lose its heat, and then, well, I didn't plan it, I didn't know what I'd do, I just knew that canoe was mine and I could do what I wanted with it. In the field next to the auction yard was a pile of wood, half chopped, and leaning near it was what I thought of as an axe, but it must have just been a short-handled hatchet. Still and all, it nearly took my foot off when I hefted it. I brought it back over by where I'd been sitting the last hour and I raised it as high as I could and brought it down on the side of that canoe. I raised it up and brought it down again. It was heavy and I was afraid of it, but once I'd made a hole I used my foot and broke the hull even more. And then I took the hatchet to another spot. I smashed up the boat my father had loved and I didn't even feel bad about it until it was all done. And then I just lay down inside the thing with holes all in it and I cried so hard I thought my eyes would fall out and I felt good for the first time since I'd overheard that conversation downstairs. "Had he been acting strangely? Depressed?"

It was near dark when I started walking home. I knew the way, but I'd come on my bike, and the bike now belonged to someone else. I had a long walk ahead. My heart began to race when a truck slowed down next to me. I thought of all the stories Joleen Rabideaux had told my mom on our porch. Young girls, taken and never heard of again. I kept my eyes straight in front of me. The truck stayed beside me. I walked faster. I heard the window roll down.

The driver said, "Hey, Loni Mae. What you doin' out here?"

It was Captain Chappelle.

He took me the rest of the way home, and as soon as he dropped me off, my mother lit into me. Where had I been all day and what did I think, coming home after dark, did she need to imagine me dead too, didn't she have enough to worry about? And where in God's creation did I leave my bike that Captain Chappelle had to pick me up on the side of the road like a runaway? But I just went to my room without answering and shut the door and didn't come out till morning and even then I was cold as steel and never told anyone what I'd done, not even Estelle.

"Short day today!" Adlai is surprised to see me back so soon.

"Yeah. Not a good swamp day," I say.

He leans over my receipt like it's the Dead Sea Scrolls. And he writes about as fast as the Dead Sea Scribes.

I say, "If you don't hurry up, I'm gonna miss the alligator wrestling."

He looks up. "I beg your pardon?"

"That sign on the road, 'Alligator Wrestling Live Noon Every Day.' I go daily."

Adlai narrows his eyes to see if I'm being sarcastic. I did go once, a long time ago with my parents. "Haven't you ever been?" I say. Next, I'll give him my oratory on kitschy Florida tourism, and how it cheapens the state and everybody involved. I'm feeling cantankerous, and well, why not share?

"It'd be interesting for a city girl like you." He thinks I'm from the metropolis of Tallahassee, because I wrote Estelle's address on his little card.

"It just so happens," he says, "that I close up for lunch. I'll go with you."

"Oh, well, I wasn't really . . . You shouldn't—"

"Why not? You're going anyway, right? I'll just tag along."

I've played tug-of-war and my feet are slipping. He has to know I was just being snide. I stare at him, and he stares back.

"Okay, I'll take your 'why not,'" I say. Maybe he thinks I'm afraid of alligators. Or of him.

I go to unlock my car, but he says, "Come on, I'll give you a ride."

Reluctantly, I get in his truck. The ignition turns over and Patsy Cline wails out her miseries.

The place is only ten minutes away. Besides the big sign, it's nothing fancy. Gravel parking lot, metal fence, ticket booth. With his back up against the chain link, that guy Garf from the restaurant loiters with his mutton-chop whiskers and his blue snake tats. He and Adlai exchange a glance.

"You know that guy?" I say.

"Yep."

"Is his last name Cousins?"

"Yep."

Adlai says no more. While I'm turned around wondering what Garf Cousins Jr. is doing here, Adlai pays our entry fees.

"No, please don't—"

"Relax," he says, and waits for me to go in.

The sparse audience proceeds up a ramp lined with Astroturf, and we lean against a concrete wall that hits us all at about hip level. We overlook a shallow concrete pit covered with white sand and bordered by a moat. It's real show biz—the strong man comes out and flexes his muscles, then taunts an adolescent alligator with something like a mop handle. The gator opens its mouth wide.

Of course, the guy doesn't bait it enough to provoke the big, scary harrumph a gator makes when it really feels threatened, expanding its chest and expelling all the air in a loud, sudden rumble. I was kind of hoping for that, actually, the sound that surely inspired stories of fire-breathing dragons. It means, *Take one step closer and you're food.* I mean, if you plan to exploit an animal, you might as well put yourself in real peril. But most of the small crowd is happy with what they get: snaggly jaws and a whipping tail, big sharp teeth and that bumpy, prehistoric snout. They're mildly terrified for the shirtless man who has lured the gator out of its fake pond.

Not that I would intentionally get that close to a gator of any size. But they do it Live Noon Every Day, so it can't be that threatening, can it? They orchestrate the show so the crowd *oohs* and *ahs* at every predetermined point. When the guy finally pins the alligator on its back and rubs its thorax to lull it into semiconsciousness, it occurs to me the whole appeal of this spectacle is vaguely sexual. Subduing a beast by turning him over and rubbing his belly until he's calm.

"I'd better get back," Adlai says, and he puts his hand to my waist to guide me in front of him. There's a spark.

"Oh!" I say. It was static electricity from the Astroturf. Wasn't it?

30

I have a few things to pick up at FSU's Strozier Library, so I park on campus and put all my change in the meter. I'm sticky and sweaty from canoeing and then standing unshaded at the alligator place. I walk across the quad, passing the bookstore and peering in at the art supplies. They haven't changed the arrangement of their merchandise since my dad bought me my first sketchbook here ages ago.

God bless him, he saw me sitting at our kitchen table one day, my tongue firmly planted in the corner of my mouth while I tried to capture the image of a wren eating birdseed on the window ledge. Daddy peered over my shoulder at my lined school paper and said, "That's pretty good, Loni Mae." The next thing I knew we were in the truck headed for Tallahassee—an hour's drive and a place Daddy avoided the way he avoided ties and shoes that pinched. But there I was, on a university campus, trying to keep up with him as he strode across the quad, a man in his thirties with no prospect of college, among kids on their way to sorority mixers and swim practice. To me, these young people were a previously undiscovered species.

Inside the bookstore, my father humbled himself to ask, "Where're the art supplies?" and the young cashier pointed us toward them.

I stroked the smooth, heavy paper in each sketchbook until I noticed my dad shifting from foot to foot like a little kid.

He said, "Well, which one, do you think?"

I picked out a medium-sized vellum pad. "This one?"

He nodded, paid the college girl behind the register, and we left the store. My dad took his giant steps back across the quad and I followed, clutching my new precious object.

We got in the truck and Daddy sat in the driver's seat without starting the engine. He stared through the windshield, gripping the wheel, keys still hooked on his right thumb. "It's like they all know a language I don't know," he said. Then he turned toward me. "But you're gonna know it."

I looked up. Was he accusing me?

"Just don't forget." He locked his eyes to mine. "Even when you know all the college jazz, don't forget what you know now." He put the key in the ignition, let out a breath, and said, "Time to git!"

He let me bring that sketchbook to the swamp, and when he saw me watching a bird he'd get the canoe as close as he could, hand me my school-issue #2 pencil, and whisper, "Make it yours, Loni Mae."

I pull myself away from the bookstore window and toward Strozier Library. I haven't been inside here in years. It's just a brick building, lots of light in the foyer, and a couple of floors' worth of books. Nothing magical. But even before I attended FSU, Grandmother Lorna brought me here, and unlike my dad, she was perfectly at home on campus. She showed me how to lift out the heavy drawers from the card catalogue that used to occupy this open area on the first floor. Now I sit at the computer and type in a search for "herbs and herb lore." Less chance for serendipity, but also less risk for a hernia. I scribble a few numbers from the screen and then make my way toward the stacks.

The elevator gives a soft "bing," and I step out and breathe in the lovely smell of book dust. I meander among the shelves and read the spines in the section on herbs: Pliny the Elder, Dioscorides, Paracelsus,

Turner, Albertus Magnus, Parkinson, Culpeper. There's also a volume by John Gerard, slightly larger than the Gerard's *Herbal* my mother consulted.

In college I had a feminist botany professor who said that the properties of herbs have been documented largely by men, but the knowledge has been passed down in an oral tradition among women, one generation to the next. Even when girls were deemed unworthy of literacy, the rhymes they heard their mothers recite, like *I borage give courage*, or *Nettle out, dock in, dock remove the nettle sting*, made them bearers of a rich knowledge. The woman in a village who knew about herbs was called the Wise Woman.

I grab the best books from the stacks and take the elevator back down to the first floor to find Interlibrary Loan and see what treasures Delores has sent me. After signing for them and adding them to my pile, I wander, my arms weighted, looking for a place to sit. Maybe the Reference room.

I step in and there it is: the Circle of Snooze. Those deep, comfortable chairs like the ones in Estelle's office weren't tossed out after all, only relocated to Reference. I plop down and open one of the herbals. The book is crackly, dusty, and full of good advice: *Sedum* . . . *protects against lightning. . . . If a wife puts caraway seeds in her husband's pocket, he will never stray. . . .* I flip pages. *Holy Thistle . . . a cure to melancholy . . .*

I make notes.

The spells and remedies sound hazily familiar, like I've heard them in my sleep. *Yarrow is used in love charms.* Maybe I overheard them from Grammie Mae, a true Wise Woman. She once took me out in her garden and pressed some wet leaves to my face. Wisps of hair escaped her bun and shone in the sunrise. "Wash with dew from the Lady's Mantle," she said in her wavery voice, "and you will be a powerful woman."

Did it happen yet, Grammie? So many powers I'm lacking still, including the power to understand my father's end, to be honest with my brother, to connect at last with my mother. Could some herbal tidbit open a door? I turn a fragile page.

Betony . . . guards against water snakes, fearful visions, and despair. No wonder Grammie Mae used to say, "Sell your coat and buy betony." And here's something my mom might like: *Paracelsus believed that each plant was a terrestrial star, and each star a spiritualized plant.* Echoing an expression I picked up from my little niece, Heather, I whisper the words, "Way cool."

As I go through all this lore, a little rhyming poem is knocking at my brain, an herbal mnemonic Grammie Mae taught me, and which I once recited with dramatic portent, making her chuckle. What was it? Something about thyme. I close the book and stare out from my cavelike chair, past the weighty shelves toward the trees blowing outside. The words assemble themselves and I say the verse under my breath, halting at first, but gaining momentum as it comes to me:

> "*Thyme, or 'dawn in paradise,'*
> *I go there with the dead.*
> *They die by someone else's hand*
> *Whose souls sleep in my bed.*"

Carefree days, those, when we could chuckle at death. I rouse myself and get up to leave. Straining under the weight of the books, I retrace my steps across the quad. I picture my dad's work boots striding ahead of me, and that familiar spiral of regret starts up in my sternum, the one that, if I let it, can eat me alive. *Why didn't I go with him that day? Mrs. Rabideaux could have come over. I could have gone.*

I pass the bookstore again and recall I need a tube of paint for the kingfisher. Payne's gray. I make it my only thought, muttering as I push on the glass door, *Payne's gray for the kingfisher, Payne's gray for the kingfisher.* Ah, birds! Ever my salvation.

"Ma'am. Ma'am. Can you leave your books here?" It's the cashier, talking to me. I set my burden in a square cubby and she gives me a number. I choose and pay for the tube of paint, heft my heavy volumes once again, and walk toward my car, popping the trunk to set everything inside. As I walk to the driver's side, I notice my wheel has been chalked, maybe by parking enforcement. But it's a weird chalk mark, with multiple letters scrawled in white. I stoop down to see. It's like graffiti all around the black sidewall: *YANKEE GO HOME.*

31

Estelle comes to her apartment door in response to my insistent knocking.

"I think I'm being stalked," I say. "Or . . . something."

"What? Come in."

Last time we met in her office, she had on an emerald jacquard suit with a pearl silk blouse. Now she looks like a thrift-store cheerleader: mauve tennis skirt and almost-matching top. Roger isn't home.

"Who would want to stalk you?" she says.

"That's a good question." I follow her into the kitchen, telling her about the chalk on my tire. "It said: 'Yankee Go Home.' Add that to the creepy dead doves that said: 'Fly Away, L.M.,' and it sure seems like someone's trying to get me to leave."

Estelle throws a popcorn packet into the microwave. "Well, let's see. Have you pissed anyone off?"

I stare at her.

She beep-beeps the microwave into action, then looks at me. "Not that you would."

I walk back toward the living room. "Well, the bird guy, for no good reason."

"You know a lot of bird guys, Loni. Can you be more specific?"

"You know, the homing pigeon keeper, who thought I killed all his pets."

"Is that Alfie? You know who he lives next door to? Rosalea and your long-lost love, Brandon."

"Yeah, Brandon. Such a romantic barfer, I miss that."

Estelle flops on the couch and bounces a pillow on her lap. "You know, there are just average people in Tallahassee who dislike northerners. And especially people from Washington. Maybe someone saw your D.C. plates and decided to be funny."

"I don't know. What are the chances that 'Go Home' and 'Fly Away' with my initials are unrelated? Also, Lance said there were some long white hairs caught in the string that held the doves, which makes me think maybe it's Mr. Barber. As nice as he was to me when I was a child, in his present state he's volatile and paranoid and possibly violent."

"So. You think a man with a likely case of dementia followed you to Tallahassee just to write on your tire?" The popcorn is filling the apartment with a slightly burnt smell, and she gets up to retrieve it.

"Does that make *me* sound paranoid?"

"A little. But you should call Lance and tell him about it just in case."

I open her fridge. "Do you have any of those coconut patties left?"

Estelle reaches deep into the back and pulls out the box. "Please eat them. And what you don't eat, take with you. They're evil." She carries the popcorn bowl to the living room and turns on the television, our second-tier anesthetic. She scrolls through the channels but can only find boring reality shows, so she turns on a talk show, lowers the volume, and speaks over it. "So, what else do we have? What's all the evidence?"

My sweat from the walk over is starting to evaporate. "Well, that's it for the stalking. No, that's not it. Mr. Barber threatened me with a knife."

"What?"

"Well, he was about to, in the store."

"Definitely tell Lance about that."

"I will. I should have already. They kind of roughed him up."

"Who did?"

"The store clerks."

"Anyone else mad at you?"

"Well, I went to see a lady who did not want to talk to me. Phil said she was my high school math teacher, but there was no Miss Watson at Wakulla, was there?"

"No, but there was Miss Watkins—I had her for Algebra Two," Estelle offers.

"Right, me too. So that other lady might be ticked at me for knocking on her door. But I can't exactly see her stooping down to write on my tire. Other than that, who could I possibly piss off?"

Estelle smiles, noncommittal. After a moment, she says, "And how's your mom?"

"My mom?" My eyes stray to the TV screen, but I pull them away. "She suddenly doesn't like to read."

"Ouch!"

I dip into the popcorn. "But I may have found a work-around. I picked out some short passages and read them to her aloud."

"How'd she react?"

"Really well to the first one. Then bored by a few others. I mean, how could she not respond to Leonardo da Vinci?" I chew the popcorn and pull a book from my bag to read the quote aloud. "*Water is sometimes health-giving and sometimes poisonous. It suffers change into as many natures as are the different places through which it passes.*" Now, is there anything truer than that? You'd think, living next to a swamp her whole adult life would make my mother appreciate that! But she had no reaction."

"What was the one she liked?"

"Poetry. One or two lines at a time. I never thought it would be rewarding to see such a tiny glimmer in her eyes. But even if it's fleeting, I'll keep doing it, at least for the time I have left here."

Estelle says, "Good for you."

I reach for a coconut patty. "That's why I was on campus in the first place. I went to Strozier Library to find more snippets. Which reminds me—" I rummage around in my bag. "I might have found something out about this Henrietta character."

Estelle folds her knees in front of her. "Tell."

"Well, my mom talks about her in her journal." I flip to the page. "Listen to this.

> "That woman! I do not know if she got an inheritance or what, but since her means have increased, she is insufferable. Saw her in Tenetkee Drug today and she said, How y'all doin'? I told her fine and she said, If you need some maternity clothes, Ruth, I have a lady who can sew ya somethin' fine. I looked down at my big belly, stretching the buttons on one of two blouses I've been wearing over that brown skirt with the stretch panel. I don't remember Henrietta herself looking so fashionable when she was pregnant, but she has begun to act like the matriarch of all the women in town, the wealthy older cousin. I said, Thank you, Henrietta. That's sweet of you. Then I bought my calamine and got out of there."

"Hm." Estelle stares at the ceiling. "So she was someone who had kids not much older than us, maybe . . . and she came into some money. Maybe she left Tenetkee to go buy a bigger house somewhere else?"

"I don't know," I say. I put the journal back in my bag. "I wish my mother had included her last name and maybe an address."

Estelle picks up the popcorn bowl, inspects a kernel, and rejects it. "Not to change the subject, but how's that Adlai guy?"

"Not to change the subject?" I look at the screen. The talk show host is welcoming another guest—some TV star I can't name.

Estelle says, "Just wondering if you've cornered him yet."

"Right," I say. "I go once with the guy to alligator wrestling, and you think it's time for me to pounce on him. Get real." I put my hands to my knees and stand up.

"No, seriously." She pulls me back down to the couch. "As fantasti-cally romantic as a gator show must have been for your first date,"—she raises an eyebrow—"what you have in common is canoeing. Why don't you ask him to come along with you one day?"

"Estelle."

"And park the canoe in some shady, out-of-the-way place—"

"Estelle, shut up."

She turns her palms upward. "I'm just being encouraging!"

"About awkward, meaningless canoe sex?"

She laughs. "Who says it has to be awkward?"

"Estelle, these are your fantasies, not mine." On the screen, the TV star crosses one ankle over a knee and looks down, then up at the host.

Estelle says, "Okay, so what's your idea of fun?"

"What is this, Truth or Dare?"

She waits.

"If I tell you, will you stop asking me questions?"

She nods.

"Okay," I say, "here's my idea of fun. First, the right guy. Second, many previous dates. Finally, at the right time"—I take a breath and spit it out fast—"a white canopy bed with starchy sheets over a firm mattress." We both laugh.

Estelle says, "And the canoe guy, fulfilling all your dreams."

"You said we wouldn't talk about it anymore." I look at the TV screen. "Who is this guy being interviewed? He looks familiar, but . . .'"

"Why don't you just start a friendship?" Estelle says. "Ask Adlai to show you the finer points of canoeing."

"Hey, I am trying to watch this very important interview with this person who . . . I don't know who it is, but I'm sure he's interesting. So quit interrupting." I stare at the screen.

Estelle bores a hole in my temple with her gaze.

Finally, I turn. "Estelle, I'm not going to ask Adlai the finer points of canoeing. He has sketchy . . . associates. I think he hangs around with that Garf Cousins Jr., who is scary. Anyway, I *know* the finer points of canoeing. And I never get into a canoe with a man unless I'm feeling extremely patient."

"And this is because . . ."

"Because there are guys who think canoeing is about power. They want to steer, they want to put muscle into it, they want to prove they know more than you do. They miss the point. Canoeing isn't about control, it's about cooperation."

"So how do you know the Hairy Man won't *cooperate* with you, if you know what I mean?"

The studio audience is clapping now, and the credits are rolling. I'll never know who that actor was.

Estelle barrels on. "The problem with you, Loni, is that you have impossible standards that no man will ever live up to."

"The problem with me is I hang around with someone who starts sentences with, 'The problem with you is . . .'"

"And also, that you run from every relationship that looks promising."

"I do not, Estelle. Name one."

"Andrew Marsden."

"My college boyfriend? No. I did not run. I was prudent. He was a risk taker."

"That cute guy in Arizona your roommate's cat didn't like?"

I look up at the ceiling. "Cats can be very perceptive. They understand people's true character."

"The man you asked out in D.C. but avoided when he wanted to see you on weeknights?"

"He told me my working late was interfering with his schedule. Sorry, but he just didn't understand the Smithsonian."

"Loni, you're a runner. Face it. You run from relationships."

I pick up the remote and browse through Estelle's saved shows. "You recorded a *Beverly Hillbillies* episode?" Estelle is the one who first introduced me to this show when we were undergrads—even before I wrote about it for class.

"Saved it for you, dear."

I hit play, and Flatt and Scruggs twang out the theme song.

Estelle says, "Hey! Maybe Adlai's secretly a millionaire, a Jed Clampett type."

"Shut up! You think I would date Jed Clampett?"

She cuts her eyes at me.

I eat another morsel of chocolate and coconut. "Jethro, maybe, but not Jed."

She smiles. "Yes, Miss Jane."

High culture. It's what keeps our friendship alive.

32

I'm nearing the end of my fourth week in Florida, and I only need the barest groceries because I'll soon be leaving that sterile little apartment and going back to my real home. I'm in the cereal aisle of the Tallahassee Winn-Dixie when I look up and see the same lady I saw walking on Sullivan Road near the museum—the one who looked like Joleen Rabideaux. She's puzzling over two jars of baby food.

I throw a box of Shredded Wheat in my shopping cart and roll up next to her. "There are just too many choices, aren't there?"

She looks at me, and I'm sure.

"Mrs. Rabideaux?"

Her eyes widen slightly.

"I'm Loni Murrow—Ruth's daughter."

She takes a deep breath. "Well, I'll be ding-danged!! Look at you! You grew up to be the cutest little thing, you really did!"

She's quite a bit shorter than me.

I ask, "Do you live in Tallahassee now?"

She looks down at the two jars in her hand, then up again, "Well, I have done ever since . . . you were a girl. That's why I didn't reco'nize you! Tell me all aboutcha now."

I explain that I'm in Florida visiting my mom, when she cuts me off with, "Well, Loni, it's good to see you! I gotta get me home to

Marvin. He's no good by himself. Good running into you!" And she is pushing her cart away from me, fast, before I can ask her anything about herself, like, why baby food, and why'd you move out of your house so quick, and if you've lived here all this time, why didn't I ever run into you when I was in college or grad school? And most of all—who is Henrietta? "Mrs. Rabideaux!" I call, but she's disappeared down the detergent aisle. I race my cart after her, but every time I think I see her, she's rounding another corner. Finally, I see a full cart abandoned by the front door and hear tires squealing as a car careens out of the parking lot.

What the hell?

I take my cheddar cheese, bread, butter, six apples, milk, and Shredded Wheat back to the apartment. Then I drive to Tenetkee.

On the way to St. A's, I drive past Joleen's old house. Still deserted, sitting empty. The white paint has washed away, leaving gray streaks. The screen door hangs from one hinge. Why would the Rabideauxs be in Tallahassee and do nothing about their house in Tenetkee?

I pass my mom's house and slow down. After only two weeks in the tenants' care, it's already taken on a different personality. They haven't trimmed the hedges. Even at her dottiest, my mother kept those ixora bushes sharply pruned. We left the shears in the garage for the renters, but clearly, they can't be bothered with simple maintenance.

I proceed at a crawl until a man comes out the side door—Mr. Meldrum. He and his wife came by the day we were cleaning, maybe to hurry us along. He's round, his wife flaccid and flushed. Mr. Meldrum looks out squinting and shading his eyes, and he half-waves. Does he see it's me? I give a lame wave and gradually speed up.

At the Geezer Palace, I greet my mother. "Hey, want to explore the paths outside?"

"There are paths?" she says.

I should have suggested this before. The grounds are actually pretty nice—shady, with pine trees and benches. As we stroll, I say, "Remember Joleen Rabideaux?"

"She was a smoker," my mom says.

"Did she ever tell you why she moved?"

"Joleen Rabideaux moved? Into here? They don't let you smoke here."

"No, remember you told me she moved away suddenly, like the movers came in the night or something."

Mom says, "What are you talking about? She lives right down the road."

I stare in front of me, stepping over a line in the sidewalk.

She says, "But don't trust that husband of hers. He's shifty."

Joleen mentioned his name in the grocery store. "Marvin?" I say.

"Joleen puts up with him, but he's nosy. He's the kind that would smile while he knifed you in the back."

"Didn't he work at Fish & Game too? Did Daddy not like him?"

But I don't get an answer. Either she's not accepting any more questions or she's drifting.

"Hey, you know who came over to your house not long ago? Henrietta. Remember her?"

She turns her head away. "Henrietta never came to us. Oh no, she would not cross our threshold."

"Really? Why not?"

"She lived on the other side of town."

"Um, like, on what street?"

"High-falutin' Street, that's what." She rolls her eyes. "Must we walk this entire path?"

When we return to her room, I try again. "So, about Henrietta," I say.

She turns sharply. "Why do you keep talking about that awful woman? Now, show me those pictures you're always drawing."

I take a deep breath but do as I'm told. I pull out the bird drawings I've most recently finished—the marbled godwit, the savannah sparrow, the purple gallinule. She sits and holds out her hands to receive them. As much as I'd like to think otherwise, the desire to bring home art projects to Mom is still strong.

Though she never really cared about the birds of the swamp, she handles each drawing with care, seeming to enjoy them more for color than for information. She hands them back. "You did fine," she says in a tone that means *You tried hard and didn't fail.* It's as close as she comes to praise.

I ask once more about Henrietta as I get her settled at her lunch table, but Mom is done with that topic.

I have a little time before my own lunch with Phil at the F&P Diner, so I stop in at Elbert Perkins' real estate office, the storefront with the closed vertical blinds. I go in and shut the door behind me, but no one seems to be in. "Mr. Perkins?"

He comes to the doorway of a back room, belly leading.

"Hello, Loni, what can I do you for?"

I suppose that's a joke about sex, best ignored. "Mr. Perkins, I had a question about our lease, you know, with the Meldrums?"

Perkins pushes up to a tall metal file cabinet. "Just a second, here." He has on different boots today, snakeskin beneath the dress pants. He looks through his half-glasses at a drawer full of folders. "Here we go." He pulls one out. "Would you like to sit?" He sits, too, on the other side of a putty-colored desk. "Now what's your question?"

"Isn't there a line in the lease about the tenants and their responsibility for upkeep? I drove by this morning, and the bushes in front aren't being trimmed."

Perkins looks at me over his reading glasses. His chin has an underhang of flesh. He turns his eyes to the lease, runs an index finger down the length of the page, and finds the passage he wants. He reads: *"Tenant will keep the premises clean, sanitary, and in good condition and upon termination of the tenancy will return the premises to the landlord in a condition identical to that which existed when tenant took occupancy, except for ordinary wear and tear, and reimburse landlord' . . . blah, blah, blah . . . 'for damage to premises through use or neglect."*

"Right," I say. "Neglect. Already they've neglected the ixora bushes."

Mr. Perkins fills his big torso with air. "This mostly refers to the house itself, not the yard, per se. I mean, if it was really bad, trash everywhere, old cars, maybe . . . but they'll get around to trimming. I heard that Meldrum fellow likes to garden. They probably just been busy, honey."

Honey does not sound like a term of endearment. It sounds like *quit wasting my time.*

I say, "How long should we wait before we say something? That's question number one."

"Wait another two weeks, at least. Goodwill still counts for a lot in these parts."

As if I'm from "parts" where goodwill doesn't count.

He checks his watch. "And is there a question number two?"

Like there's so much bustling business in here. My real question number two is why has the Rabideauxs' house sat empty all these years? He would know. But I come at it from the side. "What if I were in a position to buy land?"

He raises his eyebrows. "Around here?"

"I'm just saying what if." *Now I'm not such a pest, am I?*

He gives me another seconds-long assessment. "You just want land, or you want a house with land under it?" He chuckles and gets up, straightening his long legs under that rounded front. His hems crease at the boots. He ambles back to the desk with a binder that says: "Current Listings." He sets it down heavily on the desk and then he sits. "You want right in Tenetkee, or larger Wakulla County?"

"Tenetkee, mostly. Let's start there."

He flips through, inserting a few descriptors and why the person's moving out. A job in Tampa. A daughter in Georgia.

Joleen Rabideaux's house, with its half-hinged screen door, is not in his book.

"What about the old Rabideaux place?" I say.

His eyes go to the right. "That there's a derelict property. Ownership uncertain. You don't want a place like that, honey."

Again with the *honey.*

"Just curious, is all, as close as it is to my mother's place."

Perkins takes off his glasses. "So you'd really come back from the big city and take up with us small-towners?"

I disregard the taunt. "Maybe. Do you know the story of that old place?"

He opens his mouth and hesitates a half second. "I wish I did," he says, and shows me a large fake smile. Now I know what's different about him. He's had his teeth done over. Veneers.

I sit and wait, giving him a smile of my own.

"Well, Loni, if you don't mind . . . I have another client coming in right behind you." He opens the top drawer of his desk and pulls out a ballpoint pen but leaves the drawer open. I glance down to see a handgun in a holster.

My eyebrows must arch, because he says, "You folks up in Washington don't like those, do you? Don't believe in the Second Amendment?"

"Mr. Perkins, have I done something to upset you?"

"Not at all." He gives me that Cheshire grin again and closes the drawer.

33

Phil waits for me at the F&P, whose initials *actually* stand for Franny and Pete. Franny still sits on a cushioned stool and runs the register, but she used to pad around in white, gum-soled shoes, shouting out the orders to Pete and calling every kid "sweetie"—in a nice way—before writing down the hot caramel sundae or the biscuits 'n' gravy.

When his food comes, Phil dollops hot mustard onto his plate next to his fried liver and onions. Should I tell him liver has the highest cholesterol of any food? I look at my grilled fish without any desire to eat. He cuts up his onions, mortars them with mustard to a piece of liver, and puts the three-piece package in his mouth. Who else does this?

And then, like a shaft of light, it comes to me. My dad used to eat just that way: a square of meat, a smear of mashed potatoes, a piece of carrot. It all had to be on the fork so his taste buds could enjoy it at the same instant. The tendency must be genetically imprinted on Phil. He looks up and sees me smiling. "What?"

"Nothing."

He swallows his three food groups.

I squeeze lemon over my fish. "So . . . you invited me to lunch out of brotherly affection . . ."

He smiles big. "Of course." He pauses, then dives in. "But I've also been thinking about the wallet, and this guy Daniel Watson, you know." He doesn't say the word *Dad*.

"Right," I say. "Well, Mrs. Watson slammed the door in my face."

"Hm." He cuts a new piece of meat and starts assembling another little food package. "I wonder if Mr. Hapstead, at the funeral home, would have anything to add." He pops liver-mustard-onions into his mouth.

To this day I drive out of my way to avoid the funeral home.

"Because . . . no inquest, all that." He gestures with his fork.

"Jeez, Phil! Hapstead's? I'm sorry, but . . . you don't remember how terrible it was."

"Right, Loni. You have dibs on all that is terrible."

So much for the brotherly affection. I set down my utensils lest I use them as weaponry.

But he softens his tone. "It's fine," he says. "Don't worry about it. I'll go talk to him."

I stare down at the inedible food on my plate. God knows what Mr. Hapstead could describe. Sodden pockets, heavy objects.

"No," I say quickly. "I'll go."

He looks up from his plate. "You will? But you just said . . ."

"I changed my mind."

His eyes move across my face.

I say, "Well, you and Tammy keep telling me how I don't do my part. So, I'll do this."

It's a complete and utter lie. I have no intention of ever going to that funeral home. I hate the place with a passion so visceral I can't even name it. But saying I will go might yet prevent my minty-fresh little brother from the knowledge that can result in a pernicious gray fog, ready to descend at any moment.

Phil touches his napkin to his lips and says, "Awesome, Loni. Thanks."

I hate how my little brother can be so annoying and still, one genuine smile from him can fill me right up.

Outside, we say good-bye, and he crosses the street and opens the smoked-glass door to his office. As soon as it closes, I see coming down the sidewalk that furious tornado of a girl, Tammy, her path of destruction clearly set for me. Her tight skirt and heels don't slow her down a bit.

When she gets close enough, she says, "Loni! A word."

"Tammy, how you doing?" I'm practicing that friendly thing.

She marches me around the corner so we can't be seen from Phil's building. "You trying to find out something about Mona Watson?" She's right up near me now, her hairstyle stiff in the breeze. "Because you know she's a client of mine."

Oh, great, Tammy is pissed because I hassled her friend. "Look, Tammy . . ."

She lowers her voice. "And I can find out almost anything from people while I'm doing their hair."

"You can?" I wobble.

"Mona has a weekly appointment, you know. Wash 'n' style. Phil told me you went to her house, but that's no way to get information." She elongates her words. "My methods are much more subtle."

"Thanks, Tammy, but—"

"If there was foul play, Phil wants to know. And so do I," she says.

"Tammy, I'd kind of prefer . . ."

"*Not* to get to the bottom of it?" We lock eyes for a minute. She's sweating behind her makeup.

"Um . . . wanna walk?" I say. We turn in the direction of the park, and she keeps pace with me in her very high sandals.

She says, "If you're afraid Phil is gonna find out something about your dad that you don't want him to know, let me tell you—those rumors have been going around ever since I was little." She pauses, still walking. "Phil has never talked about it. But my own mother, the week of my wedding, told me to think about what I was doing, because the son of somebody who'd go and do that might go and do it himself. I told her to stuff a smelly sock into it, Phil was my boyfriend and wasn't anybody on God's green earth I'd marry but him."

I'm caught in the wind of this information. I watch her feet and my feet moving against the sidewalk, sandals and sneakers, stepping in time. We stop, no longer in the shade of the buildings.

She touches my arm with a sharp, manicured finger. "You think you're the only one who can protect your brother from the truth, whatever it is, about your dad, but I don't want Phil to get bad news, either!" Her bangs are actually damp. "I'm for putting an end to those rumors once and for all. Now, number one," she counts with her long nails. "It's unlikely your daddy just fell out of his boat. And number two, we're hoping he didn't jump. And number three, if there was some dirty dealing, somebody in this town knows about it. And number four, if it's bad news and we don't want Phil to find it out in a court of law, you and me better work together, and fast."

I stare at her four raised fingers.

"How about this?" she says. "You do what digging you can, I do what I can, and maybe we can find all the ugly before Phil does."

I step into the park, where Tammy's heels will sink, and head toward my car. "Right. See you later, Tammy." I'm trying to get away but also trying to adjust to a new world—in which my sister-in-law wants to help me.

I drive around town trying to process what I just heard. If only I could figure out the location of High-falutin' Street, I could find this Henrietta and clear everything up. Without thinking, I pass the funeral home. It's just a building with columns. The place can't hurt me. But I do speed up.

Back in my sparsely furnished apartment, I hear a low hint of thunder. I turn off the AC, open all the windows, and lie down on the chenille-covered bed to think. The wind whips and slaps the blinds, lifting the hair on my arms. What if I did what Phil asked, and went to Hapstead's? My aversion to that place is old and deep. The last time I was there I was twelve years old, and I vowed I would never, ever go there again. The wind outside gives way to rain, just as it did on that terrible day in that awful place.

*   *   *

"Look here at Loni now, she is so brave." It's the mother of a boy in my class. I stare at the brown piping on the collar of her dress. My mother shakes her hand. On the other side of the casket, an officer stands, an honor guard.

A lady from church says to my mother, "Your big daughter, such a comfort to you." Every grown-up in town files past. "Help your mama with the baby," they whisper, as if I didn't know that, as if I didn't have Philip right there on my hip.

Tall and craggy Mr. Zenon is next. "What a big girl you've gotten to be." Behind him is short, squat Joleen Rabideaux, not much taller than me, and she says to him, "She's not a girl at all, now, she's a young lady." I've sat up in the live oak and listened to Joleen tell my mother what to do with me, how to make me straighten up, what to nip in the bud. Mostly she makes me feel awkward, but now she says, "I'm proud of you for being strong. Cool in a crisis, that's what you are." She smooths my hair and it sticks to my sweaty head.

After Joleen Rabideaux, I think maybe I can stand it all, the *braves* and the *not-a-tears* and the *good helpers* and everything they say to me, everything they say to my mother, *he-was-a-gem,* and *sorry-for-your-loss,* and just the speaking of her name. *Ruth.* For some, that's all they say. The Fish & Game people, the other officers, all ironed and fresh, each put a hand on my head, on my shoulder. It could have been them. But it wasn't. I want to ask them, He drowned, but how can that be? And what did it mean, what I heard on the stairs? "Had he been acting strangely around home? Depressed?" Explain it to me! But they say nothing, and neither do I.

I put Phil in the stroller. He starts to squinch his face in a way I know well, and in a minute everyone can smell his diaper, which means I can leave this horrible room. I put a hand on the stroller and push. People in line smile sadly as I pass. If only they knew I'm no good at this. My mother told me this morning, "You would think on the one day I actually need your help you could do something right!"

At the doorway of the funeral home stands the man who bought my fish eagle, Mr. Barber. He's not in line to console my mother. He stands away from the others and glowers at the whole scene. Before I push the stroller through the doorway, he turns and leaves.

In the bathroom, Philip howls as I change him. I'd like to howl too. I'm clammy and hot, and I just want to go out in the swamp with my dad. That's when everything becomes real.

34

APRIL 13

I have to finish the boxes *today* and get them and myself out of here. In the apartment, I do the count. Twenty more to go. But I thought of a new way to spur myself on: treat the stuff like the batches of bird skins that are shipped to Natural History and need unpacking. That's always a mixed blessing, because while I prefer living creatures, these birds are dead. *And* they enrich our body of knowledge. This task in front of me is exhausting. *And* it occasionally provides an unexpected pleasure. Like the box I've just opened, containing one of Phil's kindergarten assignments: construction-paper circles and a stiff yellow page with the edges cut into fringe. "I love yow Mom from Philip." He was such an openhearted boy, Phil, very attuned to others. Whenever I would walk into a room, he'd smile big and pat the floor, or the couch, or the seat next to him for me to sit down. Things changed when I left for college. It tore out a piece of me to leave him, and yet I was so glad to escape my mother's disapproval. When I'd visit, he'd be standoffish at first, then his old self, then cool again when I left. But this artwork is from before, when he had no call to guard his feelings. I set it aside for Tammy's memory book.

Tammy. I can't believe what she knows. *Those rumors have been going around for years.*

Beneath Phil's artwork is a shirt box. When I lift the top, I inhale rose petals and must, the air in Grandmother Lorna's old house. Inside are gloves—long, short, embroidered.

I told my mom to stuff a smelly sock in it.

Two more round boxes yield hats from the sixties—a delicate wire scaffolding covered in velvet and silk leaves, a navy-blue toque with a net. Ruth kept these remnants of her own mother, whom she shunned, just as she disdained my father's true-crime paperbacks, but kept every last one.

You think you can protect your brother from the truth, whatever it is, about your dad?

I take the hats to the bathroom mirror, straighten my back, and lift an imperious chin as I try them on. Heather didn't know her great-grandmother, but with these in her dress-up box, she'll have a hint.

Grandmother Lorna could be haughty. She used to throw luncheons for her women friends, who wore stockings and low heels and discussed politics and the cultivation of roses. On those days, she'd often invite me up to Tally to help. The ladies made cooing noises when I set down their salads, or when I filled their teacups from the silver samovar.

While they sat and talked, I excused myself and went into the sunroom and picked up a magazine from the side table. "Smithsonian," it said. At the bottom of the first page was a signature, *S. Dillon Ripley.* At the top was a sketch—a building with round battlements and the words "The View from the Castle." Mr. Ripley wrote about going to the Tidal Basin early in the morning to look at birds, and I pictured my own high weeds and spongy ground, and heard the chattering notes of birds I knew. I read his column and then paged through the whole magazine, lingering on each photo.

After the ladies left and Grandmother Lorna had rested, she took me to the FSU library and said, "Borrow any book you want."

I said, "How 'bout a magazine?"

She lifted her eyes to the ceiling.

I told her which magazine, and she said, "Oh!" and parked me at a table in the periodicals stacks. While she graded papers from her Greek and Roman mythology course, I looked at back issues of *Smithsonian* bound together in heavy red covers. I learned about animals and gemstones and people living in jungles. But what sent a tingle up the back of my neck was a story about artists who worked at a museum and did nothing all day but draw birds.

After the library, I helped Grandmother Lorna tidy the sunroom. I said, "Grandmother, how did my mom meet my daddy?"

Usually when I brought up my dad, she'd raise one eyebrow and say, "He does, does he?" But that day she stopped fluffing a couch pillow and stared off into the distance. She spoke like she wanted to rewind the past.

"Your mother had just finished her junior year at FSU. She was editor of the *Flambeau*, and doing piano recitals all over Florida. She had a promising musical career in front of her, you know. But one day she came home from her job at the ice cream shop with a certain brightness about her, as if she'd been running. She began staring off into space and forgetting to practice her piano. She worked a great many extra hours scooping ice cream. I suspected something, but didn't make a fuss because I thought I knew all the Florida State boys who might have caught her interest. I should have been more attentive. As you may know, your father did not attend college." She paused. "He was in Tallahassee for a training course. Gun-handling, or some such. After his course finished, I thought that would be the end of it. But he began to take the bus from Tenetkee to Tallahassee every Saturday."

I didn't interrupt. I watched the straightness of her back and the smoothness of her blue-gray hairdo as she moved around the room.

"That boy was so pitiably in love with your mother," she said, "because he knew a girl like Ruth would never go for him." She paused and turned her face toward me. "And to everyone's surprise, not least mine, she did." She threw down the last couch pillow with a thump.

My grandmother had her virtues. She was just a snob. She thought of my father the way—well, the way I think of Tammy.

You and me better work together.

I lift out the last hat. It's delicate, and remarkably like a bird skin, with overlapping feathers and a few tail tufts accenting the front. Ring-necked pheasant, male. And there's the double edge. A good-looking bird gave its life for a hat. A difficult grandmother led me toward a career I love. And as much as I might resist it, the sister-in-law I've snubbed for years is offering me her help, and I need to say yes.

I get in the car and point myself toward the canoe shop. The swamp is the only place I can get any clarity. Plus, I've got to finish Estelle's drawings and I need some inspiration. I pass the sign Alligator Wrestling Live Noon Every Day, and feel again the spark from Adlai's touch.

One of the herbals I brought home from the library had a fascinating chapter on herbs and their connection to desire. For Elizabethans, a bundle of rosemary helped arrange an assignation, and an apple suggested libidinous intent. I picture Adlai's reaction to a sprig of rosemary left on his counter, or a juicy Fuji. Better yet, a "Florida butterfly" orchid from the swamp, since the same herbal had an entire page on the sensual properties of the orchid. It called the flower female—"open and inviting"—the root, male—"tuberous and reaching"—and the entire plant "hot and moist in operation."

Would Adlai scold, on seeing the orchid taken from its habitat? Or would he touch the petals softly, thank me in a whisper, and lead me to a white canopy bed in a sunstruck clearing in the woods . . . ?

I make a left turn at the shellrock road without noticing the yellow Chevy coming full speed toward me in the opposing lane. He blares his horn, flooding my brain with adrenaline, and I punch the accelerator, kicking up gravel and avoiding a collision by half an inch. The Chevy's horn Dopplers away behind me, and I breathe hard, feeling my heart pound.

I proceed down the gravel road, hands clutching the steering wheel like a new driver. I park, take a few deep breaths, and thank evolution for the flight response. And now it's time for my frontal lobe to kick in. I was nearly smashed to bits just now because of a stupid, impossible fantasy that will go no farther than the interior of this car. When I go in there to rent a canoe, I will be businesslike. Customer-like. Plants and birds, and nothing more.

"Well, if it isn't my canoeist number one." Adlai shines me a big smile as I enter.

Resist. "Hello," I say. He might be any other stranger. I know nothing about him. He could be married, the father of seven children. I glance at his bare left hand. He probably has a thousand unforgivable character flaws. He associates with scoundrels. I hand over my credit card and wait for him to get the canoe.

He folds his arms.

I act as if he's not studying me, not waiting for me to say something else. I turn to look at the bottles of bug spray, pick one up, and read the label.

"Alrighty, then!" he says, and gets up.

Good. He's doing his job, and I'm doing mine. I'm here only for the birds.

From the dock, he pushes the canoe off with an extra-hard shove.

"What the . . ." I snap my head around.

There he stands, fists on his hips, elbows out, shaking his head. I paddle away fast.

I take several byways before I understand where I've gotten to. I hug the shore of a lake so wide it has channel markers, so it must be part of a well-traveled, deep cut waterway. A shiny new speedboat comes through, throttle open wide. The clever name painted on the side is *Real Estate Perks.* I look up and see the driver: Elbert Perkins. Long legs, big stomach. How does that guy make so much money selling property in a town as small as Tenetkee? The wake from his boat nearly swamps my canoe, until I turn the bow and manage to paddle perpendicular to the inconsiderate waves, up and down, up and down.

At the next cut-in, I find a narrower channel with mangroves overhanging the water, dappling the surface with their shadows. I recall paddling back to the fishing camp with my father under such branches, pulling the water toward me and feeling the boat move beneath us, mostly from my dad's strong J-stroke.

"Psst," Daddy said from where he sat, and I turned. He didn't stop paddling, but he motioned with his eyes and the smallest flick of his head, indicating something over his right shoulder. I looked up. Two dark birds glided in silence behind the canoe. They seemed enormous, they were so close. When they saw me looking, they banked and landed in the shadows of the trees. "Night herons," my father whispered.

He gave me the birds, and he gave me the swamp. At some point he stopped trying to teach me the finer points of fishing. He saw what I liked about the place and supplied a way to describe it. "Pond chicken," he'd say, at the movement of something purple in the reeds, or "Kingfisher," when a small rocket flew past and ahead of us, close to the water.

Once, in the same tone of voice, he said, "Swamp girl."

I turned, quick, to see.

"That's you, Loni Mae." He looked at me sideways and laughed. Shafts of sunlight shone through the Spanish moss above him. "Or no. I got a better name for you. The Marsh Queen."

I pushed air between my lips and smiled, but after that I sat straighter, reached out farther, and drew more water with my paddle.

I come around the curve of a hardwood hammock to witness two herons, a great white and a great blue, having what looks like a territorial dispute. I slow the canoe. Another white heron stands in the shallows a short way off, either fishing or waiting to see who'll win. The white and the blue keep flying up, each trying to warn the other off, angling their wings so the light catches them first one way and then another.

I sketch them fast, trying to record the unintended grace of their motion as well as the force of their intention. While they're concerned with power and territory and fishing rights, they have no idea how stunning the exchange makes them look. The blue heron, in particular, shows me the richness of her color from every angle.

They finally settle in the shallows at a slight remove from each other, and I put away my sketchbook. By the time I get back to the dock, I'm buzzing with a tired euphoria.

Adlai offers a hand up, but his face is neutral.

"I just saw the loveliest sight." I step onto the dock.

He turns his back and walks inside.

At the desk, I actually open my sketchbook and show him the two herons.

He looks at them, looks at me, and says, "Uh-huh." He holds my credit card between his two fingers.

What a jerk. Is he trying to get back at me for ignoring his overtures this morning? I slap the sketchbook closed, grab my credit card, and leave.

I can't wait to get back to a place where people are friendly and the climate at least has "mild" within its range. A month in this heat has surely melted my brain.

35

I stop in to see my mother. The cast is off her wrist, and they've started physical therapy, but she's not happy about it. I've brought some books with me, but she's not in the mood.

"Well, PT is work, Mom. It's not supposed to be fun."

"Thank you for the encouragement," she says, rolling her eyes.

"Mom, can I just tell you something? You have done that to me so much in my life . . ." My throat snags.

"Done what?"

"That thing with your eyes. Like what I have to say is totally worthless."

"Well . . ."

"No. Not well. It isn't nice. And I'd like to ask you not to do it." My voice wavers. I have never said anything so plainly.

She turns away from me, as she always has.

There's a knock at the door. Mariama opens it halfway and circles a hand toward her chest.

I say, "Excuse me, Mom," and go out into the hallway.

"I am sorry to interrupt," Mariama says.

"No problem." I shut the door behind me. "I'd rather talk to you. How's everything going? How is *your* family?" She told me before about her college-age son, studying computer science.

She smiles, clearly glad to be asked. "Everybody is doing good. Hale and hearty, thanks be to God."

"And your son is still acing all his classes?"

She smiles. "Half of what he says about tech flies over my head. I only hear the whoosh."

We both laugh.

"But about Ruth," Mariama says. "She needs more knickahs."

"Knickers?"

"Panties. Underthings. She only has two pair."

"But I brought ten new ones. I even ironed in the nametags."

Mariama pauses. "Hm. She might be getting confused and throwing them in the bin—I mean the trash—instead of the dirty laundry. We'll look out for that. But in the meantime, could you bring some more?"

"I'll do it right now."

I take a nice long drive and pull up at the mall. Here at Governor's Square, Tallahassee's big indoor celebration of American consumerism, elevator music plays, fountains burble, children shout, and clashing perfumes waft from cosmetic departments and kiosks. Folks amble slowly toward everything they don't need—three stores for sparkly headbands, four stores for insanely priced purses, and nineteen stores for shoes with excruciating heels. *Come in! Buy the unnecessary! Accumulate junk!*

I beat a path to Macy's for white cotton "Hanes for Her" briefs. If I bought my mother any other kind, she'd be scandalized.

"Yes, I need a bag," I say.

I take the Macy's escalator two toothy steps at a time, until I find myself at eye level with the back pocket of a pair of Levi's, male. Finally, something in the mall I can appreciate. As he gets off the escalator, the guy stops to see where to go next. Oh no.

"Well, hello," he says. It's Adlai, with the same bored look on his face he had for me yesterday.

"Oh!" I say. "What are you doing here?"

He gives a half-laugh and plays with his beard. "I beg your pardon?"

"I'm sorry, I . . . I'm just so used to seeing you, you know, with the canoes." I put my semi-transparent bag behind my back.

"Yeah, I *really* love my canoes. But I'm actually allowed to go other places."

"Sure, yeah, just . . ." I exhale loudly. No words. I try to get the focus off my own stupidity. "Um . . . what'd you buy?"

"That's kind of a personal question," he says, opening the bag in his hand. "I got a shirt and tie. How 'bout you?"

"Oh yeah, just some"—I keep the bag behind me—"stuff for my mother." I clear my throat.

He nods, his top teeth biting his lower lip softly. "Well, it's good to see you, you know, out in the world. I'd hate to think you only existed when you were near canoes."

The world loves a smartass. "Likewise." I turn to go.

He calls, "See you next time you reappear, huh?"

"Right."

I step out into the parking lot, still a little flustered. Why don't people just stay in the categories I put them in?

There's a Panera across the way, and I walk toward it. I'll take Mom's essential equipment to her after one more stop. I haven't seen Captain Chappelle since the hospital, and I hear a voice in my head—hers—saying, *Don't ask what you can do, just do something.* For my mom it would have meant a casserole. For me it's a container of takeout soup.

Back in Tenetkee, I carry my warmish Panera bag up the three steps to Captain Chappelle's porch and breathe in the honeysuckle. He comes to the door looking a little thinner, but his face is healing and looking closer to normal. He's still the strong man my father knew.

"Captain Chappelle. How are you feeling? I brought you some soup."

He takes a moment, then pushes open the screen door to let me in. "I do not deserve such kindness."

"Sure you do. I'm afraid it's gone a little cold, though. Would you like me to heat it up?"

"Would you do that?" He closes the door behind me. "And you sit and have some with me, now."

I find a big saucepan in his kitchen and pour in the quart of soup I've brought. I'm still wondering about what he said in the hospital, his thought fragments about the way my dad died. I'm not here to quiz the man, but still.

I find two bowls, two place mats, napkins, spoons, and I lay the table. He sits and blows on a spoonful of soup.

I try to think of some local chitchat, but for a moment we simply dip our spoons into the bowls and put them in our mouths. Finally, I say, "You're looking better."

He lets out a snort. "Ain't gonna win any beauty contests for a while."

"You know, I think your doctor suspected . . . that you'd been beat up."

He suspends his spoon above the bowl. Then he says, "Beat myself up, I s'pose. Did my usual gym routine, then cut a mess of brush from the side yard, came in, and instead of a gallon of water and a decent dinner, had a little Johnnie Walker on the rocks. With nothin' else in me, I guess it knocked me flat."

I study the bruise on his temple in the shape of the doorjamb.

"But thanks to you"—he nods in my direction—"I didn't stay flat."

I nod. *Here goes.* "Captain Chappelle, when you were in the hospital, you said something I didn't understand. You said you felt responsible for what happened to my dad. Is that because—"

"Did I say that? Those drugs they give you, they make you hallucinate. Drugs are bad, Loni, don't ever take 'em."

"No, I won't. I just—"

"What you have to remember, child, is that your father was an upstanding man, an officer of the law. A good man, unlike a lot of the scallywags he and I dealt with. And that is why I saw to it he didn't just have the standard department funeral. He had everything top of the line." He dips his spoon back into the soup.

"Thank you. I mean, I know he was a . . ." *Don't lose it.* ". . . a good man."

"And it shows, in you, darlin'," he says. "In fact, you're *very* much like your father." He gazes at me. Then he pushes his chair out and carries his empty bowl, and mine, to the kitchen.

I follow him. "But, I mean, you knew him so well, and you saw him just before . . . at work every day . . . Was he, did you notice . . . ?"

"Loni," he says, putting the dishes in the sink. He gestures for me to pass back through the dining room and toward the front of the house. "It's natural for you to want to know as much about your father as possible. Coulda been that visit from his daddy, Newt, had some effect, coulda been a thousand things . . . that made him careless. But there's a time when you have to be at peace with not knowing. There are things a man takes with him when he goes, and it's not for us to understand. Like my Stevie." He shakes his head back and forth, back and forth.

We've arrived at the front door. The man has lost his son, he's suffering, and he has no one. Despite his recent hospital stay, I can feel the strength in his shoulders and arms as I reach up to hug him good-bye. This is what it would be like to embrace my own father at this age, if he'd lived.

Back at St. A's, an older man, a resident with steel-colored hair in a military brush, stops me in the hallway. "Can you help me?"

I say, "Sure, what can I do?"

"They've got me here under false pretenses."

I look around for a caregiver, and Carleen, one of Mariama's protégés, steps in. "Guess what, Harold! The cook is looking for you. He has a lamb chop fixed just the way you like it." I wonder if taste is the last sensation the brain holds on to, that animal instinct to keep the body going. Carleen takes Harold by the arm as if they're strolling. He walks with her but turns his head my way.

My mother is not in her room. I take the soft cotton briefs out of their package and lay them on top of her dresser, writing "Ruth Murrow" in Sharpie across each band. Then I fold them and put them in the drawer.

I pause at my parents' wedding photo, my father in a simple dark suit and tie, smiling big. I turn to hear my mother in the doorway saying, "I told you I didn't want to, and yet you insisted."

Mariama shrugs her shoulders at me. "I thought maybe the sewing club . . ."

"It's okay," I say, as my mother settles into her chair.

"Mom, I brought you something." I don't mean the items I just put in her drawer. I also came armed with more books. I'm not giving up on reading to her.

"Tell that woman to quit trying to get me to—"

"Her name is Mariama." I sit across from my mother. "Here, listen. This is Sir Walter Raleigh. You ready?"

She sighs.

"*Man's blood, which disperseth itself by the branches of veins through all the body, may be resembled to those waters . . . carried by brooks and rivers over all the earth, his breath to the air, his natural heat to the enclosed warmth which the earth has itself.* Isn't that a neat idea?"

No response.

"And he's not the only one who thinks that way. This guy named William Caxton also has a . . ." I check her expression. Blank.

"Okay, let's try this one. It reminded me of Grammie Mae."

"Mae?" my mother says, with a glint of recognition.

"*Our ancestors served as guardians of practical information and mystical herb lore. They were quite often the oldest among us—the Wise Women.*"
She nods.

I pull out John Gerard's *Herbal.* "And I found a recipe I bet

Grammie Mae knew about: *Calendula—conserve made from the flowers and sugar, taken in the morning, cureth the trembling of harte, and is given in time of pestilence and plague.*"

Mom's lips move slightly upward, a hint of a half-smile. She says, "Just in case of pestilence and plague."

36

It's tax day, and Phil has been crazed with work. I did my own taxes in February, because they're simple and I try not to look at them any longer than I have to.

I text Theo to adjust my expected return date to April 23. Texting saves me from hearing his disappointment, from listening to another mention of young Hugh Adamson and his deadline, from talking about caves and groundwater, and from sensing the controlled but palpable fear in his voice of the bureaucratic parasites attempting to eat our beloved institution from the inside out.

I've also paid for another week in the apartment. There's a housing glut in Tallahassee, so Roger's friend Charlie is happy to have my rent money, even if it's temporary.

I prepare for next week's return to Washington by rising early, getting right to work, sticking to the list, and fighting distractions. I am way too busy to talk with Mr. Hapstead at the funeral home, though Phil will be asking and I will say, *Yes, I went*, and it will be a lie.

In the little studio in Estelle's museum, the morning sun edges around the closed Roman blind. The anhinga, bird number 9 on Estelle's list, has a long, curving neck that sticks up like a periscope from the water and ends in a rapier-sharp beak. The rest of the body is submerged. I fill in the anhinga's black serpentine neck and then sketch arcs in the water for forward motion. "Snakebird," I whisper, but it's Daddy's voice I hear.

"Snakebird, ten o'clock," he said, pointing.

My braids hit me in the face as I whipped my head around and saw, in front of a clump of floating weeds, the pointy black garden hose of a neck entering the water and diving out of sight.

"How can he hold his breath for so long?" I asked.

"Mystery of nature, honey. He can swim like a fish, fly in the air, and walk on the ground." Daddy cocked his head toward the water where the bird disappeared. "If I were a bird, I'd wanna be him."

The sharp beak came up a few yards on, with a wriggling fish speared through.

"See, Loni Mae, he's a better fisherman than the both of us." He winked. He knew I'd rather draw than fish. And he'd rather fish than almost anything else. Daddy reeled in his line and reached for the spinner bait, shining like a prism. "Time for our lunch, too." He set down the rod lengthwise in the canoe, lifted the picnic basket, and handed me a sandwich in wax paper. Ham and cheese with pickles. He unwrapped his. "What a woman your mama is, takin' care of us even when we run off and leave her." He gestured with his sandwich. "She made sure we wouldn't have to dive for our food."

I looked past Daddy's crinkly eyes to see the snakebird settle on a branch and work the fish around to swallow it.

On my drawing table: the black bead of an eye, the shine of the water around the anhinga, my father's snakebird. Daddy wasn't just a visitor to the swamp, he was a part of the place. The birds, the bay trees, the mangroves, were the friends he grew up with. His roots, too, reached down beneath that water.

And unto that water did he return.

I leave the drawing unfinished and get my keys. To hell with lying to my brother, and to hell with avoiding distractions. I've got questions that need to be answered. I grab my bag and prepare to break an old vow.

37

I expect a preservative smell like in the Smithsonian back hallways, but the entrance at the rear of the funeral home leads me into a simple office cluttered with papers. Mr. Hapstead, in shirtsleeves, stands writing something on a whiteboard—his schedule of "events," I suppose. His beanpole body has a slight curve to it.

It's sad, this getting-old business. My mother and her age-mates seem diminished, and I wonder if they feel that way inside. Those who aren't sick and who've kept their routine, who have their glasses handy for close tasks and don't linger at the mirror, may not be conscious of how much they've aged. Maybe that's true for Mr. Hapstead, who went to our church and was a family friend, always laconic and tactful.

"Mr. Hapstead, hi! You probably don't remember me."

He turns, squinting. "You're Loni Murrow." He pauses. "How'd you get so old?"

I laugh. So much for the tact. I wonder what else has gone by the wayside. It must be just as jarring for him to see me at thirty-six as it is for me to see a stooped old man. But if he can be candid, then so can I. "Mr. Hapstead, how's your memory?"

He leans his skinny hip on the desk. "Sharp as a tack, why?"

"I want to ask you a question about my father."

"Hm. And I thought you came because of my good looks," he says, and pauses. "Your daddy was a real decent fellow."

"Yep," I say. "You handled his . . . funeral."

"Why does everyone say *funeral* like it's a bad word? Funeral, funeral, funeral. But I'm very sorry for your loss," he adds, remembering his lines.

"Was there anything . . . unusual about it?" I teeter toward information I might not want to hear.

"Unusual? I'd have to think." He looks toward the crown molding. After a minute, he says, "It was a real nice funeral. Top-of-the-line everything."

He hasn't asked me to sit down. "Yeah, Captain Chappelle told me he paid some . . . extra."

"Did he, now. As I recall, it was a fund, collected by the Fish & Game wives. Frank must have contributed." Hapstead stares into the middle distance, maybe scanning the data in his brain. "Yup, two big funerals that year, both wildlife officers. Both top-of-the-line." He seems to switch the memory off abruptly, and sits down to open the mail.

I sit too. "Mr. Hapstead, you might not remember this, but . . ."

He shoots me a glance that says, *Watch it, missy.*

"Well, was there anything strange, you know, about the way my father died?" At least three-quarters of me hopes he's hazy on the particulars.

He sighs. "In this business, a memory like mine is a curse. People mostly don't want the details. So everything has to stay up here." He taps his temple.

"I can certainly understand that," I say. "It's just that my brother has, well, he's initiated an . . . um . . . Do you remember anything about an inquest?"

"As I recall, your mama didn't want one, and who could blame her?" He stops.

My heart clutches. *He knows.* I jump in. "And everyone knew he died of drowning, so—"

"Oh yeah, it was drowning, all right." He stares off again from behind his glasses. "But you've got to close a wound, you know, or the fluid, the embalming . . ." He turns to me. "Well, see now, you don't want to—"

"Wound?"

"On his head."

Wait. What is he saying here? A tiny light switches on in my brain, and all my childish theories rush back in. My dad, tangled in his fishing line, falls backwards from the canoe, right onto a cypress knee. I almost say aloud, *That's right! He hit his head!* For a brief second, it seems so obvious. All the rest has been a mistake.

"Mr. Hapstead, Dan Watson wrote a report that said—"

"Well, Dan Watson was the other funeral I'm talking about. Same year. Also premium-quality casket, deluxe memorial wreath, the whole shebang."

Hapstead's recalling how much money he raked in. And I'm over here in my fantasy land with the "accident," when I know without being told that my sweet father just had a day so black the swamp couldn't lift him. He weighed himself down, tossed away his wallet, and fell back from the unstable canoe, banging his head and leaving without so much as an *Oh shit, I'm a father, and I ought not to go.* The bile stirs in my stomach.

Hapstead jabbers on. "Now, with Watson, I had a real challenge. Shotgun at close range basically explodes the face, as opposed to drowning, where you still gotta deal with the skin so long in water—"

My throat burns and I rush out, letting the door smack behind me. In the parking lot I bend over and retch, loud and foul, in a green puddle. I should never have come here. I take a deep, shuddery breath, straighten up, and make a beeline to my car. I need to get the hell out of this town.

I zip past our house, and then Joleen Rabideaux's, where someone has started dumping old barrels, as if the wreck of a house weren't enough.

Almost without intention, I head toward the canoe shop. It's late in the day, and there's no real time for paddling. But I've got to replace these awful images with a different picture. Would that be the swamp, or the sight of Adlai himself? He certainly doesn't want to hear my troubles, and I don't want to share them. Mr. Hapstead, Dan Watson's exploded face, my father's pickled skin and seeping head wound. I've got to blot them out.

The sun is still hot, but low in the sky. I swish water from a bottle around in my mouth, spit it onto the gravel, chew some Dentyne. I walk through the empty shop and outside. Adlai's over by the shed, sanding and repairing a fiberglass canoe. He bends over, his back to me, wearing overalls with no shirt, the open sides of the overalls showing a well-shaped contour. Even if the man is all wrong for me, I can admire.

Is that what I'm here for? To follow my own worst tendencies? To jump into an attraction that will distract me from my confusion and horror? I've done it before, and it hasn't ended well. He's yards away, and I haven't said a word. If I walk back to my car without making any noise, he'll never know I came.

But he must sense my presence, because he turns. His look is boy-ish. He's shaved off the beard. There are tiny flecks of paint on his face.

"Hey!" he says.

"Hi."

He flushes, walking toward me. "Pardon my formal attire." No smile until I laugh.

His clean-shaven face is slender, and it's all I can do to keep from reaching up and touching his smooth cheek. "What happened to the whiskers?" I say.

"My buddy tells me they're not appealing to the ladies."

"And how many ladies are there?"

"Just one, that matters." He doesn't look away.

I do. "I was wondering . . . I mean, I was hoping you'd let me take a canoe now, just for half an hour or so."

"Well, it's almost sunset."

"Yeah." *I should not be here.*

"Sorry," he says. "It's just that, if anything were to happen—"

"Yeah, no, that's okay, I understand." I stick my hand in my pocket, and my fingers touch something soft. I pull out the Hi-Floating Bubble Gum Worm I bought at Nelson's Sporting Goods. "Here, I, um . . . brought you a present." I put the neon-pink lure in his hand. "It went through the wash, so it's very clean."

"Oh, a worm," he says. "That is so sentimental."

"I love those things." I click my front teeth together in a silly way. "Texture."

He tilts his head to the side.

"Well, see ya." I turn and walk back through the building to the parking lot. I'm almost to my car when I hear footsteps on the gravel and turn around. He's moving quickly, and he stops short to keep from bumping into me.

"Uh," he says. "There is one possibility."

He takes a step back so he's not standing quite so close. "I don't want you to think of this in a way like I'm . . . I mean, if I went with you, you could . . . There wouldn't be a problem. With . . . liability."

I assess him. Okay, so he's likable. Of course, some serial killers are likable, at first. But dammit, I'm way past likable with Adlai.

He waits for my answer. He's nervous, guileless, a teenager asking me to the dance. Canoeing with any guy has its hazards, now, doesn't it?

"Okay," I say.

He pulls his head back a fraction of an inch. "Okay!" he says. "Okay, then. We can take my canoe."

We go back through the shop and he tosses me an unopened bottle of bug spray. "Worst time of the day for 'em," he says. "As you know."

He goes to unlock the shed and when he returns, all I see coming toward me is an upside-down canoe over the head of a lovely, bare-armed body in overalls. He reaches the bank, sets the canoe down, and beams at me. "Birchbark," he says, indicating the boat.

"Yeah," I say. "You don't see many of these anymore."

"The mildew and rot will eat it up if you're not careful. It's hell to maintain, but responsive like nothing in the water." This man, both boyish and stalwart, has a clear confidence, steady like a pilot light. I finish with the bug spray and hand it to him. He smears it on his arms, neck, ears, chest. He throws the bottle into the canoe, and holds the boat still as I get in.

There are no seats, so we kneel. Me in front—reluctantly, because I'd like to know exactly how the birch handles. But it is his canoe. And I know how to be the front person.

Despite what I told Estelle about canoeing with a guy, there is another possible scenario. In the best circumstances, it can be like slow dancing, responding to the other person's movement. Right now I'm Ginger, and Fred is leading from the rear. It's better than dancing, though, because with canoeing we can switch places so the same person doesn't always lead.

As we move further from the dock, it's clear Adlai doesn't play games. In the balance between front and back I can feel his trust—our strokes are well matched, and we move easily through the water. He follows my rhythm and strokes when I do. I feel him keeping a steady, even pressure between paddle and water, and steering us subtly in the current. The surface is calm, but even in more difficult conditions, crossing a lake in a wind, for instance, or running rapids, I sense we'd do well together. We wouldn't need to speak.

38

APRIL 20

It's a Heather and Bobby day. At the elementary school, I show the playground proctor my note with Tammy's signature authorizing me to pick up the kids, and they run toward me. It's prom night at Wakulla High and the busiest day of the year at the salon. Aftercare, manned mostly by high schoolers, is cancelled. I've set aside my duties both with my mother's belongings and with Estelle's birds so I can spend the afternoon with the kids.

At their house, we have a snack and then play a few goofy dress-up games with Grandmother Lorna's hats and gloves, which I've brought. Bobby tires quickly of it and asks if I'll play tag outside. "Sure. You guys start and I'll be out in a sec." They run to the backyard while I rewrap the hats in tissue.

As I slide open the glass door to join them, Heather says to her brother, "No, Bobby, don't touch it!"

Bobby's peeking around the back corner of the house. "It's just sleeping," he says.

I say to Heather, "What's he found?" thinking lizard or frog. I go up behind him to see he has one finger about to touch the point of a massive, bumpy tail.

"Bobby, no!" I cry, but it's too late. He's made contact, and the gator curves its open mouth toward us.

I swoop Bobby up in my arms and shout, "Heather! Get inside!" I leap over the threshold after her and slide the glass door closed just as the gator reaches it, bumping the bottom of its great open snout against the reflective glass. I lock the door, put down the Charlie bar, and we three huddle together, standing back from the glass watching it thrash and bang itself up against what must look like its own reflection.

Gators can outrun humans, so thank God it was facing the wrong way in a tight space when it started to chase. After what seems like a lot of angry flailing, the monster turns and waddles across the yard. I can feel two little birdlike pulses under my grip, and mine isn't much slower.

Heather looks at me, her face still taut with fear.

"Well, that was exciting," I say.

Bobby's eyes are big.

I give him my strict face. "And now you know what happens when you touch a gator's tail."

He nods up and down, up and down.

I should call Phil. But instead I call Information to see who might help us. The operator directs me to Fish & Game's Nuisance Alligator Hotline.

We wait.

When they knock, I let the two guys in the front door. The larger man's lower lip is distended with chaw; the younger man is polite but eager to get started, a car with his engine revving. With the gator at the far end of the yard, I open the sliding door for them, then shut it again, quick. The kids and I pull up three small wooden chairs to watch. It's not unlike the live alligator show I saw with Adlai, only these men are truly in peril, and they're not doing it for our reaction. They strategically corral the animal, grasp the tail, and after several failed attempts, turn the gator over. Finally, the larger man sits on him and wraps the jaws together with a stout rope.

Then he takes out a pistol. I get up and face the kids, blocking their view, and say, "You know what we need? Popcorn! Here, come help me make it."

They show me where the popcorn popper is, and Heather climbs up to open another cabinet, but when she hears the report of the gun outside she stops. She and Bobby look at each other. Then Heather scrambles down and they run to the glass door.

The smaller man crawls out a neat rectangular hole in the wooden fence, about the size of a doghouse, and pulls the lifeless alligator backward through the hole. The canal beyond the fence sparkles with light.

"He killed it," Bobby says, and looks up at me.

I go around front, where they're hauling the gator onto the back of the truck.

"'At's a ten-footer," the large man says.

"I thought you'd try to relocate it," I say.

"No, ma'am." The tobacco in his lower lip keeps him from speaking clearly. "Once they start botherin' you, they tend to come back."

I wonder if this is true. "So you're gonna repair the fence, right?"

"Ma'am?"

"That hole you had to make in the fence . . ."

"That hole? That's where your friendly gator got in, ma'am. We didn't make no hole."

"Well, who did?"

"Don't know, but they spent some good time sawin'. 'At's a big ol' hole."

A clutch of neighbors has gathered. Along with them, the children and I watch as the men heave the alligator onto the bed of the truck, tail first. The head has one red lesion at the back of the leathery skull. Something protrudes from the mouth—a heavy-gauge line.

"This gator was caught," I say.

The young man studies the line. "So 'twas," he says.

I say, "So how do you get paid? Fish & Game?"

He turns his head to the side to laugh. "'At's our payment right there."

Lance Ashford pulls his squad car up next to the truck, parks, and gets out. The younger gator catcher says, "Hello, Officer, we are licensed by the State of Florida as official contractors to the Nuisance Alligator Division. . . ."

"Relax," Lance says. "I'm not on duty, I live here." He turns to me. "What up?"

"Look at this." I point to the heavy monofilament in the gator's mouth, then bring Lance around to the back of Phil and Tammy's lot to show him the cut in the fence, a neat, freshly sawed square, just big enough for a three-hundred-pound monster. The severed planks lean up against the intact part of the fence. He stoops to inspect it.

"Lance, someone's trying to scare me—us. And they're succeeding."

Heather and Bobby step forward to look through the hole in the fence, each placing a small hand on one of Lance's big shoulders.

"Hey there," he says, turning his head to each of them in turn. "Wanna go see my baby girls?"

As we walk over to Lance's townhome, I call Phil.

"What the hell?" he says more than once.

I assure him everyone is fine and give him the list of items from the lumberyard that Lance said they'd need to patch the fence.

I'm glad for the chance to visit with Lance's wife, Shereen, and their two little girls, and I sit on her couch and watch the four kids play. Bobby and Heather keep glancing toward me—a sort of check-in that could be for my benefit, or theirs.

By the time I get back to Tallahassee, it's seven o'clock, and I don't have the energy or inclination to eat. I just flop down on the bedspread and stare at the ceiling. If I think about what might have happened, it will undo me. Those terrible jaws, that tender flesh. *But it didn't happen*, I reassure myself. It didn't. Everyone is safe.

Still, who would do that—endanger children—and why? Is there some malignant force following me that could hurt the people I love? My mind spins like a whirligig. I reach for a distraction, some sort of reading material that will occupy my mind and stop the pinging. My mother's *GARDEN* book.

Must we start at breakfast with the sucking of the teeth and the disdain for every friendly attempt I make? I merely said, How about we go into town to buy you a new dress? and she said, What's wrong with what I have on? I said, I am not criticizing your wardrobe, dear. And then she said under her breath, Yes you are. I blurted, Could you rearrange your attitude? I am sick of it! She took off like a hurricane, slamming doors behind her. She is up in her room now, stomping. And here I sit in the garden.

Mae had a saying about anger—When thou art vexed . . . then throw the seeds . . . and ne'er heed where they fall. If basil plants are what thou need . . . then sow them with thy gall. Well, I have a packet of seeds, and Mae was rarely wrong. So for every tiny seed I thumb into the ground, I think of an insult. You puny seeds. Wretched things. You're minuscule! Wrinkly! Before too long I start to chuckle, and realize the rhyme must be an herbal cure for anger.

I suggested the shopping trip to lift a particular cloud. Last night I tried to talk with Boyd about our lost baby, and he said, Quit dwellin' on that, Ruthie! You got a live daughter in this house who needs you! So I am alone. And here I sit on my garden bench with an empty packet of seeds. Days to maturity: 66. Days to emerge: 5-10.

And what was that? A kick? Lord, it has been a long, bad time since a baby kicked me from the inside. I wait for another.

Loni was a kicker—till the minute she was born. And when they handed her to me, all squashed and puffy, feet still moving, mouth pursing, I could hardly believe in her. Boyd said, I think she's hungry. I put her to my breast, and her tugging for milk felt both strange and inevitable. She was asking for exactly what I had, and I was giving her exactly what she needed. When she was finished nursing and Boyd took her from me, he walked up and back, bouncing at the knees and patting her back, and I looked down to my arm and saw a cockleshell, an impression of her little ear on my skin.

Oh, Loni, come back to me now. Come feel this new baby kick.

I set down the journal. I didn't go see her today—too rattled by that gator. But at least I can call. I dial as I stand at my window and stare down at the stubbly courtyard. Two rings, three, four. I'm about to click off when someone picks up with a raspy breath. But no one speaks.

"Mom?"

"How DARE you!" she says.

"What? Mom, this is Loni."

Her voice is scraped raw. "I know who you are. And you will not defy me! Do you think all I care to do is chase after you—to the top of the tree or the middle of the marsh or God knows where? Get back here, Loni, *now*!"

I hold the phone away from my ear, then put it back. "Mom, listen . . ."

"And no back talk!"

"Mom."

"Don't make me come and get you! Why did you ever go in there? That's the *stupidest* thing you've *ever* done."

"Mom . . ."

"Lorna Mae Murrow, don't you speak another word to me. Just pick those boots up one at a time. Get your feet out of the mud. And DON'T tell me you can't!"

Something in her voice, something old and impenetrable, shakes me. I pull the phone away from my ear, touch the button, and disconnect the call.

Throughout high school, I had a recurring nightmare of a scolding voice repeating my name over and over. The dream drove me out of bed, trembling and wandering the house, still essentially asleep. I'd wake in the morning curled up on the braided rug in Phil's room, wondering how I got there, until I recalled the fright of the dream. I never identified the voice, but there it was in the phone just now, sharp and scorching.

I haven't thought about that nightmare in years. But all it takes is my mother pronouncing my full baptismal name, and I'm that shivering lump once again.

39

I sit in a café that borders a rectangular Tallahassee park. I'd like to sight a bird through this large picture window—a house sparrow, a wren, anything. Last night I had troubled, sweaty dreams and woke with that grayness threatening to creep in around me. The caffeine will help, but spotting a bird would provide a more reliable antidote. Tammy's chart designates me as today's visitor to St. Agnes Home, but after last night's phone call, it's just not on my happy list.

Outside, cars whiz by on Madison Street, then slow and stop at the light. One car is decidedly pink. I stand up, but the light changes before I can see who's driving.

I run out to my car, turn the ignition, and drive the way I saw that pink car heading, but it has disappeared. I reduce my speed, looking down side streets as I pass, until someone behind me honks and I quit my hazardous driving. It's time to head south.

Soon I'm passing the "Welcome to Tenetkee: Small But Proud" sign, and I try to think of yet some other way to delay my arrival at St. A's. I pull up in front of the Tenetkee Public Library, one place where my mother and I used to approach contentment—if not together, then in parallel. It was a high-ceilinged, un-air-conditioned room with a paddle fan above and sunlight streaming in. I was in the Smokey

Bear reading club, and filled a card with gold stars, one for every book I read.

Though the public library is on Main, the same street as Phil's shiny office, the buildings that used to stand to either side of it are gone, replaced by weedy lots that merge into meadow behind, giving way finally to damp, scrappy woods. Just to the rear of the library, I can see a corner of freshly assembled lumber, and what looks like a new room being framed out.

I push on the heavy front door. The public library is air-conditioned now, but it's still got the high ceiling and the paddle fan. I wander among the blond wooden shelves until I spy a stand filled with U.S. Geological Survey pamphlets. These might help me with the underground water I'm supposed to be drawing for Theo. I take a few and fan them out against a nicked wooden table.

These slender publications have mellifluous titles: Transmissivity of the Upper Floridan Aquifer . . . Tabulated Transmissivity and Storage Properties of the Floridan Aquifer System . . . Carbonate Aquifer Characterization . . . Groundwater Flow and Water Budget in the Surficial and Floridan Aquifer Systems . . . Megaporosity and Permeability of Carbonate Aquifers.

The stage-volume-area-perimeter charts are populated with numbers, and the pamphlets treat the sexy subjects of hydraulic property data, evapotranspiration, runoff, infiltration, stream water levels, groundwater flow, aquifer recharge, streamgages, stage-dependent rainfall, unsaturated zone flow, and the biogeochemical components of wetlands. Nothing visual, however, suggests itself for the drawings I'm supposedly qualified to produce. I sit and close my eyes, letting the facts go fuzzy. Behind my lids float bright heat maps dissolving into colored layer cakes, Peter Max cross-sections of striated land with earth on top and blue water as icing between the layers. I wonder how Bob Gustafson in Rocks would react to hydroporous limestone done in neon-brites. I open my eyes and put the pamphlets back where I found them.

I sit down at a vacant computer to check my email. My relationship with the internet is tenuous, especially when I'm not at the museum. I carry a dumbphone and own only a desktop computer, which sits in my apartment in Washington. In D.C., people are always asking me when I plan to enter the twenty-first century. Here in Tenetkee, no one's even brought it up.

The library's home page has a bunch of links, including one to "Public Records by County." Deeds would be in the public record, right? Maybe I can find out who bought Joleen Rabideaux's place. I click and browse.

"Mr. Tenetkee Real Estate," Elbert Perkins, said the Rabideaux place had "uncertain ownership." But I think he knows more than he's willing to say. For the last twenty or thirty years, he's handled almost every property sold in this little town.

I click on "Deeds," then "Wakulla County, Florida," and it asks for a date range and a name. I type in *Rabideaux* and guess at the year they moved, not long after my dad died. A list of things that have nothing to do with their property comes up, but I'm on the right track, because the categories are Buyer, Seller, Date, County, and Plat Number. I try a few more dates, and then I see it, *Rabideaux*, under Seller. The name under Buyer says: *Investments, Inc.*

I google *Investments, Inc.*, but I get 41,700,532 results. Everything that has those two words in it. And nothing that has only those two words in it, at least as far as I can see from the first few pages. What did Elbert's phrase "uncertain ownership" actually mean? I go back to the "Deeds" directory, put in the county name and *Investments, Inc.*, and I get several more properties. Two of them seem to be right near the library here. The two vacant lots, maybe?

I pull open the library door and go out to look at the lot next door. What used to be here? I can't remember. There's still some broken concrete and rusty rebar strewn about in the weeds. Did Investments, Inc., have intentions to redevelop, and then maybe go bankrupt?

Down the street, Phil's cranky receptionist Rosalea Newburn emerges from their office building, her stiff eighties-style hair disagreeing with the hot wind. I get into my car and crank the AC. Rosalea walks down to Elbert Perkins' real estate office, maybe to hand-deliver something, only she goes in and doesn't come out.

I could walk to the Geezer Palace, but it is so hot I instead sit and enjoy the lovely cool of my wasteful air-conditioning. After a moment, I hedonistically drive around the corner and park in the St. A's lot, bathing in the chilled air for a few minutes more and avoiding going in. By now, my mother might have forgotten last night's phone call. But I haven't.

Finally, it's time.

"Hey, Mom! How're you doing today?"

She eyes me. "Fine, dear."

Relatively lucid, no immediate hostility.

"Feel like walking?"

Outside, the sirocco wind has calmed to a breeze. Thank goodness for the shade over this path. My mother is completely silent, leaving me to initiate conversation.

"I finally talked to Theo," I say.

"Is that the boyfriend?"

I flush. How would she know . . . why would she think there's a boyfriend? "No, Mom, Theo's my boss at the Smithsonian."

"Oh."

"He gave me a drawing assignment."

"So you can go off and leave me."

Within her cloud of confusion, she's sometimes remarkably aware. "Well, yeah, I will have to go back to Washington soon, but this is something he wants me to do here. I was hoping he'd ask me to draw some rare Florida bird."

"Hm." She looks at her feet, moving slowly.

"But instead, he sends me in search of underground rivers!"

"And did you find any?"

"Well, I've done some research."

She looks up. "Did you find any?"

"Not yet. So far I've just doodled."

"Show me."

We sit on a bench and I take out three drawings that preceded the dry well of the Tenetkee library.

She says, "This one is a lizard."

"Well, cave salamander. It has no eyes because it lives in the dark all its life."

I tried to capture the way this animal inhabits the caves. It can't see, but it makes its way along the rock formations and the water running through them. This critter knows every slippery surface, every little stream of running water.

"What is this one, a cave?"

"Yeah, but it's not finished." A dragonfly settles on the armrest of the bench.

My mother hands me back the drawings. "You had a boyfriend who liked caves."

Who says her memory is gone? "That's true, Mom. Andrew."

"Yes, I liked Andrew."

I did, too. But as I told Estelle the other day at her apartment, Andrew was not for me because he took unreasonable risks. He dove, with scuba equipment, in the underwater caverns I'm supposed to be drawing. At least two of his fellow spelunkers died in those caves, just in the time I dated him. They got disoriented in the narrow passages and ran out of oxygen. People die in those caves every year because they forget which way is up and which is down.

I adored Andrew—he was my first real love affair in college. He was sweet, smart, and for a near-innocent, outstanding at the physical arts. His body was lean and muscular, and he loved me with an intensity equaled only by his desire to do dangerous things. We were kind of inseparable, and everyone thought we'd end up together. But the cave-diving made me crazy. I used to lie awake and imagine those last minutes, the dwindling oxygen, the struggle to find the surface, the miscalculation about which cramped passageway led upward. I'd dream it was me, trapped underwater.

I tuck the drawings back into my bag. "Should we go back in?"

My mother says, "Why don't you call Andrew up? He probably still lives nearby."

Sure, that's all I need, to find out that Andrew Marsden is alive and well and has a wife and three children and stopped cave diving the minute I left him. I'll just find him in the phone book, ring his house, and after child number three says, "Just a minute," I'll say, "Hello, Andrew? What do the caves look like, really? And the water. Could you describe the water?"

My mom and I enter the building and walk toward her room. She doesn't speak, so I fill the vacuum. "Did I tell you I've been canoeing?"

"Of course, with your father. You two always go off and leave me for the swamp."

Here we go again. "No, I've been going mostly by myself."

"Mostly?"

"Well, once I went with the guy who rents the canoes." I push open the door to her room.

"Is he nice looking?"

"Kind of."

Both Estelle and my mother would have me rush in. Estelle wants me to have sex in a canoe, while perhaps my mother envisions a long white veil. If I mentioned the guy who bagged my groceries at the IGA, they'd both ask, "Is it serious?"

Mom sits on her vinyl chair. "I went canoeing once with your father," she says. "Only once." She goes silent.

I'm fixing the blinds and thinking about how adept Adlai was with the birchbark. "How come only once?" I turn to Mom, but her eyes are filling, about to spill over. Whoa. Crying isn't something my mother does.

"Mom, what is it?" I touch her arm.

She shrugs my hand away. "Leave me alone!"

"What . . . can I . . . ?"

"I said, leave me alone! Can't you understand English?"

"Okay, fine!"

I walk back out into the heat. If she wants her privacy, she can have it. But why does she have to be so mean? That jagged edge in her voice is the whole reason I spent so much time avoiding this visit. And just when I thought she'd started to be nice, there it was again, telling me to *get out*. And why? Because I tried to comfort her? I don't even know what she's crying about. God forbid she'd tell me. She didn't even cry at my father's funeral. So what brought on tears today? Going canoeing once with my dad? I don't get it. I don't get anything about her.

40

Adlai puts away the last of the rental canoes and hangs up the life jackets, securing the shop before we leave. This time it wasn't me running to a guy as a salve for life's dissatisfactions. He called me. When my phone rang and he said who was calling, I was surprised. *Did I give him my number?* But of course, I put it on the little form I filled out the first time I rented a boat. I'd written Estelle's street address, but my own cell number, which retains the Florida area code from my very first phone, giving the impression I'm a Tallahassee resident. When I realized he was asking me on an actual, planned canoeing date, I thought about correcting that misconception. But the pleasure I felt at hearing his voice made me hold back. I said only, "Sure, that sounds fun. I'll bring some food."

What harm can a little date do? He doesn't need to know my life story, with all its rivulets and backwaters.

He hoists one of the heavier canoes onto its storage brackets with a clunk, and pushes it back. "No, I haven't been doing this very long," he says. "I only just came up this way two years ago. I was trying to avoid being an insurance salesman." He turns toward me, then smiles.

"I beg your pardon?" I say.

"My father and brothers own an insurance office in Broward County. Do a good business, too. But I was the oddball. I spent ten years trying to save the Everglades. And as soon as I quit, my brothers asked me again to join the company."

"Why'd you quit?"

He reaches into the back room and pulls out two ash paddles. "You mean the conservation? I was working for a state agency in Dade County, thinking I could make a difference." He props the paddles against the counter. "The politicians say they want to save the Everglades, but what they really want to save are their ever-loving backsides, and limiting growth isn't popular, so they choose dead birds and mercury in the fish. You don't want to get me started on that. I had to get out of South Florida before I became completely cynical."

"And is North Florida better?"

"Well, there's still some hope for the place, environmentally. And *I'm* better here." He makes eye contact again, gold sunbursts at the center of gray irises. What kind of geode would match that? "'Scuse me a minute," he says, and ducks into the other room.

While he changes, I wander outside. A cloud moves across the sun, offering a break from the heat. Adlai comes out and turns the key in the door, then walks toward the shed to get the birchbark. I follow, and help him carry the canoe. It's light, but I feel a bead of sweat drop between my breasts.

"Wanna steer this time?" He offers me the stern.

I steady the craft as he steps into the bow. We settle in, and pull away from the dock. Adlai has changed into a clean T-shirt in a soft shade of yellow that stretches across his broad back. His strong, even stroke is a pleasure to watch from behind. The butter-colored shirt is snug, and I observe the way his upper body moves. There's a place where the arm connects to the shoulder, a muscle that flexes when he reaches forward with the paddle to gather new water. It's the same muscle, in evolutionary terms, that in a fish connects the fin to the body or, in a bird, the wing. I watch the movement of this muscle as I stroke in unison with him, turning my paddle slightly at the end of each pull to keep us going straight toward the bend where a bay tree leans in. We paddle steadily together. Adlai points, and I steer in the direction he indicates. He knows where he's going. He's showing me parts of the swamp I've never seen. We pass through a small channel where the trees have grown low over the water like a canopy. Estelle's tunnel of love, maybe. Even in the shade, the color of the water is less brown, and getting clearer as we go. Eelgrass waves on the bottom. It's the first time I've ever seen *through* the water of the swamp.

We come out into an open area. It's deeper here, but still transparent. Ahead of us, the surface roils like a pot of water set to high. We move into it, and the canoe shimmies. Adlai takes his paddle out of the water and rests it sideways across his body. I do the same, and we drift, floating over the chasm of a spring, an icy blue that goes down farther than I can see.

He tells me this spring pumps 400,000 gallons of water a minute. "The only thing that keeps it from being a geyser," he tells me, "is the maze of caverns it has to pass through on the way up. But you probably already knew that."

"Not really."

"This one," he says, "has sixteen stories of caves from bottom to top."

"How do you know all this?"

"I studied hydrogeology at the University of Miami. We used to say the department was always in a state of flux." He waits for me to get the joke.

But I don't laugh. Instead, I stop and readjust to this new image of Adlai, the scientist.

"What?" he says.

"Nothing, I just didn't think . . ."

"You didn't think I went to college."

"I . . . I . . ."

"And if I hadn't, then what?"

He's right. I've been walking into his shop for weeks with nothing but small-minded prejudice and preconceived notions. He must consider me a complete jerk. "No, it's just, I wouldn't, I wasn't . . . ."

He looks away.

Then I get a sudden pang. "I hope you don't, um, dive the caves?"

He turns his head toward me. "I don't have that particular mental illness." He waits, and I realize it's a joke. I smile, then he does too.

We go around another bend, he points to a flat beach, and I steer the canoe that way. He jumps out from the bow and pulls the canoe up onto the sand so I can climb forward and keep my feet dry. An unnecessary gesture, but a nice one. I hand him the food, deli items bought on my way out of town. I'm not exactly known for my blueberry pie.

We climb up the bank to a hardwood hammock. The branches of live oaks above us blink with sunlight. This is the same type of dry ground where my own live oak, the one in my backyard, took root a hundred years ago. Adlai doesn't realize it, but he's returning me to my natural habitat. He's brought a faded Indian-print cotton bedspread and he shakes it out like a parachute, holding two corners as it descends. Then he kneels and takes the food from the plastic grocery bag. I wish at this moment I'd brought lunch in a proper picnic basket like Dorothy Gale's, with wicker flaps on either side.

"Looks good," he says, in spite of the mean packaging. "Cucumber salad . . . pastrami, is it, on rye? I like pastrami." He reaches into his rucksack. "I brought some killer gingerbread from the bakery near my house, and a couple of tangerines."

"From your backyard?"

"No, from the IGA. I do have a tree, but they're not in season." He looks at me as if to say, *Don't you know that?*

Of course I know that. But something's causing my brain not to function.

"These must come from Chile," he says.

"*Tangerinus chilensis*," I say, and he smiles.

We're a couple of children on an outing. The speckled canopy encloses us like a clubhouse. No one else allowed. We eat hungrily, and our conversation, with mouths full, is mostly sounds. "Mmm." "Yum." The gingerbread is dark and moist and full of molasses.

When I'm finished eating, I lie back and look up at the branches of the live oaks, stretching over me like protective arms. I inhale and pretend Adlai and I are the sole owners of this hardwood hammock, the only ones who know its worth.

"Now you know what got *me* here," he says. "How did you come to this place?" He still thinks I live in Tallahassee.

"Me? Well . . ." Should I tell him I'm not of this place anymore? The back of my brain nags me to tell the whole truth. The rest of me says, *Just enjoy the moment.* "Adlai, my boy, this is my native soil." I like the sound of his name on my lips.

He lies on his side and leans toward me. His voice is low. "Nice place you have here," he says.

We kiss, like we're trying something we've heard about but have never done.

After a few minutes, there's a pattering on the leaves above us. We ignore it, consumed with the wetness of lips and impervious to the wetness of skin. But when the sky opens up, we have no choice. We separate, laughing, and gather up the picnic as quickly as we can. We take shelter at the base of the largest live oak, stretching the cotton bedspread out over our heads.

"Do you mind the rain?" he says.

I shake my head. "No."

"Good," he says, and together we watch it pelt the swamp.

41

For three days straight, I've been sorting, thanks to a combination of a stimulant—Colombian coffee, and a numbing agent—a rented TV. The apartment came wired for cable, but I haven't wanted the distraction until now. The only way I can keep from being mesmerized by the screen is to watch something I've seen before. Then I can listen with one ear, occasionally glance at the action, and get on with what I have to do. I've been mostly watching the Nostalgia Channel, leaving it on into the wee hours as I decide: trash, treasure, or thrift store. I've been cutthroat with the junk, and I just have to get it all out of here before I rethink any decisions. After five and a half weeks in Florida, and before I run out of money, sanity, and good judgment, I've got to get back to my actual life.

Of course I'll be sorry to leave certain things behind. That kiss from Adlai, for one. I've had to ignore several of his phone messages since then. But it can't be helped. I don't live here, and I don't need that kind of complication right now. As it is, that picnic made me forget to ask Theo for another extension. On Monday I got a text saying: "What's up?"

When I called him to scrape and bow, he said, "Listen, Loni. Every time you call to say you're staying longer, our man Hugh can barely disguise his delight. All I can say is, you better have your heiney back here by May 10."

I open a carton we hauled from the closet shelf in my old room. Tubes of colored beads, a Knitting Nancy, ten jacks with a desiccated rubber ball, and a small silver key. At the bottom is an old *Smithsonian* magazine. I open it and read Secretary Ripley's column. How different I am from the girl who first picked up this publication. Who knew then that I'd actually meet Ripley himself?

He retired years before I started working at the Smithsonian, but he still maintained an office in the Castle, and worked on special projects of his own choosing. Theo was one of his protégés and knew I idolized the man. Early in my tenure, I was drawing a lesser yellownape (*Picus chlorolophus*), a complicated green bird with an exquisite yellow ruff at the back of its head and neck. I was concentrating on depicting the dash of red at the crown exactly as it appeared on the bird skin, when I looked up and who was standing in my doorway with Theo but a tall, affable-looking fellow I would never mistake for anyone else. Here was the ornithologist, adventurer, art historian, and political adept who'd revolutionized the Institution. If I'd had some advance warning, I could have made some brilliant comment. But it was like a chance meeting with Bruce Springsteen. What do you say? *Hey, man, I like your work.*

I put down my paintbrush as Theo introduced us, and I said, "It's a real pleasure to meet you, sir."

"Likewise," he said, and looked over my half-finished version of the yellownape, then lifted the tag on the specimen with two fingers. "Nicely done," he said.

Theo—God bless him—said, "Ms. Murrow is one of the finest young bird artists in the field, Mr. Secretary."

Ripley looked at me with more attention and said, "Always good to find a kindred spirit."

A kindred spirit! Inside I leapt and hopped. Outside I smiled calmly and said, "Thank you, sir."

After they left, the walls of the room vibrated for another quarter of an hour.

Later that day, I had to go over to the Castle to talk to one of the archivists, and my route took me past his office. His door was open, and he called out to me, "Murrow, isn't it?"

I backtracked and he waved me in.

He had books and papers strewn across his desk. "I'm putting together a history of the Institution." The room was paneled with dark wood, but a shaft of sun from the skylight illuminated an old map on his desk. "Did you know that during the Civil War, when an attack on Washington seemed imminent, our scientists were told to evacuate and they took with them the Smithsonian family heirlooms?" His face shone with both knowledge and a childish delight.

I raised my eyebrows.

"Bird skins and precious eggs!" He tapped his pen in the middle of his desk. "Imagine scuttling out of here with what you consider the dearest artifact in the collection. What would you take?"

"Wow. I hate to think of the museum ever being under threat," I said.

"But if you could preserve only one item."

I stared off, mentally running through the museum's inventory.

He said, "Well, I've ambushed you. No need to answer now, but you ponder it when you're here late at night, drawing under that goose-neck lamp," he said. "Theo tells me you're quite dedicated."

I didn't know what to say to that, but the Secretary filled the silence.

"In the old days, the senior scientists also stayed into the night, but that was because they actually lived in the upper floors of the museum. When I started here, a few of them were still wandering the halls in their nightclothes."

"*Picus chlorolophus*," I said.

"I beg your pardon?"

"That's what I'd take with me. The lesser yellownape. Unless you were able to get to it first, sir. Theo told me you collected that bird yourself."

A smile crept onto his face. "Good to know it would be under your protection."

The Secretary left Washington after that, and I attended his memorial some time later. But my encounters with him shine like a gem, perfectly lit. I've heard that families stay together by reciting old stories. In a long tradition, from the egg-clutchers to the bathrobed hall-wanderers, from Ripley to Theo to Delores Constantine—my Wise Woman of the Botany Library—the Smithsonian family has put its arms around me and still holds me tight.

I put the old magazine on the "treasures" pile, get up to make another pot of coffee, and see I'm running low. There's a market about half a mile away, and it would do me good to stretch my legs. I get my bag and keys and open the apartment door to a strange sight: Estelle, getting ready to knock.

"Hey." I take a half step back. "Isn't there a security door? How'd you get up here?"

"Oh, someone propped it open. I just walked in." She sashays past me into the bare apartment, wearing peach-colored board shorts and a white T-back with flowers embroidered all around. She surveys the room. "I like your decorating scheme. Early American Cardboard."

"Haha." I haven't invited her over for this very reason. No soft rugs in my place, no earth tones, no throw pillows. Just boxes.

She stretches out on the paisley love seat, the only piece of furniture in the room. She must know I've been avoiding her, because after I specifically told her I wouldn't get involved in her textbook project, she wangled it so the illustrations I'd already agreed to would appear in the book. And then, because of page limitations, she decided I should draw the last four incongruous birds all on one tree, which I refuse to do. But here she is anyway, making herself at home, expecting me to act the hostess.

"I can offer you water, skim milk, or coffee."

"Since when do you drink coffee?" She gets up and wanders over to the bedroom and peers in, pokes around the tiny kitchen, presses a button on the old answering machine and makes it beep, then notices the bird skin I've set up on the wobbly Formica table, along with a preliminary sketch. "Huh," she says. "You prefer drawing here?"

I don't answer.

"You know," she says, "you *are* being unreasonable about those last four birds."

"Darling," I say, an edge creeping in, "Bad science is bad science. And a pileated woodpecker, a bald eagle, a blue heron, and a sandhill crane would never, ever inhabit the same tree."

"So that's why you're drawing on your crappy kitchen table, rather than in the nice studio I've supplied you?"

My caffeine high makes me a little too ready to fight. "Don't click your tongue at me. I'm right on this one, Estelle."

She turns. "They're fifth-graders. If they get a fanciful drawing here or there, it means we don't leave anything out. What's the difference?"

"When did you get so sloppy?" I say.

She looks down at her outfit.

"Not your clothes. Your precision. Your attention to detail. Your . . . Estelleness!"

She walks over to the window, looks out, then plops back down on the love seat. Her face crumples.

"What?" I exhale.

"Roger doesn't want to have kids."

I sit down next to her. "Have you been talking about marriage?"

"No, we've been talking about kids. Anyway, I don't know how we'd have them. He travels all the time. I've spent the last five years asking him where he's off to now."

I nod. "Had you never discussed children before?"

"I thought we had. But tonight he made this . . . declaration." She turns toward me suddenly. "Tell me honestly. What do *you* think of Roger?"

I hesitate. "I don't know. He seems fine, I mean—"

"He can be sarcastic."

I nod again.

"That can get old fast. And what if he's sarcastic with our children?" She stares off.

"But he doesn't want—"

"That can be hard on a kid's self-esteem." She gets up and paces. "Should I give him the boot?"

"Estelle, that's not a question I can—"

"Didn't we always say we'd both have girl-children, and they'd be best friends?"

"Yeah, but we also both planned to marry all three of the Hanson Brothers." I start to sing the one Top-40 hit of their heartthrob career. "MMMBop! Bopa doo mmmbop . . ."

"Right." She stares at me without really seeing and puts her hand on the doorknob. "Now, you know, I need those last four birds to show to the publisher. So get to work on that all-purpose tree."

Man, she can switch fast. So much for our agreement not to mix personal and professional. There's a breeze when she slams the door.

I abandon my trip to the market. I decide instead to capitalize on my vexation and my remaining caffeination to get the damn birds over with. I shut off the TV and wad up some paper to stick under the wobbliest table leg. I try to ignore the voice in my head screaming, *This isn't right!* I want the woodpecker in flight, with its flap-pause-dip, flap-flap-pause-dip stutter stroke. But Estelle wants him on a tree, so I outline the tall red cockade and imagine the rat-a-tat he'd make on his chosen food source.

The underground water and caves may not get done. Even four different birds on the same tree have to be easier than inanimate water and rocks. While I work on the woodpecker, I also scratch on my doo-dle page: a plant, a fish, a canoe in water. Pickerelweed behind. My mother's back. It's not a memory. I never saw my mother in a canoe. It's just speculation, a way of wondering what brought on the rarest of Ruth Murrow phenomena—tears.

My phone rings, and I answer, my attention still on the drawing.

"Loni," says a nasal female voice.

"Yes?"

"It's me, Tammy."

"Oh! Hi!" My sister-in-law has never before called me on the phone.

"So, Mona's weekly wash 'n' style is Friday at three thirty. Come down to the salon before that, and we'll see what we can find out."

"Wait. . . ." It takes me a minute to connect what she's saying to her recent offer of help. *I can find out things while I'm doing people's hair.*

"But . . . won't the kids need picking up?" I stand up and pace the room.

"Nope. Aftercare."

This might just be a diversion for Tammy. But her story of telling her mother to "stuff a smelly sock into it" makes me list over in her direction. Maybe she's more than just spandex and hairspray.

"So get yourself here at three and watch a master at work."

"But if I'm there, why would Mrs. Watson—"

"Oh, you're gonna be hidden, don't worry."

I go back to the table and survey my two drawings. What's happening to the world? Four random birds on the same tree, Tammy calling with an offer of help, and my stone-faced mother in tears. Beneath Ruth's floating canoe I've drawn a cross-section of water-filled caves, layer upon layer, a honeycomb of streams running through the porous limestone.

In the research I've done for this assignment, I've been reminded why these underground rivers can be so dangerous, and not just for aquatic spelunkers. The water flows along serenely until it erodes the terra firma above, causing a collapse, and into that sinkhole go houses, trees, and anyone mistaking that spot for a safe place to stand. Like the guy on *The Florida Report*, one minute asleep in his bed, the next minute vanished, never to be found. Everywhere I step in Florida, it could happen to me. Slurp-slop and I'll be gone.

42

"Loni?"

A young woman with light, wavy hair stands before me in the Tenetkee Public Library, where I've returned to soak in the atmosphere and do a little more research. I have no idea who this person is.

"I'm Kaye Elliot," she says. "I went to school with your brother."

My mind goes through a thousand pictures in a half second, and stops at one, a blondish, mussed-up kindergartner in tights and rain boots shoving a crinkled paper into my hand as I stood waiting for Phil to run out of his classroom. The bearer of the note, out of breath, said, "I'm Kaye, and Philip needs to call me so he can come over and play." When I opened the scrap of paper, I saw a scribbled phone number. I've always admired uppity women, whatever their age.

The grown-up Kaye says, "Loni, it's so good to see you! I'm the librarian now." Like her younger self, she's still a little breathless. "My official title is 'media specialist,'" she says, "but I hate that. I always wanted to grow up to be the librarian."

"And here you are. Good for you." I sound like my mother, but I mean it.

She asks about my life and pushes a lot of, "Wow!" into the air when I describe my job.

I say, "Is the library adding a new room? I saw some work going on behind the main building. . . ."

"Yes! Mr. Perkins donated money for an expansion."

"Elbert Perkins?"

She nods her head.

Where does that guy get his money?

"Now, if there's anything I can help you find," she says, "just let me know."

This curiosity and unselfish desire to search, a universal trait of librarians, has always made me grateful, and when I mention the caves, she suggests a few sources I haven't yet explored. As she points me toward them, I say, "Hey, do you take book donations?"

She nods, eyebrows raised.

I wave my thanks to her when I leave, pulling open the heavy door. As I start down the steps, I notice a sharp pong of unwashed scalp and wet dog.

"Hey there!" It's Nelson Barber, his white hair looking even wispier, if that's possible. There are bits of food stuck in his scrofulous beard. The last time I saw him he had a sharp hunting knife in his hand.

"Got a minute?" he says.

The least threatening version of this question could still trap me for hours. "Hi, Mr. Barber. Actually, I've got three minutes, and then I have to go." I take a step back. "By the way, you didn't happen to saw a hole in my brother's fence, did you?"

"Heh-heh," he says, "I heard about that. J.D. come by and shot him a hunk o' gator meat, is what I heard."

"J.D.?" The man with the chaw.

"Forget about that," Nelson says, and moves closer to me, rambling in a low, confiding voice, "What I want to tell you is, how slow and sneaky they were, takin' my store. You saw 'em. Bit by bit, that's how they do it. Elbert told me to refinance. Attractive interest rate. Bunch a hogslop." He scratches a scab on his cheekbone. "'Expand the warehouse!' he tells me. 'Buy more stock! Compete with the chains!' Then the economy started to tank, and he says, 'Source things out! Mortgage your house!' That house I'd been in for thirty-six years! 'Rent out the warehouse!' he tells me, and then, 'These guys'll work for a song. Enjoy yer life a little, take time off.' Turns out, it was a conspiracy! Bunch of thugs. Wanted the warehouse for other things. You know what for?"

"No, sir, I sure—"

"Number one most moneymaking deal in Florida."

I wait.

"Know what that is, don'tcha?"

"Um, tourism?"

"Drugs! Contraband!" he spits. "Elbert and his upstanding partner nobody's got the guts to name, them guys and their many minions . . . and you know who else? Franny and Pete—code name F & P—they tried to poison me with their nasty-ass food! Not only that, but the dentist tried to pull out all my teeth! Did I tell you that? And your brother, who ain't even a real accountant, got his degree by mail order, he better move his ass and start filing my complaint with the IRS! They're the ones got the dentist to take out all my teeth. That quack ought to be tarred and feathered! His balls cut off!" A wisp from the top of Nelson's head lifts in a sudden breeze.

I'm squinting and hoping he doesn't have a knife. I don't want anything cut off of anyone. "I'm so sorry, Mr. Barber, but I have to be somewhere, and I'm already late. Bye, now!" I turn away from him and toward the sidewalk, glancing back to be sure he isn't following me.

He mutters and moves the other way, past the new construction behind the library and across the field toward the woods. Barber seems to appear and disappear quickly, probably because he knows all the little waterways and how they're connected. The stream down by those trees must lead to the larger swamp.

Mr. Barber thinks everyone's against him, right down to my own brother. Was it Phil's private parts he was threatening, or the dentist's?

He's even paranoid about two of the nicest people in town, Franny and Pete. And he has something against me, for sure. *Yankee Go Home!* Was that him? And the doves? He might not be wrong about Elbert Perkins steering people into unsupportable mortgages, but Elbert didn't single-handedly make the economy tank.

Well, none of it is my business, and it *is* time for this Yankee to go home. I pass the state capitol building and pull up at the Tallahassee Science Museum. I'm still fighting with Estelle over the last four drawings, but I might as well turn in the ones I have.

She sits behind her desk in a corporate uniform—navy blue jacket and matching earrings. The skirt and shoes under the desk are surely an identical navy blue. I smack my drawings of the belted kingfisher, the yellow-crowned night heron, and the anhinga down on her desk.

She looks them over carefully, critically, and I try not to get distracted by the touch of appreciation in her face. When she looks up, I say, "And about those last four. I'm almost finished with the pileated woodpecker, and I've put him on a dead tree, where he belongs."

"Yes, and . . ."

"Next, I'll be drawing the bald eagle. Which nests in a *live* tree, not a dead one."

She stands. "And never, in its entire life, does it set its little talons down on a dead tree?"

"Ergggggggh!" I say, and turn to leave.

"Where are you going?

"To Bridget's studio. Remember her? Bridget? Your real bird artist? I can't wait for Bridget to have her baby, come back, and tell you off. And while I'm down there pretending to be Bridget, I'll be burning through those other three birds!" I leave her office, pound down the hall, and raise the Roman shade.

Bald eagle, bald eagle. I try to draw it on the tree with the woodpecker. But I just can't. So I start the bird with no environment at all.

Because of its status as a national icon, the eagle is always in danger of becoming a cliché. While its image advertises patriotism and the

American way, the actual meat-and-bones animal has a stark fierceness that has nothing to do with the symbol. Its feathers are often awry, and its small eyes carry an expression of sharp accusation. As I draw the dead bird before me, I try to inhabit the living bird I once saw sailing across a perfect sky.

The sun was in my eyes, and the eagle was far above us, but it coasted into a pocket of bright blue, calling out in a high peal.

Daddy set the canoe paddle across his knees.

Without lowering my eyes, I said, "How high do you think he can go?"

"As high as he wants." Daddy's neck was bent back. "I envy him, Loni Mae. He can get away from 'bout anything."

"I'd like to fly like that," I said.

"You'd come back, though?"

I looked away from the bird.

Daddy wasn't grinning, wasn't making fun. "'Cause Mama and Daddy'd miss you if you flew off and forgot us." His eyes caught mine.

I put down the pencil. *And what the hell did you do?*

My father understood me in a way no one else ever has. So why didn't I understand him? What did he want to get away from? And why couldn't he stay to see me through?

My phone vibrates. That will be Estelle, nagging me from down the hall. "What?"

"Hey." A man's voice. Adlai.

I should have checked before I answered. I knew when we finally spoke I'd have to come clean, tell him it can't go any further. The picnic was fun, but that's it. I don't live here, I won't live here, so it's pointless.

"Where you been?" he says.

"Oh, I don't know, busy."

He says, "Just hoping we could find some more bad weather."

Damn, I like this guy.

I say, "That was a pretty nice picnic."

"Yeah." He leaves a space for me to say just how nice.

But I do not. In the silence, I try to envision letting this go further, being open, for once, to the unknown.

"You know," he says, "canoe rentals have dropped significantly the past couple of days."

"Are you trying to tell me you need my business?"

"You could say that."

A good-looking guy is asking me to go canoeing, and I'm trying to wrestle four stupid birds onto the same tree. What kind of a choice is that? I grab my keys, ignore my better judgment, and head for the canoe shop.

43

I try to act like the picnic, the kiss, never happened. A man and a woman, both in floppy hats with drawstrings, are paying for the canoes they used. When they leave, Adlai stands and smiles. "Shall I close up?"

"Sure," I say. "But I don't want to affect your bottom line. . . ."

He raises his eyebrows.

Why, when I'm with someone I like, do I do stupid things like that slip out? I try to qualify it. "I mean, in a negative way."

He laughs. "You can affect my bottom line, if you want."

"I didn't mean to say that, exactly." I laugh too.

"I'll go get the birchbark," he says.

"I'll come." *Ergh. I should stop talking.*

He smiles, but he's too polite to respond to that one.

I follow him into the tight space of the shed, where the canoe sits on a waist-high rack. He grabs both gunnels but must not realize I'm directly behind him, so when he lifts the boat he knocks me back against the wall.

"Yikes!"

He turns his head, quickly setting the canoe back on its supports to tend to me. "I'm so sorry, are you all right?"

I'm still standing flush against the beam, and he touches the back of my scalp. "Did you hit your head? Any blood?" He knows there is not. In a softer voice, he says, "Can I make it better?" and kisses my temple, then my cheek. I lift my chin and he kisses my mouth. We're tentative at first, and his lips are soft. I don't know how long we stand there kissing in the dim shed. At some point I'll remind him about the canoe, and the fading light, and what we're missing out on the water. But not quite yet. Somehow what's important is not outside this cramped space, not any further than Adlai's soft, wet lips, the taste of his tongue, and his hands cradling my head like a precious object.

I pull him close.

He whispers, "You are doing something to me, Loni Murrow."

"Likewise, Adlai Brinkert."

He draws a deep breath, then kisses me again.

It is almost full dark outside. He pulls away and leans back against the canoe on its struts. His chest expands and he exhales through his teeth. "Okay," he says. "I have to think. With my brain. Which is a little difficult at the moment."

"Likewise," I say.

He grins. Shakes his head side to side as if to clear it.

"Hey, you asked me to come down here," I say, smiling.

"And did ya?"

"I did. Only for the canoeing."

"Which . . ." He glances out the door of the shed.

"It's too dark for now." I take a step toward the doorway to look out.

He comes up behind me, encircling my waist with one arm. "Maybe tomorrow."

"I'm walking to my car now," I say.

He drops his arm. "Okay. Yeah. Good." He follows me out of the shed, back through the canoe shop, and out to the parking lot. I open my car door and stand behind it.

"That was kind of fun," I say.

He nods.

I get into the driver's seat and shut the door.

He motions for me to roll down the window. "Okay, then. Bye."

He leans down and gives me a little peck on the lips, then another, and then we're making out again, him leaning down and me with my neck in an awkward position, but I do not care. He is the best kisser.

Finally our lips separate and I say, "Okay. Gotta go. Yeah, gotta—"

He holds his face level with mine, skin almost steaming.

"Yep," I say, "bye!" I turn the key and he straightens up.

I slowly drive away.

There's very little light, but in my rearview I think I see him raise a hand to wave.

44

In the back room of Tammy's salon, my nose stings from the starchy, ammoniac smell of hair dye. When I stick my head out from behind the curtain separating her workroom from the main salon, she says, "Get back in there! Mona could arrive any minute."

I twiddle my thumbs and look around. Tammy's right about one thing—if I wanted the scoop on anyone in Tenetkee, this is the place. Before the lull, I heard about two affairs, one boob job, and a set of elderly sisters fighting over their father's small fortune. For the moment, though, it's quiet. I rummage in my bag and open my mother's little *GARDEN* book.

Again this week Boyd's daddy came around drunk and banging at the door shouting, Let me in, boy, or I'll whip your sorry ass! Boyd and Loni were gone, and I stayed quiet till he left. I hope Newt never comes back. Whenever he shows up, Boyd's silence deepens.

I'd like to comfort my own husband, if he would talk to me. But he won't. Last night I went to bed ready to give right up. At midnight I woke to an empty bed, rubbed my eyes, and saw Boyd framed by the window. Come, Ruthie, he said. Got to see these stars. I put on my slippers and went over, and he moved me in front of

*him. He was warm behind me. He put his hands on my big belly
and we stood awhile, looking up and listening to the crickets sing
their song. Under the clear night sky, we watched the outer reaches
of space and felt this child move in my inner space. We did not talk,
but we were there, together, paying attention.*

The salon's front door opens and I hear two women come in. I
peer through a quarter-inch crack between the curtain and the wall.
It's Tammy's best friend, Georgia, along with Mona Watson. The
young woman and the older woman have a similar body type, but
Georgia's puffy hairstyle is a bit more updated than Mona's Sandra
Dee tease-out.

It could be coincidental that Georgia is here, but I suspect Tammy
invited her. Georgia sits and picks up a *People* magazine while Mona
takes her place in the chair. At the mirror, Mona and Tammy decide
what to keep the same about the flip-do. There's some murmured chitchat during the hair wash, and then Tammy seats Mona again and
says, half to Georgia and half to her client, "Isn't that awful about poor
Claudia Applegate, losing her husband? He was so nice, and then so
young? Mona, did you go to the funeral?"

Mrs. Watson adjusts her black drape. "Oh, it was sad."

Tammy removes the towel from Mona's neck. "You just don't like
seeing a fella go so young! Wasn't Claudia's husband a relative of yours?"

Mona says, "By marriage. He was a second cousin to my Danny."

"Oh, that must have been hard for you," Tammy coos.

Mona goes right where Tammy steers. "It was, I tell you. The whole
thing reminded me of my Danny's funeral, Lord love him. He was
young, too, when he died."

"God rest him," Tammy says. "How did you ever get through it?"

She's immobile under Tammy's scissoring hands. "Well, honey, if
you must know, I was heavily sedated—and I suppose the same was
true for Claudia, there. Of course, it wasn't my idea, the sedatives, but I
thanked my stars for the man who gave me the pills."

"It wasn't a girlfriend?"

"No, my husband's boss, Frank. He was a saint. Even picked up part of the bill for the arrangements."

Georgia folds her *People* back on itself. From the chair where she sits, she says, "That Frank Chappelle *is* a nice man." She lowers her voice to almost a whisper. "And handsome, too."

Mrs. Watson doesn't say anything.

Tammy says, "What a shame he's all alone, with no one to look after him. I heard his wife ran off and left him years ago. Didn't she have a boyfriend in Mobile or something?"

"Honey, the way people talk and get it wrong," Mrs. Watson says, fluffing her drape. "He was the one running around on her."

I prick up my ears.

Tammy says, "Really?"

Mrs. Watson almost chuckles. "He was a saint to me, but I guess not to his wife."

Where does this woman come off, making insinuations about Captain Chappelle?

She keeps going. "I mean, I don't like to get into anyone else's business, especially someone who helped me out in my tough time, but Rita Chappelle was my friend. And when she found out her husband had a floozy in Tallahassee, she packed up the children, took them to her mama's, and didn't look back."

I have half a mind to go out there and tell her what to do with her lying gossip.

Tammy says, "No! A floozy in Tally?"

"There were rumors about him and some local ladies, but that was a bunch of hooey. No self-respecting woman would have an affair in a town this size."

Tammy says, "I just can't believe that nice man was a rounder! So Mrs. Chappelle just started a whole new life?"

"Yeah, it was sad. They seemed so good together. But like I always say, you just never know what goes on between people."

"That's a fact," Tammy says.

Through my quarter-inch gap in the curtain, I can just barely make out Mrs. Watson's damp head. "And Rita didn't go to no Mobile, she went back to Panama City. I really missed her when she left. Fish & Game wives get close, you know."

"Did she remarry?" Tammy moves around Mona and blocks my view.

"No, she's still Chappelle, just like she was still in love with Frank. I heard he used to go visit her, even after the divorce. I kind of hoped she'd forgive him and come back to town. Might have been better for young Stevie."

Tammy says, "Losing that boy must have been hard on Frank."

"'Specially the way he died," Mona says. "Poor thing, Stevie really did try to turn his life around. He musta just fell off the wagon again. And that mother and child in the other car. Now there's a sad story. They were on their way to Disney World!"

There's a pause while everyone takes that in.

Mona says, "Anyway, after Stevie's funeral, I brought Frank a casserole or two. I felt sorry for him, all alone, and Rita being so bitter at the funeral."

Tammy says, "The ex-wife?"

"Well, I'm sure you heard. The scene she made? She said it right out where everyone could hear, 'Our boy's dead because of you!' and whatnot."

"No!" Georgia says.

"But after about the second casserole, Frank sorta got the wrong idea, if you know what I mean. So I stopped visiting. After my Danny passed, Frank was very kind to me, and I just wanted to repay the favor. But I suppose everyone is complicated in ways we can't know. My Danny did have his quarrels with Frank. Toward the end, they were butting heads all the time. But why am I going on? You don't care about any of this old ancient history. And me getting all worked up."

"Here, honey," Tammy says. "Take a tissue."

In the back room, I dip one small end of my hair into a pot of white paste and wonder what color it will turn. This is so not my scene, the salon, the gossip and mean-spirited hearsay, the skulking in back rooms listening for God knows what. The more I hear, the more muddled I get. It's like trying to draw a bird I've never seen and finding a feather or an eggshell, but not the bird itself. And then a bunch of birds I haven't come to see flit around and distract me.

Tammy's doing the last swoop on Mona's hair. I told her beforehand to ask about Henrietta, the person who wrote the pink letter. And she still needs to ask about the form signed by Mona's husband, Lt. Daniel J. Watson—*Wallet found on land . . .*

Instead, Tammy says, "Bye-bye, Mona, see you next week!"

Mrs. Watson leaves, and I wait a minute, then emerge from behind the curtain. Tammy sweeps up fine little hairs from the floor.

"Tammy, the two questions I was hoping you'd get to . . ."

"Now, you're next," she says, and plops me into the chair.

"What? No, Tammy, really."

"Don't worry, I'm not gonna change your style, just trim your split ends."

I've always hated getting my hair cut. It takes so much time, and for what? I want it long. But even though I've seen Tammy's creations, I don't get up from the chair. Maybe I'm too startled by the offer, or too confused about what I just heard.

She sprays my hair with something from a squirt bottle. "Don't worry, I never give anyone a style that doesn't suit them. For instance, Loni, do you still have that complete set of Beatles LPs you bought at Final Vinyl in Tallahassee?"

"I beg your pardon?"

"And the actual turntable you bought to play them on?"

I nod. "Well, yeah, but—"

"So, you see, that gives me information about how to do your hair. Linda McCartney style, 1968 through '70. Not blond, of course, but like her, parted straight down the middle, just a little trim to your ends."

Is she making fun of me? "That's how I already wear it."

"No, because you don't trim your ends." She combs and inspects the tips of my long hair. "What did you dip into back there?" She snips and continues, "Okay, so what did we learn? It doesn't sound like Mona was boinkin' Frank Chappelle."

"Did you think she was?"

Georgia looks up over her magazine. "So why'd he buy her a house?"

I turn toward her. "What?"

"Rumor has it," Georgia says.

The Tenetkee rumor mill. It may be the only thing keeping the town standing. But is this any of Georgia's business? I do hope Tammy hasn't talked to her about every single aspect—

"Loni, please keep your head still." Tammy puts two fingers to my skull.

"So you think Frank Chappelle bought Mrs. Watson her house?" I ask.

"Pretty expensive gift to give just out of pity," Tammy says, combing my hair over my face and parting it, a straight line of pressure against my scalp.

"Wait," I say. "Who says Frank bought her the house?" But I'm just a head being worked on. They are deaf to me.

"And then," Georgia says, "why didn't Mona's husband get along with Mr. Chappelle?"

Tammy combs my hair back off my forehead. "That's what Loni's gonna ask his wife, Rita."

"What?"

"Mrs. Chappelle. She might remember something no one else does." Tammy holds her pointy comb at an angle while she talks down to my reflection. "I found her for you. Now you need to pursue the lead. You heard Mona. Rita's in Panama City, and her name is still Chappelle. So look her up! Remember, this is a fifty-fifty deal. I do some, you do some."

I glance up at Tammy's reflection in the mirror. She sees herself as a private eye from a novel—maybe *H is for Hairstylist.*

I say, "I don't understand half of what you two are talking about."

Tammy glares down at me with her eyebrows together. This could explode so quickly.

I backpedal. "I mean, I appreciate . . ."

She goes back to combing and snipping.

"Tammy," I say, "all I wanted to know from Mona was about that piece of paper her husband filed . . ."

She completes my sentence like a teacher telling me what I've gotten wrong. ". . . *And* why Frank Chappelle paid for her husband's funeral, *and* why he bought her a house, for goodness' sake."

"Are you sure he bought her the house? And paid for the funeral? Because according to Mr. Hapstead . . ." The name catches in my throat.

"What, they took up a collection? Please. You got to have rich people contributing quite a bit to make it add up to a nice funeral and a *house*. And don't forget while you're in Panama City—ask Mrs. Chappelle why Frank and Dan didn't get along."

"No," I say. "The collection was only for the funeral."

Georgia pipes up. "Loni, Dan Watson was murdered in cold blood, and it's never been solved. Your daddy, God rest him, died in what they called an 'accident.' But what if it wasn't? What if it was murder? Your daddy could have been a victim of the same gang."

There's that little light again, illuminating my brain with another *what if*. It would be so tempting to jump into this elaborate conspiracy my sister-in-law and her friend are trying to construct. Professor Plum, in the conservatory, with the candlestick.

"Could we stop this right now?" I say.

Tammy frowns at my reflection.

"I think, just, for everyone's sake . . ."

She gets all polite. "Loni, how old was Phil when you left home for college?"

"He was starting first grade, but . . ."

"Right." She spins the chair away from the mirror so I'm facing her. "He is grown-up now, big sister. A lot younger than you—no offense—

but Grown. Up." She takes two strands of my hair and pulls them down next to my chin, checking them for evenness. Then she leans in and snips. "I told you. Neither of us wants him to hear info that's nasty *and* untrue. And if the truth is bad, well, he can handle it, whatever 'it' turns out to be." She gets behind me and straightens my head with her fingers. "Maybe 'it' will turn out to be different from what anybody thinks. I'm for the pursuit of truth. How 'bout you, Georgia?"

"Yes, ma'am."

Tammy does a few more snips, then spins me back around toward the mirror. "Voilà!" she says.

I look at my reflection. "Wow," I say. "That looks kind of good." All she's done is straighten my part and trim the ends, but somehow it's better.

"Now," she says, "quit puttin' your hair in a ponytail every day."

"I don't always . . ."

"What the ponytail says to the world is 'I can't be bothered with fixing myself up. I have nice hair, but I'm keeping it back where you can't see it.'"

Did she just give me a compliment?

"If you have a special occasion, now, I could do you some magic." She winks at me in the mirror. "Say, for a wedding. You might like a French braid tucked under, simple but elegant. Oh no, for you, spiky, right? Lotsa gel? Ha. Ha. Just a little joke, Loni."

I laugh. We've misplaced our usual roles. I'm woozy from the spinning chair, the smell of ammonia, and a growing and mossy confusion. But even if I don't know what it all means, I suppose I still have more information than when I came in.

45

I flick my newly trimmed hair over my shoulder as I walk the two blocks from my place to Estelle's. After the salon, I took a whole load of boxes over to Goodwill, where I'm now on a first-name basis with the volunteers. All I have left is to decide about the most precious books, draw the water-filled caves, and finish the last four birds.

In spite of our tug-of-war over those "final four," I'm hoping Estelle will actually, this time, stick to her promise of separating work and friendship. Popcorn night is a ritual we've had since middle school, and as I knock, I pray to be received *not* by Estelle the troublesome curator, but by Estelle the friend, the person I've known since the first grade, who witnessed almost every milestone in my young life. Please.

She opens the door wearing a frothy white A-line vintage dress with ruffles around the neck and bell-shaped sleeves, and floats onto her oatmeal-colored couch. I remind myself that on most fronts she is still my closest ally, and soon we'll return to our untainted long-distance friendship.

She has set out popcorn, a tiny bit of chocolate, and a steaming pot of herbal tea. She says, "Okay, update me on your life."

A part of me relaxes. We won't be talking about work. "Well . . . I went someplace I promised I'd never go again."

"Monkey Jungle?"

"No, Estelle. Nothing so benign. I went to the funeral home."

"Oh. Sorry."

"Yeah, that's what the funeral director said. *Sorry for your loss.* But are you ready? I found out something both weird and surprising."

"What?" She gives me her full attention.

"My father had a head wound."

She cups her chin in her hand.

"And here's something even more shocking. Are you ready? Tammy wants to help."

"With what?"

"Well, for one thing, she cut my hair."

Estelle looks at my head.

"And, she got wind of all these stray, confusing details about my dad and had me listen in while she did that Watson lady's hair, the one who wouldn't talk to me."

Estelle wobbles her big bell sleeves. "So, what did you find out?"

"Well, surprise! Tammy didn't ask any of the questions I told her to. And now she's pressuring me to talk to another lady, only this one lives in Panama City. But I don't really want to go."

"Even if it might help you find stuff out?"

"Strangely, I'm just not that fond of having doors slammed in my face."

"Would it help if I went with you?"

"No, and let's talk about something else now."

"But you said Phil was about to do something stupid—"

"I know, and I brought it up, but . . ."

"Okay, then, let's hear about Adlai." Estelle stretches one pedicured foot out on the couch, point, flex.

I sigh.

She hits my arm. "Come on, spill."

"There's nothing to tell. It's like high school. Lots of kissing."

"Where?" she says.

"On the lips!"

"No, I mean, at his house?"

"Oh, I'm not going to his house." I reach for the popcorn bowl.

"You're telling me he hasn't even suggested . . . you know?"

"Oh, Estelle, leave me alone. He's just a nice guy. Nothing more."

"I got it. He senses you're weird about sex, so he's being considerate."

"I am not weird about sex. We've only gone out a few times. Anyway, I can't start sleeping with him and then go back to D.C. What would that accomplish?"

"So don't leave."

"Right. But how inconsiderate of me, just talking about myself. How are things with you and Roger?"

"Forget Roger, I want to hear about Adlai."

I let out a breath. "Well . . . let's see. He said he'd help me with some drawings."

She swivels her head, fast.

"Not *your* drawings. The Theo stuff, the caves and the underground rivers. He knows a lot about them."

"Okay, so you've told him about the Smithsonian, and Washington. How did he react?"

I look toward the TV, which is still off. "I . . . um . . . I told him I'm doing some long-distance work for them."

She looks at me like I've murdered someone.

"What?" I say. "That's not untrue."

"You're a shit!" Her eyes go wide. "You have to tell him where you live."

"I know that."

"You have to be honest with him," she says. "And then it can grow from there."

I set down the popcorn bowl, trying to stay calm. "Listen to me. We've had a few dates. We've talked about groundwater. We've kissed. A lot. That is it. I'm not entangled."

"*Entangled* does not always mean physically." She stares at me.

I get up and retrieve the TV listing from across the room.

Estelle stands up too. "This is why you're trying to finish everything up and get out of town, isn't it? Because you know something good could happen, and you just couldn't stand that. So you're doing what you've always done. You're running."

I wheel around. My skin is clammy. "Shut up! If I don't get back to my job, it'll be gone!"

She looks me straight in the eyes and separates every word. "No. You are running. Because you are afraid."

Her words hit a bullseye at the center of my chest. I stare back at her. "Estelle, shut up! I've gotta go." I grab my bag and walk out her door.

46

It's early in the morning, and I've climbed out of bed to reach for my sketchbook. I sit on the floor, knees folded to chest, the side of the mattress supporting my back, and I draw the blue heron flying up and protecting her territory. The purest images come as I wake, and I need to catch them before they disappear. As I sketch, the old story my father used to tell echoes in my brain. No wonder the fairy queen of the marsh chose this bird to inhabit. The heron is regal in her blue, asserting her will with shimmering, outstretched wings.

After Daddy died, every time I chanced to see a blue heron, I made a wish. She was the queen of that realm, wasn't she? She could cross the invisible line between the land of the living and the land of the spirits. I asked her to bring him back. That was a noble wish, wasn't it? Any task she asked of me, any sacrifice, I would do. When I understood that would not be granted, I wished for her to take him a message, that I missed him and thought of him every day. Had she done it? The only impossible task I'd been asked to perform was living without him. Then, I wished that he would send me a message back.

After years of silence, I stopped wishing. I turned to other, unstoried birds of whom I could ask nothing, birds I could capture on paper, or in a wide, shallow drawer. Natural History has bird skins of blue herons, but I have never sought one out, never touched or drawn from one, and won't. Yet here is the living, regal heron on my sketchbook.

My back starts to ache, so I rise from the floor and get dressed. When I unplug my cell, I see I've missed a call from Delores. That's interesting. I hit *Reply*.

"Delores, you called me?"

"Hello, Loni. Yes. I was talking to your boss," she begins. "He's concerned about you."

"Yeah, I'm concerned about me, too. But not to worry. I'm nearly done here."

"It didn't take two weeks, did it?" The phone rustles as Delores multitasks.

"Delores, did you call to say, 'I told you so'?"

"No, that's just a side benefit."

"Well . . . ," I say.

"Well, if you're nearly done, then that's good. Does your mother think you're nearly done?"

"I keep telling her."

"And what does she say?" The clacking of computer keys.

"Guilt trip."

"We all like our trips, don't we?"

"I bet you've never guilt-tripped your daughter." This is more personal than we usually get, but it's out before I can pull it back. Maybe the distance, maybe the phone, maybe the relief of Delores' familiar voice has made me cross the breach. "I mean, here's the thing, Delores, my mother would never come halfway and ask what's important to me, or what I love."

"Have you done that for her?"

That stops me.

"Let me tell you something, Loni. I have made mistakes as a mother. I know, hard to believe, but there it is. I guarantee your mother has too. And it's possible she regrets it. But if she'd like to approach you in some other way, you might have to open a door."

"Hm." I leave a small silence. Delores has given me career advice before, but she's never pried, never butted in. Given both our circumstances, and the rarity of a comment like this, I'd best listen. "Delores, what does your daughter do?"

"Uh . . . she designs things for . . . satellites. Yes, that's it."

"In California?"

"Mm-hm. Why?"

"Just wondering."

"She was always a stargazer. Didn't care for chlorophyll and photosynthesis, where my head was most of the time. She hated my work."

"Because it took you away from her?"

"Uh, she never said why."

"Hm. Hey, I learned something about stars, recently. Actually, it was from one of the herbals you sent me through interlibrary loan. Maybe you could use it on your daughter. Want to hear it?"

"Shoot."

I locate and flip through the notes I made that day at FSU in Strozier Library. "Here it is. *'Paracelsus believed that each plant was a terrestrial star, and each star a spiritualized plant.'*"

"Sounds pretty woo-woo."

"Yeah, but maybe a connection point."

"Okay, I gotta go, Loni. Check in with HR, will ya? And give 'em a progress report. Theo's afraid you're gonna miss your deadline."

"Thanks, Delores. You're the best."

"Right. Ta-ta."

I plop down on the bed and stare up at the ceiling. Delores called for practical reasons. But her other advice is what I need to follow. *Honor your mother. Go halfway. Open a door.*

I get up and grab a few books I've marked with stickies to read to Ruth, shove them in my bag, and step out the door. Something crunches beneath my feet. I'm standing on birdseed. A line of it stops at my apartment and proceeds down the steps. *What the hell?* I follow the trail down the stairs, a neat little line out into the foyer and down the long walkway to the street. The seed is dispersed a bit on the concrete where the birds are enjoying it, but the line gets thicker, and I follow it all the way to the sidewalk, where it ends at my car. My front windshield is soaped, and in the dried white coating is written: *D.C. HERE I COME!* The rear windshield has a brown film on it. I put my nose to it and sniff. Someone has smeared *shit* on my window.

I stomp up the Town Hall steps and bang open the doors of the Tenetkee Police Department. "Is Lance Ashford here?"

Lance comes out to the front desk.

"I want to get a restraining order," I say.

He takes me back to his desk and sits me down. "All right, Loni, calm down. Now who needs restraining?" He raises one eyebrow.

"Nelson Barber, that's who! He's insane."

Lance takes a form from a vertical file. "Has this person assaulted you or touched your person?"

"No, but he *has* held a knife in a threatening way." I tell him about the weird trail of birdseed and the current state of my car. I remind him about the dead pigeons, and the chalk on my tire. "And don't forget about that hole in my brother's fence. Bobby could have been killed by that gator!"

A few other officers with nothing else to do come over and listen.

Lance looks down to his form. "Aside from the knife in the store, did you see this person perpetrate any of the . . . pranks?"

"Pranks? These are not pranks!"

Lance says, "Loni, would you get over yourself and let me fill out the form?"

I look at the guys standing around. "This is a private conversation," I say, and they move off. I turn to Lance. "You can't do anything about it, can you?"

"I can file this report. But we'd have to catch the guy actually doing something to restrain him."

"How about checking the stores to see who has bought twenty pounds of birdseed?"

"That's a fine idea," he says. "And unofficially . . . I'll keep my eyes open."

My phone buzzes. *A. Brinkert*, the screen tells me. "Gotta go," I say. I walk outside by the Town Hall pillars. I shouldn't even answer. But I do. Maybe I'm still shaky from the morning's trouble, but my insides flutter like a teenager's.

"What would you say to dinner at my place?" Adlai's voice is even.

I swallow. Everyone knows what that means. "Sounds nice, but do you like Lebanese food? Because there's a place in Tallahassee called Zahara . . ."

There's a pause. "If you're worried about me trying something funny, it's just dinner."

I really shouldn't. I should go home, sweep up the birdseed, and prepare to get out of town. Instead, I go home, take a broom to the now-scattered line of millet, flax, and sunflower seeds on the sidewalk, walkway, steps, and hall, then shower and get ready for my date.

I put on a bunch of makeup to cover my freckles, then wipe it all off and opt for just a touch of blush. I put on my nicer jeans and a decent top, and that will have to do.

Ugh. I hate dates. When you call it a date it has more chance of being mediocre than anything. So why am I so nervous? I can do the cheery banter, the conversation-making, even if it's a false version of myself. I'd really like to drop that for once.

Adlai's house is near a lake bordered by rushes. Live oak trees adorned with air plants and Spanish moss shade frame bungalows built in the 1920s and '30s. I don't tell him about my very weird, bird-seedy day. Instead, I let him give me a tour of the house. He shows me the renovations he's done, expanding the kitchen and putting in a bank of windows and French doors along the back.

"This is nice," I comment idly. "Your contractor did a good job."

"Well then, I thank you."

"You didn't do this all yourself."

He nods. "I'm the only contractor I know who's completely honest."

"Yeah," I say. "I wonder sometimes if real honesty even exists anymore."

He turns from the window. "I certainly hope so."

I raise my eyebrows. I'm the one who didn't want stupid chitchat. "So how about you? Have you achieved complete honesty every minute of your life?"

He leans against the butcher block counter. "Every minute? Not a chance. I was a bad kid. Checkered youth, and all that."

"And what about now?" I think of that guy Garf talking to Adlai in the canoe shop.

"Now?" he says. "My number one rule is: Never lie."

"Wait, never? You *never* lie?"

"Want to see the rest of the house?" He turns and walks to the stairs.

We ascend and he shows me the roof he raised to make an airy, light-filled bedroom. It has the feel of a tree house. But of course, here I am in his bedroom. Seduction itself is frequently based on half-truths—self-deception at the very least. If he kisses me, I'm leaving. Because I know myself, and I know it won't stop there.

"Are ya with me?" he says. He's already halfway down the stairs.

"Oh, right," I say. "Yeah."

Built-in bookshelves line the staircase, and as I descend, I read the spines: *Bleak House. Tales of the Argonauts. Plato's Republic. Field Guide to the Sierra Nevada. The Seminoles of Florida. Life of Pi. How to Read Water. Complete Works of Lewis Carroll. Angle of Repose.* If a personal library is like a fingerprint, then I like the hands that collected these books.

Downstairs, we continue the conversation about truthfulness. "So you're telling me you never tell one lie."

"Most people think that's a good thing." He walks toward the open kitchen.

What I don't say is that I myself have a few lies going. One big lie of omission to Phil, about my father's "accident." Another, maybe tacit lie—reading my mother's journal without telling her. And Estelle would call me dishonest right here and now for forgetting yet again to tell Adlai where I really live.

"Yes, of course it's a good thing," I say. "Veracity makes for a civilized society. But most people slip every once in a while."

"Think about it," he says. "Just deciding to tell the truth all the time means you've got less chaos. It makes life simpler."

I lean on the counter and watch him pull food from the fridge—chives, tomatoes, squash. "Okay," I say, "but what if somebody gets a really bad haircut and says, 'How do you like my hair?' What do you say then?"

He turns on a burner and pours olive oil into a skillet. "I smile real encouragingly and say, 'You got it cut!'"

"So you avoid the question."

"Look," he says. "You may have noticed I'm not exactly a chatterbox. When I do say something, it might as well be true."

But if he omits unpleasant truths, is that so different from what I've left out of my conversations with him? He tosses cut-up vegetables into the skillet.

"Okay," I say. "How about this. What if your boss gets a facelift and he's so different he's almost unrecognizable?"

Adlai turns. "Has this happened to you?"

"Not at all."

"Well, imagining that I actually had a boss, I'd say, 'Who are you and what have you done with the other guy?'"

I laugh, and he lets out a short guffaw. He takes a wooden spoon from a drawer and stirs the contents of the skillet, covers the pan, and says, "Just a few minutes now. Want to take a load off?" He gestures toward the couch and sits next to me, not too close, not too far.

"So, tell me about your family," he says, turning a conversational corner.

"Oh." I pause. "Well, I have a brother in Spring Creek, just outside Tenetkee." He seems to want more. "A mother right in Tenetkee." A pause. "My father's dead." I study the weave of the couch.

I can feel icicles forming on our previously warm conversation. But if I told him my story, even if I knew it well enough myself, he'd be appalled. So I detour. "What *I'm* interested in is hydrogeology."

He takes up the change. "Well, it may not sound like it, but it's a very useful degree. For instance," he says, deadpan, "no one's gonna sell me Florida swampland for a bargain, unless Florida swampland is what I want." He waits for my smile. "And when I did my trip across the state—"

"You mean across Alligator Alley?"

"No, woman, not in a car, in a canoe."

"You crossed Florida in a canoe? The whole state?"

"Only once. I was raising money for the conservation group I told you about. Anyway, it gave me a lot of time alone, and I got to thinking about all the water in this state, above ground and below, and I thought, it's a generous thing, water. It sustains so many complex systems. Plants, animals, birds. Us."

He stares into the distance. Then he looks back to me. "You don't get bit by that many mosquitoes on one trip without having it change you." He smiles. "So here was my epiphany, one night, watching the sun set over a small lake I may never find again. I'd already spent ten years on the policy side of conservation, staying current on the science, testifying before land-use committees and city council meetings, debating the issues with people just this side of brimstone, and waking up at night thinking about how greedy and clever and shortsighted and downright stupid some people could be. Just before I left on the trip, I'd been asked to run for office myself. I stared across the lake that night and knew that propelling myself across all that water under my own power was teaching me something about simplicity. The next day I adjusted my route, resupplied in Moore Haven, and started heading north instead of east."

I imagine him in his birchbark canoe, the muscles in his shoulders pulling at the water, stroke after stroke.

"The whole time I was paddling, I felt like the water was drawing me toward someplace specific. I didn't know where, but I was ready to follow. And when I'd almost run out of supplies, I found the canoe shop with a 'For Sale' sign. Could have been hunger and fatigue, but I had a strong sense I was in the right place at exactly the right moment. So I went home, figured out the financing, and bought the shop."

"Well, I'm glad you did," I say, about to make a crack about the discounts I've been getting.

But he stops me, gently cupping my face in his hand. "I'm glad, too." He strokes my cheek with his thumb and says, "Lucky me." He leans closer, but just then the kitchen timer beeps.

"Dinner," I say, and get up to move toward the table.

After we eat, complete with a crème brûlée he made himself, I say thank you and he walks me outside. I'm careful not to touch him, and he must sense my caution, because when we get to my car, he gives me a shy kiss good night, and simply takes my hand. I draw him closer, and then we are kissing deeply, time disappearing as we stand under the live oak trees with the Spanish moss cascading down. Before I die from want, I have to stop this, but not just yet.

At last we separate, breathe, and I reach for my keys. "Dinner," I say with more emphasis than I intend, "was delicious."

47

APRIL 30

Leaving the Geezer Palace today, I'm distracted again by the TV's noon news, murder and mayhem, and the same yellow-haired reporter I've seen before. Just as I start to turn away, the reporter's name comes up at the bottom of the screen. I look back, but it's already disappeared. Did it say Rabideaux? As in Joleen Rabideaux, my mother's neighbor? The reporter is about my age. But Joleen didn't have any kids.

I stare, watching the reporter's lips move. The Rabideauxs did have a niece who used to come down from Tallahassee, and Joleen would bring her over to play with me. She had a funny first name like Kicky or Khaki, and she didn't like the outdoors. I'd try to get her to play my usual pretend games at the edge of the marsh, acting out my favorite stories from *Journeys Through Bookland*, but she insisted we go inside, where she would dump her boatload of Barbie dolls on the braided rug in our Florida room and stretch shiny bathing suits over their weirdly twisted arms, all the while telling me scary gossip about children being taken by swamp men and enslaved. She sounded just like her Aunt Joleen hashing over all the terrible headlines on the porch with my mom.

Could this TV reporter be that kid? She's telling about a horrific local murder, and a whisper of a smile plays around her mouth.

Mariama comes up. "Mm. Mm. Mm." She shakes her head. "A crazy world." She pronounces it "weld."

The shot switches back to the anchor, who says, "Thanks, Kacki."

The big sign outside announces "Tallahassee NewsChannel 5." I enter the lobby and approach the gleaming receptionist's desk. A petite woman in her twenties wears a delicate headset. Lights blink on a console. "One moment please," she says to a caller, pressing a button and looking up at me.

"Hi. I wanted to leave a message for Kacki Rabideaux?"

The receptionist presses a button and I hear her voice over the loudspeaker. "Kacki Rabideaux, please come to the front desk. Kacki Rabideaux to the front desk, please."

"Oh, I didn't mean . . . You didn't have to . . . Is she here?"

"Don't worry, she'll come. I don't have much power in this place, but they all come running when I do that." She smiles.

And she's right. In a brief moment, Kacki's in the lobby, looking at the receptionist, then at me.

"Kacki?" I expected to have more trouble reaching her.

"Yeah, hi." She shakes my hand. She's bigger and more brightly blond than she looks on TV.

"Hi! I'm, uh, Loni Murrow."

"Okay." She moves over toward the curving white couch. "Here, have a seat. So do you have a problem with a company, something you want Contact 5 to investigate?" She folds one ample leg under the other.

"Contact 5? No, I . . . um . . . you wouldn't remember me, but we used to play together as children. In Tenetkee, when you came to visit your Aunt Joleen."

There's a pause. She pulls back her head.

I keep talking. "My parents had the place on the marsh not far from your aunt and uncle's. Loni Murrow."

She seems to rummage around for the memory. Then her voice tarnishes. "Oh yeah, I remember you. 'Nature's Child,' my aunt used to call you." She puts one arm over the back of the couch.

"Really?" I say. "Huh."

"Well, it's been a lot of years. Did you move away?" Her eyeliner, top and bottom, is perfect, her jawline burnished with blush.

I nod.

"And you're not needing me to go after some crooked company on the air?"

"No, actually, I saw your aunt in the grocery store, and I wanted to get back in touch with her."

She drops any vestige of the public-pleasing persona. "Yeah, well, I'm in touch with her every day, her and her two-hundred-pound oak table and her wall-size mirror and the forty-nine African violets she treats like her children. Every one of them has a name." She stops and looks for my reaction, then goes on. "Not like a plant name, but like, Herman, Prudence, Dick! She actually calls one of them Dick." She laughs. "I know it sounds mean, and she is helping me out. She and Uncle Marvin came down from North Carolina when my baby was born five months ago. I won't bore you with the cute pictures. But Aunt Joleen said they were only moving in 'temporarily.'"

"Really? So she hasn't lived in Tallahassee all this time?"

"Not for years, till now."

That's not what Joleen told me in the grocery. "Well, I would love to go visit her. . . ."

Kacki eyes me. "Do you think you could get her to move out of my place?"

"Maybe they could buy back their old house," I say. "You know, do some renovations . . ."

"You think I haven't suggested that? Aunt Joleen acts like it's radio-active. She says she needs to stay with me to take care of my baby. But just between you and me, it'd be a whole lot easier if she lived at her own house and just came over when I went to work."

"Well, maybe Mr. Perkins could find her a different—"

"Elbert Perkins? The real estate dude? Also radioactive."

"Hm," I say. "Well, in the meantime, do you think I might call, or . . . or visit?"

"On one condition." She leans forward. "Please try to convince her she should live someplace else? I'll give you my address." She gets up and swipes a blank sticky note from the receptionist without asking, scribbles on it, and hands it to me. "Don't mind the mess, it's their fault. And you can see my baby Amber! Tell her I say hi."

"Right. Thanks, Kacki. Any special time I should go?"

"Nope! They're there twenty-four/seven. They treat my place like it's their doomsday bunker. Uncle Marvin is sittin' in my chair right now, I guarantee, with the remote in his hand. I haven't changed the channel myself since I gave birth."

I push open the glass door. "Well, nice seeing you."

"Yeah, sure," she says, and disappears inside.

48

The home is a prefab, good sized and well maintained like its neighbors, with a crisscross fence marking off a small raised porch, and a twirly wind catcher in the front, spinning in the breeze. It's in the neighborhood on the other side of the woods from the Science Museum. I tap a hollow knock at the door. In a minute, a wide little head pushes aside a yellow curtain. Joleen. Her eyes expand. The curtain covers the window again and she says, "Who is it?"

"Hi, Mrs. Rabideaux. It's Loni Murrow. We saw each other in the grocery store?"

The door opens a crack.

"What do you want?"

"Just to come in and chat, if I could."

Her eyes go left, right. "Anybody with you?"

"No, ma'am."

"How'd you find me?"

"Kacki said to come on over."

"Kacki?" The space between door and doorjamb gets a half inch bigger. "Well . . . come in, then, I guess." She opens the door quick and closes it almost before I'm all the way inside.

A male voice calls, "Who is it?"

"Nobody, Marvin!" To me, she says, "Have a seat, why don'tcha?" I'm in a tiny living room with a short couch and a big chair. Kacki's right. There's too much furniture for this small place. And I see at least some of the African violets, lining the bookshelf and crowding the side table.

"I like your plants," I say.

"Aren't they the best?" she says, smiling for the first time. "Temperamental. They let me know when they're upset."

On the floor are some baby toys, a blanket.

"So now, whatcha got?" She sits and presses her palms to the knees of her beige knit pants.

I take the adjacent chair. "Oh, I just wanted to visit."

"Hm."

I sink into the upholstery. I'm here to find out what Joleen knows about my father's death, and also, who is Henrietta? "So," I say. "You moved away for a while?" A warm-up.

She stops and thinks. "What did Kacki tell you?"

"Just that you came back to help with the baby."

"Oh, just *wait* till she wakes up! Baby Amber looks just like her mama. She is so sweet. Except when she cries. Then she screws her face all up and gives you the what-for." Mrs. Rabideaux laughs. I remember that laugh now, the wrinkled nose and the teeth together, eyes closed.

"Would you want to come visit my mom, ever, Mrs. Rabideaux?" It's not really why I'm here, but Mom might like to see her.

"In Tenetkee?" Her eyes get big again. "Well . . . one day, maybe." I can tell she doesn't mean it.

"Mrs. Rabideaux, are you afraid of something in Tenetkee?"

"Who me? No!"

I wait until she speaks again.

"It's just that, we left in kind of a rush. And some people are still mad at me for not . . . telling them we were leaving."

"Why *did* you leave so fast, Mrs. Rabideaux?"

"Well now, Marvin had his surgery, the gallbladder, and then he got another job, and, the usual things, you know."

"But you moved out of your house in the middle of the night?"

"No."

"Would you want to move back into your old house?"

"Oh, dear, no."

I open my mouth, but she goes on.

"We're just here for temporary, you know. Just to help out Kacki."

"But in the grocery, didn't you say you'd been living in Tallahassee since I was little?"

"Did I say that?" Her eyes go to the ceiling.

Why is she telling me two different stories?

Marvin appears in the doorway with a napkin tucked into his collar. He's strongly built, but thick around the neck and middle, with graying hair parted on the side and slicked over.

"Who are *you*?" He still has the deep voice that always made people say he should be on the broadcast radio, not just the Fish & Game two-way. Funny to think how important those two-way radios were for my dad and the other officers in the days before digital.

Joleen gets up. "Now Marvin, this is Loni Murrow, remember, Ruth and *Boyd* Murrow?" She slows down on my father's name.

He stares at me. "You're the daughter." His lips don't quite close after he says it.

I nod.

"Shit," he says.

"Marvin, you go back and finish your sandwich. And watch your mouth."

He turns around and goes back toward the other room.

"Don't mind him and that foul language." Joleen's fingers play with the lace doily over the arm of the couch. "Oh, I think I hear the baby!"

I hear nothing.

She gets up and leaves, then comes back in, bouncing up and down with a small, sleepy baby in her arms. "This is Amber! Say hi, Amber!"

Of course, the child is too small to do anything but stare in an unfocused, bobbly-headed way, and the bouncing only makes little Amber even more unfocused.

"You'll have to excuse us. Baby needs to eat. Don't you, baby? It was real nice seeing you, Loni. Now, don't tell the folks in Tenetkee you seen us, right?" Her eyes hold mine. "It's awkward, like I said."

I nod as I get up. "Hey, Mrs. Rabideaux, do you remember someone named Henrietta? Because I found a note from her . . ."

She gets that saucer-eyed look again. "Oh, no, me oh my. Nobody that I can think of." With tiny bouncing steps, she moves me in the direction of the door.

I turn. "Listen, before I go, would you mind if I asked Mr. Rabideaux . . ." Mr. Rabideaux appears in the living room doorway again, minus the napkin. "Mr. Rabideaux. I had a question for you about Dan Watson." I pull out the incident report. "See, he signed a report that said—"

"Get out," he says.

"Sorry?"

"I said get out!"

I look to Mrs. Rabideaux. She shrugs. "Well, nice seeing you, Loni, you better just . . ." She scoots me toward the door. Then, looking out the yellow curtain first, turns the knob and nudges me out. "Toodle-oo!" she says, and slams the door behind me.

I stand outside and watch the curtain swish back and forth until it comes to rest. I knock again. "Mrs. Rabideaux!" I rap harder. "Mrs. Rabideaux!"

There is no response.

I pound my feet back to my car. Mrs. Rabideaux definitely knows Henrietta. It was clear in the way she denied it. And Dan Watson's name sure pressed a hot button for Marvin.

What are they afraid of?

49

MAY 1

Just as I pull into a parking space at the Geezer Palace, my phone buzzes. A text from Theo: "Update?" The man does not do long messages.

I let my thumbs hover. "Making good progress," I respond. "Back soon."

I can tell he's typing, but I wait and wait before his message pops up: "It is now May."

"Back soon," I type again.

I'm determined to make my last few visits with my mom upbeat, even if she's unable to give me any of the warmth I might hope for. Today I've brought her an old poem from a guy named Barhydt, who visited Florida in the 1800s. I tuck the volume under my elbow and go inside.

"Hi, Mom!"

She doesn't respond.

"Mom. Hello!"

She sits in the vinyl chair, dressed in an aqua sweater set, but she might as well be a mannequin in Velma's dress shop window. Her eyes are focused somewhere beyond me. I try to penetrate the armor a few more times. "Mom. Mom?"

Nothing.

Well, I guess staying positive is pointless. Even on a good day, which today decidedly is not, there's precious little I can do to change the prevailing wind. Maybe the mature response is to quit trying.

I throw old Barhydt back into my bag and pull out my sketchbook. I flip through all the incomplete pictures I've drawn of my mother— her back at the piano, her back in the garden, and several imprecise versions of the young Ruth at the clothesline in the rain. I still don't really know her, and probably never will.

I go to look for Mariama, but she's busy with another resident, so I get a cup of coffee from the machine and flood it with Cremora and sugar. As I've learned, I could go back to Mom's room in ten minutes and she might be perfectly fine. But in the meantime, what do I do? I have her journal in my bag, never meant for me to read. I sit in a cushioned chair in the lobby and take it out.

My mother's voice in these pages is just as complicated as she ever was in real life. But if she's sitting blankly and giving me nothing, maybe the journal is all I've got.

My circle planting is growing, and my squares of thyme and lemon balm hold their shape, for now. This garden is so different from the straight rows I planted at first, carrots and onions and cabbages. Mother Lorna came down here in a silk scarf to say, loudly enough for Boyd to hear, You mean he expects you to farm? I shushed her, but she went on in full voice, Ruth, moving to the country doesn't mean you have to <u>be</u> country.

She considered "being country" her worst insult.

Well, I was proud of my neat Beatrix Potter rows. The blight took the carrots, but the onions held on, and so did the cabbages, which proved useful in a terrible way. Joleen said, Put those cabbage leaves right in your bra. Dries up the milk. I took her advice, desperate to relieve the fullness and pain, my body reminding me every second of the baby who should have been at my breast. After the hospital, Boyd and I couldn't stand to be in the house, so we dropped Loni off at Mother's. The ruckus that girl put up—ten years old and wailing—Mama! Mama! I had to close my ears.

Boyd took me to the fishing camp, but he did not fish. We canoed around, and all was quiet, except for that awful bird—it sounded like a baby crying. At night, while Boyd pushed the cots together, I reached into my brassiere to replace the wilting cabbage leaves with the fresh ones I had brought. I pressed them against my weeping breasts, and we tried to laugh. Cabbage leaves! But no laughter could lift the weight of that absence. In the night, that horrible bird called out, three short bursts, then five, six. Wailing over and over. In my fractured sleep it was the baby. She hadn't been killed by the fall, just wanted to be fed. Why wasn't I feeding her? And then the dream changed, and the cry was from Loni, calling from Mother Lorna's doorway, Mama! Mama! Not my fault!

I look up without seeing. Not my fault? It says, *killed by the fall.* I read it once more. And right there in the lobby, something I must have known all my life, and at the same time refused to know, subsumes me like a sinkhole. I am Alice, falling and falling, fragmented images appearing around me in the dark: A pair of flat loafers, stepped down in the back. Two small yellow Wellingtons, stuck in mud. The stream, a plank for a wobbly bridge. A ten-year-old girl determined to walk through the marsh. One step, another, grass up to my eyes, sharp against my skin. The third step sinks. I try to pull it up, but the other foot sinks too. Mud holds me tight. A mosquito sings in my ear, bites my arm.

"Loni! Lunchtime!"

I twist around, see her at the bottom of the tree. "Mama! I'm here!" She looks around.

"Here!"

"Lorna Mae Murrow! What are you doing?"

She's on the other side of the creek.

"Pick up your feet and get out of there." Hands on her hips.

"I can't."

"Pull at the top of your boot."

I try, but it is stuck fast.

She stands and glares at me a long second. Then she starts across the board I laid across the stream for a bridge. She is so fat lately, and she makes the plank wobble. Her shoes flap in the back. She tightrope-walks over.

"Stretch your arms up, Loni, and lean back." Her hands squeeze mine and pull. My feet slip out of the boots and the wet ground soaks my shorts.

"Now, get up and follow me back over the creek."

She steps back onto the plank, but it slips, and she slides in slow motion down the muddy bank until she bumps to the bottom, sitting on the creek bed in water up to her middle. The creek is not deep. I slide down the bank to help, stumbling facedown. She is trying not to laugh. We sit there, both of us drenched, and we begin to giggle.

But a few days later she started having pains, bad ones. She called Joleen, who told Marvin to get my dad on the two-way. Daddy screeched into the yard, carried my mother to the truck, and told me to go to the Rabideauxs'. He pulled out of the driveway fast.

I spent two long days at Joleen Rabideaux's in a bedroom smelling of warm plastic and old radio parts, wondering why my parents had abandoned me. And then suddenly I was at Grandmother Lorna's, standing by her wrought-iron screen door.

Daddy said, "Mama doesn't feel good, Loni Mae. We'll be back for you on Monday." Mama would not look at me.

"Don't leave me," I said, and turned to my mother. "Mama."

But the wrought-iron screen door slapped against the casing, clicking shut and locked.

"Mama!" I called, grasping the wrought iron and shaking it. "Mama!" They were walking away, and she would not turn around. I knew I was too big to cry, but my sobs were high-pitched and slurpy. "Mama!"

I must have dropped these pictures in a deep well, hoping never to see them again. But here they are, courtesy of one *GARDEN* journal. How could I not have made this connection before? Here, in my mother's careful penmanship, our entire troubled, mixed-up history falls into place like the tumblers of a locked safe. This is the reason I could never please my mother. Her little chick fell from the nest. And I gave it a push.

A thin, gray-haired man runs his walker over my toes, and the lobby of the Geezer Palace rematerializes. I get up from my seat but do not go back to my mother's room. Instead, I stumble out to the bright, burning blacktop of the St. A's parking lot and drive away. I pass the vacant Rabideaux place with its graying shutters, and then I pull into the driveway of my old house, the scene of my crime.

Mr. Meldrum comes around from the back, pulling off gardening gloves. In his white T-shirt, he's an egg in overalls.

I get out, rubbing my sweaty palms on the sides of my jeans. "Hello." I muster a flatline cordiality. "I was just driving by, and . . ."

"Well, Phil was here yesterday. Fixed a little drip for us upstairs. The hot-water knob wouldn't shut for love nor money. . . ." Mr. Meldrum's cheeks are pink.

"You're gardening," I say without affect.

"Yeah. Come on back if you want. Got a lot to do before we lose the sun."

I follow. Why am I here? Maybe to see the stream and the mud, to confirm my own culpability. Or maybe I'm here for the healing herbs.

"I got my crop of Early Girls here. . . ." We round the corner of the house, and he indicates a row of scrawny, staked tomato vines. "And then four rows of hot peppers over here."

"Wait, where's the herb garden?" My mother's orderly geometrics have given way to mounds of dirt, a few struggling plants. This is not the yard we relinquished mere weeks ago.

"Ah, well, Lorraine and I, we're not into the herbs. We couldn't tell you what's a herb and what's a weed."

"Oh." I turn away. "Oh, no."

"What is it?" he says. "You sick?"

"I have to go." I lurch toward the car, mumbling. I look back at what used to be my home, and reverse my car without looking. All Ruth's treasures torn out by the roots. What will I tell her? *Sorry for your loss?*

No. I will not tell her a thing.

50

MAY 2

The morning sun slices through the apartment's blinds. I throw my arm across my face and lie still as a corpse in the unwashed sheets. The robot in my brain says, *Work.* I force myself up and stumble toward the rickety Formica table.

Pencil. Blank sheet. Dead bird. Dead tree.

Outside, the sun blazes. Inside my skull, heat lightning.

Draw. Florida sandhill crane. *Last one.*

I make a line. Two. Three. I bargain. If I stay out of bed, I can lay my head on the table.

What I need is self-heal. From the garden. But the garden has been slashed and burned.

The wall phone rings. Who knows that number? Can't think. Another ring. Three times. Four. A baritone "hello." The previous tenant lives on in his outmoded machine. "You have reached—" *Beep.* "Hi. It's Estelle again. I called your cell, but you must have it on mute. Call me when you get in?"

She knows I'm in. She wants a bird. Four birds. On a tree. I sigh. Another ring. Machine clicks and whirrs. "Hello, you have reached—" The tape hums, beeps. *Stop calling, Estelle.*

A pause. A man's voice. "Hey." Pause. "Just wondering what happened to you yesterday. I thought we were supposed to . . . Hell, I hate voice mail. Just call and tell me if we're still on for tonight."

I lift my head, stand, walk to the wall, pick up the handset. "Adlai."

"Hey," he says. He waits.

I wait.

His voice says, "So, should I . . . Are you . . ."

I say nothing.

"What's going on?" His voice at the end of a long tunnel.

"What's going on," I echo.

He waits.

I speak. "Should I tell you the truth, or a lie?"

"I beg your pardon?" Dead air. "Loni, you're sounding kind of weird. Should I call back later?"

"No." I hold the heavy receiver. "You don't want to talk to a liar."

"Whoa," he says. "Are you in some kind of trouble? Do you want me to come up there?"

"Please don't."

"Oh." He doesn't say anything for a second. "Sorry, I guess I'm missing something."

"Yeah."

He waits. "Are you, uh, givin' me the shove?"

"Sounds like it."

There's a long silence. Then a click.

I walk out from the kitchen. Sit on the paisley love seat. Minutes pass. Too bad he called. No taking it back. *What's going on?* he said. What could I have said? *Just found out why my mom can't stand me. But y'all have a nice day.*

I sit and stare. Like sitting under a cloud.

Are they weeding? she'll say. Oh, yeah, Ma. They're weeding. Gettin' all those dang weeds right on out of there.

Estelle calls again and talks to the air. "Loni, I'm sorry. You don't have to put all four birds on one tree. Just return my call. Please do not be mad at me." She's mixing work and friendship like she said she wouldn't. Poor Estelle. Don't take it personal-like.

I still have on pajamas. I bargain. I can go back to bed if I bring my sketchbook.

I prop the pillow, grip my pencil, close my eyes. I didn't say I had to draw.

After a few minutes, I open my eyes, and my hand moves. It begins to outline a bird—the one that can swim and walk and fly. Not for Estelle. Only me. The bird perches with wings open to dry like a cape, beak pointing upward. Water, earth, sky. *Anhinga anhinga*. The bird that fears no element.

New blank page. Red receding hairline. Bustle of rump feathers. Florida sandhill crane, dancing in short, stubby grass. Where it belongs.

I flip again. Hand works faster than head. Four birds, same page. Woodpecker. Eagle. Blue heron. Crane. Each in its own habitat. I add details, get the *gizz*.

I rest my head back. One thing, at least, is set right.

Darkness for a while. Then, eyes open to slits. Hand moving again. A leaf, large and rough, a thorny stalk, blue flower. *I borage bring courage.* Then a saw-toothed leaf. Lemon balm. *Soothe all troublesome care.* Marigold—*cureth the trembling of harte.* Perhaps their medicine will cross through the cell walls of my drawing hand.

The plants grow into a schematic, a garden, geometrically arranged. I consult the crackly herbals by my bed. Chamomile, catmint, sorrel. In Latin: *Matricaria chamomilla, Nepeta X faassenii, Rumex acetosa.* I get out of bed, retrieve my colored pencils, come back.

The smell of earth fills the room. Root and flower and loam. Decay and regeneration. Mullein and comfrey, costmary, feverfew, betony. I sink into the earth, below verbena and lavender, descending as I draw.

I work all day. I fall asleep among books and sketches, wake in the night, and push them to the side. When the sun comes back, I draw more. The phone rings and the machine beeps and I don't listen. I keep drawing. I will give my mother a piece of what she lost.

At midnight I know I will not sleep.

When the sun shines pink through the blinds, I shower. Dress. Point the car south. I taste the dry-mouthed hunger of no sleep, day for night, the scratchy eyeballs and the racing heart. I roll down the windows. On the passenger seat, I touch the drawings, now in a heavy paper folio. They must not fly. This is a new *GARDEN* book. Intended for its proper owner.

But one stop first, to mend something I broke.

51

Adlai stands on his threshold with me outside. He hasn't yet shaved. His T-shirt is wrinkled. Has he slept in his clothes?

"Hello." He is formal.

"Hi."

He waits.

"I wanted to catch you before work," I say.

He stands two feet of wooden porch away. "And you're here because?"

I breathe. "Because I fractured something . . . I value."

"Uh-huh." He doesn't move.

I nod my head up and down, up and down.

"So what'd you lie about?" he says.

"I beg your pardon?"

"You said you were a liar. Did you tell me a big lie or a lot of little lies?" His eyes narrow, like I'm the bank robber come to dynamite his safe.

"Look, everybody lies. You're the only pillar of truth I know."

"Me and the woman I end up with."

Oof. "All right, well, I came here to apologize, because when you called, I was upset about . . . something else."

He stares hard.

"And just now I was thinking, if I came back to grovel, you might consider . . . still wanting to—"

"What'd you lie about?" He stands like a guard at the gate.

"What did I lie about? I lied about my address."

"What?"

"I don't actually live here . . . in Florida."

He turns his head to the side, then back to me. "So where do you live?"

"Washington."

"Hm. So it's *not* a borrowed car. And you live there, like, all the time."

I nod.

"I get it. You're what they call an adventurer."

"What?"

"And I'm part of the adventure."

"Wait. No. I am not . . ."

Behind his eyes a door slams shut.

I stammer, "That is not . . . You obviously have no idea . . . I do not . . ."

His silence is a mirror. I see myself, arms flailing, face flushed, hair in tatters.

"Bye-bye, Loni," he says, and steps inside his house, closing the door with a gentle *click*.

I stand there for a minute, then turn and walk down his porch steps. *Shit*. All the way to the car, I curse myself for losing this lodestone of a man.

I get to the driver's side door, stop, and look up. No. I should pound on his walls, scream at his window, cause a scene. Tell him I tried *not* to fall for him. But nothing I say will do any good. I open the car door, get in, and pull away fast. When I'm halfway down the block, my phone vibrates on the passenger seat, next to the booklet of drawings. He's calling to say, *Come back*. I don't take my eyes off the road. "Hi," I say.

"Hey, did you forget our breakfast?"

It's not Adlai. It's Phil. "What?" I take a minute. "Breakfast? No. I mean, no, of course I didn't forget." Except I did, completely.

"I'm sittin' here at the Egg House. How far are you?"

"I'm like, right around the corner," I lie.

"Okay, I'll see you in a minute, then."

It's good to have someplace to go. I park in front of the Egg House and hurry in, banging the door louder than I mean to. I scan the place. Phil stands and waves. I go over and give him a big hug. He doesn't know what to do with that. We sit.

The service is prompt, and within minutes I'm stuffing my face with pancakes and eggs.

Phil stares at me. "Are you all right, Loni?" he says.

"Yeah, sorry, I just forgot to eat last night." And maybe all of yesterday.

"Okay."

"Why?" I ask. "Am I acting strange?"

"No, nothin'." He lifts his neat little breakfast sandwich. He doesn't have to push anything around on his plate, because he has the sausage, cheese, egg, and starch all in one bite. He chews it up and then says, "I, uh, got that address, you know, the one in Panama City. Tammy said to print you out the map to Mrs. Chappelle's."

He pushes a sheet of paper toward my plate. Step-by-step directions. "Probably best just to show up, not call first."

I let out a sigh. "Oh, that." But I don't touch the paper.

The restaurant door pops open, letting in a rectangle of light, and a small boy with a crew cut shoots toward our table. "Daddy!" Bobby catapults himself at Phil.

Tammy click-clacks behind. "We just came from the Minute Clinic. You know why your son's throat was so red? He's got a stash of Jolly Ranchers somewhere near his headboard. And he's going to show me exactly where it is when we get home. Right, Bobby?"

Bobby looks at me, then her, and nods.

Tammy looks at the map next to my plate. "So you're finally keepin' up your part of the bargain?"

I put the paper into my bag. "Right."

Tammy herds Bobby off to school, and I reach for the check.

Phil says, "Can I ask you a favor?"

I look up. What new, nearly impossible task have he and Tammy devised for me?

"Can you try not to fight with Mom?"

I straighten up, let out a breath.

He waits.

"Phil, do you think I don't try, every time I see her, not to fight? I do not like fighting. Mom, however, sometimes seems to enjoy it."

"Hey," he says, "you'd be cranky too, if you were in her position."

"Thank you, golden child who never does anything wrong in her eyes."

"Hey, she was tough on me, after you left home."

"Please."

"Well, she had shit to be unhappy about. She'd lost her husband, had to raise me by herself, teach those squeaky band classes."

"She did always come home in a bad mood from those."

"She wasn't always easy on me, but at some point I quit taking it personally."

"That's very mature of you."

"Anyway, I saw you two every time you came home, like two cats full of static electricity, rubbing past each other and jumping back, fur all standing on end. And I decided I didn't want what you two had." He taps his fork on his empty plate. "And now that she's . . . you know—"

"Losing it."

He nods.

Poor Phil. I thought it was hard for *me* to realize I was a grown-up. He's only been adulting for a few years himself, and he's watching his mom fade away.

"All I'm asking," he says, "is that you make an effort."

I bob my head. "Yes," I say.

Phil goes back to work and I take the check to the front. As I'm coming out the door of the Egg House, a very short person accosts me. Joleen Rabideaux.

"Was that young man your brother?" she says. She clutches my forearm with her small, stubby hand.

"Uh, yeah," I say.

"And he works for that law firm, don't he?"

"Well, he shares office space . . . um . . . How are you, Mrs. Rabideaux? Nice to see you."

She looks left and then right. "They've ruined our house, you know. If you want to check somethin' out, check out our house. Investments Ink, my eye."

"Really? Who owns it now?"

"Bunch o' thugs. Bought it up, ruined it."

"Hm. That's what Mr. Barber said about his—"

"Nelson Barber?" Her nails dig into my arm.

"Yes. Ow."

"Where'd you see him?" The whites of her eyes are visible all the way around.

"Well . . ."

"No. Don't tell me. I don't want to know anything. I just passed by, saw you in there with your lawyer brother . . ."

"He's not a—"

"And just wanted to say don't pay no mind to my Marvin. He's got the arteries, you know. Don't always say what he should. Now, I shouldn't of stopped. Don't tell anyone you saw me." She turns away, the purse on her forearm swinging behind her.

"What? Why not?"

She looks back. "No reason! Just passin' the time of day. Toodle-oo!"

"But Mrs. Rabideaux!" I chase after her. She's a brisk little walker for her age and size. "Mrs. Rabideaux!"

I catch up to her, but Marvin has their Buick running, and she gets in.

"Truly," I say, "I'd like to figure some things out. Can't we just—"

"Toodle-oo!" she says again, and Marvin starts to pull away.

Before I know what I'm doing, I'm pulling open the back door and getting in. Marvin is gaining speed, and the door is still not closed.

"What the hell you doin'?" he shouts.

I pull the door shut and turn toward the front seat. "Mrs. Rabideaux, you've got to tell me who Henrietta is."

"Don't know no Henrietta!" she shouts.

"I think you do."

Marvin turns his head away from the road and toward me. "You better get outta this car before I throw you out!" He swerves and Joleen screams. Marvin looks to the front.

"Why did y'all move away?"

Joleen says, "You're gonna get us killed!"

Marvin shoots her a look. "Woman, shut your mouth!"

Joleen looks to her husband. "I will not! Maybe she wants to get us killed. Maybe she's in with them! I saw her goin' into the house."

"What?" I say. "Look, all I want to know is how my dad died."

Joleen takes a breath and turns toward me, mouth open.

Marvin says to her, "You better zip your lip, Joleen. I told you we should never of come back here! That lawyer brother of hers could be in on it too. He ain't gonna help us."

"Mr. Rabideaux," I say, "what are you so afraid of?"

Marvin stomps on the brake and the Buick fishtails. From under his seat, he produces a pistol. "Get out of this car or I'll shoot your fool head off. I ain't afraid of nothin'. Call *me* a coward. Get out."

I open the door. "Look, this has all gone a little too far."

"Get!" Marvin says, steadying the weapon.

I exit the car on the side of the road in the middle of nowhere.

Joleen looks back at me as they speed away.

52

For twenty minutes or so, I walk back in the direction we came from. I see no sign of civilization. It seemed like only a few minutes passed while I was in their car, but I was too preoccupied with the craziness of the ride to watch which turns Mr. Rabideaux took. I must be somewhere in the wildlife refuge. This small road surrounded by pines is not one I recognize.

On another day, I'd be up for a walk, but I didn't sleep last night, my personal life is in ruins, and I was just threatened by a man with a gun. Heat pummels the top of my head. Still, I keep moving.

Far behind me, I hear the sound of a car. I know all the terrifying stories about hitchhikers found naked and partially buried in the woods, and yet I turn and stick out my thumb. I can't make out the car, but as it approaches and slows, I drop my hand and smile. It's a Fish & Game Suburban, and behind the wheel, a friendly face.

I hop in. "Captain Chappelle, Oh my God! I'm so lucky this is an area you patrol."

"Loni Mae, how'd you come to be walking here?"

"I had kind of a . . . wild encounter with Joleen and Marvin Rabideaux."

His front wheels are out on the road, and he stops. "Are they back in town?" His eyes go to the rearview, the side mirrors. "Well, that's good news." He accelerates. "I always liked that Marvin. Didn't he have some health problems?"

"I think so, yeah."

"Marvin. He used to hunt gators, back before they were endangered. Just a hobby, of course." He smiles. "I wonder if he's still doin' that."

"I wonder."

"So what did ol' Marvin have to say for himself?" Captain Chappelle turns down the squawking dispatch radio.

"Well, he wasn't too happy with me."

"No?"

"I was asking him, well, some of the questions you and I talked about. You know, about my dad."

The wheels hum on the pavement. "And what'd he say?"

"Not much."

He nods, two hands on top of the steering wheel. From where I sit, his face looks all healed up.

"How are you feeling?" I say. "You're looking a lot better."

He just nods.

I say, "I tried to ask Marvin about Dan Watson, that report he filed, but Mr. Rabideaux—"

"Watson?" He seems surprised at the name. He leans forward on the wheel, then sits back.

"Yeah, I guess I saw that report after you had your . . . fainting . . . spell. Basically . . . well, I think I have it, if you want to look at it. I just wanted to ask Mr. Rabideaux if Officer Watson would file a report that wasn't true."

"Dan Watson was a fine officer, like your daddy. And like your daddy, he died in the line of duty."

"Oh, Captain Chappelle, come on. We both know my father did not die in the line of duty." The palmettos rush past.

"Exactly what do you think you know, Loni Mae?" He looks away from the road for just a second.

"Everything," I say, though that's far from true.

His uniform shirt shows circles of sweat. "Listen, honey, what your daddy did, he did for you kids."

"How can you say that?"

There's a long silence. Captain Chappelle does not answer, but a muscle in his cheek twitches.

Finally, I speak. "The only really confusing thing is that report of Daniel Watson's, it—"

"What report are you talking about?"

The two sheets, stapled together, are still at the bottom of my bag. I pull them out, and Captain Chappelle slows the truck, pulling over on the shoulder cushioned by pine needles. He pats his breast pocket for his reading glasses and puts them on, studying the paper like it's written in ancient Sumerian.

We are surrounded by wilderness, and I still don't have my bearings. Captain Chappelle mutters something under his breath.

"Sorry?" I turn back to him.

He grips the paper. "I don't know where you got this, Loni, but it is fraudulent. Dan Watson's been dead and buried a long time now." He sets the form down and puts the truck in gear.

I fold it back up. "Well, Mr. Hapstead said—"

"Hapstead?" He looks at me as he pulls back onto the road.

"Yeah, Mr. Hapstead, at the funeral parlor. He remembered a head wound on my dad. Can that be right?"

"Well now, you've run into a great many folks on your visit." He glances in the rearview. "I suppose . . . it was such a long time ago now, I can't remember all the details, honey. I guess we figured your daddy fell out of his boat somehow. Hit his head when he fell . . . maybe? It pains me to think about it." He drives a little farther, then turns onto a dirt road. "I just have to check something down here, you don't mind, do you?"

"No, of course not." We bump along for a while until the trees give way to an open area and some water. Captain Chappelle gets out of the car.

"Had a report of some illegal traps down here." He wanders around, surveying the area.

I get out and look over the pond, which opens onto another waterway. I wish I knew where I was. A canoeist enters the pond, and I wave. Could it be Adlai? For a half second, my heart lifts. The man paddles toward us and I see it's not. But he comes up nearly to shore. I say, "Great day, isn't it?"

"Yeah, when you're in the shade," he says. He has on a large-billed khaki hat.

Captain Chappelle is behind me. "Shit," he says.

I don't think I've heard him curse before.

"Let's go." His voice is severe.

"No traps?" I say.

"What? No. No traps. Just a fuckin' guy in a canoe." Something about this place seems to have irritated him mightily. Maybe it was a false tip. I slide back into the Suburban, taking the incident report from the seat and putting it back in my bag.

By the time we get back to the Egg House and pull up next to my car, Captain Chappelle seems more himself. He idles the truck. "Now Loni Mae, I know you still have questions about your daddy. Probably always will have. Of course, he had his moods. If he was extra low that day, that week, that moment, he did not let me know. I wish I could have stopped him. Your mother probably wishes she could have stopped him. Maybe even you might have changed his fate that day, asked him to stay home."

Ouch.

"Like I asked Stevie to stay home the day he died. But continuing to ask that same question over and over again, honey, it just ain't healthy."

"But Dan Watson . . . his report seems to imply—"

"Poor Danny. Also a closed book, unfortunately, God rest him."

I would sit in this Fish & Game vehicle forever if he would just give me the answer to the question *why*.

"Just think of your dad as I do, Loni Mae. A stand-up guy, true to the end."

I reach over to hug him. "Thank you for being his friend," I say, and I get out of the truck.

53

The landscape of spiky palmettos recedes in my rearview. Maybe Captain Chappelle is right, and I should let it all be, make peace with the unanswerable. That little folder of drawings still rests on my passenger seat. I was in such a hurry to take it to my mom, as if a stupid art project would have any effect at all. But my mother, too, is part of the unanswerable.

It's time now for me to return to my orderly office, all my paints in color-wheel succession and people around me who direct their curiosity at worthwhile pursuits. In Washington, the past is irrelevant, so it can't find me there. Once I turn in Estelle's last drawings, dump the rest of my mother's junk, and say good-bye, I can get back to my real life.

As I open the apartment door, I inadvertently kick a large envelope that skids under the love seat. A note scrawled on the outside says: *Just a few revisions—hope you don't mind! Estelle.*

I look through the changes she wants me to make and set the package down on the kitchen table. I'd really like to pick up this rickety piece of furniture and throw it out the window. But it will have to serve me just a little longer. I fix the wobble one more time, push some papers into a pile, and sit down to work.

Corrections are *not my favorite.* But I will get them over with, and then I will leave.

Number 1. Yellow-crowned night heron. I think of this one as a schoolmarm in a feathered hat. *Please shorten the plume and clarify the wing pattern.* I do it. I don't care. I don't let myself disagree. I refine the tweed-like crosshatching on the wing and pull the plume back.

Then I check my cell. No voice mail, no texts. I get up and press play on the old hulking answering machine. Nothing. Approximately thirteen times since I left his house, I've dialed part of Adlai's number. But it's time to stop being a teenager. I'm leaving town. It's over. I met someone who isn't suited to me, we kissed a lot, and that's it. I'll forget him when I'm back in Washington.

I work on the corrections and then glance at my watch. It feels like I've been working only a minute, but it's been hours. I move on to the next one. Kingfisher. *Please widen the breastband.*

A loud buzz shakes the apartment and stops. It repeats. *What is that?* Then I realize. Though I've spent weeks in this austere apartment, I haven't met a single neighbor or ordered even a package. And when Estelle came over, she just waltzed in through the propped-open security door. So no one has ever pushed the bell for 2C from downstairs. I find the previously silent intercom and speak into it.

"Yes?"

"It's Frank. Could you buzz me in?"

"You're pushing the wrong button," I say.

I go back to the table. The buzzing resumes. Maybe it's an intruder who just presses every bell until someone lets him in. I walk over and speak again. "Look, you've made a mistake. You're pressing 2C."

"Loni Mae, it's Frank Chappelle. Just go on and buzz me in."

"Oh! Captain Chappelle? What? . . ." I try to find the button I should push, but it doesn't seem to do anything. I say into the intercom, "Just a minute." I slip on a pair of shoes, take my keys, and start down the stairs. What's he doing here? How does he even know where I . . . I must have told him. Right—standing in his garden. I said, *Calhoun*

Street. The building's called "Capitol Park." Sounds like a big green meadow, or a seven-storey garage, ha! And of course, my name is on the mailbox downstairs: "L. Murrow, 2C."

I wave at him through the glass door in the vestibule.

"Hello, darlin'!" He smiles as I unlock the inside door. He's changed from his Fish & Game uniform into an ironed striped shirt and khakis.

"Welcome!" I say. "I'm surprised you came to see me!"

"Well, Loni Mae, I was thinking about the talk we had this morning, and I had to drive up here anyway, so I hope you don't mind me dropping by."

"Not at all. Come on up! I've dropped in on you a fair amount, haven't I? I just didn't know you came to Tallahassee that much."

His step on the stairs is slower than mine. "Yeah, I'm on a couple of state boards here."

"Oh." We reach the landing. "Do you have a meeting today?"

He nods. "Comin' up at four o'clock. A dull one." He cracks a smile. "But seeing your sweet face twice in one day takes the edge off."

Before opening my apartment door, I say, "Now, it's very humble. I'm just surviving on the furniture the previous tenant left." I turn the key. "Can I get you . . . a glass of water? Sorry, I don't have much in the fridge."

"Water's fine, Loni Mae."

I look forward to never hearing that nickname again. I go into the galley kitchen to pour his water, and as I take the pitcher from the refrigerator I'm looking at Chappelle's young face. My drawing of that newspaper clipping where he gave my dad an award is still held up by the little plastic fridge magnet. And next to it is the back of the receipt with my father's handwriting:

Frank > Elbert > Dan
Walkie-talkies
who else?

I look out at Frank, sitting on the paisley love seat.

He says, "Yeah, when I was first married, Henrietta and I had a little apartment like this."

I spill the water from the pitcher. "Henrietta?" I look from the glass to Captain Chappelle. "You mean Rita . . . ?" I wipe off the counter, wipe off the glass, and bring it to him.

"Yeah, Rita. Short for Henrietta. When we were young, she had long hair and thought of herself kind of like the singer Rita Coolidge—who was a hometown girl, you know. A few years older than us." He sips from the glass, looks around for a coffee table, then sets the glass on the floor. He sighs. "Yeah, well, all that changed. I hear she's gone back to her full name. My ex-wife, that is. We don't speak more than the odd unkind word."

Henrietta's signature floats behind my eyes. Chappelle pats the place next to him on the love seat.

Instead, I pull over a plastic chair from the kitchen table and set it across from him. *Henrietta is his wife.*

I say, "Henrietta, she's—"

"Ruling bitch of the world, if you'll pardon the phrase."

I hate it when men use that word. "Right," I say. "So . . . um . . . you're . . . you, um, serve on some boards up here?"

"Yeah, state licensure boards, that sort of thing. As I get closer to retirement, I figure they'll keep me active, keep my brain working, you know, give me something to study on."

I nod. *Henrietta is the woman who left Captain Chappelle. Took his children away.*

Captain Chappelle turns his head to the side and pulls his lips together. "Loni Mae, I feel bad. I feel bad because you've been asking me for something, and I've been putting you off."

I say nothing.

"It isn't pretty. Not one bit of it. But this morning after I dropped you off, I got to thinking. Maybe you got a right to know." He takes a deep breath. "I wish I didn't know it myself, but in the end, your father saved my life, and for that I'll always be grateful. After all of it, he was a hero."

"A hero? I don't understand."

"And that's because you didn't know what was going on. Be thankful. You were young, and it wouldn't of been right for you to know."

Henrietta's letter said: *There are some things I have to tell you about Boyd's death.*

"It pains me to tell you, honey. Like I said, what he was doing, he did for you kids. At least, I hope he did it for you, and not just out of greed."

"I beg your pardon?"

He inhales deeply. "Your daddy and that snake Nelson Barber had a deal going with some fellas we in law enforcement call scum. Rest of the world might say drug dealers. Some low-flying planes would drop bales of stuff in the swamp, and these fellas would retrieve it."

Those bales. "You mean my dad—"

"No, honey. Boyd just watched so I didn't come up and stop them. Me or any other law enforcement."

I grip the arms of the plastic chair.

"That's all he did. He did not get involved beyond that. Barber was more into the business, probably recruited your daddy."

I focus on a muscle in Chappelle's jaw. Tense, release. Tense again.

"Now, don't condemn him, honey. Like I said before, he knew it was wrong, but he did it to have a little extra for you all. One day he just didn't do his job good enough, didn't hear me comin', and I came up and surprised 'em." His eyes scan mine. "See now, you don't want to know this."

I move my mouth to speak, but nothing comes out.

"What I want you to keep close, darlin', is this. Okay, he did some things that weren't on the up-and-up. But when the bad guys went after me, he protected me. They knocked him cold, bludgeoned me, and ran off, leaving us both to die. Only I was inside my boat and he was in the water. Why they didn't just shoot us both in the head, I'll never know. When I came to, your papa was already gone. Expired." He rubs his face with his hand. "I put 'On Duty' on that form because I owed him something for saving my life. Why make you all suffer for what he'd done?"

I say nothing. Every polluted image I've ever conjured swirls around me: my father's waterlogged body, a weighted fishing vest, his wallet flying toward land, the cypress knee. And now, new pictures: floating bales, a receding plane, faceless men in a speedboat, the blood from the back of my father's head.

Nelson Barber said, *They got to him.*

It can't be true. It can't. That wasn't him, how could it be? He couldn't have been the man I knew at home and also . . . this. Or could he? Was this the source of his silences, his dark days?

Chappelle is still speaking. "He did it for you kids."

I hoped something else happened, that my father didn't kill himself. But not this.

Captain Chappelle has stood. He has his arm around my shoulders and he's leaning over, holding me upright in the chair.

"I shouldn't of told you." He lets go. "But I didn't want you hearing it from someone else. Since you been talkin' to so many folks, I didn't want you asking the wrong people, having it come out, and then more people thinking ill of your father. He was a good man. He just did some bad things." Chappelle stands up straight and moves toward the door.

I get up. "But, but—"

"I'm sorry," he says. "I know you got a good life up north, Loni Mae. I don't know, maybe it's better to let people lie in their graves."

I walk with him, see his hand on the lock, watch the door open, look up at Captain Chappelle. "But how did he—"

"It's hard to understand, honey, how a man like your father could do bad things. Just know, deep inside, he was good. He made a mistake, that's all, and unfortunately, it killed him. I knew you wouldn't give up till you heard the truth. So now that you know it, you can go back to your life and remember the good."

I need to inhale but can't seem to draw a breath.

He says, "You gonna be okay? Want me to stay?"

I shake my head, watch him leave, and shut the door. I lean back as I close it. *No.* I pace the length of the apartment, door to kitchen and back to the door. Bedroom to kitchen to love seat to window to door. "No! No no no no no no no." It's the only word my lips will shape. I circumnavigate the apartment fifteen, sixteen, seventeen times. My feet move and my hand slaps the wall. "No!" On my sixteenth or eighteenth pass, I hit the kitchen table with my balled fists. Papers go flying. I stoop to pick them up and smack each paper down one by one. I want to break this fucking table, collapse its wobbling legs. I pound it with a pencil drawing. My pathetic budget. A printed sheet of directions. *PANAMA CITY, FL*, it says. I snatch it up.

54

Panama City is sandy and windblown and partly under construction, with its old-timey amusement park near the beach, the Ferris wheel and roller coaster still operational in spite of an endless struggle against salt and rust. They call the shoreline the Miracle Strip, implying that it survives not on the strength of its kitchenette motels and graying tiki huts but rather on the kindness of divine Providence, just as the fishermen out at the end of the long pier pray and wait bareheaded, no matter the weather, to reel in their own miracle.

I stop for gas and rack up more debt on my credit card. I consult the printed map.

All along, Mrs. Chappelle is the person I've been seeking. I haven't spoken to this woman since I was a kid. Her ex-husband has called her the reigning bitch of the world, so she might be harder to talk to than Mona Watson and Joleen Rabideaux combined. Still, there's that letter. There was something she wanted my mother to know. Was it the same awful news I just learned? Or is there even more?

The Mrs. Chappelle I remember was friendly, at least before her divorce. She was one adult who spoke to children as people. My mother drilled me to use my best manners at the annual Fish & Game barbecue at their house.

I knew to say, "Is there anything I can do to help, Mrs. Chappelle?"

Once, she said, "Well, now, I guess you can help me with the punch glasses, Loni Mae."

She and I went into the kitchen together, and she asked what I wanted to be when I grew up. "Because girls have to have careers now, just like I tell Shari, in case Prince Charming takes his time arriving." She laughed.

For some reason I told her what I'd told no one else. "I'm hopin' to be a natural history artist. I read about it in a magazine called *Smithsonian*, and it's a real job."

"Like illustrating history books?" she asked.

I said, "I don't know why it has that name, 'history.' It should just say 'nature artist.' It's drawing birds and bugs and plants and such."

She turned from what she was doing at the counter and looked at me, like she no longer saw a little girl, the daughter of a man who depended on her husband for work, but instead saw a person with a good idea. She said, "Well, I like that. And you better let me know once you got there. I want to hear all about it." She pressed her lips together and nodded, holding my gaze another steady couple of seconds before she took up the punch bowl.

I pull the car over to look at my printed directions. I'm a mile inland in a middling neighborhood of one-storey frame houses. I drive a few more blocks and see a pearl-pink Coupe de Ville parked on the street and I pull up behind it. The house has white pebbles in the yard instead of grass.

I knock on the door, and Mrs. Chappelle opens it. Her face is lined, but she's got a certain pep my own mother has surrendered.

"Yes?" she says.

I could still say, *Oops, wrong house!* But I'm frozen.

She sets her lips in a line.

"Mrs. Chappelle," I say, finally. "I'm Loni Murrow."

Her face falls almost imperceptibly, then perks back up. "Well, of course you are." She takes a breath, hesitates. "Come in, dear." She sits me down on the couch and goes to the kitchen. When she comes out, she hands me a glass of lemonade so sweet I can't take more than the first sip.

"You've grown up real nice. Were you in the same grade as Shari? No, of course, you were younger."

This is what Southern manners are all about. They keep us on the surface, keep us from talking about things that matter. The deep wells under Mrs. Chappelle's eyes are partially hidden by makeup, but no makeup can cover that shade of dark. She sits down in a rose-colored wingback across from me.

"Mrs. Chappelle, I was so sorry to hear . . . when Stevie passed."

"Well, thank you, dear."

There's an empty silence.

"Mrs. Chappelle, I'm bothering you, I know. And I apologize. I just . . . have to—"

"Did your mother send you here?"

"My mother? No."

"Maybe I shouldn't have told her." She puts her fingertips to her cheek. "But with Stevie gone, I had no more reason to keep that lie going."

"You mean you've seen her? Recently?"

She nods. "I went to . . . the Home."

"And you told my mom about the . . . the drug people?"

"Yes, I suppose she told you everything." Mrs. Chappelle looks down at her hands.

"No, she didn't. My mother . . . forgets. Captain Chappelle is the one who . . . told me. He didn't want to." A sharp pain prickles my throat, and my chest feels like a cave.

"Oh, my darlin'," she says. "What did that man say to you?"

"He said my dad, my dad was . . ." I'm a blubbering idiot. She comes and puts her arm around my shoulder, the way a first-grade teacher might. The lightest sort of touch.

"Let me guess, now. I bet he said your daddy was helpin' the drug fellas."

I nod a first-grade kind of nod.

"I see." There's a long silence. "And then, did Frank tell you something like, he found out, and told your daddy to stop?"

I sputter, "He said the drug guys attacked him, attacked my father."

She leaves my side and walks across the room for a box of tissues, which she places before me. I take one and blow my nose.

Mrs. Chappelle—Henrietta—inhales deeply. "Well, that last part was right, at least."

"What part?"

"Your father was attacked by somebody helpin' the drug fellas." She stands by the wingback chair.

"So, it definitely wasn't an accident."

She's looking me dead on now. She shakes her head no.

"And it wasn't . . ." I cough out the word. "Suicide?"

"Oh, certainly not. That's what I wanted your mother to know."

"But my father, did he . . ."

"Your father had way too much faith in Frank Chappelle, I know that. For all his time at Fish & Game, Boyd would never have judged Frank as anything but upstanding. People who are honest never do think the folks they admire can be so far from what they seem."

Everything is in motion, and I'm between what I know and what I don't know. "Wait. When you say 'honest' . . . you mean my father?"

Henrietta nods.

"And *not* Captain Chappelle?"

She moves her head side to side.

I take a sip of the syrupy lemonade. This woman clearly despises her ex-husband. Is she bitter enough to lie?

She comes over and sits in a rocking chair next to the couch, but leans forward instead of back. She looks down at her folded hands. "Loni, I tried to tell your mother . . ." A heaviness comes over Mrs. Chappelle's thin face. "You see, Stevie . . . Frank brought his own son into something so vile—" She breaks off. When she recovers, her voice has an edge like a knife blade. "And it took my boy over."

She starts to speak again, her voice low enough that I have to scoot to the edge of the couch to hear. "You make deals with yourself, so you can sleep at night. I had hope that Stevie could break free of it all. Well, I suppose in a way he has." She leans back and closes her eyes, letting the rocking chair center itself on its rungs.

I'm lost. The woman is in pain, and she's not making sense.

Mrs. Chappelle props an elbow on her armrest. She looks at the carpet. "When our earnings first started to increase, I did not ask where the money came from. I grew up pretty basic, and I liked the little extras. But then some unsavory types started acting like they knew me from somewhere. And finally, my husband took a mistress, because he could afford one. That's when I left. I chose poverty and my pride. But it wasn't because I was too upright to take drug money, which is what it turned out to be. I thought I could protect my children, but Stevie wanted to be with his father, and the minute he turned eighteen, he went back there. Frank took him into his filthy business. His son, who thought the world of him."

"Wait. You mean Captain Chappelle was getting drug money?"

She nods again.

"And my father?"

"Boyd knew nothing about it. He might have been the only one in that office who didn't know. Or maybe he had his suspicions, and that's what made him dangerous."

Those directions, in my dad's handwriting, to the Fish & Game Law Enforcement Division. That officer who was locking the door said " . . . whistleblower complaints, that kind of thing . . ."

"I just can't believe Captain Chappelle . . ."

"Oh, that man is so smooth. He will smile and charm you while he stabs you in the heart. Believe me on that."

"So . . . do you know what happened the day my father died?"

She waits a long time. "Loni, I wasn't there. And I wouldn't consider my source a reliable one. I had already left that vermin Frank Chappelle, but he came here drunk the night it happened, thinking

I would give him comfort. After the girlfriend got tired of him, he'd come down here once a month or so and beg me to come back. He said no one could ever soothe him like I could. The sweetness act almost took me in. Until that day. He showed up drunk out of his mind, telling me his version of what happened, the version where Frank didn't mean to kill your daddy, only knock him out. Where he didn't mean to leave Boyd floating facedown and bleeding from the head, it just happened. Where God was going to forgive him, because it was an accident. I should have turned him in then, I should have called the state police. But he'd already drawn Stevie deep into it. I did not speak because I thought I could protect my son, keep him from prison. Turns out my sweet boy was not only working for those fellas, he was their customer, too. He might have been safer in prison."

I'm so close to the edge of the couch I have to plant my feet or I'll pitch forward.

She says, "It was like a switch went off inside me. I couldn't bring your daddy back, and I couldn't tell anyone without implicating Stevie. So I kicked Frank out of here before he could tell me any more of his twisted version of events. From that moment, I devoted every bit of my energy to getting my son away from Frank, away from that business, and into a program. Stevie tried, he did. More than once. He wanted to do better. But the poison kept drawing him back." She puts a tissue to the wrinkled skin around her eyes.

I take out the faded receipt I pulled off the refrigerator before leaving the apartment, my dad's writing on the back:

Frank > Elbert > Dan
Walkie-talkies
who else?

"Mrs. Chappelle, does this make any sense to you?"

She looks at it and nods. "Those three were all in on it somehow. I don't know everything, but if you want more detail, Loni, you'll have to talk to someone who might have gotten a more reliable account of what was going on amongst them, and what exactly happened the day your daddy died."

"And that would be . . . ?"

"Dan Watson's wife. Mona. She and I have never spoken of it, but I believe she is the only person alive who might have heard a truer retelling from her husband."

So Dan Watson *was* there that day. And Mona knows but refused to tell me.

I drive fast through Tate's Hell Swamp, stopping only once for flashing blue lights behind me and a Florida Highway Patrolman who takes his swaggering time to write me a ticket. While I wait, a beat-up blue pickup races by. I take the citation, drive 55 until the patrolman is out of my sight line, and then speed up again.

You got a good life up north, Loni Mae. That's what Frank said. In other words, *Fly Away, Loni Mae.* Or more succinctly put, *Yankee Go Home.* Did Frank put Nelson Barber up to smearing my car windows? *D.C. HERE I COME!* Or was it Nelson Barber at all?

I smack open the door to Tammy's salon. Mona's weekly appointment is already underway. Her vulnerable neck is leaned back over the sink, and Tammy is dispensing warm water over all parts of her little head. I peek over Tammy's shoulder, making sure Mona sees me before I cross the room. Tammy's friend Georgia is there too, catching up on gossip with a few other ladies who wait their turn. I take a seat on the far side of the salon. Mona says to Tammy in what she thinks of as a whisper, "I know she's kind of related to you, but I don't like that girl."

From where I'm sitting, I say, "I can hear you, Mrs. Watson."

Georgia and Tammy both look at me. So do the other women. In my hometown, if you're being talked about within your hearing, you're supposed to act like you're deaf. People are shocked when you don't pretend.

Mona lifts her head from the neck rest of the sink and looks at me. She sits all the way up.

Tammy grabs a towel and does her best to keep Mona from dripping water all over the chair. "Now, Loni," she says.

I don't move from my seat. "Well, Tammy, I just want to know why Mrs. Watson doesn't like me." Everyone in the salon is listening.

"I'll tell you, young lady," Mona says. She has drops of water on the shoulders of her drape. "For one thing, your fake Yankee accent."

"Oh, is that all?" I say.

"And what gives you the right to swoop in here from up north and dredge whatever you feel like dredgin'?"

"Now, Mona," Tammy says, trying to conceal her delight.

"Mrs. Watson," I say. "I'm actually here to get my hair cut, but what luck I find you here, because you know who told me to talk to you? Rita Chappelle. Also known as *Henrietta*."

Mona stands, the drape flying up behind her. "She doesn't even live here." She takes a step toward me. "You don't know where she lives."

"Oh, but I do. I just came from Panama City, Mrs. Watson, and our conversation had everything to do with you. Your husband, things he was doing that he shouldn't have."

"You . . . You're just like your mother!" She comes up to where I'm sitting. "So high and mighty. You think you're better than us!"

I stay in my chair. "Mrs. Watson, tell me, your husband—"

"My husband was a wonderful man!"

I pick up an emery board from the table next to me and attend to my raggedy nails. My hands are trembling, but not my voice. "Let's be polite and say your husband made some bad choices. But he wanted to do the right thing."

"He always did the right thing!"

"Now, Mrs. Watson." I shake my head. "Mona."

"It was all your daddy's fault! Why Dan wanted to get himself in trouble over your stupid, dead father is beyond me."

I force myself to stay seated. "He saw my stupid, dead father die."

"So stupid," she says.

"He picked up my daddy's wallet."

"Did Henrietta tell you that? Because that's a damn lie. Danny wasn't even there."

I take out the wilted accident report. "No, ma'am. This sworn statement from your husband says he was there. He put this in the file himself."

"Because he wanted to get out of it!" She notices the other ladies in the room. She looks around at them, her eyes wild. "Well, he didn't want to end up dead, like stupid Boyd!" Her red face shows fear at what she's revealed.

I pretend a calm I do not feel. "And he thought he had something that could get him free of Frank."

"Don't mention that name to me," she hisses.

"Captain Chappelle, that nice man? Bought you your house?"

Her lip curls. "I deserved that house, and if you think you can come here and change what happened twenty-five years ago . . ."

I stand now. "Can't change it, Mrs. Watson. Can only tell the truth."

"Truth! A lot of good that'll do. Gets people in trouble, that's all. It's better not to know."

"So," I say. "Dan picked up my father's wallet, which went flying when Frank hit Boyd from behind. A canoe paddle to the back of the head?" Henrietta didn't mention which blunt instrument was used. But I can see by Mona's face that I've guessed right. And that she knows the story. She heard it from a reliable eyewitness, her husband, Dan.

"And my dad was left unconscious, to drown in the swamp." I don't phrase it like a question.

Mona's wet hair drips from her cheeks to her slumped shoulders. "Who told you?"

Dan must have relayed all of it. But after he was shot in the face, his wife conveniently forgot the details. Took the house and shut the hell up.

Tammy does not chide me to be quiet. She stands back, listening. Mona looks at her, then to Georgia, then to the other women in the salon. "They'll take away my house! It's all I have!"

Tammy approaches her. "Now, Mona." She puts her arm around Mrs. Watson's shoulder and removes the towel from around her neck. Hardly looking down, Mona gets her purse. Still wearing the salon's drape and oblivious to her own unstyled, damp hair, she walks out the door.

Tammy watches Mona from the window to be sure she's out of earshot, then lets out a whoop and high-fives me. She's grinning like she's just won the lottery.

The other women in the salon sit with their mouths open. Tammy announces that their appointments will be rescheduled. They're eager to leave anyway, and go tell the story to anyone who will listen. Tammy turns around the "CLOSED" sign and bundles me out the door. She drives the two blocks to Phil's office and shepherds me out of the car and past Rosalea. Tammy is gleeful about the horrible news that somehow proves her right.

We sit across from Phil, and Tammy does most of the talking, except when she wants me to say something about what Mona or Mrs. Chappelle said, and then she says, "Tell him, Loni, tell him."

When I speak, Phil gives me the most profound attention of his life. He writes down everything I say, acting as his own secretary in this most private of matters. His jaw moves as he writes. Is he angry? Shocked? Is he imagining, as I have for years, what our father's last moments must have been like? Only this time, for once, maybe it's the truth. Daddy comes upon the drug runners and tries to stop them. Chappelle and Dan Watson are there to smooth the process, to protect the criminals from law enforcement. But my dad doesn't see his so-called friends. He has his firearm in one hand, the wallet with his badge in the other, and he's whacked from behind by his good buddy, that not-so-nice man, Frank Chappelle. The gun goes in the water, and the wallet goes flying. In the chaos, Chappelle doesn't notice the wallet.

Somebody did, though—Dan Watson, on land, also complicit until he saw what Frank was capable of. Dan must have picked up the wallet and stowed it. He filed that report two months later. Was he trying to get out of Chappelle's dirty business? Was the report an insurance policy, something to hold over Frank? Watson never got a chance to do more than put his addendum in the file. A week later, he was shot in the face. And unbeknownst to Chappelle or anyone else, that piece of paper sat in the public record for twenty-five years, until my brother and his friend Bart came upon it. If my mother hadn't been so blindsided, if she hadn't bought Frank's story, considered him such a trusted friend—just as I did, as everyone still does—if someone had just investigated, they'd have found that piece of paper and gotten curious. Maybe they'd have found good old trustworthy Frank Chappelle.

Phil scribbles on a legal pad. After everything has been said, he writes some more. He says to no one in particular, "I've got to get Bart in here. We need to contact the prosecutor."

Tammy speaks, agrees with him, maybe, although I can no longer hear their voices. The room dims to a pinprick. All I can see is that killer, in his house, offering me juice. That killer, smiling his million-dollar smile. That killer, showing me his camellias, his fucking rhubarb. That man who consoled me about the "bad things" my father did. That man who left my father to breathe brown water into his lungs. He's surely also the "poacher" who shot Dan Watson at point-blank range.

Phil writes, his attention trained on the legal pad.

"I gotta go," I say.

I walk back to the salon parking lot like a zombie. I get into my car, quiet and calm and burning with hatred for Frank Chappelle. I'll kill him with my bare hands. I'll find the sharpest knife in his kitchen. I'll scoop out his innards like he's a bird specimen. I'll set his house ablaze and listen to his screams. Yesterday I wouldn't have thought myself capable. But murder is pulsing through me and all I want is to strangle that man, rip his head off, when I think of the way he acted like our protector, tried to ingratiate himself with my mother, got us to trust him without question.

The sun is setting when I reach the house with the cascading vines. On his neighbor's front lawn lies an abandoned baseball, a mitt, a bat. I grab the bat and walk up Chappelle's porch steps. My thumping heart is a ball of phosphorus, burning so hot it may exit my chest. I bang open the unlocked door without knocking and grip the bat with two hands, shouting, "Chappelle! Frank!"

If I'd been with my father the day Frank whacked him, I might have done something to prevent it. Created a distraction, called out a warning. Now the only remedy is revenge.

"Come out from wherever you're hiding, you sack of steaming . . ." I kick open the bedroom door. Empty. I go into every room, every closet, even the garden, but Chappelle is simply not at home.

55

I have to tell someone, I have to be with someone, I have to fall and have someone catch me. I go to the canoe shop, but it's closed, locked up tight. I drive to Adlai's house, not because I want him to take me back, but because I need somewhere to go, someone to keep me from finding Frank Chappelle and bashing his brains out. I knock and then I pound, but Adlai does not come to the door. There's a braided rug on his porch, and suddenly I am so tired, all I want to do is lie down. I curl up on the rug, just for a minute, letting the warm wind tickle the hair on my arms. I can hear the swish of the reeds on the lake nearby. Then, for a while, there is nothing.

"Loni. Loni."

I open my eyes, and there he is, this lovely vision. I've died and he's the angel Gabriel.

"What are you doing?" Adlai says.

I try to sit up straight and I taste the worst breath of my life. My hair falls in my eyes, and I push it away. I'm sweating, and my face feels mashed, indented with the braided carpet pattern.

"I don't know," I say.

"What's happened? What's the matter?" he says.

"You weren't here."

"I went looking for *you*," he says.

"You did? But I thought you were through with me."

"Apparently not." His face is at eye level. His arms are close to mine.

"I was in Panama City," I say. "Tate's Hell Swamp. Then here."

He says, "I'm glad I found you."

"On your own front porch."

He looks down. "Well, you know what they say about looking for your heart's desire."

He can't mean me. I say, "I almost killed a man today."

"You did?"

I nod, then shake my head. "No, I mean, he wasn't home."

He takes out a roll of Pep-O-Mint Lifesavers and rips away some of the foil, directing it toward me.

"That bad, huh?" I say.

He nods.

I take the minty circle and put it on my tongue. "After my breath is better, will you just hold me?"

"I think I could manage that."

I stand, still unsteady. We move into each other's arms, and I press the whole length of my body against him. He smells like boxwood in a warm wind. We stay like that for minutes.

His breath tickles my ear. "Care to come in my house?"

He turns his palm upward and gestures toward the door, like that time at the dock when he said, "Your chariot awaits." It's the same hand that reached for me at the hardwood hammock, bringing me into a place where I belonged. I finish the breath mint, touch his face with both of my hands, and kiss him. And Lord o' mercy, he kisses me back. We stay there on the threshold for a few long, delicious minutes, and then Adlai pulls back. He lifts a finger and says, "Don't you play with my feelings."

I say, "If only it were just play." We pass through the doorway and up to Adlai's tree-house room, to his featherbed nest. Only the warmth of him matters. I do not speak, do not tell him about my awful day, do not discuss a thing. Tonight, I say only what can be said without speaking, and he answers in a way that is beyond words.

56

MAY 5

In the morning, I wake first. Leaf shadows play on the sheet and dance across Adlai's smooth chest and face. His lips gather in a gentle pout. I get up, dress, and slip out silently.

The live oak tree, the one casting shadows against his windows, moves in the wind. I stand at its base and listen to the sound. The tree is ringed with periwinkles, and I stoop down to pick one, noticing a break in the flower bed that leads to the trunk. The knots and low branches are so clearly climbable, I can't resist. I pull myself up and use each foothold to reach higher. I arrive at a thick, horizontal branch and sit crushing periwinkle petals beneath my nose.

The sound of footsteps gives me a start. I look down and see Adlai. He's pulled on his jeans but left his chest bare. My startle becomes a thrill.

"Hi!" I say.

He tilts his head back. "I thought maybe you'd left me."

I shake my head no.

"May I?" He steps up, reaching and pulling with his forearms in a way that tells me he's climbed this tree before. We sit next to each other without touching, but the air between us is charged. He leans back against an upright limb.

"So, Loni. Time to tell all."

I begin to talk. It starts as a trickle but becomes a stream—all that I've held back, and all I haven't known until now. I tell him backwards, Mona Watson and Henrietta, Frank Chappelle and my father. I tell him about the journal, about my mother's garden, about the lost baby. I swallow hard. I change position on the broad branch. I edge toward him and lean against his chest, taking care not to send us both toppling. He puts his arms around me, and I talk until it's all been told. For a minute he's quiet. I expect him to say, "You are one messed-up chick." But instead he says, "See how good the truth feels?"

I smooth the hair on his arm. "I guess you've always been the most truthful person in the room."

"Not quite."

I turn my head to look up.

He says, "Don't worry. It's been many years."

I sit straight. "Hm. You've been holding back information. Come on, Brinkert. Out with it."

He looks to the side, maybe deciding if he can trust me, after all. "I think I did mention my checkered youth."

I nod.

"Settle in. It's kind of a long story. I don't tell many people."

I lean against him.

He moves his hand up and down my arm. "And it ain't pretty."

I don't say anything.

He says, "I started smoking pot in high school, you know, hung out with the stoners, lied to my parents. Now weed's legal most places, but back then, not so much."

I stay quiet.

"To support my . . . recreational use, I started dealing. First a little, then a lot. My source got to know me. He told me he'd buy me a ski boat—a Stingray—if I'd make a few runs, Lauderdale to Bimini and back. That sounded like a real bargain, stupid as I was." He leaves a long silence, shaking his head side to side.

"I didn't know the guy had done this before, roped other teenagers in, but minors were less suspect, more likely to be out for a joyride in their daddy's boat, that whole bit. The Stingray was sweet. It was love at first sight with that boat. I couldn't wait to take my friends skiing. But before that, there was the matter of becoming a smuggler, though my source never called it that. 'Just a couple of runs,' he said. He showed me how the boat was tricked out with false panels. I made the first crossing in a little over three hours, and found the folks I was to see on the dock in Bimini. They refueled the boat and loaded me up with ten large bales and a couple kilos of cocaine—which I hadn't expected—all stowed away in the boat's clever compartments."

I try to imagine Adlai as a naïve teenage drug trafficker.

"It all went fine until I came back into U.S. waters and the Coast Guard flagged me down. They came alongside the boat and boarded. I never knew how keenly I treasured my freedom until those long twenty minutes. They left without making any discoveries, just said, 'Good day, young man,' and I kept on slow till they were out of sight, and then I fired that boat back outside U.S. waters. I opened the panels and dumped all the drugs over the side, and after that I came back in and scuttled that beautiful Stingray on the reef off Jupiter Island."

"Wow," I say. "That's some bad trouble."

"I took a float and swam in to shore, and then I hitchhiked back to Fort Lauderdale and waited for the police to come arrest me."

"And did they?"

"They did not. But if they came tomorrow, I'd tell the truth and face the consequences."

"But you were underage."

"Yup."

"Well, I don't think they'll come and get you now. What about the guy who bought you the boat?"

"He was a teacher at my school. Mr. Hawley. He presided over detention. He had very little to say to me after that, except for once in the hallway when no one else was around, he shoved me up against the wall and said, 'You little douchebag.' Another teacher rounded the

corner, and he pretended like he'd been disciplining me for some infrac-
tion. 'And don't let it happen again,' he said. I can tell you I avoided
getting detention for the rest of my high school career. And no one
higher up in the drug-dealing chain ever came after me either, thank
God. Mr. Hawley probably mortgaged his house so he wouldn't have
to confess his bad judgment to his own supplier."

"And nothing else ever happened?"

He shakes his head.

"You are so lucky."

Neither of us says anything for a few minutes.

Then I say, "So that's what made you give up lying?"

"Not immediately. In fact, I lied right away to my parents, because
I didn't go out of the house for a week. I told them I had the flu.
I sat in my room with the air-conditioner turned off and sweated. I
thought about what could have happened and what might yet happen.
My neighbor Prescott came over one day, because he hadn't seen me in
school. We'd carpooled in elementary, but I'd been hanging around a
different crowd since then. Without being specific, I told him I'd been
reassessing my life.

"He said, 'I do that every Sunday, man.' Turns out, Prescott was
a Quaker. So he invited me to a Sunday meeting. Mostly, the people
just sat there. Every once in a while, someone would stand up and say
something, but the meeting was primarily about the quiet. I kept going
with Prescott and his family. The Quakers have this idea that you just
always say the truth, and it's as simple as that. It seemed pretty radical
to me at the time, and I wanted to see what that kind of honesty felt
like."

I nod.

"To the rest of my crowd, this was totally uncool. None of the stoners would talk to me after a while, and that hurt. 'So like, what's our
friendship based on?' I said. And they turned their heads to me and
blinked.

"So I hung with Prescott and a few of his friends. My family didn't understand the Sunday routine, but our relationship improved, so they didn't object."

I shift against his chest. "Good to know that's possible . . . improved family relationships."

"I'd like to meet *your* family," he says, his chin resting on my scalp.

And with my lust-addled brain, it actually seems like a good idea.

The leaves rustle and flutter. We stay up in the tree a little longer, enjoying the wind. Then we climb down. Adlai, still barefoot, guides me to a part of the lake fed by a spring and protected by reeds. We leave our clothes on the limb of a tree. This natural pool is clear, and we lower ourselves in, open our mouths, and taste the sweet water.

On our way back to the house, damp inside our clothes, we pass my car. There, still on the passenger seat, is the visual corollary to my mother's journal. "Can I show you something?" I say.

He gives a tiny nod.

I unlock the car and feel the pent-up heat, reach across my art kit for my handmade book, and bring it inside. I narrate each page for him, and when I'm done, he turns his face toward mine.

"What?"

He touches my hair. "I think you're showing this to the wrong person."

57

There's a pre-rain light show in the distant clouds as I pull into the St. A's parking lot. By now, Phil will have had Frank arrested, so I can leave retribution to the state. I will give my mother this little book of drawings, and then I'll call Phil for the update.

Mariama sees me in the hallway. "Loni, I want to tell you, your mum is having a very good day. Perhaps her best."

"Yeah?"

"She joined the gardening group!"

"Well, that is good news. Thank you, Mariama."

I open the door to my mother's room. She's looking through her chest of drawers but turns when I come in. "Hello," she says. "What's that you've got?" She lifts her chin to indicate the folder of drawings under my arm.

We sit on the edge of her bed and she leafs through the pages one by one. I've recreated her lost garden as I remember it, aided heavily by her *GARDEN* book.

"Isn't that nice," she says at the schematic. "Why does it look so familiar?"

She turns to the next drawing, and I point. "There's rosemary. For remembrance." I look at her face. "There's lemon balm. Heals wounds, you know. There's lad's love. Blessed thistle. Sage."

She nods her head, "Um-hm," like I'm reading off a list, reciting a phone number:

555, um-hum, 7253, um-hum. She looks through the whole folio, holding each drawing by its edge and turning it over carefully. She sets the last page down on its face. "Thank you, Loni," she says, having given the requisite attention to my school project. It might as well be a turkey made with the outline of my hand.

I stand up. "Did you see the borage? '*I borage bring courage,*'" I say, reciting the quote from Gerard.

She looks at me as if I'm an odd child.

I throw myself against the back of the vinyl chair across from her. It's not that she doesn't like it, she just doesn't get it. She doesn't understand that I'm giving her something she's lost. She doesn't even know she's lost it.

The rain begins, pounding against the window. My mother starts a story about Bernice, down the hall. Bernice this and Bernice that, and Bernice fell, and someone picked Bernice up. I'm hardly listening. With everything that's happened in the last forty-eight hours, my energy is beginning to ebb. I thought the little book might do something for my mother, for us, but nothing really can.

"And do you know Bernice didn't even—" In the middle of a sentence, she stops, looks again at the drawings, and then at me, as if a light has come on in some previously unlit room. "You read my journal," she says. The light turns white hot.

Maybe I didn't think this all the way through.

She pulls her lips together. "I should have told you to burn my things."

I'm still caught in that spotlight.

Her jaw is moving, and she strains to get up from where she sits. I stand to give her a hand, but she shakes me off.

"Don't help me." She turns to face me. "Listen, you, I'm your mother, but that doesn't mean you own me. Who told you my things were yours to paw through? Do you think you can just help yourself to whatever you want?"

Right. I *have* been pawing through her things. And she's calling me out for it in the familiar, accusatory voice that has always set my teeth on edge.

"Some things are still private, still mine!" she says. "Don't you have things you'd like to keep private? Yes! Because you never tell me anything!"

"Hah!" I say, a simple exhalation of breath. "Hah!" Lately I *have* been telling her things. She just can't remember. And why is she so lucid all of a sudden? Because she's fighting. Disapproval of me is so ingrained that it sharpens her mind.

"Well, guess what?" I say. "Maybe I shouldn't have read it, but I'm *not* sorry, and I'm *not* apologizing."

"That is hateful!" She turns away. "Lord, I could use a cigarette." She roots around in the drawer of the bedside table, where, to my surprise, she actually finds one.

"Give me a light," she says like she's in a barroom.

"They don't let you smoke in here. You told me yourself. And what's more, you don't smoke!"

"I don't smoke in front of your father!"

"Mom, about Dad," I say, "I have to tell you—"

"So many things he wouldn't let me do. Smoke, talk . . . Only things I had were my plants in the garden and that ratty old notebook you sniffed out. Your father refused to talk to me about . . ."

She falters, and I supply the ending. "The baby. The one you lost."

She spins her head toward me with a look of alarm, as if I've opened a wound so private, she must close it immediately. She turns away again, showing me her back, thin and bony and frail.

"You missed that baby the way I miss Dad," I say, and it rushes into the room like a surge of water, Daddy's soaked body being hauled onto a boat, the face lolling. I never saw it, yet it's as real to me as a memory. In this moment I want his living voice, his smile. I want him back, and know it cannot be.

My mother drops the unlit cigarette and turns toward the window. I have to lean in to hear what she's saying. "Sometimes I am half-awake, and feel for Boyd in the bed and think, he is out doing his swamp time. And then I open my eyes and it hits me fresh, like I have just found out he will never lie next to me again." She presses on the windowsill.

I should stay with her in that grief, share it in the same moment for once, but it's too hard. So I teeter instead toward the ledge where my mother and I first fell apart. "And the baby?"

She turns, comes close, and locks her eyes to mine. Her words are slow and deliberate. "Loni, that sadness got all tangled. I wanted to know why I lost her, and no one would tell me for sure. She could have been dead inside me even before I fell."

"But you blamed me."

"And then I forgave you."

"Oh really? Did you tell me that? Did you talk to me about *any of it?*" My face tingles and my voice goes rough. "Did you ask *my* forgiveness, for treating me . . . the way you did?"

"Then your daddy went, and I barely knew how to hang on." Her gaze drifts.

If I were kind, I would let her off the hook. But I won't. She may never be this present again. I wipe my nose with the heel of my hand. "It wasn't fair." My breath comes broken and choppy.

She steps toward me and cradles me. She says into my hair, "I wish none of it had happened. I wish I had not lost that baby. I wish I had been a better mother to you. If you took on that blame, you can take it off right now." She pulls me gently away from her and holds me by the shoulders, separating each word. "It was not your fault."

After a minute, I say, "Do you still think about her? The baby?"

She turns again and faces the window. "Like your dad," she says. "Just when I think I'm done, the grief comes and gets me."

The rain outside is gusting sideways. My mother looks out at the storm. In the stoop of her shoulders, I see the young Ruth under the clothesline, surrendering to sorrow.

58

When the rain lets up, I go out to my car. I sit for a long time, looking out at the street, seeing without seeing. It begins again to pour. Other cars drive in, swing their lights around in the pounding rain, and park. A silver Cadillac passes in front of me, pulls up in front of the F&P Diner, and turns off its lights. It doesn't register at first, but then I realize whose car it is. But it can't be. Chappelle has surely been arrested by now. Phil was going to see to it. Lightning cracks close, and the driver is illuminated, sitting in his car, waiting for the storm to let up.

A strobing rage shoots through me. Why is he still free? He thinks he can drive around town and go where he wants? After killing my father? Letting me grow up thinking my dad left us on purpose? Seeding that rumor through Tenetkee for two generations? I get out of my car and cross the street.

Frank opens his car door, unfurls his umbrella, and stands up. "Well, hello, Loni Mae!" He is fake-charming, ready to trade recipes for rhubarb pie. "Why, you're getting all wet!" He moves toward me as if to share his umbrella. "Come into the diner and I'll buy you a cup of coffee."

"Shut up!"

"What?"

"Don't call me sweetie, you . . . you . . . fucking worm!"

"Loni Mae, now, I believe you've gone crazy, girl."

"You killed my father!"

From under the umbrella, his eyes scan mine back and forth, back and forth, half recognition and half question. Then he smiles like a matinee idol. "Now, Loni Mae, I know you don't want to believe the worst about your daddy, but—"

"I talked to your wife! I talked to the people who know what you did."

His face changes then, and he is no one I have ever known. His is the face of an enemy. "Well, that's too bad for you now, isn't it?" He catches my wrist. For an old guy, he's got a very strong grip. The pain is intense. It's possible the small bones in my hand and wrist will break.

"I shoulda took care of you the other day, when I had the chance." He starts dragging me toward his car. "If it hadn't been for that fuckin' guy in the canoe, I coulda left you in the forest preserve."

I lean all my weight back, but I'm on the losing side of this tug-of-war.

"I told you not to go unearthing the past, but you don't mind your elders, do you?"

I start to scream, but because of the rain, no one hears. Everyone is indoors. "Getting rid of me won't do any good!" I shout. "I've told everyone in town! I talked to the state police!"

Though it's not true, it shakes him for a second, and he loosens his grip just long enough for me to wrench my hand away and run. He grabs for me, but he's old, and I'm young, and I run faster than I ever have, dashing back toward the Geezer Palace, toward my mother, and safety.

The sky cracks and rumbles. I splash through puddles in the parking lot, and I throw myself forward. The sliding glass doors of the St. Agnes Home part, delivering me with some force to the terrazzo floor. Water pours from every surface—my skin, my shoes, my eyes, my ears. The indoor air is cold, and the hair on my arms stands on end.

I get up and turn around, peering through the glass, through the rain. The Cadillac is gone. I stand for a long time without moving. A woman comes to the front desk. I turn and see her staring.

"May I help you?" she says.

She has a question on her face, but she's on the surface and I am underwater. What have I done? Everyone I love is in danger now. Anyone I might have told. I have to call Phil. My phone, my bag, everything is in the car. I ask the woman if I can use the handset from her switchboard. She directs me to a wall phone.

I call my brother. "Why isn't Frank in jail? I thought you went straight to the prosecutor!"

"Loni, calm down," he says. "They're gathering all the evidence before they arrest him. They don't want to alert him in case he runs."

"Then I've done something very stupid." I tell him what has happened.

"I'll be right there," he says.

I hang up and call Panama City Information for Henrietta's number. "Mrs. Chappelle," I say, "you should probably get out of your house." I explain why, then hang up and go back to the receptionist.

"Listen," I say. "If anyone comes looking for Ruth Murrow . . ."

She looks at her computer screen.

I raise my voice. "No, listen to me!"

She looks up.

"This is life and death." I have her attention. "If a man named Frank Chappelle—tall, older, but extremely strong, maybe in a uniform—if he comes and asks for my mother, he's to be denied access, no matter how official or how convincing he seems. And have your biggest security people ready to help you. The man is a murderer."

The receptionist looks alarmed, but that's not enough. I go find Mariama and tell her.

"Don't worry," she says. "I have dealt with killahs before."

I study her face. She is not speaking figuratively.

Her dark eyes hold mine. "I told you where I came from."

I do some quick math. In the '90s, around the time my world was shattered by my father's death, Sierra Leone was brutalized by civil war. Mariama would have been a young adult, watching everything around her being blown to pieces. I learned it as a fact in a college classroom. Mariama lived it. How little thought I've given to the life of this woman I've come to depend on.

She glances toward the door of the dementia unit. "That door can lock from both sides." Her gaze comes back to me. "We will keep Ruth from harm."

59

Phil bursts into the lobby. "Loni!" He looks to Mariama. "Oh, hey there," he says, and takes a quick breath. Does he even know her name? "Loni, I'm taking you to a secure location." He looks at me and blinks. "Come on. We'll leave your car in the parking lot. I called Lance, and he said he'll surveil the place from his patrol car." Phil is half-panicked, half-energized. I'm glad he wants to kick butt now, but he should have done it yesterday. I wish to God Chappelle was already behind bars.

Phil burns rubber all the way to his house—the "secure location." The sky has cleared, and the kids are out in the yard by the patched fence. Phil, Tammy, and I sit in the dining room. My brother drums a pencil on the blank legal pad before him. "Now, we have to make a plan," he says. "Number one, Loni, you have to get out of town. You're the only one Chappelle is sure knows the entire story."

"Well, me, and his ex-wife, and any one of those women who sat in the salon waiting for a trim. They've surely spread the news by now."

Phil leans back in his chair. "Hadn't thought of that. But I suppose it could work in our favor. He can't kill the whole town."

Tammy says, "See there? Gossip can be a force for good. Course, he can always just say you started a nasty rumor."

"Which he knows something about," I say. "But why can't they just arrest him? They know what he did."

"As the D.A. explained it to me and Bart, they've got no murder weapon, and the body's been in the ground for twenty-five years. Right now, all you got is two old ladies talking, and one is his ex-wife, who's got a grudge. So, on the murder, there's not too much yet to go on. But I did do a little tax research." He smiles.

"And?"

"Seems like Frank and Elbert Perkins are partners in a shell company called Investments, Inc. And they've been pretty clever, but if I'm able to follow the whole path, I suspect we'll find so much tax fraud, those two will likely never get out of jail. If we can get them into jail, now."

"I'm sorry," I say. "I'm an idiot." I let out a long breath.

Phil says, "Okay, back to the plan. Where do you think you'll go?"

"I'm not going. He might come after you, or Mom—or the kids, God forbid!" The alligator in the yard—it's so clear now. That had to be Frank.

Sweat dampens Phil's hairline. "Let's not panic. Maybe we keep the kids home from school a couple of days, say they've got strep, nothing to raise alarm bells. Right now, though, it's likely Chappelle is scared, and he may run. I think Mom's safe. He'll assume she can't remember anything, which is at least eighty percent right. You talked with the folks at St. A's, right? And Lance said he'll have a twenty-four-hour detail on the place. I also talked to Bart. . . ."

I roll my eyes.

"Now I know you're not thrilled with Bart, Loni. But he's having his firm's P.I.'s watch Chappelle's house. You already called Mrs. Chappelle? She could be under serious threat."

I nod. "And cursing my ass, for sure."

"Maybe," Phil says. "But you're the one I'm most concerned about. If he comes for anyone, it'd be you."

Tammy says, "So we got to get you on your way, Loni. Want a sandwich for the road?" She gets up and moves toward the kitchen.

"Well thanks, Tammy." She's actually being very nice. No one has sent me off with a sandwich for the road in a long time. Maybe they're right. Maybe it's time for me to do what I do best. Run.

When Phil drops me back at my car, both of us look around in anticipation of an ambush.

He says, "Now, don't go back to your apartment in Tallahassee. That's the first place he'll look. Where you gonna go? Want me to follow you a ways?"

I give him a big-sister look.

"All right," he says, and gets back in his own car. "But wherever you go, call me. And stay safe."

I do drive out of Tenetkee, but I stop at Adlai's house.

Again in his leaf-shadowed room, I lie next to him and recount what's happened since I left.

"Just stay here with me," he says. "That guy Chappelle doesn't know me well, and I don't think he'd connect the two of us."

"Because we're an unlikely couple?" I say.

"Are we?"

Then I think of Nelson Barber. *You rent this piece a crap from that sonofabitch Adlai Brinkert?*

I sit up. "Who owned the canoe shop before you bought it?"

"I don't know. I never met them. I dealt with a holding company, Investments Real Estate, or something."

I sit up. "Investments, Inc.?"

"Yeah, something like that."

"And Elbert Perkins handled the transaction?"

"Yeah, why?"

I get up and start dressing, tripping over my pant legs. "Shit. Shit shit shit."

"What?"

"Elbert, Frank, Investments, Inc. They're tied together. So if Elbert knows you, and Frank knows Elbert, and they understand that you and I . . ."

I'm trailing clothes and buckling my belt as I go downstairs. Adlai stops to put on his jeans, then follows behind. I say, "I'm putting you in danger just by being here."

I get to my car and throw in what little I have. Adlai doesn't know that in my sweatshirt I've wrapped a very sharp cooking knife from his kitchen. For protection.

"Where you gonna go?" he says.

"The best thing I can do is hit the road, and let it be known around town that I've gone. Hopefully, Frank will follow me."

"I thought you wanted to hide from him."

"There's no hiding from that guy. I don't want him to catch up, but I do want to draw him away from here so he can't hurt anyone I love." I'm thinking mostly of Bobby and Heather, but Adlai's eyebrows arch.

By the car, he pulls me close and kisses me.

I push him gently away before our good-bye becomes another hello. "I'll come back," I say.

At the gas station, I fill up the tank, purchase a jumbo coffee and a few cans of Red Bull, and consider my strategy.

My first stop is at Elbert Perkins' real estate office, where I sit in the car and scribble a friendly note, occasionally glancing up and around:

> *Hi, Mr. Perkins!*
>
> *I'm driving back to Washington tomorrow. But I'm still interested in buying a little plot of land nearby, so please call if anything comes available!*

I write down my D.C. work number. I'm hoping that telling Elbert I'm going is just like telling Frank. Only I'm not going tomorrow, as I've written, I'm going in one second, to get a good head start.

It's already dark by the time I slip the note under the door and hit the road. This is not my best time of day. But I'm eager to cross into Georgia, because then maybe Frank will too, and doesn't something become a federal offense once a criminal crosses state lines? Or, if he finds me, maybe I'll be the criminal, turning toward him with Adlai's kitchen knife. The longer I drive, the more confused my reasoning. Maybe I've overdone it with the caffeine.

On about midnight, when I've passed a sign for Vienna, Georgia, and the cold coffee is just about gone, I catch a glimpse of a silver Cadillac two lanes to the left and a little behind. My pulse picks up.

Over in the slow lane, I keep a discreet distance, letting the Cadillac pass but never getting directly behind him. I can't see in his windows and hope to God he hasn't noticed me. He pulls into a rest stop, and I keep going. If that was him, he must not have seen me. I floor the gas.

I've had to pee for the last hour and a half and finally I just have to stop, even though it will give him a chance to catch up. I splash my face. Sleep deprivation and too much coffee have made me delusional. Chappelle could be anywhere. He might be waiting outside the ladies' room right now, ready to choke me dead, or he might be somewhere in North Dakota, counting his money and laughing. I look at myself in the distorting mirror. If he's still close by, and if he catches up with me, I will be forced to use that knife to defend myself. And then what? Will I go lead a normal life? I turn off the tap and skulk back to my car.

I have to be rational. I work at the Smithsonian, and my eight weeks of leave are nearly over. I do not want to lose my job, I do not want to die at the hands of a known murderer, and if I can avoid it, I don't want to become one. At Macon, I head for I-20, which will take me to I-95 north. I'll be in Washington in ten hours. I can leave this mess behind me and go reclaim my life.

In other words, I will run away, as I have always done. I ran from my father, the last day of his life, when he asked me to go with him. I ran from my mother, away from her grief, away from my own. I ran from my little brother, from his dependence on me, his love for me, when he looked up and said, *I don't want you to go.* I've run from every romantic relationship that has ever looked promising, and I will run from Adlai. I will run from my family, from my hometown, from my father's killer.

Just outside of Augusta, I realize I'd better get a hotel room, because I just saw an ironing board cross the road. I'm falling asleep at the wheel. A tall sign off the highway announces, "Motel," and I take the off-ramp. I find the motel parking lot, but it's unclear where the office is. I drive alongside a couple of two-storey buildings. On the second floor, cracks of light escape from between crooked curtains. Many of the broken windows are patched with cardboard. Rusty cars fill the parking spots. As beat up as this place is, it seems to be at full occupancy. It's the middle of the night and lights are on, yet there's a strange silence. I finally pull up to a plate-glass window with "OFFICE" painted in an arc. I surely don't want to stay here, but I need to use the restroom again. No one sits behind the desk. I venture past it into an open area and spy the door marked "Ladies." I push open the door and I'm met with the reeking smell of shit. I try the first stall, but it's the offending toilet, not only full but smeared. The next stall over, the porcelain is less filthy, but the pipe that should connect the toilet to the wall is gone. The third stall has no toilet at all. What is this place?

I come out and see a man wandering in the large room. He turns and smiles at me. Nearly all his teeth are gone and the few that are left are brown. "Outta order," he says.

I nod and do everything I can not to sprint to my car.

I speed back to the highway. What was that awful place? There were people there. "No Vacancy." It's a slow dawning, because I'm so naïve, and my regular life is far from the worst it could be. That was the last stop on the road to an addict's hell. There's a name for a place like that. I saw it in a magazine. Abandominium. Those are the people poisoned by the likes of Frank Chappelle. It's just money to him, money he'll kill for. But to the folks in those rooms, and so many like them—his own son—it's life at the end of the road.

I touch my turn signal at the next exit, get off, and turn around to go back south. I'm done with running. I need to make everyone see what that guy has done, how utterly amoral the "upstanding" Frank Chappelle really is. I will make him pay.

Even though it's 3:00 a.m., I've got a second wind. My phone is plugged in, and it starts to buzz, buzz, buzz. Who's calling me in the middle of the night? I press green.

"You have caused me a world of hurt."

It's Chappelle.

"Frank?"

"And you're gonna get a world of hurt in return."

"Where are you, Frank?" And how does he have my cell number? But of course, I called him, called and called, when he was lying wounded on his kitchen floor and I was actually worried about him. When I had no idea who he really was. Maybe he *was* beat up. Who knows what kind of people he's in business with? My relentless concern fed my cell number, over and over, to his caller ID.

"Where are you?" I say again.

He growls. "Don't you nevermind where I am. I know where you are, and that's all that matters."

My blood stutters toward my shaking fingers. He doesn't know. He's bluffing. He can't know where I am, because I'm in between places, the southbound no-man's-land of the flat highway in the middle of the night.

I shout, "You're going to pay for . . . hello?" But he has hung up.

The road moves beneath me. Can he really know where I am? If he talked to Elbert, he'll think I'm still in town, ready to leave in the morning. Maybe he thinks I'm at that bare little apartment in Tallahassee. I'd like to be there, because I need to lie down and rest. I'm not thinking right. My mind is too, too tired.

On the highway, someone behind me turns on their brights. I'm in the slow lane going two or three miles over the speed limit, so what the hell do they want? I stick my hand out the window and signal for them to pass. Instead, the car accelerates and comes close to my bumper—so close I have to speed up, too, so it won't hit me. And speed up, and speed up, and speed up.

Oh my God. I let my guard down. Somehow Frank has tracked me. He waited until I was exhausted, and now he will kill me with his car and make it look like an accident. I keep my eyes on the rearview, but all I can see are the brights, close on my tail. When I look forward, I'm about to hit the slow-moving car in front of me. Without checking, I swerve into the left lane. So does he, staying inches behind me.

When the right lane is clear, I switch over quick, hoping for a turn-off where I can screech into a Waffle House, a Cracker Barrel, anyplace, jump out of my overheated car, scream and get help, or, if I have any guts at all, turn and defend myself. As I look for an exit, the brights move to the left, and the car begins to gain on me in the passing lane. I look over, wild-eyed, expecting to see the barrel of a gun.

Instead, four college boys in a Toyota Corolla hoot and laugh, giving me the bird—frat guys, driving high or drunk and acting criminally idiotic. Their taillights strobe into the distance.

I put on my right turn signal and pull over on the shoulder until the car bumps to a stop. I rest my sweaty forehead on the wheel.

When the vein in my temple quits throbbing, I speed up gradually and pull back onto the road. But I take the next exit, which is Crawford-ville. There's a Crawfordville, Florida, near Tenetkee, so maybe Craw-fordville, Georgia, is a safe place. I follow the sign for the Comfort Inn. I can't drive anymore tonight. Could Chappelle have hired those boys to harass me? To make me pull off here? Now I am *very* paranoid.

As I fill out the hotel registration, though, I look down to the floor next to me and see a pair of boots and the crease of dress pants, just like Chappelle's crony, Elbert Perkins. My heart flapjacks, and I shoot my eyes toward his face, but it's only a wizened old man in a cowboy hat. Still, when I get to my room, I double-lock the door and push a heavy chair up against it.

In the hotel bed, my eyes droop, and I'm carried along a nice stream until other pictures float toward me—Frank and Elbert on the lam, the sharp edge of Chappelle's knife against the bleeding rhubarb, a canoe paddle to the back of the head. It's not the most peaceful sleep of my life.

When the sun hits my eyes, I wake, even though I've only had a few hours' sleep. I call Phil, who tells me neither Chappelle nor Elbert Perkins has been seen or heard from. Then I close the blackout curtains, get back in bed, and call Adlai. I hear cereal hitting a bowl, the scrape of a chair. He's at the breakfast table.

"You okay?" he says.

I tell him I'm coming back. I don't talk to him about danger, or fear, or my renewed desire for Frank's demise. I only want the soothing sound of Adlai's voice. I make him talk to me all through his breakfast. When we run out of things to say, I get him to read me the box scores, the fishing report, the extended weather forecast. When he's done with that, I say, "Tell me about water." There's a silence. I can hear him locking the door of his house behind him, getting into his truck, heading for work.

He says, "Tell you about water."

"Yeah, you know, facts. Figures. Stuff that might bore the typical listener."

"Hm. Okay." I hear the ignition of his truck, and he puts the phone on speaker. "Let's see. Did you know that Florida averages a hundred fifty billion gallons of rainfall a day?"

"Every day?" I'm starting to get sleepy. This is a good bedtime story.

"Uh-huh. And all told, two quadrillion gallons of water are movin' through the Floridan aquifer right now."

"Keep talking." I like the sound of his voice.

He recites a few more facts. Then he says, "Are you still there?"

"Um-hm."

"Rest up, Loni. See you soon."

I sleep most of the day behind the dark curtains. The Comfort Inn wants to charge me for two days, but I wheedle them down to a day and a half.

I start to drive south again, and after Tifton, Georgia, I take the back roads. When I cross the line into Florida, I see a sign for one of those gun shows where it's ridiculously easy to become a woman packing heat. I pull off the road and pay to go in. I browse the tables and contemplate Adlai the Quaker and nonviolence versus Frank the scabrous snake and self-preservation. A man at one booth tries to sell me a $7,000 gun that fires a thousand rounds a minute and still, miraculously, is not considered an automatic weapon. "So no restrictions on its sale!" The salesman, dressed all in camo, smiles big. "You *need* one of these!" I pass table after table, overwhelmed by all the means to kill. I imagine Frank and his associates coming here and walking out with a carload of merchandise. When I pass through the exit doors and into the waning sunshine, I am empty-handed.

It's dark by the time I get to Tallahassee. I don't go to my brother, and I don't go to Adlai. It's me Frank wants, and I won't draw him toward anyone I care about. I push the paisley love seat up against the bolted apartment door. I take off my shoes and get under the chenille, fully clothed. The kitchen knife I stole from Adlai is next to me, still wrapped in the shirt. My mind bubbles like a double boiler with visions of Frank storming in and finding me more prepared than he expected. My hands and hot forehead pulse. I stay vigilant. I scoot down in the bed. I put my head on the pillow, but he will not catch me unawares. I close my eyes, but only for a second at a time. Then two seconds. Then three. Before I know it, morning has arrived, and I've slept like the dead.

60

The birds start to sing even before the light lifts the darkness. I'm groggy, but intact. No one has killed me in the night.

I get up, move the love seat away from the door, and try to clear my head. I've refused to run from the person who frightens me the most. Now what?

I sit on the love seat and survey the apartment. Sketches of birds are taped to the wall. The anhinga, inhabitant of three elements: earth and water and sky. Studies of the final four: sandhill crane, blue heron, bald eagle, and the woodpecker with a red pompadour. Did I ever deliver the finished pictures? I check my portfolio and see them there, safe and waiting.

Five heavy book boxes, all sorted, sit on the floor, waiting to be dropped off. After 9/11 people said, *If we live in fear, the terrorists win.* Frank Chappelle won't keep me from delivering drawings, nor from finishing the quotidian task of donating these books. And if he comes after me while I do, I will not run.

I carry the book boxes down the long path and out to my car. On every trip down and back, I scan my surroundings.

I'm struggling under the weight of the third box when a man walks deliberately toward me on the sidewalk. I almost drop the books. He's not Frank, though. It's a barely recognizable Nelson

Barber. He's had a haircut, a shave, and his red-checked shirt even looks clean.

"Where the hell you been?" he says. "Here, let me help you with that box." He tries to take it from me, but I hang on to it. "Give it to me, dammit." He wrestles the box from me. "Now where you want it?"

I point to the back of my car.

He places the box gently down in the trunk next to the other two. Then he looks up. "So that Frank Chapelle ain't the saint you thought he was, huh?"

I shake my head.

"Got more of these boxes to carry?"

I nod, walking back toward my building.

He walks with me, and for some reason, I let him. "Ever hear of a company called Investments, Inc.?" he says.

I nod.

"That's the way they took it from me, you know. Elbert and your daddy's so-called friend Frank. Got everyone to believe I was crazy. Started the nastiest kinds o' rumors. Said I was takin' little girls into the storeroom and—"

He breaks off, his head vibrating and his teeth set.

"No better way to get folks to hate ya . . . 'cause nothin' you can say to that foul lie will ever make them stop wondering." His lower lip shakes.

As delusional as he might have seemed before, I know now he's telling the truth. By the time the last box is in the car, he's more or less filled in the details my brother had only begun to suspect. Investments, Inc., was how Frank and Elbert laundered the drug money, how Frank kept himself in Cadillacs and other luxuries, and how Elbert Perkins became such a goddamn philanthropist. It's not the conspiracy theory of a raving old man. It's the truth.

"Mr. Barber," I say. "I'm sorry I didn't pay attention . . . before."

"Humph."

"And that I suspected you of . . ."

"Of what?"

"You know . . . pranks."

"What kinda pranks?"

"Well, like Alfie's homing pigeons . . ."

"You thought that was me? Missy, you been gone from this county too damn long. Everybody knows Alfie's neighbors hated those birds. Shittin' all over their lawn furniture."

". . . And then someone wrote on my tire in Tally, and vandalized my car here . . . sprinkled a line of birdseed from my door to my car . . ."

Birdseed. Like the kibble in my high school locker. Didn't Estelle say Rosalea and Brandon lived next door to Alfie? When I ran into Brandon the day of the murdered doves, he was laughing behind his hand. Plus—he works at the feed store. I'm so stupid.

"Well, you don't still think I did those things, do ya?"

"No. . . ." I shake my head. "I thought for a minute it was Frank, but . . ."

"So all is well between us," he says. "Sort of."

"Do you need a ride somewhere?" I ask.

"No, darlin'. I got my truck. Anyways, I'm late for my . . . anger management—them county social . . . whatever . . . sons o' bitches. They're all right, though." He walks away from me and shoots me a grin, showing that dark spot on the side where a tooth is missing. Then he puts one finger in the air and shouts backwards, "That gator, now, that was probably Frank!"

As he climbs into his truck, a sudden breeze blows the tops of the trees, and I look up. Rain is coming. I close the lid of my trunk, open the driver's side door, and get on my way.

Before I reach Tenetkee, the skies open, racking up another installment in our region's 150 billion daily gallons. Before Adlai fed me that fact, I never thought about exactly how much water fell, only that my windshield wipers were always beating against it and it was forever pooling in the lowlands.

I pass the "Welcome to Tenetkee" sign. Before I do anything to cut my life short, I have to preserve my precious cargo. Kaye Elliot has plans for a special area in the Tenetkee Public Library she's calling the Murrow Collection. It's just a recess in the wall that used to house the VHS tapes, but the arrangement will allow my family's books, the quiet heartbeat of my childhood home, to remain together under a stout roof.

I park outside the public library and wait for the downpour to sub-side. A woman with an umbrella and a couple of heavy plastic grocery bags approaches the library but doesn't go in. Instead, she picks her way through the vacant lot to the side of the building and disappears around back. Why you'd walk into a muddy field in heels is beyond me. The rain slackens, but I give it a few minutes. The woman comes back toward the sidewalk, empty-handed now, folding up her umbrella. I see it's my frenemy, Rosalea Newburn. I'd like to shake her by the shoulder pads and say, *You jerk! And if you and Brandon had anything to do with that gator, I will kill you!*

But of course, as perverse as Rosalea and Brandon might be, Nelson was right. That one was probably Frank. And if I talk to Rosalea now I'll blow it, like I did with Chappelle. This time, she and her disgusting husband won't even know what hit them until they're in a court of law, answering to charges of criminal harassment.

Rosalea sees me getting out of my car and startles. "Well, hey, Loni!" she says like Miss Frickin' Congeniality.

I bite my cheek. "Hey." She toddles away in her muddy heels. I force myself to stay the course, grabbing a book box, looking over each shoulder, and pushing open the library door with my back.

In the Tenetkee library's main reading area, a school group bustles about like word-hungry insects. Kaye Elliot talks with the teacher but glances my way. She excuses herself and comes over to take the box from me. As she does, I see my niece, Heather—it's her class in here. I wave, and she waves back with a happy breath of surprise.

I make a few more trips to my car. The sun is sucking up water droplets, making the air thick and damp. I go back into the air-conditioning and set a box down. I'm sweaty, but there's one more box to retrieve. As I turn to go out, Kaye approaches. "Loni, I'm excited to get these organized! I just have to finish up with the class. Can you do me a favor in the meantime and get some metal bookends from the storeroom? It's the second white door back there." She points toward the back, pantomiming two rectangles. "Not this door," she says, pointing to one of the shapes she's drawn in the air, "but this one." She points to another spot on her air drawing. I'm not sure I get it, but I wander down the hallway and see the two doors. Of course, I pick the one that goes not to the storeroom but to the outside, where the new addition is being built.

Looks like construction has been suspended. Maybe because Elbert Perkins, the main benefactor, is a fugitive from the law. I inhale the smell of new lumber. There's just a plywood floor, a small portion of which is covered with a half-roof, but the rest of the platform is open to the sky.

In the damp open field beyond the addition, six or seven white ibis poke the ground for insects among yellow hawk's-beard and dandelions. I step out for a better look. I'll get the bookends in a minute. One of the ibis hops up onto the new foundation, gives me a look, and hops off. A backhoe, sitting dormant, has made a wound in the earth, leaving a large gulley below the edge of the built-out platform. This morning's rainstorm has left a pool of muddy water in the rut. Mosquito heaven. Way at the bottom of the field are those tall cypress trees, a clear indicator of water at their feet. Something blue floats across my sight line and a heron lands in the distant trees.

But back to my task. Storeroom. Bookends. As I move toward the open door, there's a rustling behind a stack of plywood in the corner's deep shade. Probably a river otter come up from the stream, or a beaver who's strayed. An empty plastic grocery bag, just like the ones Rosalea was carrying, floats up on the breeze. And then a figure stands up from behind the stack of lumber. He is gaunt and hungry looking, with a scruffy beard, but when he attains his full height, he is unmistakable.

My brain says, *This is someone I wanted to kill.* But my heart pounds out, *This is someone who wants to kill me!*

"Hello, Loni Mae," he says, smiling. He picks up a claw hammer from on top of the stacked lumber.

Frank Chappelle is trapped, and there's nothing more dangerous than a cornered animal. I shout toward the open door, "Kaye! Call 9-1-1!" Has she heard? I move to get inside, but Frank is quicker than me. He grabs me by the arms and drags me out toward another stack of two-by-fours near the edge of the platform. Adlai's butcher knife! Where is it? It is still in my car, useless. Frank forces my back to bend at a painful angle over the piled wood. He raises the heavy claw hammer high above his head. This is it.

"Aunt Loni!!"

Frank looks toward the doorway and I scramble out from underneath him. Heather has come out, and he moves quickly toward her, knowing that by hurting her, he can hurt me worse than death. She darts away, but he swings the hammer hard at Heather's sweet head. "No!" I shout, and grab a yard-long piece of two-by-four from the pile. I swing like it's the Softball World Series, and the flat of the wood catches him behind the ear. He stumbles, taking a few staggering steps to the edge of the built platform. He teeters, then falls over the lip. The hammer lands in the grass, and Frank makes a splash, landing face-down in the gulley filled with rainwater and good Florida earth.

I drop the plank and run to Heather, her body splayed on the plywood floor, her back unmoving.

"No!" Snot is running down my nose and my jagged breaths will not pull in enough air. I fall down next to her and stroke her hair. "Heather? Heather, baby?" She is too, too still.

Time slows. We lie there for what feels like forever. Then I hear a small, muffled voice. "Aunt Loni?" Heather turns her face toward mine. She is calm, like we're at a slumber party, snug in our sleeping bags, side by side on the floor. "Can we go inside now?"

61

In Washington, I have a favorite bench by the fountain in the National Gallery sculpture garden. Today I take refuge there to watch the eight arcs of water rising slowly from the circle's edge. They grow together until they're almost higher than the trees, then shrink steadily to nearly nothing. And repeat. My sketchbook is open on my lap, but I do not draw the fountain. Page after page shows a man being struck, spinning, and falling, blood flying from just below his ear.

After everything, Lance Ashford took me, cradling Heather, back to Phil's house. I stayed with her until she was settled at home, and until I was assured that, at least physically, she was fine. On Phil's doorstep, Lance said to me, "Now, Loni, don't leave town."

But I did. Lance and the others might think I ran from justice, but that's not it. I drove fourteen hours straight, my brain on autopilot, until I hit D.C. morning traffic on the 14th Street Bridge, Thomas Jefferson standing tall in his rotunda on my left, the sharp slant of the sun reflecting off the dome. The trip was not about running. It was about showing up for work. I needed to be back by May 10.

On my way to Theo's office, I passed the desk of Hugh Adamson, budding political operative, who has been happily counting the days until I became a tick mark on his "Elimination" chart.

"Morning, Hugh," I said, smiling. He drew his eyebrows into a pinch.

When I reached Theo's office, I tossed a set of drawings onto his desk. "There's your water."

He looked up. "You're back!"

"In a manner of speaking."

"No talking in riddles, Loni. I've been limping along for two months with expensive freelancers, and your inbox is overflowing."

"In more ways than one." I turned to go to my studio with its colors all in a row.

"Hold on there. Before you go anywhere, sit down and explain yourself." He smoothed his mustache and leaned back in his chair.

My gaze traveled over his head to a spot on the wall. "Theo, please just give me a minute to adjust."

I went to my studio, grabbed a blank sketchbook, and came directly here to the fountain.

I flip the page away from acts of deadly force and begin to draw the eight perfect arcs, the double row of European lindens behind them, and the neatly chiseled circle that describes the border of the fountain. But I scratch at it with my pencil, disturbing the perfection, making the circle uneven. It becomes an overgrown pond, teeming with cackling moorhens and long-legged wading birds. Kingfishers zoom across, and pintails ripple the surface. There's even the beginnings of a dam at the far end, with what could be a beaver's head popping up just above it. The rise and fall of cicadas fills my ears as I draw. Soon moss hangs from the linden trees, cypress knees stick up from the water, and on the far side, through the morning mist, a male figure takes shape, shirtless in overalls, mouth turned up in a gentle smile.

A waft of air just above my head makes me drop the pencil and brush at the part in my hair. A flesh-and-blood pigeon has buzzed me and landed on the neat fountain's edge, waking me to the real.

The fountain's arcs persist in their pattern. The pool's borders are firm. I am here where I belong. I made it back by the deadline, restored to the job I always dreamed of. I've reentered the embrace of my vast Smithsonian family and the logical lines of Washington, D.C., the city laid out as both a circle and a grid. All is in order. This is my life.

So why, if my drawing hand always tells the truth, does this page in my sketchbook show nothing but a wild mess, snakes and gators and a roiling surface?

A chill blows across the circular pool, prickling my skin. I look up. Across the fountain, a man with a barbecue belly and a cowboy hat moves quickly toward me. If Chappelle can't kill me, his co-conspirator, Elbert Perkins, can. I get up and hustle toward Constitution Avenue and its sidewalk full of people who might slow him down.

"Excuse me," I say. "Excuse me." I dart around tourists with small children, a fellow on a scooter, two grandmothers laughing.

I reach the museum and push my way through the crowded exhibits. I check over my shoulder as I pass under a life-size green turtle, and hurry through the sharp fish bones of the Ancient Seas. Just past the open jaws of a giant shark, I reach an entrance to the back hallways and cast around in my bag for my key card. Where is it? The cowboy hat bobs above the crowd, heading my way. I swirl my hand through the bedlam of my belongings and finally touch the card, rectangular and smooth. I press it against the touchpad, and—*beep!*—I'm inside the locked door. I peer out through the small rectangle of glass to see the hat continuing toward me. Is it really Elbert? I don't linger to find out. Within the byzantine passageways, I choose a route not back to Birds, but to Plants.

Delores Constantine sits behind her desk surrounded by botany books, as ever, the curly phone cord winding from the receiver at her ear. When she hangs up, I blurt, "Delores, I need you to tell me what to do!"

Delores looks past me. I turn to see a tall, smiling woman.

"Loni, meet my daughter Aubrey."

"Oh, wow. Hey, hi."

Aubrey shakes my hand vigorously. "Nice to meet you."

I turn toward Delores. I've never seen this woman beam, but her cheeks are pink and there's no other word for it. "I'm taking the afternoon off," she says, "and we're going over to Air and Space."

"Wait, Delores. *You're* taking the afternoon off?"

"There's a first for everything, Loni. Aubrey's going to explain to me how all those machines work." Some of Delores' glow dims as she says it, but it shows up instead in her daughter's face.

Then Aubrey says, "Mom, is the restroom to the left or the right?"

"Left."

Aubrey ventures out into the hall.

I lower my voice. "She's here!"

"On business, but I'll take it."

"And, it seems . . . good. How did you—"

"Number one, I'm going halfway, while I still can."

"And number two?"

"I decided to save my advice for people who ask for it, like you. So what is it you so desperately need help with?"

I look down at my open sketchbook with its boggy, snarled, alluring mess, and I understand. There's nothing Delores can tell me that I don't already know.

I have to go back.

62

MAY 17

So am I a murderer? My self-defense immunity hearing seems to say no, because I walk out of the courtroom. Chappelle did not die, entirely, from the blow to the head. The official cause of death was drowning, even though when the EMTs went to work, the water he'd inhaled in that deep puddle poured out of him, and his bleeding head was stanched. They took him to the hospital, but he did not last long. When the judge asked about my role, I spoke only of Heather, the claw hammer, and the pretreated lumber. On Bart Lefton's advice, I omitted the fact that I carried a butcher knife across state lines in case I needed to slice the deceased in half. I also did not tell the judge about the night I entered Chappelle's empty house with a baseball bat in my hands and murder in my heart.

Bart tells me I will not go to jail. "Thank you," I say, and walk away from him, my feet moving, my mind blank. My only fear now is what killing Chappelle might have done to my soul.

Adlai, who sat through the proceedings in the fourth row of the courtroom in a starched white shirt, a tie, and khakis, moves toward me in the parking lot, his face stony. I can smell the Noxzema and water. He is freshly shaven. "Need a ride?" His stern manner tells me what's coming.

My brother and sister-in-law watch me climb into this man's truck. I am an automaton.

Adlai, Quaker and pacifist, drives without speaking. We are over. I accept that.

"It is okay," I say, after a time. "I understand. You believe in non-violence."

He nods.

"So, it makes perfect sense why you don't want to . . . continue . . . being with me."

He slows the truck and stops it by the curb. "I do believe in non-violence." He looks at his hands on the steering wheel.

I close my eyes and prepare for what he's about to say.

"But, Loni, if I'd been there with you, I'd have probably done worse."

I open them again.

Adlai turns his head. "They'd have put me in anger management there with your friend Nelson." He quashes a smile and puts the truck in gear. "So, where you want to go?"

The question baffles me. Where *do* I want to go?

But I point, and he follows my directions: *Turn right. Straight. In here.* We pull up to Concrete World, with its paving squares and birdbaths, its plaster ducks and deer. They're comforting. I understand them now, frozen and inert.

"This is where you wanted to go?"

"No, but it was on the way. And I like this place." We sit there for a while without leaving the truck. Then it comes to me. What I wanted to share. "Did you know I plan to build a liquor store across the street?" I pause.

"A liquor store?"

"I'm going to call it Spirit World."

He looks at me, his head at an angle. He glances at the Concrete World sign. "Are you telling a joke?"

"Not very funny, is it."

"Maybe on another day. We can work on your delivery."

He starts the engine, but before he pulls out I see a man standing by a birdbath, running a hand across its lip, his arms covered with blue serpents and knives. "Are you friends with that guy?" I say.

"Who, Garf? Yeah. Tough looking, right? He's really a marshmallow. Smokes a little too much weed, and keeps trying to get me to invest in a legal marijuana farm—which I will never do—but he's a master canoe builder. Made my birchbark, in fact. I, uh, I've asked him to make another." He glances at me. "Just in case."

I say nothing.

Adlai backs up the truck and points it toward the road. "Where to now?"

We head south until I point and Adlai pulls in at a familiar driveway. I get out and knock on the door of my own house. "Mr. Meldrum, I was wondering if I could show the backyard to my friend?"

From the truck, Adlai gives a single wave.

Mr. Meldrum looks at me like I'm a rabbit asking to nibble his tomato plants. "Well . . . I guess."

From between their frilly curtains, Mr. and Mrs. Meldrum watch me showing Adlai the live oak and the marsh. When the curtains fall back to cover the window, I go over by the untended borders, where the property creeps into chaos. I keep my eyes on the ground, foraging for plants that might have survived the Meldrums' herbal pogrom. I find mint, some lamb's ears, and a bit of comfrey. I pull these feral herbs up by the roots, holding them like a nosegay, and feel a glimmer of life.

I'm weeding, not stealing. I'm uprooting what the Meldrums consider botanical junk. As I gather, I tell Adlai what I know about the properties of each plant. And for some reason, maybe the clump of Spanish moss I've picked up, I tell him the story my father used to tell me about the Marsh Queen, beautiful and terrible, with hair of moss, and eyes like shafts of sunlight.

He repeats, "So she would grant a noble wish . . ."

"Yes, but only in exchange for the nearly impossible task."

"*Nearly*," he says, "being the operative word."

I put the herbs behind my back and wave at the fluttering kitchen curtain. "Thanks!" I call. At the side of the house I pull up another weed, the orange cosmos that looks like a marigold, only wilder.

Mr. Meldrum appears on the front porch as we reach the car, to give the illusion he hasn't been watching out the back. He tips his index finger from his forehead.

We stop at the garden store for a cedar window box and some soil. On the bed of the truck, I put the pilfered herbs in a neat row and surround the roots with loam. Adlai sprinkles in the darker potting soil, and I press it around the small plants, inhaling the mineral scent.

Back on the road, the truck moves fast and the sun flashes through the pines onto Adlai's white shirt: *flash-flash*, like a light going on and off. It's time to take Adlai to meet my mother. Good news, rare as it is, ought to be shared.

Tammy and Phil must have picked up the kids after the hearing and driven straight to St. A's, because they're already strolling the grounds with my mom when we arrive. From a distance I can see Ruth chatting and smiling. Phil gives her a simple joy. He's her baby.

Adlai takes my damp hand in his dry one as we approach. Phil and Tammy stare. My mother says, "Loni's here!"

The kids run up from where they were playing on the lawn, and Heather gives me a side hug. I stoop down and squeeze her tight, holding her an extra minute. Then she takes her Gramma's hand. I want to pull them all close and never let them go. But we're not that kind of family.

Adlai puts a hand to my shoulder.

"Right. Phil, Tammy, Mom, I'd like you to meet Adlai Brinkert."

Adlai shakes hands with my mom first, then Tammy. The handshake with Phil is larger, a "Hey, man, glad to know ya," white-boy handshake, where the hand swings wide until it connects with the other man's palm. I usually find the pose overdone, but in this case it's strangely comforting. I introduce him to the children, who act shy.

He stoops down so he's no taller than they are. "I am very pleased to meet you both," he says. He stands and says to my mother, "Ms. Murrow, would you care to sit down?" Offering his arm, he leads her to a picnic table in the shade. Tammy follows, still staring at Adlai. My brother and I stay behind.

Phil taps his fingers rhythmically against his pants pocket. "Didn't know you had a boyfriend."

I nod. "I . . . yeah . . . I actually . . . do."

He bobs his chin, then changes the subject. "Did you hear they hauled in Elbert this morning? He was squatting in some abandoned fishing camp in the swamp. Frank was with him until . . . well . . . you know. We gotta watch tonight's news. Bart says the arraignment's this afternoon. Do you know on top of everything else, those two dumped a bunch of chemicals from a meth lab into the swamp?"

I shudder.

"Nice, huh? Lotta side businesses. The old Rabideaux place and Nelson's Sporting Goods were raided this morning too—both major drug depots." Phil half turns, sucking in his breath. "And you know who else was in on it? Rosalea! That damn girl was boinkin' old Elbert Perkins! She's been leaking our accounting records and the law firm's private files to Elbert, and she brought those groceries to Frank, thinking he'd share them with her decrepit boyfriend. Bart's law firm is throwing the book at her."

I'm glad for that, and hope, with a little help, they'll pull in Brandon as well.

"Wow." I nod. "I'm . . . gonna go sit down." But then I turn back. "How does Heather seem?"

"A little shaky."

"Phil, I am so sorry."

"Loni, you saved her life. You don't need to apologize."

"But if I—"

"Shut up, sister. You're fine."

I start across the grass toward the picnic table. The whole day has been too much for me. I see again the recoil of Frank's head, blood flying as he spins, a two-by-four falling heavily from my hand.

I reach down and take off the low pumps I bought for the hearing, returning myself to a more natural state. The grass is sharp and hot against my liberated feet. One fact begins to seep into me, an idea I could never before access. My father didn't mean to leave us. He's still gone, and we cannot get back a single lost minute. But his heft and warm breath were stolen, not surrendered. He wanted to come home.

Phil catches up with me. "Oh, and one more thing. It's now quite possible that the state owes us even more than we thought." His eyes sparkle with numbers.

Heather and Bobby come tug at their father to play, and he relents. I watch Heather. She doesn't look my way, and I don't want to push the *Are you okay?* business, but I will follow up.

I reach the picnic table and sling one leg, then the other, over the bench next to Adlai. As I sit, my mother says, "Oh yes, mint will colonize the whole garden unless you contain it." Adlai raises his eyebrows at me and asks Mom for more gardening advice. She only drifts a little. "You know about pinching the small flowers off the basil, don't you? And culling the lad's love? Otherwise it gets rangy."

"How did that lad's love get its name?" he asks, and takes my hand beneath the table.

During my mother's long explanation, Tammy sits across from Adlai in a trance. Either she's fascinated with him or amazed I've attracted a man. Or maybe it has nothing to do with us. It could simply be an effect of trauma. It was, after all, her six-year-old daughter who was nearly killed.

"Hey, Tammy," I say, breaking the tractor beam. "I'm thinking about doing a memory book." The idea has only now occurred to me. "I'd like to pull together some photos of my dad. Have any pointers?"

She seems to wake up. "Really?"

"Maybe you could get me started."

She swivels toward me. "Well . . . the thing is"—she rests one elbow on the table—"you have to tell a story. With pictures. You decide what the story is, and how you want to tell it." She pauses. "I mean, it's not always easy to see what should go with what, but when you hit on the right combination, Loni, it's almost . . . like magic."

"Cool." Asking one simple question shows me how I might have made things easier between us all along. "Tell me more."

She does, so I only half hear when my mother says to Adlai, "Did you think of that? Clever fellow."

Adlai puts his hand to my waist. "I didn't make the connection. Your daughter's the clever one."

"I am?" I say.

"I was telling your mom about 'Rock-a-bye.' You know, the cradle in the treetop, the bird in the nest. . . ."

I scrunch up my face. *Did I tell him that?*

My mother looks at me. "And when will you two start gathering twigs for *your* nest?"

I freeze. "You know what?" I say. "I just remembered something I left in the car."

The others move toward the building, and Adlai walks with me back to the parking lot. Next to his truck, he puts his hands on my hips and pulls me gently toward him. "If we ever do build a nest together, Loni Murrow, let's not use twigs, all right?"

I get a pang of fear in the lowest region of my torso that quickly changes to desire. I take in a breath and let it out. "You're so darn practical," I say.

He smiles first.

"Now let's get the plants." I turn and unhook the tailgate.

We grab the cedar box full of herbs. Before coming inside, we plant the tall, apricot-colored cosmos just below my mother's window.

It might be rangier than the composed calendula, but this one gangly stalk will produce half a dozen flowers within a week.

Inside, we stop in the rec room to throw water on the mint, the comfrey, and the lamb's ears. I lean on the upright piano, used for jaunty renditions of "Happy Birthday" or "Keep on the Sunny Side."

I say, "I wonder if my mom would ever play the piano here. I mean, once her wrist is all healed."

Adlai lifts the window box from the counter. "From what you've told me, she might wait till it's dark, then steal down the hall and play a nocturne."

I put a hand to his smooth jaw.

The plants have perked up, and we carry the window box to my mother's room. I set it on her sill. "From your garden," I say.

She looks at the plants and then at me.

"I snitched 'em." I take her *GARDEN* journal out of my bag and slip it into her hands while Phil turns on the little TV.

We hear Kacki Rabideaux's voice over footage of Elbert being led into a courtroom. "Perkins was arraigned in court today on charges of money laundering, drug trafficking, and fraud. Also arrested was Perkins' alleged lover, Rosalea Newburn Davis."

When the story is over, I get up and switch off the TV, just in case there are stories about other courtrooms, self-defense hearings, that kind of thing. "Time to go!" I say. Phil looks at me with a question, then puts an imaginary phone to his ear, and I nod. He and Tammy and the kids say their good-byes.

Adlai and I walk my mom to the dining room. Before we leave, Ruth tells Adlai, "Loni's my wild child, you know." She hugs me good-bye, puts her lips close to my ear, and whispers, "Rock-a-bye, my baby girl."

We get back in Adlai's truck and I stare into the middle distance. Way too much is traveling through my brain. Adlai leans over, and when I turn, he kisses me softly on the mouth. He tastes like salt and spearmint and something elemental, like a smooth stone.

When we drive on, my mother's words echo—*baby girl*—and I see the impression of a cockleshell, my newborn ear, on her young arm.

My car is still parked in front of Bart's office, where I left it this morning. That seems like a very long time ago. We pull up behind it and Adlai lets the truck idle. "I . . . uh . . . I haven't asked you how it went in D.C."

"I'm gonna stay for a year," I say.

He lets out a sigh. "Well, I guess I can visit."

"I mean down here," I say.

"A year? Down here?" A smile breaks over him. "Well, that's good news!"

"Yes, it is." I smile too.

Delores, the Wise Woman of Botany, told me while I was in Washington that every seven years, employees of my pay grade are entitled to a sabbatical, and I'm two years late in taking mine. She helped me fill out the form. I listed my purpose: "to study the birds of the southeastern United States with an emphasis on the marshlands of Florida."

Hugh Adamson sputtered an objection, but he couldn't do a thing. Apparently, the sabbatical is a long-standing Smithsonian policy that would actually take an Act of Congress to reverse. I didn't write on the form my other intention: to freelance, get my name out there, and see whether Florida is where I belong.

In the driver's seat of his truck, Adlai is smiling, almost holding his breath. "Follow me home?" he says.

Before I get out, he takes my face in his hands and kisses me again.

6 3

Rivers which flow perpetually . . . return into themselves,
and what has flowed away in their going, they give back by
returning.

—Adelard of Bath, Quaestiones Naturales

The courtyard below my window gives off the pungent tang of Surinam cherries just come into fruit, attracting starlings in profusion. They rattle, whistle, and whirr. I sit at the drafting table I bought almost a year ago, at the beginning of this sabbatical. I'm working on a new drawing of my mother beneath the clothesline, trying to capture in halftones the line of rain as it approached like a sheet across the marsh. I think I've finally got her face right. I've changed the perspective—no more bird's-eye view. She's in profile, my father opening the screen door, coming toward her in the wind.

During the past eleven months, my personal drawing has provided a balance to the paying work. Because I'm eager to refine my own drawings, I procrastinate less on the natural history work and achieve the *gizz* of a bird more quickly. I'm still a stubborn perfectionist, just more efficient. I have deeper questions to get to, and answers I might only reach with my drawing hand.

On the wall next to my drafting table, I've mounted a rectangle of gray Homasote, a porous panel like a bulletin board, only much larger. On it I pin drawings, ideas, and studies. I spend most nights at Adlai's, so this apartment has become more of a studio than a living space. But last night I began this picture and didn't want to stop, so Adlai stayed over and made me happy in my own bed for a change. I often go with him to work, drawing from live birds as opposed to dead skins. In these last eleven months he's seen my short fuse, my stubbornness, and all the disadvantages of being with me, yet he's still around. For my part, I've listened to an astounding number of screeds about the systemic pollution of Florida's groundwater, and I've learned several new ways that absolute truth can be a disadvantage. But almost every night, we share with each other the substance of our days. If I demand honesty from my drawings, Adlai requires it of everything in his life, including me. It hasn't been easy, but it's given me a clarity that's only possible near the source of a spring.

During Elbert Perkins' trial, my dad's name came up frequently. My father would have been proud to hear what his friends and neighbors thought of him. After one of those days in the courtroom gallery, I came home and the loss of him washed over me.

I said to Adlai, "Why did I have to be so stubborn? The only thing he wanted was for me to learn to fish, and I wouldn't do it."

Adlai pushed my hair away from my damp temples and said, "Never too late."

The most damning testimony came from Marvin Rabideaux. "Danny Watson wasn't no dummy," Marvin said. "Once Frank and Elbert come up on him, Danny locked the 'transmit' button on his two-way." Marvin, the dispatcher, heard the whole nasty dispute and the loud boom that ended it. "Joleen and me, we got outta town that very night. Otherwise, we'd of been next."

I turn to the picture I'm working on, the one by the clothesline. I've drawn the house and the yard, the healing herbs, the marsh, and, behind it, the swamp. In the drawing, my mother and father are on the verge of touching. I use gouache to splash the picture with rain and color.

The floor at my feet is littered with discarded studies. Not crumpled, not tossed, just superseded. I've never been given to collage, but I begin to pick them up and tear them so that each piece contains only one element. My father's thumbs, nicked from the fishhooks, his muddy boots, his face shining with stubble. Little Philip's doughy hands. It's satisfying, this act of ripping, but it's not destructive. I pin each fragment to the gray board, move them around, play with spatial relationships, then stand back. I move the creek, the tree, the marsh, juxtapose an old sketch of the fishing camp, a crying bird's nest, an egret. I'm silently laughing to myself, playing. It's a jumble on my wall, but it's got shape, and direction. It's like the Cracker Jack toy with tiles that move around within a frame until the picture is achieved, all but one empty square. And so I leave an empty space—for the lost baby. Her absence brought about that *GARDEN* journal, pulled my mom away from me, pushed me toward my dad.

And what of the young girl in the window? I've been on the outside for a long time, but this admixture calls for participation. I sketch a narrow pair of shoulders, and a long ponytail hanging down between them. I tear the paper around the edges and stick the drawing in place. Does it mean I'm giving the viewer my back? Maybe, but only to shine a light on the main players—a mixed light—bright and revelatory, with patches of shadow. It says, *Follow me into this place.*

Adlai emerges from the bedroom, closing the door softly behind him. "I'm going to work," he says.

I hardly look away from the wall. "Okay." I give him a dry-lipped kiss good-bye and turn my attention back to the collage.

But after the apartment door clicks shut, I grab a hat, my sketchbook, and a thin volume of Whitman poems with a passage I can recite later, maybe by heart, for my mother. I run out the door. "Wait! I'm going with you!"

Adlai is already halfway down the long path to the sidewalk, but he turns at my shout.

I run at full speed and pass him, reaching the street before he does. I throw my things in the cab of his truck and turn around. He's smiling, still ten yards away, a little sleepy and taking his time, baffled by my energy.

I put two hands over my left shoulder and cast an invisible fishing line in his direction. I reel him in, spinning my right hand fast. Maybe he is my nearly impossible task. Maybe this life is the granting of a wish.

From the cab of the truck, the Whitman passage rises up in me like steam from the marsh, and I slow the handle of the invisible reel.

"What are you doing?" Adlai says.

I recite, *"Now I see the secret of the making of the best persons, / It is to grow in the open air and to eat and sleep with the earth."*

"Eat and sleep with the earth," he repeats, putting his arm around my waist. "I'm for it."

I lean in close, breathe him in, and know I'm home.

ACKNOWLEDGMENTS

Many thanks to Kathy Abdul-Baki, Milagros Aguilar, Barbara Bass, Jody Brady, Jeremy Butler, Clive Byers, Ellen Prentiss Campbell, Will Carrington, Sylvia Churgin, Jim Dean, Rocco DeBonis, Simone Deverteuil, Gaela Erwin (for the bird skins), Barbara Esstman, Suzanne Feldman, Audrey Fleming, Leslie Frothingham, Renee Harleston, Toby Hecht, John Helm, Susan Jamison, Elva Jaramillo, Karin Johnson, the late Randall Kenan, Caroline Liberty, Alice McDermott, Laura McDougall and all the McQuilkins, Sally McKee, Tom Milani, Debbie Mitchell, Kermit Moyer (for his constancy and good judgment), Julee Newberger, Michael O'Donnell (oh patient, patient man), Bill O'Sullivan, Janet Peachey, Anna Popinchalk (who lent me her room), Jocelyn Popinchalk (friend and fellow birdwatcher), Danielle Price, Ruth Schallert, Myra Sklarew (for all her warm encouragement), Davina and Jack Smith (for their book collection), Sarah Dimont Sorkin (for years of insightful reading and inspiration), Sara Taber, Alice Tangerini, Henry Taylor (for crucial lessons on precise language and honesty of speech), Lisa Tillman, Julie Tombari (for the fiblet), Cary Umhau, Kristin Williams, and of course to Emily Williamson, my wonderful agent. A million thanks to my editors: to Jackie Cantor for her remarkable eye for story and her particular enthusiasm for this one, and to the sensitive and astute Rebecca Strobel. The rest of the team at Gallery/Simon & Schuster—Aimee Bell, Andrew Nguyen, Lisa Litwack, Alysha Bullock, Barbara Wild, and Lisa Wolff—all made this book better. And Jessica Roth's energy helped get the book to hungry readers. Thanks also to Abby Zidle and Danielle Mazzella Di Bosco.

For early interest in my career, thanks to Miriam Altshuler, Jeff Kleinman, Sally Arteseros, and the late Richard McCann. Thanks especially to the Virginia Center for the Creative Arts—that spare and magical place—for the many visits that have nurtured my writing and this project in particular.

Two books, Lesley Gordon's *Green Magic: Flowers Plants & Herbs in Lore & Legend* and Linda Ours Rago's *Mugworts in May: A Folklore of Herbs*, proved particularly helpful on the subject of herbs and herb lore, and the National Audubon Society Pocket Guides to the Birds were a pleasure to consult, along with Roger Tory Peterson's classic *Field Guide to the Birds* and Richard ffrench's (yes, with two small *ff*'s) *Guide to the Birds of Trinidad and Tobago*, among others. I also gathered information from the wonderful website of Cornell University's ornithology department, AllAboutBirds.org, and from the American Foundation for Suicide Prevention (afsp.org), a source of assistance and hope for people affected by suicide.

Many thanks to Richard Heggen, Professor Emeritus of Civil Engineering at the University of New Mexico, who compiled the most exhaustive compilation imaginable of references to subterranean water, *Underground Rivers: From the River Styx to the Rio San Buenaventura, with Occasional Diversions*, and made it available in PDF form online through the Internet Archive.

Some information about the Smithsonian was gleaned from an article by Larry Van Dyne titled "Uncivil War at the Smithsonian," which appeared in the *Washingtonian* March 2002, and tidbits about the history of the Institution were gathered from James Conaway's *The Smithsonian: 150 Years of Adventure, Discovery, and Wonder*.

Research assistance was provided by the Florida Fish and Wildlife Conservation Commission, most notably Officer Kathy Chidsey

Merritt; by Bob Hoppman and Mark J. Nowicki, experts in things financial; by Gayle Share-Raab, hat aficionado; and by Smithsonian Librarians Gil Taylor and Katrina M. Brown. Thanks to Greg Wright for the Geezer Palace, to Jim Cozza for agreeing to stop for a swamp tour and for the drowsy driver's ironing board, to David Gardner for "Keep on the Sunny Side," to Mary Beth Guyther for two well-timed herons, to Mary Proenza for the technique of sketching photographs, and to artist Rolf Ness for working with me as I first developed the live oak seed for this story. Many thanks also to the librarians in the Rare Book and Special Collections Reading Room of the Library of Congress as well as Peter Armenti in the Main Reading Room for their tireless curiosity and enthusiasm as they helped me track down original sources. Most essentially, thanks to my family, close and far, for their ongoing love and support.

ADDITIONAL READING AND REFERENCE

Adelard of Bath (1080–1152). *Quaestiones Naturales.*

Back, Phillipa. *The Illustrated Herbal.* London: Chancellor Press, 1996.

Barhydt, D. Parish. "Ahyunta." *The Dollar Magazine* 7, no. 42 (June 1851):263.

Burnett, Charles, ed. *Adelard of Bath, Conversations with His Nephew: On the Same and the Different, Questions on Natural Science, and on Birds.* Cambridge: Cambridge University Press, 2006.

Callery, Emma. *The Complete Book of Herbs.* Philadelphia: Running Press, 1994.

Coffey, Timothy. *The History and Folklore of North American Wildflowers.* New York: Houghton Mifflin, 1993.

Conaway, James. *The Smithsonian:150 Years of Adventure, Discovery, and Wonder.* 1st ed. Washington, DC: Smithsonian Books; New York: Knopf, 1995. Chapter 10, "A Wind in the Attic."

Dowden, Anne O. *This Noble Harvest: A Chronicle of Herbs.* New York: Collins, 1979.

Elias, Jason, and Shelagh R. Masling. *Healing Herbal Remedies.* New York: Dell, 1995.

ffrench, Richard. *A Guide to the Birds of Trinidad and Tobago.* 2nd ed. London: Christopher Helm, 1992.

Florida Department of Environmental Protection. "The Journey of Water." www.floridasprings.org.

Gerard, John (1545–1612). *Herball or General Historie of Plants*. Imprinted at London by Edm. Bollifant for Bonham Norton and Iohn Norton, 1597.

Gordon, Lesley. *Green Magic: Flowers Plants & Herbs in Lore & Legend*. New York: Viking Press, 1977.

Heyman, I. Michael. "Smithsonian Perspectives." *Smithsonian*, June 1996.

Marshall, Martin. *Herbs, Hoecakes and Husbandry: The Daybook of a Planter of the Old South*. Tallahassee: Florida State University, 1960.

Nelson, Gil. *The Trees of Florida: A Reference and Field Guide*. Sarasota, FL: Pineapple Press, 1994.

Perkins, Simon. *Familiar Birds of Sea and Shore*. New York: Alfred A. Knopf, 1994.

Peterson, Roger Tory. *A Field Guide to the Birds East of the Rockies*. Boston: Houghton Mifflin: 1980.

Peterson, Wayne R. *Songbirds and Familiar Backyard Birds East*. New York: Alfred A. Knopf, 1996.

Piercy, Marge. "To Be of Use." In *Circles on the Water*. New York: Alfred A. Knopf, 1982:106.

Potterton, David, ed. *Culpepper's Color Herbal*. New York: Sterling, 2002.

Rago, Linda Ours. *Mugworts in May: A Folklore of Herbs*. Charleston, WV: Quarrier Press, 1995.

Raleigh, Sir Walter (1552–1618). *The History of the World, in Five Books*. London: Printed for T. Basset, etc., 1687.

Reynolds, Jane. *365 Days of Nature and Discovery*. London: Michael Joseph, 1994.

Ripley, S. Dillon. "First Record of Anhingidae in Micronesia." *The Auk* 65, no. 3 (July 1948): 454–455.

———. "The View from the Castle." *Smithsonian*, October 1983, 10; December 1983, 12; and April 1984, 12.

Snell, Charles Livingston, Harold Darling, and Daniel Maclise. *This Is My Wish for You*. Seattle: Blue Lantern Books, 1995.

Thoreau, H. David. *Journal.* Edited by B. Torrey. Boston and New York: Houghton Mifflin, 1906), 1:438.

Van Dyne, Larry. "Uncivil War at the Smithsonian." *Washingtonian,* March 2002.

Walton, Richard K. *Familiar Birds of Lakes and Rivers.* New York: Alfred A. Knopf, 1994.

Whitman, Walt. *Leaves of Grass.* 1867. "Song of the Open Road," section 6. The Walt Whitman Archive. Gen. ed. Matt Cohen, Ed Folsom, and Kenneth M. Price. Accessed May 21, 2021. http://www.whitmanarchive.org.

Wilder, Thornton. *The Bridge of San Luis Rey.* New York: Albert & Charles Boni, 1927.

Author's note: Readers may observe that I've played with time in two isolated but significant details. First, Secretary of the Smithsonian S. Dillon Ripley would not have overlapped with Loni's tenure at the Institution, even as an emeritus, but he was such a towering figure in the modern history of the Smithsonian, and in my imagination, that I decided to include him in the narrative nonetheless. Second, the National Aquarium, housed on the ground floor of the Commerce Building on 14th Street in Washington, D.C., closed some years before the action of the novel, but for the purposes of the story, I kept it open. Wishful thinking, perhaps. My apologies to the sticklers.

The

MARSH
QUEEN

VIRGINIA HARTMAN

This reading group guide for The Marsh Queen *includes an introduction, discussion questions, and ideas for enhancing your book club. The suggested questions are intended to help your reading group find new and interesting angles and topics for your discussion. We hope that these ideas will enrich your conversation and increase your enjoyment of the book.*

INTRODUCTION

For fans of *Where the Crawdads Sing*, this "marvelous debut" (Alice McDermott, National Book Award–winning author of *The Ninth Hour*) follows a Washington, D.C., artist as she faces her past and the secrets held in the waters of Florida's lush swamps and wetlands.

Loni Murrow is an accomplished bird artist at the Smithsonian who loves her job. But when she receives a call from her younger brother summoning her back home to help their obstinate mother recover after an accident, Loni's neat, contained life in Washington, D.C., is thrown into chaos, and she finds herself exactly where she does not want to be.

Going through her mother's things, Loni uncovers scraps and snippets of a time in her life she would prefer to forget—a childhood marked by her father Boyd's death by drowning and her mother Ruth's persistent bad mood. When Loni comes across a single, cryptic note from a stranger—*"There are some things I have to tell you about Boyd's death"*—she begins a dangerous quest to discover the truth, all the while struggling to reconnect with her mother and reconcile with her brother and his wife, who seem to thwart her at every turn. To make matters worse, she meets a man in Florida whose attractive simple charm threatens everything she's worked toward.

Pulled between worlds—her professional accomplishments in Washington, and the small town of her childhood—Loni must decide whether to delve beneath the surface into murky half-truths and either avenge the past or bury it, once and for all.

The Marsh Queen explores what it means to be a daughter and how we protect the ones we love. Suzanne Feldman, author of *Sisters of the Great War*, writes that "fans of Delia Owens and Lauren Groff will find this a wonderful and absorbing read."

TOPICS & QUESTIONS
FOR DISCUSSION

1 From the first chapter, Loni is beholden to a strict timeline set by an unsympathetic boss who can't wait to fire her if she goes a second beyond the allotted family leave time. Have you ever encountered a workplace conflict? How did you handle it compared to how Loni did?

2. Loni's world revolves around the animals and vistas of the Florida wetlands. How did this environment contribute to your reading experience? Were there any scenes or details that stuck with you as you read?

3. When Loni has to think through something difficult, she turns to drawing or canoeing to make sense of it all. What are your coping strategies for puzzling through hard situations?

4. Phil's wife, Tammy, enjoys making scrapbooks containing important photos and memories, and she transforms Loni's mom's old photo albums into one of these creations. How do you preserve memories and photographs?

5. Loni and her brother, Phil, initially have different attitudes around the mystery of their father's death. Loni believes it's better to not know what you don't know, while Phil wants to dig for buried truths. Which side were you on as you were reading?

6. Loni finds her mother's journal and starts reading, curious that it may hold the key to untangling their complicated relationship. Would you have read the journal, knowing it was never meant to be shared?

7. Loni and Estelle struggle to balance friendship with the work obligations that turn their relationship into that of boss and employee. What advice would you give them in Chapter 41 when Estelle asks Loni to draw "four incongruous birds all on one tree"?

8. In Chapter 49, Loni realizes that her mother's herb garden has been torn up. She decides not to tell her, instead immortalizing the garden in her drawings. Why do you think this garden was so important to Ruth, and how does this moment represent a turning point in their mother-daughter relationship?

9. As Loni and Adlai get to know each other, their relationship deepens and their principles align. How do you think Adlai's value of truth affects Loni's understanding of her father's passing?

10. In Chapter 54, we encounter a tragedy of addiction and heartache. What do you think motivated Rita Chappelle to share these details with Loni?

11. The book contains a twist ending—when did you first begin to suspect the true story behind Boyd Murrow's death?

12. The story ends with Loni spending additional time in Florida, but the door is left open around what happens next. Do you think she will permanently relocate to Tenetkee or return to her Smithsonian family in D.C.?

ENHANCE YOUR
BOOK CLUB

1. Loni Murrow connects with the world through her drawings, allowing her to connect with the "pond chickens" and other wildlife in an intimate way. Look out your window and create a drawing of your own. Discuss what that process felt like and why you chose that particular plant or animal.

2. The setting of *The Marsh Queen* is incredibly vivid—you can see the Spanish moss, feel the sticky heat. Step outside and create a sensory map of *your* setting. What can you see, feel, hear, and smell? How does this set the backdrop for your story the way Florida swamps set the background for Loni's?

3. Loni and her mother use easy-to-recall rhymes about herbs to connect across the time and memories that have forced them apart: "*Lemon balm soothe / all troublesome care / reviveth the heart / and ward off despair.*" Research plants native to your area and try your hand at a rhyme of your own that describes their properties or appearance. Share them aloud.